The Shadow Queen

THE

SHADOW

QUEEN

SANDRA GULLAND

Doubleday

New York   London   Toronto   Sydney   Auckland

The Shadow Queen is a work of fiction inspired by the life of Claude des Oeillets, daughter of the actress Alix des Oeillets, and confidential attendant to the Sun King's mistress, Madame de Montespan.

www.doubleday.com

DOUBLEDAY and the portrayal of an anchor with a dolphin are registered trademarks of Random House LLC.

Library of Congress Cataloging-in-Publication Data
Gulland, Sandra.
    The Shadow Queen / Sandra Gulland. —First Edition.
        pages   cm
    1. Louis XIV, King of France, 1638–1715—Fiction. 2. France—History—
Louis XIV, 1643–1715—Fiction. I. Title.
PR9199.3.G7915S53 2013
813'.54—dc23   2013013829

ISBN 978-0-385-53752-0 (hardcover)
ISBN 978-0-385-53753-7 (eBook)

Book design by Maria Carella
Genealogy designed by Jeffrey L. Ward
Jacket design by Michael J. Windsor
Jacket photograph © DEA/DAGLI ORTI/Getty Images

MANUFACTURED IN THE UNITED STATES OF AMERICA

10 9 8 7 6 5 4 3 2 1

First Edition

In memory of my father, Robert Zentner
(1917–2013),
whose lovable eccentricities are reflected
in several of the characters in this novel.

Everything that is deep loves the mask.

—Nietzsche, *Beyond Good and Evil*

CONTENTS

HISTORICAL NOTE

In 1651, France was a country torn asunder, buffeted by violence and discord. The country had been at war with mighty Spain for sixteen years. As well, the King (thirteen-year-old Louis XIV) and the Queen Mother (Anne of Austria) were engaged in a civil war with powerful members of the French nobility—including the King's uncle and cousins.

The violence was such that the royal family fled Paris, taking refuge in the southwestern town of Poitiers. From there they intended to amass an army and fight their way back to Paris.

Those outside the world of the Court—in essence, most everyone in France—did not understand the reasons behind the constant warfare, did not know, in fact, who their enemy really was. All *they* knew was disease, violence, and hunger. Their only fight was to survive.

Act I

Winter Swallows

*(1651, near Poitiers,
in the southwest of France)*

CHAPTER 1

inter was coming—I could smell it. Even so, we headed north, following a cow track across a barren field, away from all the lawless soldiers.

Onward. I shifted little Gaston onto my right hip and set my eyes on the far horizon . . . Onward toward Poitiers, where we might earn a meal performing for crowds. News had spread that the King and Court were there, mobilizing for yet another battle.

We had seen the aftermath the day before, corpses rotting in the sun, pickers crawling over the leavings like flies on a harvest table. A sparkling brass buckle, a dagger with a carved hilt, a hat plume, three bone buttons—treasures that could be traded for food.

"We are players, not scavengers," my father said gravely, turning me away. "There are things we do not do, things we *will* not do."

His reproach stung even now.

I pulled the patched woolens up over Gaston's head to protect him from the cold. He hummed in sleepy protest, sucking on his thumb. Father was right, I knew—we were players, and proud of our calling. We might be hungry, but we would never beg.

I glanced back to see Bravo pulling our cart of costumes and props, our kettle and precious embers. The donkey never stopped, but he never increased his pace either, even when wild dogs threatened.

My parents lagged far behind, hands linked, singing their favorite song, "Le Beau Robert."

My belly cramped, but not from hunger. Was my time upon me?

My courses had started some moons before. Father and Mother had been jubilant. I must make a formal vow! they theatrically declared, as knights had done in days of old.

I'm a girl, I objected. The ceremonial swearing to uphold the code of chivalry marked a boy's transition into manhood.

My parents—loving any excuse to perform—insisted that it was a perfectly suitable rite to mark *their* daughter becoming a woman.

So Father and I had acted out the ritual before our audience (Mother, with Gaston in her arms)—first the silent prayer, and then the sermon. It had all been pretend, but we were players: we took pretend to heart. I wore a red robe of nobility over a white tunic, symbolizing purity. My hose and shoes were black, symbolizing death.

"Swear not to traffic with traitors or give evil counsel!" Father recited the Code in his booming player's voice. "Swear to observe all fasts."

"I so swear," I vowed. We were often without food. I was well accustomed to want. Ours was a life of fasts.

"Swear never to betray a trust."

"I swear." Thinking of Gaston, so credulous and sweet.

"Swear to do what is right, whatever the cost." This last Father said gently.

"I so swear," I answered, my hand over my heart.

He tapped my shoulders with our stage-prop sword, dubbing me the Good Knight Claudette, binding me to my vows. A burden, and a blessing.

THE CLOUDS CLEARED as we came to a valley. The sun lit up a meadow dotted with frosted marigold. I lowered Gaston to the ground, my arms aching. He was small for five, but even so, carrying him was heavy work. Giggling, he teetered on his feet. I caught him before he fell.

"Careful, Turnip," I said, pressing my face into his neck, inhaling his sweet scent, so curiously like fresh bread (making my stomach rumble). Mother and Father fanned out, foraging for dried berries and grasshoppers, which we ate greedily after removing the heads, legs, and wings. I kept Gaston near. It was a relief that he'd finally learned to hold his water and hinder-fallings, but he was still a baby at heart.

I worried that he was so clumsy, spotted with bruises, worried that he'd yet to talk the way other children did—children who teased him cruelly, calling him an idiot, a simple, a fool.

Yet Gaston was far from simple. I'd never won a game of Mill against him! On our wanders, he always seemed to know the right direction to go (when the rest of us were lost), and although he couldn't talk, he knew when we misspoke a line during a performance. He was a puzzle I couldn't solve. Mother feared a witch had put a spell on him. Father suspected that the worms we suffered now and again had gotten into his head. But I thought otherwise. I worried that it was something I might have done to him myself, looked away when I should have been watching.

WE FORDED A river at a crude plank bridge, coaxing Bravo over with a bit of parsnip. In the shallows, we drank and splashed our faces. Mother caught minnows and we gobbled them down live. She chewed one for Gaston, making it soft, luring him to eat.

The land was made of chalk and limestone, forgiving and malleable. "There will be caves in these parts," Father said, kicking his toe into the dirt. It was time to think of shelter for the night. In a cave, we would not be so exposed—to wind, wolves, men.

A narrow path led up to a ridge, which was surmounted by an enormous cross. Its surface gleamed in the fading light.

"Compliments of the Company, no doubt," my father said, frowning.

The Company of the Blessed Sacrament.

The Company of the Devil, he'd once dared to call it. The secret society did good works by day, but attacked Jews, Romas, and players by night—all demons in their view, enemies of the One True Faith. Even some priests were of their number, preaching the stoning of players on festival days.

We were goodly Christians, so why did the Church scorn us? Why could we not take Communion or be buried in hallowed ground? Why were we excommunicated, forbidden the comfort of Heaven?

I lifted Gaston into my arms and began the climb up the mountain. He hummed, one long high note, fixing his moon eyes on me, unblinking. His voice was plaintive and high, enchanting to hear. I hummed along with him, the notes vibrating through my head and chest, twining with his. My sweetling—my very own treasure.

THE SUN WAS about to set when we found the opening to a cave. Remnants of a wolf carcass, charred logs, and a sharpened stick were evidence that the site had been home to humans before. An overhang offered protection from inclement weather.

The slope was wreathed in frost-withered vines, clematis, and primulas. On the far side of the valley, atop a rocky height, I could see the city of Poitiers. Church steeples rose above a cloud of smoke.

"Perfect," Father said, regarding the vista. At the edge of a steep incline, we wouldn't be taken by surprise.

The floor of the cave was wide and dry, the walls smooth. Holding a rush candle, I saw crude images of large animals painted onto the stone.

Gaston made echoes in the cavern as I hauled in the basket of bedding. "Come help, Turnip," I sang, for he understood words best when put to tune. He ran to me, stumbling. "Doucement, mon petit!"

Outside, Mother set the tiny wood statue of the Virgin in a rock nook and arranged her tokens around it: a bouquet of dried carnations, a corn-husk doll, a chipped teacup, a rusty key. "How delicious is pleasure after torment," she recited in a deep and melodic voice, quoting a line by the great playwright Corneille.

The familiar words rang out across the valley. We might suffer from want, but at least we had poetry.

he next morning, Father and I set out back down the mountain, picking our way around boulders and rugged outcrops. "Tracks," Father noted as we passed a pond ringed by trees and bushes. Deer tracks: we would be back.

Our intention was to go into the city and approach the Court, offering to perform lofty passages from the Great Corneille as well as some light entertainment. The young King—no older than I—would likely be bored and desirous of amusement. If we succeeded, we would be rewarded well.

As we got closer to Poitiers, we saw caves much like our own, many of them occupied. Some had gardens and plank doors, but most were hovels. Bone-thin children held out their hands. I delighted them with a flip; at least I had that to give.

Soon the path widened and we were joined by others—peasants going to market, three youths on a mule. We followed a road edging a river until a bridge came into view. Six heads were set on pikes at the top of a tower.

Father hung a tin cross conspicuously around his neck. "I've only five deniers," he told me—not much in the way of a bribe. We pushed through the mewling beggars to join the long line of people waiting to get into the city.

"Where are you from and what business do you have here?" a pudgy guard asked when we finally got to the gates.

At least that's what I thought he said. Every town and village spoke a different patois.

"French, Monsieur?" Father suggested as the guards took our satchel for inspection.

Another guard, this one with a thick black moustache, made a so-so gesture. "This Christian town is," he informed us in broken French, regarding us suspiciously. "No beggar, no Jew, no Roma."

Father explained that we had come to the fine town of Poitiers to visit his old aunt, who was breathing her last. He made a sad face and pressed the cross to his heart, miming grief. His best shirt of embroidered cambric showed under his jerkin.

The moustached guard shrugged at his partner, who had opened our satchel. He held up my slapstick with a puzzled expression. My heart jumped, fearing he would take us for players.

"To amuse my cousins," I explained. The wood slats, held together at one end, made a splendidly loud noise, perfect for comic skits. I demonstrated the motion with a snap of my hand.

The guard copied my gesture and jumped at the *clack* the sticks made. He laughed and gave it to the other guard to try. *Clack! Clack! Clack!*

The plump guard wanted to do it again himself. *Clack! Clack!* He laughed like a child with a new toy.

I was relieved when he put the sticks back in the satchel and waved us through.

WE HEADED UP the hill, through the narrow, congested streets and into the heart of the ancient city. I paused at a stable yard. "Should I change?"

Father nodded. "I think we're close."

I slipped behind a wall, taking care where I stepped. My breeches were baggy around my hips—I stuffed my skirts into them and slipped on the short jacket, pulling up my stockings and tightening the twine on my big boots. Last, I applied a cream of chalk powder mixed with egg white to my face, then patted on just a bit of (precious!) flour. I secured the wig under my chin with a frayed ribbon.

I did a duck walk back out to the cobbled street and saluted my father. He grinned, every part of his face smiling, his brows lifting like the outstretched wings of a bird. Mother told me I looked just like him. I had his thick auburn hair.

"Don't move," he said. There were three men standing in front of a tavern across from the stable yard. They watched as Father shaped my smile with some of the red clay we'd found near Roussillon. Then I did a flip for them.

"Chapeau! Formidable!" they cheered.

A line of hooded men in black appeared in procession, carrying crosses and chanting like droning bees in a hive. The Company? Big, ragged holes had been cut in the cloth for their eyes. One man turned to stare, his eyes rolling ghoulishly. I lowered my head and signed myself, praying in fear as they passed.

THE PALAIS DE JUSTICE opened onto a crowded square with a scaffold at its center. I clambered after my father, heart racing.

The vast guardroom was like a church: dark, cold, and echoing. Thick tree trunks were burning in four enormous fireplaces at one end, yet they gave off little heat. A long plank table was heaped with the remains of a feast. A wave of longing came over me as I gazed at the leavings: a fish stew, something that smelled like partridge and cabbage potage, a platter of beignets (Mother's favorite).

Two spaniels and a greyhound snapped and growled under the table. The greyhound's snout appeared, and a beignet was gone.

Hunger made warriors strong, Father said. Swallowing, I stepped back.

After inquiries, Father was directed to a city magistrate who in turn told him to speak to Monsieur le Duc de Mortemart, charged with arranging entertainments for the royal family. We went through a small courtyard where a number of soldiers were smoking pipes and passing an earthenware crock between them. I stayed close behind Father, following him through an arch into yet another courtyard, and then another. On the far side, four guards leaned beside a double door.

"I wish to see Monsieur le Duc de Mortemart," Father announced in his aristocratic voice—the voice he adopted for playing the parts of kings.

Yawning, a young guard with a hint of a beard opened one door. I made an exaggerated clown bow, but he didn't smile.

Flushing, I climbed two steps at a time, joining Father in a dark antechamber off the landing. We waited beneath a tall window of Venetian glass; covered with soot, it let in little light.

One Ave Maria, two, three . . . On the fourth, a footman appeared and ushered us into an elaborately furnished room with a high ceiling and a great hanging candelabra. Candles had been lit despite the hour. A coat of arms was painted on a china vase: a shield with a menacing blue snake curled in the lower quadrant.

A man in velvet and old lace looked up at us from a desk covered in papers and scrolls: the Duke. The coat of arms must be his, I surmised. His shaved head was covered with a skullcap; a wig hung over the back of a chair. I wondered if he was a knight.

The footman gestured: step forward.

Father put down our satchel, bowing and greeting the mighty Monsieur le Duc de Mortemart formally, in Latin.

"Spare me," the Duke groaned in French. His lips were stained red and his cheeks rouged. From the cracks in his face powder, I suspected he'd been napping. He had the manner of a man under water.

Father explained in his most melodic French that we were players, members of an acclaimed acting troupe. The tragedies of the Great Corneille were our specialty, but we also excelled in comedy, skits perfectly suited to engage the interest of the thirteen-year-old King.

"With your indulgence, Monsieur?" Father handed me the slapstick and we launched into a skit, one that involved tumbles, jumps, and my thundering sticks. I ended our demonstration with a *triple* flip. I bowed, breathless and triumphant, Father looking on in astonished wonder.

"Get these devils out of here!" the Duke growled, holding his temples.

THE FOOTMAN ESCORTED us roughly out the door, tossing our satchel after us.

"How tragic to be a humorless man," Father said amiably at the landing, but I could see the worry on his brow. Our plan had failed.

I put the slapstick back in the satchel. "I'm sorry, Father."

"Nil desperandum," he said philosophically. Never despair. "You were magnificent, Claudette. A triple! I didn't know you could do that."

We emerged into the enormous guardroom. The dogs were sleeping on a sunny patch of stone, the table ravaged. Father headed for the doors, but I lingered, snatching a few of the remaining beignets. At least we would not return to Mother and Gaston empty-handed.

"Do you do enchantments?" It was a girl's voice, directly behind me.

"Excusez-moi?" I concealed the beignets before turning around.

"I asked if you do charms." The girl spoke French with a refined aristocratic inflection, somewhat archaic. I guessed her to be ten or eleven, a few years younger than I was. Her long, golden curls were tied up with extravagant silk ribbons, framing an astonishingly pretty face. Spots of pink had been painted on her cheeks and her enormous sapphire-blue eyes were lined with kohl. She looked like a heavenly creature.

"Certainly," I stammered, disconcerted by her noble bearing. An elderly woman, a governess by her dress, hovered about ten paces back.

I glanced toward the doors. Father was talking with a guard and seemed in no hurry. "And tricks of the tumbling kind," I said.

"I make faces." The girl blew out her cheeks and extended her neck, widening her eyes to make the face of a ghoul.

"That's magnificently ugly," I told her, and made a wide grimace in return.

"You have good teeth," the girl said, miming my frightening grin.

We were like animals, courting.

"I live in a magical kingdom," the girl boasted.

"I live in a magical cave."

"Oh," she breathed. "With bats?"

I nodded, of course.

"Do you do magic there?" she asked, switching to schoolgirl Latin.

"Vere," I responded in Latin.

"Then you must know how to cast spells."

"Why?" I asked with a mysterious look.

"I want to kill my governess," she said, in whispered French this time.

I laughed.

"I do not jest."

I saw Father's silhouette in the doors, the light of the sun behind him. His hands were on his hips: he was ready to go. I gestured that I would be right there. "All I can offer is a chant," I said, to appease, dictating a nonsense rhyme I'd used once in a performance:

We put out the light,
We render its death,
Violent light, the light is dead.

"Ring a bell before you say the words," I added, bowing and slipping away.

"WE'RE IN LUCK," Father told me outside on the wide stone steps. "There's to be a hanging soon—it would be a good crowd to play to. I found out where to go to get permission. Who was that girl?"

"I don't know," I said, looking out across the square. Flags flew from a château slightly down the hill. That would be where the members of the royal family were staying: the King, his brother, and the Queen Mother. I felt awed to be so very close. So close, and yet impossibly far. I had dreamt of playing before the royal family, dreamt of a purse of gold. "She wants to kill her governess."

Father guffawed. He was still laughing as we left through the city gates.

aston sang out when he saw me, throwing up his arms to be lifted. I made our rubbing-nose greeting and he giggled, lightening my spirits.

He'd been lining up objects in order by size outside the rocky cave entrance—a pile of rocks, Mother's hat, one of my socks, a wooden stirring spoon. His "projects," we called them. It was a curious diversion, but it gave him great satisfaction, and at least we always knew where to look when something was missing.

"They refused us?" Mother was indignant.

"*He,*" Father said. "Monsieur le Duc de Mortemart."

"I think he was unwell," I said, letting Gaston down. From too much in the way of spirits, I suspected. "The sound of my slapstick nearly killed him." The thought made me smile.

"We can always perform at the market in town," Father told my mother, reassuring her. "There's going to be a hanging."

"I have a surprise," I said, to change the subject. I didn't like performing at executions; Gaston didn't sleep well after.

Mother stepped forward as I withdrew my treasures, four sugary beignets. I tossed one in the air and twirled, catching it behind my back.

"Claudette, you didn't." Father's tone was scolding. *We are players, not scavengers.*

"They were going to the dogs," I said in protest, shamed.

LATER THAT AFTERNOON, Father and I returned to the pond where we'd seen the tracks. We hid in the bushes on either side, he with his knife and spiked club, me with the pistol, a heavy flintlock that tended to shoot left of the mark.

I got out the horn and shook out some black powder. Only three lead shots left. I opened the pan cover and tipped powder from the flask, filling it carefully to the brim: too much and it might explode—I'd seen the handless soldiers. I closed the pan, blew on it, and gave it a whack to make sure there was no powder on the surface. Finally, I tipped a shot into the end of the barrel, used the ramrod to push it in and pulled back the spanner until the serrated wheel caught, checking to see that the flint was held securely in the beak of the cock piece.

Then I waited, nestling into a place between some tree roots, the flintlock supported by a branch, listening to the busy insect world, the birdsong, the wind-rustled leaves . . . listening for a stealthy approach through the grass. Making myself invisible.

A twig's crack sparked me alert. A young buck appeared between two oaks, his eyes black pools. His antlers were spikes, not yet branched. He wasn't big, but his meat would be tender.

I took aim, allowing for the quirks of the old firearm, and braced myself for the kick-back.

The shot rang out across the valley. Father spun on his heels, his knife in one hand and his club in another. A bloom of red appeared on the hart's chest as he thrashed to the ground.

"Bravo!" my father cried out as he drove his knife into the animal's heart: a mercy.

FATHER AND I washed in the pond before hauling the carved-up carcass up the hill on the waxed cloth that doubled as our stage back-drop. I took the antlers, as well, for Gaston to play with.

Mother had a good bed of red coals going in the fire pit, and in time we were rewarded with the divine smell of roasting meat. She cautioned me to eat slowly, not to gorge, but I couldn't resist.

In the gloaming, we saw a cloud rise in the air, particles of dust set alight by the setting sun. Bravo's ears pricked forward.

"No horses or pack mules," Father said, tilting his head. His eyes were going, but his ears were still good.

"Boys," I said as they came into view on the path below. Young ones in broad-rimmed hats. I could see their bobbing heads, rag bags hanging from poles over their shoulders. There were about twenty of them, I guessed, their hobnailed boots clattering on the stones. Gaston protested as I held him back.

"Welcome," Father said, his hand on his knife.

"Hail," the boys chimed sweetly.

"I am Pilon," said a boy at the head, stepping forward.

He was a thin-faced country lad, tall as a haymaker's rake, with a heart-shaped birthmark on his cheek. He spoke a local patois mixed with some French that was difficult to understand, but through gestures and mime we were able to communicate.

They were from villages near Bordeaux, to the south, he informed us, and they were headed for Paris. They had been contracted by their parents to begging organizations for the winter.

"Remember, Nicolas?" Mother asked my father, her voice tender. "We used to see beggar boys swarming into Paris every fall. Winter Swallows they were called."

Pilon nodded. In exchange for what they earned begging, they would be taught the catechism, given food and a bed. In the spring, they would return to their families to work the fields.

There are wolves in these parts, he warned us. Werewolves. They had seen evidence of one by the river.

"Louléerou," one of the young Swallows said in the language of the Périgord, his eyes round with fear.

Loups-garous. I glanced at Mother. The moon was nearing full. Some men were known to be strangely overcome by a fit at such a time, jumping out a window and plunging into a fountain or well, emerging covered with fur and running on all fours.

"Sleep with us tonight," Mother suggested.

"And eat," Father added, offering to share our bounty.

By the firelight, the boys' cheeks glistening, I did a clown skit, delighting them with my tumblings. Their laughter echoed across the dark valley.

OUR CAVE WAS full that night with sleeping children. I woke in the dark to comfort one of the youngest, who was weeping softly into his ragged knapsack. It was his first time away from his family: that much I could understand. I longed to reassure him, tell him how grand Paris would be, the wonders he would see there. I feared for him, in truth, well knowing the dangers that lay ahead, the greed of city flesh-mongers for young boys.

Sleep, I gestured, and the innocent closed his eyes. I made a sign of the cross over him, my knight's blessing.

orning dew covered everything with sparkling glisten. Clouds blanketed the river valley; I looked out over a vast white plain. A hawk circled, gliding.

"We're in Heaven, sweet-love," Mother said, stacking sticks on the embers.

"Amen," Father said, breaking up fall-wood for the fire.

Gaston crawled out of the cave wrapped in wool.

"A loup-garou!" I tossed him giggling into the air.

Pilon and his tribe emerged, their bundles tied.

"You must eat before you go," Father offered, hauling down the remains of the carcass from the high branch of a tree.

As we sat by the crackling fire sucking on bones, I noticed Bravo tip one ear forward. I looked down the path. Riders on horseback emerged from the blanket of cloud.

Father stood beside me, squinting. We weren't as isolated as we had thought.

"Five riders on horseback," I said. "Two riding sidesaddle." And wearing full face masks. Women, then—with a small escort.

"Aristocrats," Father said uneasily.

I looked behind me, but already the Swallows were scurrying the carcass out of sight. Our cave was likely on some mighty lord's land.

"It's not a hunt party," Father said. "I don't hear dogs."

The group disappeared behind a rock outcropping, then reappeared. One of them proceeded up the path while the others stayed behind in the shade of an oak.

"A mere child," Father said with relief in his voice.

Her golden curls gave her away. "It's the girl I was talking to in the guardroom of the Palais." She was wearing a red jacket over a matching skirt, topped by a tiny man's hat. (Charming.) Her black pony's mane was tied up in ribbons, its leathers studded with silver.

I smoothed my apron and tossed back my long braids, regretting not having coiled them up properly under a cap.

The girl whipped her horse sharply and it leapt into a canter. "Stop," she commanded when she reached our cave, her voice muffled by her mask.

The Swallows approached, mewling, holding out their hands. Pilon whistled a warning and they disappeared into the bushes, fast as squirrels.

The girl's horse stood, its muscles quivering to dislodge a fly on its neck. It pawed a hoof in frustration and was rewarded with a thwack from the girl's bone riding rod. I stepped forward and brushed the fly away. "Mademoiselle." I curtsied. Four fingers of exquisite lace showed at the wrists of her jacket. I'd never seen such finery—not up close.

She tipped up her mask. "You said you lived in an enchanted cave." She regarded the site with disdain.

"Enchantment is by nature invisible, Mademoiselle. How may I serve you?"

"I must speak to you—alone." She glared at Father, who was hovering. He tipped his battered hat and backed respectfully away. "My governess didn't die," she hissed, pointing her riding rod back at the elderly woman among the group of riders. "I recited the words and rang the bell, just as you said. I need something stronger. I need poison."

"Such costs a great deal," I said, ever willing to prolong fantasy (the heart of the player's craft), though unsettled by the girl's seriousness.

"I don't have coin. I'm not allowed."

I was surprised—even I had two deniers.

I felt Gaston's little hand at my fingertips.

"A dwarf-boy?" the girl asked with interest. "I asked my father to buy me one, a black one."

"This is my brother," I said.

Gaston stared, humming in puzzlement. "Can you bow to the princess, Turnip?" He swooped off his cap. (Well done!)

"I'm not a princess," the girl informed me. "I am Mademoiselle de Tonnay-Charente, third child and second-eldest daughter of the Duc de Mortemart."

I curtsied again, even lower this time. I knew an opportunity when it presented itself. "Your father, the esteemed Duc de Mortemart: is he not the gentleman who arranges entertainments for the royal family?"

She dipped her chin.

"There will be no need for coin, Mademoiselle. Persuade your father to put our names forward as players before His Majesty and the Court. If we are hired to perform, I will have something for you."

LATER THAT DAY, as Mother and I were boiling bones and beans, a man came cantering up the hill, his horse in a lather. He wore embroidered livery of the old school, clearly of the Court.

"We might as well be on the high road," Father said with a sigh.

I hurried Mother and Gaston into the cave, then peeked out. The man leaned down to hand a scroll to my father, then turned his horse and clambered down the rocky slope.

Father sauntered back, examining the parchment. He raised a fist in a cheer.

Good news? We emerged into the light.

"We're to perform!" He did a jig, waving the document in the air. "For the *King*."

Zounds. I'd promised poison.

"And the Queen Mother?" Mother pressed her hands to her cheeks.

"Everyone!" Father kissed her tenderly on the forehead, as if she were a child.

"Will they pay?" I asked, ever the practical one.

"A goodly amount, no doubt . . . eventually." He looked back down at the paper, squinting, holding it out at arm's length. "We're to stage *The Cid*."

"*All* of it?" *The Cid* was Corneille's greatest play—the greatest play ever written. "But we're only three players," I said, mentally counting off the characters: four women, seven men, possibly more. There was a page as well, I recalled. Might Gaston be able to manage that role? I doubted it.

"We've performed it many a time," Mother said.

"True," Father said, "but that was before."

Before . . . Back when we'd been a full troupe, before Courageux and the others had forsaken our craft in favor of a bed and a crust of bread.

We squatted by the fire to puzzle it through. Most of the scenes had no more than three speaking characters at a time, so with changes of costumes and the occasional use of narrative summary, we might just be able to do it. "It's the King's desire," Father said. It might as well be God's command: the King was God on earth.

"The hard part will be casting," Mother said. "If I play both the heroine and the Infanta, what will happen in the final scene, when both appear?"

"Claudette could play the Infanta," Father said, scratching the scenes out in the dirt with a stick. He himself could play the governess by binding up his beard and using a mask. "That isn't done in serious theater, but we're going to have to be inventive."

"I'm to play the princess?" Being tall—tall as a unicorn, Father liked to say—I usually performed in travesty, as a man.

"A tall Infanta will be majestic," he assured me. "But you'll also play the Count, of course—opposite me for the duel."

Father and I always played the fight scenes, which audiences loved. We were nimble and strong, and we knew our moves well.

"Or we could simply not perform the duel," Mother suggested. "It's not in the text."

Gaston cried out in protest, clapping his knees.

"The King will love it," Father said.

WE HUDDLED AROUND the campfire, wrapped in patched blankets and remnants of fur as I read *The Cid* out loud. Slowly I turned the worn gray pages of the precious play-script, copied from a copy of a copy. Father had taught me to read so that I could prompt them through their lines. *The Cid* had been one of my first accomplishments.

My parents didn't need much prompting for *The Cid,* however. Fifteen years before, they had been members of the Marais theater troupe in Paris for the play's opening run. Father had the part of one of the minor nobles and Mother the Infanta's governess.

Father mimed being struck by Cupid's arrow when he'd seen Mother for the first time.

"You wooed me with beignets," Mother said, flushing. They'd taken the stage name *Oeillets* after the carnations she'd worn in her hair when they were wed.

"I knew your weakness," Father said with a sly smile.

THE MOON THAT night was full and bright. *This dark brightness that falls from stars,* I whispered, reciting my favorite line from *The Cid*.

I pulled our costumes out of the wood trunk and spread them on some rocks to air: my harlequin costume, Father's nobleman garb, Mother's bodice and skirts. The rent in her sleeve would have to be mended, I noted.

I went through the masks, hats, vests, ruffs, and veils—with these we could create a variety of characters.

Our one backdrop of a palace would have to suffice. Candles usually indicated a night scene, but we couldn't afford such luxury; the cutout moon would do. I looked through the props we used for Corpus Christi plays and set aside the Our Lord cloak, two horsehair beards and a tin crown. I kissed the wooden sword with which I'd been dubbed the Good Knight Claudette and set it aside as well. We would need it for the duel scene.

I held up one of the gowns Mother wore for princess roles. It was a lilac brocade with deep lace trim—worn, stained, and tattered. I'd found it in a used-clothing market stall, plunging my hand into the pile of musty, buggy gowns until I felt the telltale texture of fine cloth. I'd mended and patched it, stitching tiny satin stars along the frayed hem. They flashed like fireflies in the moonlight.

I pressed the gown to my shoulders and danced a slow, stately pavane, rising on my toes and swaying slightly, enjoying the feel of the slithery fabric in my hands. The gown smelled of sweat, but also, just faintly—at the neckline—of Angel Water. I pressed the cloth to my nose, inhaling the hint of myrtle in that aristocratic scent. I imag-

ined the woman who had once worn this elegant gown, imagined her
maids clustered around her, arranging her ribbons as musicians played,
a table laden with foodstuffs. The blessed world of the nobility—
a world without hunger, without want.

I looked up at the stars, crushing the gown to my heart.

Heaven is to live a life of freedom, my father liked to say.

Heaven is to live in Art, Mother would chime.

Give thanks, give thanks, give thanks.

I smoothed the lilac gown out over a rock, aching at its luxuriant
beauty. The world of the blessed was a heaven, surely—but a heaven I
would never know.

he square in front of the Palais was festooned with banners and flags, as if for a pageant. I was relieved that the scaffold was no longer there.

We led Bravo through an arch to a field crowded with carriages and wagons. Servants were carrying chairs, stools, and benches through two big doors into the back of the Palais. Father explained to a guard that we were players for the Court, displaying the document with the Duc de Mortemart's signature. We were directed to leave Bravo and our cart in a weedy corner, assured that our trunk and props would be brought in. We eased nature and headed for the doors, nervous about the impending performance—for the King!

Armed soldiers were checking everyone, even the servants. "Father, your letter," I said, and we were waved through.

"Mary help me," Mother whispered, crossing herself as we came into the guardroom. "It's as big as a cathedral."

Big as a cathedral—but noisier. Servants were setting out benches, their shouts echoing against the stone. Gaston clutched my hand, his mouth agape. I wiped the drool from his chin. He looked dear in the little page costume I'd made him from scraps.

Enormous fires were blazing; even so, I could see my breath. A white-breasted barn swallow swooped back and forth across the wide expanse of the hall, flitting from one high window ledge to another.

"That must be our stage," Father said, heading toward a platform at the far end, hung with tapestries. Candles set along the rim had already been lit.

"We have a problem," Mother said, accessing its height.

Suddenly there was a shuffling silence. I turned to see everyone bowing as the Duc de Mortemart and his entourage entered. He was wearing a long blond wig that matched his thin moustache. Layers of velvet and fur enlarged him. Servants stepped well back as he passed.

"Where are the rest of you!" the Duke demanded from a distance, his face an alarming shade of red.

Two men followed behind him—secretaries, I guessed, by their ink-stained sleeve laces. *Ay me.* Behind them were the old governess and the girl, who stared at me expectantly.

Father took off his hat and made a courtly bow in the low and sweeping Italian style.

"Your damned troupe—where the hell is it?" The Duke glared at little Gaston, who was sucking on his thumb.

"Four of our members came down with an unfortunate and violent grippe this morning, Monseigneur," Father said.

I glanced away, shamed. A knight did not tell untruths.

"You are to perform!" the Duke sputtered in a fury.

"I assure you that we will enact *The Cid* without disappointment," Father persisted.

"We do have one problem, however." Mother stepped up to the Duke, her hands on her hips.

"Alix—" Father said, but she shrugged him away.

"In order to perform for His Majesty, we need to be able to get on the stage." She pointed at the platform, which was higher than her head.

The scaffold, I realized, my heart sinking.

OUR COSTUME TRUNK was delivered shortly after; it served as a means to get on the stage. Even so, we had a lofty climb.

I got Gaston settled under the platform with his sound props—pot lids for the duel—before spreading our hats, wigs, and shawls on the floor behind a screen. Once that was done, I helped Father hang our painted backdrop of a palace interior (only slightly stained from dragging the buck carcass).

The smoky hall filled with muted laughter, the sounds of people milling in, resounding with murmurs and exclamations. Musicians struck up their ill-tuned string instruments. There was an air of grand events about to happen.

I set our tiny reflecting tin on the back edge of the scaffold and lined up the pots of lead paint, chalk, red clay, flour, and soot. My hands trembled touching the burnt cork to my brows. Where was the King now? I adjusted the lace ruffle of my neckline in the mirror, the set of my horsehair wig, my princess crown. The bodice was tight and the skirt, although lengthened, still short. I felt a little ridiculous in lacy lilac, in truth.

To get my mind off my uneasiness, I reviewed the things Mother and Father had taught me about the arts of fascination, the player's craft:

invention (especially when things go wrong);
attitude (as suited the role);
elocution and pronunciation (no mumbling);
memory (please).

And *gesture,* I reminded myself, pressing my hand to my forehead, palm out, to indicate despair. I stood tall, imagining myself a princess, confident and demanding, born of an ancient race. I thought of the Duke's daughter, the crisp way she spoke, the music of her cultivated diction. My heart stirred, recalling the way she sat on her horse so surely, the pride of nobility in her blood. And then I thought of my deceit, the promise I had made.

"They're seating men on the platform," Father exclaimed with a blubber of frustration.

In cities, noblemen paid handsomely for the opportunity to display themselves on a stage, but I was surprised that it was allowed for a private Court performance.

Trumpets sounded: the royal family! The sound of shuffling chairs was deafening as everyone stood. I peeked around the scaffold. *Stars!* The King, his brother and their mother were being seated directly in front of us, flanked by richly adorned courtiers.

The King looked small in his throne chair. He sat very still, as if playing a role. Although only thirteen, he looked the part. I wondered if he had to practice in order to achieve a commanding air. Born to be King, it would more likely come naturally.

Finely dressed ladies and gentlemen came and went, and for a moment I thought I glimpsed the girl again, but then lost sight of her.

A trumpet sounded—once, twice, three times.

Mother appeared from behind the screen, a wig in her hand. "This is too big, Nicolas."

I groaned.

"It comes down over my eyes," she persisted, her voice tremulous.

She did this every time, becoming tearful before a performance!

"It's the same one you've always worn," Father said, tying on the apron he wore for his first scene as a governess. He took the wig and sniffed it. "It has your lovely scent." The scent of the dried carnations Mother crushed and rubbed into her hair.

Drum rolls sounded. The Duc de Mortemart began to address the crowd, introducing the performance. The audience, loud as patrons in a crowded tavern, slowly silenced.

"Come, my sweetkin," Father said, slipping the wig onto Mother's head.

She smiled to hear the endearment. The danger had passed.

In spite of his skirts Father managed to leap onto the scaffold.

I pushed Mother up from behind. "Can this be true, Elvire?" I heard her begin, her voice warbling only a bit. "Have you changed my father's words?"

"Non! He esteems Rodrigue," Father answered, pitching his voice high (as governess), but loud, so that it would carry. "He approves your love for him."

Mother's next line was assured. I breathed a sigh of relief. The fantasy world of the play had taken hold. Once in a role, she was steady. I stooped down and squinted into the dark under the platform. "How are you?" I hissed. I didn't like Gaston being down under a scaffold. Where men had so violently suffered, their spirits surely lingered.

He turned from the tapestry skirt and gave me his *I'm happy* sign: right hand up, fingers spread.

I could hear the low rumble of voices above, the noblemen seated on the stage muttering amongst themselves. (In front of the King!)

"Nonetheless, my soul is troubled," Mother cried out, and they stilled. Her voice, so low and melodic, was full of emotion.

"Come, Turnip, we're on next," I said, backing out on all fours.

held Gaston's hand, listening for the end of the first scene.
I was not a thirteen-year-old girl, quivering with nervous-
ness about playing before the King—I was a princess, the
Spanish Infanta, as noble and proud a young woman as ever there was.
I shifted the tin crown, which was giving me a pain in the head.

The scene ended and Mother and Father reappeared. "You were
perfect," Father told Mother, kissing her lightly before lifting his skirts
and climbing down onto the trunk.

"Was it frightful?" I asked.

"Only at the start," Mother assured me. I handed her up a cap and
apron. She played my waiting-maid in the next scene.

Gaston hummed a quavering note. I looked into his staring eyes.
"When you're on the stage, all you have to do is stand there until I say,
Go to Chimène," I reminded him.

I climbed onto the scaffold, trying not to think of the doomed
criminals who had breathed their last on these planks.

MOTHER AND I exchanged a look—*Ready?*—and stepped onto
the stage, Gaston following close behind.

"Page, go to Chimène," I commanded Gaston, my voice breaking. I wiggled my fingers and he bolted, tripped, and scrambled away,
giggling in spite of himself. (But he'd done it! His first stage performance!)

"Chimène is late for her daily visit," I said, remembering to stand
at an angle in order to address both Mother and the audience at the

same time. I dared not glance at the King lest I faint. Nor could I turn my back to him.

The noblemen on the stage were murmuring amongst themselves. My mouth went dry; I bit my tongue to raise saliva. "My sweetest hope is to lose all hope," I croaked.

Gaston tumbled back onto the stage as if pushed from behind.

"Chimène is here?" I asked. He scrambled back out before I could say, "Go now."

WE MANAGED WELL through several scenes—then it was time for the duel. I was to play the Count who had offended an old warrior, Father the old warrior's son, defending his father's honor.

I stepped onto the platform opposite Father, my hand on the hilt of my wood sword. I pushed my right foot forward, my sword point high: On guard!

The audience stilled.

Observe. Take time. Have patience. We'd practiced dozens of times, and yet now, before such an auspicious audience, I froze.

Father broke the spell by lunging and I leapt to my defense.

Thrust, cut, lunge, feint.

Gaston, under the scaffold, clanged the pot lids as Father and I leapt back and forth across the stage.

Father made the final, fatal lunge, as rehearsed. With a cry of piercing agony, I dropped my sword and fell back. He held his weapon to my chest and I died dramatically as he appeared to plunge it in. The audience gasped!

I FOLLOWED FATHER off the scaffold as Mother stepped to the candles to narrate a summary of what followed. In spite of her carrying voice, she was drowned out by jeers. The sound of chairs and benches being moved was deafening.

I glanced at Father. What was going on?

Mother clambered back down onto the trunk. "The Queen Mother left with the King and his brother, and now everyone is going."

"But why?" I didn't know what to make of it.

"Come on out, lad," Father told Gaston, stooping. "Bring the pot lids."

Gaston emerged out from under the scaffold, his face and hands smudged.

"We appear to have lost our audience," Father explained.

"Count yourself blessed if that's all you lose," a low voice growled behind us. We turned to see the Duc de Mortemart, attended by his two secretaries. (I was relieved that his daughter was not with him.) "How could you!" Mortemart sputtered.

"Monsieur le Duc, please be so kind as to inform us of our offense," Mother said with a respectful curtsy.

"It is against the *law* to duel."

I glanced at Father, confused. Duels were what audiences liked best.

"Monseigneur, this is a play," Father began diplomatically, unsheathing his carved wooden sword, "and this weapon hardly qualifies."

The Duc de Mortemart pulled in his chins. "Dueling is forbidden in every form, even on the stage. This was recently signed into law by His Majesty."

"Respectfully, Monseigneur," Father began again, being careful not to look directly into the face of a superior, "how is a player in the provinces to know?"

Truly! I thought, picking up Gaston.

"You have flouted His Majesty's command *to his face*." The Duke's cheeks were quivering. "I suggest you get your brood out of town before I have every last one of you publicly flogged—beginning with your little idiot."

WE PACKED UP in a panic, but even so, the sun was starting to set by the time Bravo was harnessed and our cart loaded. I tucked Gaston into the folded backdrop and covered him over with costumes, hoping he would sleep.

We passed the massive church, its brightly colored façade catching the last of the light. I stopped for a moment, listening to the bells for evening Mass calling out the performance of the miracle: wine turned to blood, bread to flesh. A miracle forbidden to us, as players.

I followed after my family down the narrow cobbled street. From behind the stable wall where I had changed into my clown costume only days before, three men in hooded cloaks appeared, masked.

"Father?" I called out, my heart lurching.

"Players," I heard one of the men snarl.

"A demon and his trollop," said another as they began to circle.

They speak French, I noted with an odd detachment, too shocked to think, much less move . . . until I heard my mother scream.

One of the men had hold of her. She was thrashing against him, but he was laughing, as if it were a game. With a shout, Father tackled the man from behind.

Gaston's head popped up over the edge of the cart. "Hide!" I called out to him, falling down on the cobbles in my haste. I scrambled back onto my feet. "Help!" I screamed, hoping that there were men in the tavern nearby, hoping they would hear me.

The two other men had pulled Father off. Mother was still struggling, but the big man held her. I kicked him in the backside. He let go of Mother and I kicked him again, aiming for his codpiece. He grabbed me roughly by the hair.

Two of the men had Father down on the cobbles. Helpless, I heard the sickening sound of heavy boots, my father's grunts of pain.

"Alix, don't!" he cried out as Mother flung herself at his attackers.

"Hey!" someone yelled. Men emerged from the door of the tavern across the road, hefty laborers. "Leave off!" "We'll roast your balls!"

With a wrench, I was pushed away. Cloaks flapping, the masked men disappeared down a dark alley. I swayed on my feet, panting, my teeth chattering.

Mother was down on the cobbles beside my father. His eyes opened. Merci Dieu. "The devils," he said, struggling to sit.

The men standing at the door of the tavern cheered.

"Nicolas, I was so—" Mother began to weep.

"You were a fury," he said with a weak chuckle. "You too, Claudette. My women."

I picked up his hat and dusted it off. The feather had snapped at the spine. "Where are you hurt?"

Father touched his forehead. "It's just a bump," he said, putting on his hat. He winced and pushed it back off his forehead.

One of the men, drunk as a wineskin, staggered over with an earthen mug of what smelled like warm grog. He said something kindly but incomprehensible.

"Bless you," Father said, downing the mug.

I became aware of Gaston whimpering. He was standing in the cart, throwing out props.

The men gestured for us to come inside the tavern.

"Thank you," my father said, "but—" And then his eyes rolled back.

CHAPTER 7

We headed north again, eating stolen apples as we walked. Father had recovered, but toward midday the swelling on his forehead got bigger and he could no longer wear his hat. He covered himself with the hood of his cloak, like a penitent. "I'm praying for you," he said, making light.

That night, camping in an abandoned stone hut, Mother and I watched him. "I'm fine," he insisted, but it was clear the injury pained him, and twice in the night he cried out in his sleep, overtaken by specters.

In the morning, there was a blush around my father's wound and his left eye and cheek were swollen. Mother gave him half a dram of dried lovage root, an herb under the sign of Taurus. I suggested he be bled.

"But no cuts," she insisted: only leeches.

At a pond fringed with reeds, I showed Gaston how to stir up the shallows and scoop the leeches up with a spoon. I held the tin as he slipped each wriggling dark body in. The leeches had long brownish stripes down their backs and speckled underbellies.

By the time the sun was high, we had caught thirteen, one as big as my thumb. Gaston hummed a tune as we headed back to the camp; I wished for his lightness of heart.

Mother washed Father's wound and then patted it gently dry. I showed Gaston how to pick a leech up by the middle and hold its small end to the inflamed area.

"But not *on* my eye," Father joked.

Gaston laughed with delight to see Father draped in leeches.

Then we all watched, entranced, as the slimy creatures fattened and began to drop off.

MOTHER SET UP the Virgin with her relics: the corn-husk doll, the chipped cup, the key. The dried carnations I put under my father's pillow of straw to keep bad dreams away. That night he did not suffer pain. Mother knelt by the Virgin and prayed, offering thanks for the miracle.

"Don't waste your time." His voice sounded thick, as if his tongue were swollen.

I looked at Mother's little Virgin propped in the corner. Her eyes were cast down, avoiding my gaze.

And indeed, the next morning Father was feverish again and dis-tressingly weak. He'd developed a harassing cough in the night, bring-ing forth a rust-tinged froth.

"Don't worry," he said, touching Mother's hand.

I insisted she stay with him while Gaston and I went to a nearby village market to perform. We were sorely in need of money for a healer.

GASTON AND I passed through the village gates and made our way to the market. I found a spot near the fountain. Heart heavy, I tumbled and juggled and made a clatter with the slapstick. Then I played the wood flute while Gaston hummed. Perhaps our poor spirits showed, because people gave us a wide berth.

I reminded myself of my parents' teaching: *invention, especially when things go wrong.* Father insisted that we were players, not beggars, yet I was desperate to save him. I covered my clown costume with my cloak and told Gaston to stand silently by my side as I held out the cup, crying in a plaintive voice, "In God's name, help us, I beg you, we're orphans." It was not chivalrous to beg—much less lie—but this was no time for a knight's scruples.

The bells rang for evening prayer; it was time to head back. I lingered, watching the well-dressed families enter the glow of the church. We'd gotten a meager three deniers—not nearly enough for a healer, but enough for a prayer.

The village priest stood inside the church door, welcoming his parishioners. He frowned when he saw me and put out his arm.

I was barred?

He made the sign of the cross in front of my face—as if I were a devil! "You're a *player*." Gesturing at the costume just visible beneath my cloak.

"We go into churches all the time," I protested. As players, we couldn't take Communion, but we liked the singing, and some churches had wonderful organs.

"You mock the Eucharist in feigning to *choose* what you feel." He was short, but righteousness seemed to inflate him. "Only Christ has the power to choose what He feels, only Christ can *choose* to suffer. And He chose for us! A player will never cross the threshold of this sacred realm, and especially not your"—he sneered down at Gaston— "your idiot boy, son of the Devil."

I spat in his face.

I STOOD OUTSIDE the church doors, stunned by what I'd just done, anger still coursing through me. I crouched down beside Gaston. My thoughts were turbulent, both furious and dejected. I must learn to dissemble, not give way to choleric passions. "That was a bad thing I just did." I'd been taken over by a demon, surely. Perhaps the priest was right.

Gaston hummed, sucking his dirty thumb, his eyes tearing.

"I'm sorry," I said. He gave way to tears as I embraced him. Had he heard what the priest said? Had he understood? "Come, Turnip, we're going back home," I said, wiping his cheeks and taking his hand.

Home: a stone hovel.

I looked back with longing and anger at those within the church: warm, well-fed, blessed. How easy it must be, I thought, to live in the realm of the chosen, to fatten in the certainty of Heaven.

other was weeping when Gaston and I returned to where we were camped, tearing at her hair like a madwoman. "Nicolas is not getting better," she wailed, covering her face with her hands.

Gaston began to cry again, frightened to see Mother in such disarray.

"You must go back to town, get the priest," she said, gripping my arm. "Nicolas must renounce. If he doesn't, he—"

"I know, Maman." If a player didn't renounce the stage before he died, he would go to Hell. "But I will not speak to that priest!" Ever! Wrath and remorse surged through me, stirring up my blood.

And then I realized what it was that my mother was saying: Father was *dying*? I rushed to the hut, stooping to squeeze through the entrance. "Father?" I felt his foot—uncovered—and heard him faintly moan.

The stench of the infection was suffocating. I must not up-heave! I turned to the opening, for control, then crawled back. I could see him better now, the light of the setting sun illuminating his face. One side was swollen. His eyes, sunken into his skull, were bright.

I reached for his hand—so hot! Mother is right, I thought with swooning dizziness.

"Claudette," Father said, strangely matter-of-fact and without difficulty. "Tell me a story," he said. "Something funny." His smile was grim, but sweet.

I can't, I thought. "You tell one," I said, lighting a rush candle. "Tell me a story about the glory days." A story about the time before the wars and famine—a story of long, long ago, before theaters had to close because there wasn't even flour to powder a player's face. A story of the golden time *before* all that. "Tell me of the Great Corneille," I said.

"He applauded me," Father said, brightening.

"I didn't know that," I lied. My parents regarded the playwright as practically a saint.

"I think he rather fancied Alix," he added with a weak chuckle that made him cough. "Your mother has a talent for the stage," he said, recovering, "a God-given gift, I swear." He paused to catch his breath. "Oh, Lord," he groaned, but the convulsion passed and he was still.

Too still, I thought, fear chilling my blood. "I'm going to get Mother to sit with you," I told him, crawling toward the opening. I felt sick at the thought of facing that priest—after what I'd done!—yet I knew I must. If Father didn't formally renounce the stage, he would spend eternity in Hell, suffering pains worse than being torn apart by a pack of wolves.

"Don't disturb your mother," Father said.

"Someone needs to be with you."

"You're here."

"But I have to go into the village, Father." I would have to be repentant: that would be the hard part. But I could do it. I *was* repentant! I would play the part truly, with all my heart.

"Whatever for?"

"If you don't . . . if you . . ."

"It's dark," he said patiently. As if I wasn't talking any sense.

"I know. I'm not a child."

"Verily, Claudette, you are not, but I have authority over you. I forbid—" He swallowed and tried to lick his lips. "I forbid you . . . to leave my side."

"You must renounce!" I cried, weeping now.

He was silent for a time. "You think I'm dying."

I did not answer.

"I see," he said with a defeated tone. "Well—" He stopped, gasping for air like a drowning man. "I guess I'm not much of a player then," he said finally, recovering.

I clasped his burning hand. He *was* dying, and he knew it. This somehow made it true. "I spat at him, Father."

"At a priest?" His voice incredulous.

"Oui," I admitted, ashamed.

He chuckled meekly.

So I did have a funny tale for him after all. "He wouldn't let me into the church." And called Gaston son of the Devil. I dared not tell my father that. "I wanted to say a prayer for you."

"The ruffian," Father cursed, his breath labored again. "He'll be the one to burn in Hell."

I saw Father's rosary in the blankets and offered it to him.

"You're going to have to have more sense, Claudette," he said, running the beads slowly through his fingers. His breathing had calmed. "Your mother—she loves you and Gaston so much, but she's . . . she's not always strong. You may have to be the one to look after her and our sweet little fool. I'm sorry."

I heard an owl hoot in the silence.

"Promise me," he said.

I didn't answer right away. I knew that this was a sacred moment, knew that my words would have to be true. "I promise," I said at last. *To never betray a trust. To do what is right, whatever the cost.*

"Once the wars are over, go to Paris," he said, closing his eyes. "Look for Courageux."

I remembered Courageux. He'd been a member of our little troupe, a funny man who played the buffoon.

The rosary slipped out of Father's grasp, slithering into the grass bedding. "Paris," he said with a long sigh. "It was always my dream to see Alix play there again."

He fell silent. I leaned forward, my hand on his chest.

"I'm going to rest now," he said.

I retrieved the rosary and laced it between his fingers. His breaths came fitfully for a time, and then stopped.

ACT II

THE TRAVESTY PLAYER

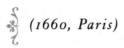 *(1660, Paris)*

CHAPTER 9

he room was dark and smelled of rat—but we could live with that. Anything to get out of the cold. Approaching Paris, we'd walked the river ice.

From the look of the blackened bricks, the fireplace smoked, but at least there was one. There was even a swing hook over the grate. The storage closet would be just big enough for Gaston to sleep in—soon he would be fourteen, too old to share a bed with his mother and big sister. And although the chicken butchery in the courtyard would be smelly, we might be able to get cheap meat from time to time, poultry not good enough for the market, but fine for our cauldron.

"I'll take it," I told Monsieur Martin, setting my cracked leather valise on the rush-strewn floor. We'd been living near Rennes when peace had finally been proclaimed, working on the country estate of an impoverished noble—Mother hired on as a necessary woman emptying chamber pots, I at the looms, Gaston cleaning the soot-clogged chimneys. It was a miserable existence, the steward cruel, and so, with our New Year's gifts of coin in hand, we'd set out for Paris, wending our way slowly across the war-ravaged fields on oxcarts and hay wagons, once even riding in the undercarriage of a post chaise. Everyone, it seemed, rich and poor alike, was swarming back into the city.

"That will be three months in advance," Monsieur Martin said, appraising me in a way I'd come to know rather too well. A woman of twenty-and-one, I was considered attractive in spite of my height, my small breasts and big feet.

With a theatrical show of despair, I sat down on the valise and looked up at him. A man gained ground by pressing a point; a woman by a show of submission. "*One* month, Monsieur?" I flashed my excellent teeth. We'd once been so desperate I'd considered selling them. The toothless rich were willing to pay handsomely.

My other treasure was my virginity, and I'd thought of selling it too, years back, to the steward's hunchback son. I had refrained, holding out—I told myself—for a higher bidder. Now I fancied myself ruler of an impregnable realm.

Impregnable, indeed! I was wearing every bit of clothing I owned: three chemises (one flannel, two with long sleeves), four skirts (one of heavy wool and another quilted felt), two bodices, three fichus, and two caps. Plus my father's old leather jerkin and two pairs of wool socks I'd knit myself, layered under his boots. *Plus* mitts, a hooded cloak, and a thread-thin lavender shawl, for ornament. Even so, I was cold. I pulled the shawl snug around my neck.

"Two," Monsieur Martin said. He was misproportioned, only his right arm muscular—from swinging a mallet, I guessed—a stone-mason by the look of his hands.

I took off my mitts and felt through the side-slits of my many skirts to the leather coin sack underneath. I pulled it out onto my lap, working the stiff lace. I frowned looking over the coins, counting, feigning difficulty with this simple task. I had more coins in my valise, but we would need them to buy bread, wood, and ale. We'd been warned that the water in Paris would make us violently sick, even when boiled and filtered through sand. "I have only enough for one month, Monsieur, but I will be a good tenant." Not mentioning Mother and Gaston.

"You seem like a nice enough girl." He leaned in, no doubt assuming I was setting up for trade.

I put out my hand, palm up—the universal pleading position, players call it. "*One* month?"

Monsieur Martin's hand on my shoulder was heavy. He could snap my neck should he choose. He roughly caressed my wrist as he took the coins. His nails were as black as his two teeth.

"It's agreed then," I announced in a carrying voice.

The door creaked open and Gaston peeped in, his blue eyes bright. He sang a hopeful, questioning note. His voice, yet to change, was high-pitched, that of a girl. Short, with chubby cheeks, he looked younger than his years.

Monsieur Martin stared, taken aback.

"This is my brother, Gaston," I said, stepping aside for him to edge into the room with our horse-hide traveling trunk and carpetbag. I motioned for him to put them down beside the dismantled table.

I heard shuffling footsteps. "And our mother, Madame des Oeillets," I said as Mother entered the room, panting from the climb.

"Mercy sakes!" she exclaimed breathlessly. Her plaits had come loose, giving her a wild look.

"The Widow des Oeillets," I added, although she did not look the part. She was wearing two frilly mobcaps and her dressing gown was on upside-down over her cloak. Its empty arms trailed after her like a noblewoman's train. Father's death years before had shaken her, beyond repair I feared. She'd become unsettled.

"Enchantée, Monsieur," she said, bending one leg and dipping with the extravagant air of a great lady. Gaston, unsure, tried to mime her.

"How many are you?" the landlord demanded.

"Only three, Monsieur," I assured him, with a watchful eye on Mother, who was now trying to prize open the leather trunk. "We're clean, quiet, and—"

"Weary me no more!" I heard Mother mutter as she wrenched open the trunk and started pulling out the contents, spreading them over the rushes: her small linens and patched stockings, a stained chemise. "Let me creep into the silence of the night to weep."

Clean, quiet—and just a little mad, I thought with chagrin, glancing apologetically at our new landlord.

"Madame, isn't that a line from *The Cid*?" he asked, stepping forward.

Mother looked up, bewildered.

"You've seen the play, Monsieur?" I asked, hoping to distract him.

"Three times—at the Petit-Bourbon."

I handed Gaston the leather bucket and gave him a denier to get water from a carrier. Eagerly he clambered out, clunking down the narrow stairs. "Are there many theaters?" I asked Monsieur Martin. One of the first things I planned to do now that we were in Paris was to try to find Monsieur Courageux, as Father had suggested. Our former troupe player might be able to help us find employment.

"Non, hélas! And now there is talk that even the Petit-Bourbon is to be taken down. The Bourgogne is said to be one of the best, but it's some distance from here and costful I'm told. There used to be another one, the Marais, but it burned."

Wasn't the Marais the theater my parents had played in? I looked over at Mother, but she was still rummaging through the trunk. I cringed to see the mess she was making.

"It's a pity. The Petit-Bourbon is a fine theater," Monsieur Martin went on, ebullient now. "I also saw *Cinna* there, but *The Cid* is my favorite. There hasn't been a new Corneille play since the great play-wright retired."

"Ah, here she is," Mother exclaimed, lifting up the tiny wood statue of the Virgin.

"My mother played in *The Cid*," I said, judging from Monsieur Martin's enthusiasm that it was safe to reveal our background. "In the original production."

"You're a player, Madame?" the landlord asked, his voice awed.

"*No,* Monsieur," Mother said, standing, looking around for a place to set the Virgin. "I'm decidedly not."

"*The Cid,* Maman—you had a part in the original production."

"It was only a small part," Mother said, setting the Virgin in a corner and placing trinkets at her feet: the rusty key, a dried carnation, the chipped teacup.

"Not *that* small a part," I said, crossing my arms. We'd had to sell our costumes in Nantes, the slapstick, tin crown and wood sword at a country fair near Saint-Nazaire. Stories of the glory days were all I had left. "You played Leonora—"

"The Infanta's lady-in-waiting?" Monsieur Martin pressed his wool cap to his heart. *"Do you wish to live in the land of dream?"* he recited in falsetto.

"Non! I will compose myself—in spite of my grief," Mother answered, giving the Infanta's correct response. (Though her wits had scattered, her memory for verse remained wondrous.)

"Would you happen to know of a player named Courageux, Monsieur?" I asked on impulse.

Monsieur Martin shook his head, his mouth downturned.

I was about to ask if he knew of any charity schools (for Gaston), but I was silenced by a woman's sharp voice calling up the stone stair-well.

"Ah, it's the boss—my wife." He turned at the door. "I'll send my boy up with wood."

"Thank you, Monsieur!" I said, but already he was gone, whistling down the stairs.

"I can't find the corn-husk doll," Mother said, sitting back on her haunches.

"It's in the carpetbag," I said, prying open the shutters of the one small window to the cacophony of hawkers below. I looked down at the jostling crowd. The elevation dizzied me. Paris! I had at last ful-filled my promise to my father.

Finally I spotted Gaston carrying the leather bucket, slopping water in his cumbersome way. He was becoming a young man; he was going to need a place in the world.

CHAPTER 10

Nil desperandum. Never despair.

In Paris, flour was five times what we were used to paying; even a sack of beans was dear. What resources we had were running out. I became sleepless, my mind spinning through the dark hours.

I'd asked everywhere, searching for Monsieur Courageux. I'd looked for work as a washerwoman, milliner, or seamstress, knocking on the doors of service entrances to the private grand hotels, and even the more humble back-alley merchants—fighting off more than one advance due to the assumption that any woman who worked was a prostitute. I'd quickly discovered that it was impossible to get almost any kind of employment without a guild certificate—and guild membership was not only hard to obtain, but expensive as well. I could do many things—just not, apparently, for hire. I could read and write, I was a qualified letter-writer, but the genteel vocations were closed to women. I was going to have to be, in Father's word, *inventive.*

"We'll go to the bridge today," I told Mother. "Gaston and I."

She glanced up from her knitting. She'd been working on a shawl since before the New Year, using ends of darning worsted together with scraps of carpet thread, twine, twill, and leather. The shawl got longer and longer, uglier and uglier, but was never pronounced finished.

I took up my sack, heavy with stones. "You stay, Maman. There's beer and bread."

I led Gaston through a maze of dark alleys to the river. He sang a frenzied melody, jogging to keep up.

I paused, waiting for an opportunity to cross the roadway. Coaches, carts, and horses were coming in all directions. Mercifully, the rain had let up. Mercifully, it wasn't snowing.

"New?" he stuttered.

The Pont Neuf, I guessed he meant, the new bridge. Over time he had learned to form a few simple words. With schooling, I was confident he could learn more. "No, we'll try the Pont Marie," I said, once we were over the mud-rutted intersection. There would be more people on the wide new bridge, but it would be crowded with licensed stalls—and officers of the law.

He pressed his hand to his forehead, then waggled a finger: *I'm not worried.*

I smiled and puckered my nose at him. Really, he was so sweet. "I've got an idea." It had come to me in the night—*Thank you, Father!*— a plan that would not only feed us, but possibly even enable me to hire a teacher for Gaston and eventually enroll him in an apprenticeship program.

The vista at the river revealed a vast sky, blooming with dark clouds. To the right, the towers of Notre-Dame on the Île de la Cité were shrouded in mist. To the left was the Pont Marie, leading to the Île Saint-Louis.

Most of the river was still ice, but pocked now, softened by the rain. In stretches I could see black water, turgid and swollen, foaming. It roared through one of the arches of the bridge. A barrel, tossed up by the turbulent water, shattered against the piles.

"Here comes another one," I heard someone behind me say.

People cheered as a second barrel exploded into splinters, thrown up against the bridge by the surging water.

I watched for a chance to cross over the roadway, but it was thronged with carriages and carts, men on horseback. A four-horse carriage manned by men in livery raced past, the driver cracking his whip. "Careful," I said, holding Gaston back. I'd seen a woman run down by a team of horses the day before.

A homeless family emerged from the riverside, dragging a soggy canvas. They waded fearlessly into the traffic.

"Is the river rising?" a hawker of oysters called out.

"Not yet," the beggar woman answered. The rain clouds parted. "Ah, sun," she said, tipping her face to the sky.

· · ·

THE PONT MARIE was more like a street than a bridge, lined on both sides with houses in ill repair. Shutters hung from hinges and some windows were boarded over. Both sides of the road were crowded with hawkers and beggars, whores and charlatans, gangs of ill-shod children. From one of the windows—Chez Gilbert—came a chorus of sawing and hammering, carpenters singing as they worked. The sudden warm weather had made everyone joyous.

I headed up the steeply sloping bridge, pushing my way through to a small spot beside a stand in front of a jeweler's shop. *Fortunes 4 sous,* a sign said.

A plump woman, humming cheerfully, fussed over the rosaries, saint images, and good-luck charms spread out on a little table.

Gaston hummed along with her in harmony.

"Lovely," she said, beaming at him. She was wearing a heavy cloak in a sickly shade of goose-turd green. But for a hairy mole on one cheek, she was pretty as a posy.

"He likes to sing," I said, wishing I had four sous. I would have liked to know my fortune. Would I ever marry, have a family of my own? "Is it permitted to set up here?"

"I've the license, but I'm happy to share the space if you're willing to watch over my table when I'm reading the cards."

"Certainly!" I said, taking a waxed cloth out of our sack and spreading it on the cobbles, making it smooth. I set the wooden Mill board on it and gestured to Gaston to sit down in front of it. He looked puzzled but did as I asked. I set out the stones, the dark ones on his side (his favorites), the light ones on the other side of the board.

"Trust me," I told him, propping up a sign I'd made: *1 denier to play: 3 if you win.* Gaston had a curious talent for the game.

oon a boy stopped by. He was tall and gangly, bone thin, his hair uncut and his clothes rags. "Don't," I said. He was clearly impoverished. "He'll beat you."

"Impossible," he insisted, but soon discovered otherwise. Even so, I refused his coin.

Next was a girl with her mother, then a miller and a maid, and then some shopkeepers and a number of others, mostly men. Gaston won every game, of course. The last was a group of four roughs. "Hey!" they exclaimed, seeing their chance. They threw down their coins, one after another, then skulked away defeated, their pockets empty.

I counted our earnings: fifteen deniers. I sent Gaston to get oysters from a vendor, cheap fare.

"Does he always win?" the fortune-teller asked, standing and stretching. Madame Catherine, she'd introduced herself. She'd had quite a few customers that morning telling fortunes.

"Oui," I admitted proudly. I'd never won a game of Mill against him. (Ever!)

"Yet a simple," she observed.

I noticed she offered remedies for a variety of ailments, from worms to faint sweats—a dragon's blood cure for colds, another concoction for pain of the piles. "Have you a cure for such a . . . malady?" I asked on impulse.

"No, but I know of a woman who got a mute to talk," she said, "and a girl, dumb as a donkey, she got to read and write Latin."

My heart sang to hear of such miracles. "How much does she charge?"

"Quite a bit—nine livres?"

A lot, certainly, but not an impossible sum—especially now with coins in my poke, Gaston's winnings.

Suddenly Madame Catherine whistled—shrilly, like a man. Gaston looked our way. "Call your brother back," she told me with some urgency.

Puzzled, I gestured to Gaston, and he shambled toward me grinning. Approaching, he opened his fist, revealing a gold louis.

I'd never seen a coin so big. It hadn't even been clipped. "Where did you get this?" I asked uneasily. Sometimes Gaston took things. He wasn't a thief, he just didn't understand.

"No doubt from that tall man," Madame Catherine said starkly, "the one with the children."

A break in the carriage traffic parted to reveal an elaborately dressed man standing with three girls. The tallest one stood staring at us. She had a large birthmark on her cheek. "With the girls?" I asked, weighing the gold piece in my hand.

"They're boys—but dressed as girls."

It took me a moment to understand.

"The Bird Catcher, we call him," Madame Catherine said, signing herself.

I recalled the country boys who had stayed with us in the cave near Poitiers, headed for the city. Winter Swallows, Mother had called them.

"Friend," Gaston sang.

HEADING HOME, GASTON in tow, I stopped abruptly. "You are never to take anything from a stranger!" He was such a trusting soul, it frightened me. The city was rife with predators. "The coin that man gave you was like honey: he was trying to lure you into a trap."

Gaston's eyes rounded.

I should have flung the coin in the river, as a lesson to him, but we needed it, needed the beans and bread it could buy. "Do you understand?"

He blinked his eyes at me (meaning "oui") and made a rabbit nose (meaning "non").

So: *oui et non*. I sighed.

A coachman called out in warning as a four-horse berlin turned into the street. The horses stopped to avoid upturning a fish cart. I glimpsed the face of a young woman inside, her golden earlocks adorned with ribbons, a single strand of pearls tied at the back of her neck. Gaston sang a troubled note, taking off his woolen cap. She looked like a creature from another world—yet a creature who was somehow familiar.

The heavy horses trotted smartly on, their harnesses glittering with brass, their headlocks beribboned and tails braided. The coat of arms painted on the door was intricate, a shield of red, blue, and white designs, a coiled blue snake in one quadrant.

The carriage slowed to turn onto another street, followed by two lackeys. "Tell Maman I'll not be long," I said, giving my brother the satchel of stones to take back. "I'm going to buy food."

THE CARRIAGE HAD stopped in front of a trimmings shop on the rue Vieille du Temple. It was not far from our room, yet another world entirely, a world of luxury trade. There was even something of a walkway, so that people might more easily stop to examine the fine goods offered for sale: a yellow-tinted collar edged with needle lace, a leather hat adorned with an ostrich feather, a bolt of silk satin worked with gold thread.

I watched from the corner as a footman in a buckram-stiffened cloak opened the carriage door and set down a carpeted stool. He extended his gloved hand to help the young woman step down. With a fur muff under one arm, she extended her booted foot, turning her toe out as if dancing. I caught a glimpse (just that) of her ankle. With a little hop, she alighted and handed her muff to the footman. She turned her back as an elderly servant with a crooked spine climbed down after her.

I could not take my eyes off the young woman. *Could* it be her? She was wearing a blue velvet traveling cloak, its satin-lined hood lightly covering her head. She fussed with the muff the footman held, and I realized that there was a little dog inside. She touched its nose with her gloved hand.

Behind me, there was the sudden thunder of rubble being tipped out of a cart. Startled, she glanced my way. I caught my breath. A froth of golden curls framed her white, oval face. Her beauty was heart-stopping, her large blue eyes intelligent and curious. She looked to be a few years younger than I was, so perhaps nineteen? That fit, too.

My princess. *Could* it be?

She swept into the shop, followed by her creeping waiting woman.

It began to rain again, a soft drizzle. Men in elegant dress pressed to pass. I stood close against the wall. The footman looked in my direction, regarding me with suspicion.

I turned, bumping into a woman coming out of a milliner's shop. "Nom de Dieu," she cursed me with scorn, as if touched by the plague.

Her maid, encumbered with parcels and her mistress's fox-lined cloak, sneered. On impulse, I shouldered her into the muck and snatched the cloak . . . and then *ran*—ran for my life through the narrow, twisting alleyways.

Trembling, I paused for breath, clutching the heavy cloak. What had come over me! Cloak-thieves were executed, their heads boiled and displayed on pikes. Seeing the young woman again had bewitched me.

I promise, Father! I won't do it again.

IN THE MARKET, I quickly traded the cloak for a sack of beans, three loaves of bread and a small keg of beer, watered and bitter. I could have easily bartered for three times all that, but I was in haste to have it out of my hands.

It was raining again and falling dark. With Gaston's winnings I bought a good-sized ham, saving the Bird Catcher's coin for the rent.

I made my way back through the labyrinthine maze of narrow alleys. In the morning, I would make amends, repent, begin anew. In the morning, I would take Gaston to the bridge, play for winnings, get the name of that miracle healer from Madame Catherine. In the morning . . .

Approaching our building, I stopped. A crowd had gathered. Beyond, I saw a shimmering expanse.

Water?

"The river is rising high!" a street-caller cried. From somewhere a woman was screaming for help.

waded into the courtyard, sloshing through water covered with floating chicken feathers. The workers were stacking cages of squawking birds onto the slaughter table. Even the path to the privies was swamped. (I didn't like to think about that.)

A rat swam past the winding stone stairs. Monsieur Martin and his wife could be heard yelling in their room, piling up goods. Tenants were huddled on the landing, frowning down at the water, a girl holding a squirming terrier.

"What's happened?" I called up, alarmed.

"It's the river," one of men said, his accent rough. "It's rising."

The *river* water—all the way here?

"But it won't come any farther," he added. "It never does."

"THE RIVER IS overflowing," I announced as I came in the door. Mother was slumped where I had left her, her knitting all around her. "I'm sorry—did I wake you?"

"Is it time to eat?" she said, rubbing her eyes. "Did you have a pleasant afternoon?"

I took in the silence. "Where's Gaston?"

"With you?" Mother said, gathering up her needles and scraps.

"He's not here?" How was that possible? "Maman, he must be here."

She looked puzzled.

I leaned out the little window: the street below was a river now.

It had happened so quickly! People sloshed through the yellow water with children in their arms. But no Gaston.

What had I done? "I'll go find him."

"I'm coming too," Mother said. "I haven't been out all day."

I groaned. This was not a pleasure outing! "Maman, stay. It's miserable out." And dangerous. "Someone should be here when he returns."

This, at least, she accepted.

I plunged down the stairwell, trying to contain my panic.

I waded out into the street, the muck-filled water now at my thighs. I made my way back down toward the river—back to the corner where I had last seen Gaston—crying out his name. The murky water was rushing into the narrow streets and alleys in waves. Garbage floated in a cesspool of sewage.

I dodged horses pulling carts laden with possessions. The water was inching toward my waist. The current was surprisingly strong; it took an effort to push forward.

I feared I might faint from the stench. The light was falling, the water was rising, and Gaston was not to be seen. I turned back, praying he'd somehow returned.

HE HAD NOT. I broke down, sobbing, peeling off my disgustingly wet clothes. My teeth chattering, I stood naked in front of the fire as Mother washed me clean with a cloth, tsking all the while. "He will be fine," she said. "His father will look after him."

This thought made me weep all the harder.

THERE WAS NOTHING we could do but pray. Even if I had known where to look, the water was too high, too dangerous. We set up an altar for the little Virgin, surrounding her with Gaston's things: his bent-up, worn Saint Francis card, his two marbles, the rag doll he slept with. His favorite Mill stones. I even made a line of objects. (And discovered how hard it was. Was a glove bigger or smaller than a sock?)

Restless, I ventured back down the stairs, holding a rag over my nose to keep out the pestilent vapors. The water had reached the seventh step. We were trapped.

"We'll just have to wait it out," I told Mother, looking out our little window at the scene below, searching, ever searching for a sign of Gaston. Where could he be? He wouldn't have gotten lost; finding his way was one of his curious talents. Something must have happened.

A man calling out "Ferryman!" poled a makeshift raft of scraps. A neighbor propped a ladder against an upper-story window and carried a screaming girl onto a tippy boat. His wife handed him down an infant, then perilously climbed down herself.

I wondered where my princess lived. I imagined her asleep in a big feather bed, wrapped in the finest clean lawn chemise. Her belly was full and she slept without fear of rats. The sleep of the blessed.

As night fell, I couldn't sleep for the howling of abandoned dogs, the ceaseless church bells ringing alarm. I felt weak knowing that Gaston was somewhere out there, alone: knowing what the virulent floodwaters could bring—cholera, fever, plague. Had Father guided us here, only to die of contagion?

Or *worse,* I thought, thinking of the Bird Catcher.

I PACED AND prayed for days; the nights, too, were restive. I had finally drifted off to sleep when I was startled awake by a thunderous sound. I sat up, staring into the dark. Had I not felt a tremor?

I slipped out from under the covers and groped my way in the dark, creeping along the wall. I felt for the window latch and, fumbling, managed to creak open the shutter.

The light of the moon illuminated the rooftops, now covered with makeshift shanties and webbed with a maze of laundry lines hung between chimneys and turrets. The flooded street below was dark, reflecting the stars above. But for the barking of a dog, all was still and silent. Had I dreamt the explosion? Tainted food could do that, cause dreams to come to life.

From far off, I heard splashing and the low rumble of men talking. The light of a single lantern appeared, drawing near. A rowboat was making its way up the street, furnishings and crates piled high in the bow. Two men sat perched in the stern, one holding the oars, the other a lantern.

"Messieurs?"

They looked up. They could not see me in the dark.

"I heard a noise." I did not have to speak loudly to be heard.

"The bridge," one of them answered.

"The Pont Marie gave way," said the other.

Goodness: the *bridge?*

"Two arches out—and all the houses on it."

Gone? I thought of Madame Catherine: she, her husband, and children lived on that bridge, over the jewelry shop. I felt sick at the thought that the kindly woman might have perished—but then gasped with foreboding. Had Gaston sought shelter with *her?*

DAYS LATER, I woke to bells ringing. I fumbled open the shutters. The morning light was bright, the air cutting and cold. And there, far below, was the *street,* its cobbles dislodged. A muddy boat sat stranded. People were clustered around a bonfire at the corner, a man and a woman dancing on the stones as a boy played a fiddle.

And then I saw *him,* his lilting walk. He was with a tall, thin boy. "Gaston!" I screamed.

"Gaston?" Mother pressed behind me, weeping for joy.

I cried out again, and this time he looked up.

The boy, his companion, disappeared down an alley, fast as a whippet.

"Don't move," I yelled down. Don't. Move.

aston winced as we embraced him. "You're bruised?" There was an ugly welt on his cheek. "What happened!" He pressed his forehead against mine.

"Where does it hurt?" He was favoring one arm.

"Men," he stuttered with difficulty. "Mill."

I caught my breath: I recalled the face of one of the roughs Gaston had won against, recalled his threatening look as he'd slunk off with his companions. "It was that gang of boys, Gaston, wasn't it."

He mimed their tight fists, a kick.

"I'm so sorry!" I raged at my stupidity. He'd been attacked—and it was my fault. I'd set him up to play against strangers, knowing they would think him dim, *knowing* they would lose. I'd played them for fools and taken their money, not thinking of their outrage. Not thinking that it was not the *knightly* thing to do. And then I'd abandoned Gaston to chase after a foolish dream. Merci Dieu, he hadn't been killed! "Who was that boy you were with?"

"Friend," he sang.

No matter how I questioned, that's all he could reveal. Clearly, he'd been looked after, but how he'd managed to survive would have to remain a mystery.

WE HEADED DOWN the rue Vieille du Temple. Deep gashes in the street were filled with stagnant water, rich with the stench of waste. The sky was dark from the fires set to cleanse the air with smoke.

The drink shop at the corner of the rue Vieux Chemin de Charenton was filled with refuse, the kegs ruined. Dogs growled over meat rotting in a butcher's shop. We passed the mud-filled trimmings shop where I had seen my princess in what seemed like another lifetime.

A shoemaker was piling his ruined wares in front of his shop. He pulled out a pair of men's red-heeled boots that he thought might fit me. (Me of the big feet.) "Made for a courtier," he said, "once upon a time."

In such heels, I felt like a giant. With a playful cry, I hefted Mother up over my head and carried her screeching down the street like a performing muscleman. Gaston giggled and clapped. He was with us again; he was *safe*. We had emerged into another world, pestilent and wrecked, yet joyful with deliverance.

A CROWD WAS gathered on the quay, staring at the now-placid river, its banks piled with garbage.

"God have mercy," Mother whispered, signing herself . . . for half of the Pont Marie *was* gone.

I stared incredulously at the gap. How many houses had fallen away? Twenty? At least. I thought of the lives lost, thought of all the men, women, and children who had tumbled into a watery grave as they slept. I thought of the fortune-teller, Madame Catherine. Dead now.

Carriages of the curious passed by, their eyes wide with wonderment. A somber group of masked men in hooded cloaks and swinging large brass crosses cried out that the flood had been a sign of God's displeasure, a punishment for our sinful ways. Nearby, a stand was doing a brisk business selling hot chestnuts and beer. Already, carnival stalls were being set up in preparation for Mardi Gras. Not even devastation could stop Parisians from reveling in Fat Tuesday, the festival of indulgence before Lent. No: for Mardi Gras there would be nothing but celebration—and why not? People had lost their lives to the raging torrent. The survivors had cause to dance.

IN THE MORNING, our stale, hard bread long gone, I made to crumple its news-sheet wrapper for the fire. Then—*Thank you,*

Father—I laid it out flat. It was yellowed and brittle, a playbill of a theatrical performance, *The Triumph of Peace.*

At the Marais Theater.

The Marais was the theater my mother and father had performed in, the one Monsieur Martin said had burned down. The date of the production was past, but not *that* long past. More important, the location was revealed: "rue Vieille du Temple, across from the Capuchin monastery."

Our rue Vieille du Temple? Not far.

AT THE CORNER of the rue Vieille du Temple and the rue de Thorigny, the cobbles emerged dry and clean from beneath a skin of slimy mud, a realm untainted by the flood. Ahead, on the left, people were camped—the bewildered newly homeless. Tents and haphazard shanties filled a courtyard where children laughed and played. A nun in sandals moved slowly from one tent to another, distributing alms-bread out of a basket. By her rough garb, I knew her to be a Poor Clare—a Capuchin.

I turned, knowing what I would see. The tall, narrow building had a slightly peaked roof. A gaudy sign hung over the door: *Le Théâtre du Marais.* Tears came to my eyes recalling Father talking of this theater with such reverence. It was smaller than I'd imagined, and not nearly as grand.

The area in front of the theater was slippery with mud, the stench from an open cesspit across the road heavy in the air. The door was bolted shut. A painted sign informed me that the theater was closed until after Lent. A smaller sign below was apparently intended for the troupe: there was to be a general meeting on the twelfth just after Terce, the bells for morning prayer.

I made a note: three days.

n Thursday, the twelfth of February, I headed back up the rue Vieille du Temple. A chill breeze puffed up now and then, sending scraps flying. The river had held to its banks, but the air still reeked and there were heaps of rubbish everywhere.

My plan was to talk to the director of the troupe, offer myself and Mother as loge attendants, asking only three sous a day for the two of us. (Plus a meal, ideally.) Gaston could work odd jobs for free. That way we could keep an eye on him—and perhaps he'd even learn something.

Of course, three sous a day would never be enough. The key would be getting Mother taken on as a player eventually, and thus entitled to a cut of the take.

Approaching the theater, I held back, watching as people entered for the meeting. Some had the lean look of players, others were laborers, thick in their ways. A few lingered around a vendor selling venison pasties and burnt wine. One tight, consoling circle had formed around a woman relating a tearful account of flood rescue and loss.

An older woman in a man's wig emerged from the theater. "It's too chill to keep these doors open," she scolded, kicking away a wooden prop. "Everyone in." Her demeanor was affable, at odds with her gruff words and the curious nature of her costume. (Mother might not appear daft in such company.)

As the last of those lingering outside disappeared into the theater, I stepped forward.

"Are you here for the meeting?" the woman in the wig asked, looking up at me sideways.

"Not exactly." I was tempted to curtsy, as one would to someone in such an ostentatious hair piece, however laughable. No doubt it kept her head warm. I edged my foot in front of the door, to prevent it from being closed in my face. "I'm to talk to someone about employment." As if it had already been arranged.

"Now? Best hurry then," she said, and I slipped in behind her. She nodded toward the closet where tickets were sold. There, an old man sat hunched over a plank table, sorting piles of coins by the light of a candle. "Monsieur Pierre?"

He looked up, squinting. I guessed he might be as old as fifty. He had tufted eyebrows and a high forehead. A thick black moustache almost covered his lips. He was dressed in black with a crumpled white collar—an accountant, I surmised, by the look of him, some kind of clerk. A humble, dull, settled sort of man.

"There's a woman here to see about employment."

"Send her to Monsieur la Roque, Madame Babette," he said, not even looking up, pulling on the tuft of hair under his lower lip.

"Bonjour, Monsieur," I said, boldly stepping forward nonetheless. I slipped off the hood of my cloak and edged into the cubicle. A coal-filled brass brazier was set on the table, giving off a welcome heat. A half-empty flagon of milk was perched on a shelf. "I'm of a theatrical family—between my mother and me and my strong brother, there isn't any stage work we haven't done." I was talking too fast; I coached myself to slow down. "My mother and I could be loge attendants, but we can also help build, sew, paint sets. I can do sums, *read;* I know how to prompt." The room smelled of cheese and garlic, which sharpened my hunger. (How long had it been since I'd eaten cheese?) I feared my stomach would growl.

"The troupe has all the hands they need," he said, returning to stacking coins.

"I can juggle." I looked around the tiny chamber for objects I could use to demonstrate.

"The Marais does not perform farces anymore." On the word *farces* he revealed a hint of a stutter, the way Gaston sometimes did.

"We will work for a mere sou or two," I persisted, already lowering my price. "You would not regret it, I promise you."

"We employ too many as it is." He rolled a stack of coins into a square of cloth and placed it in a wood box, tapping it in to fit.

"My mother is a wonderful actress," I pressed on. "She performed *here,* at this very theater."

"I advise you not to tell false stories, Mademoiselle," he said tiredly. His eyes were watery but bright. "This theater has been closed off and on for some time."

"Monsieur, I speak the God's truth! It was a long time ago, around the time that the King's cousin was publicly baptized." I didn't know the year, but I recalled Father saying that La Grande Mademoiselle had been nine at the time, and had screamed with laughter when dunked. Gaston, as a child, had to be distracted with a reenactment of the story the few times he was bathed—it was the only way we could get his hair wet.

"Your mother must be of an age," he said with a bemused expression, putting the box into a trunk and locking it with an iron key, which he pressed into the side of his boot.

How old *was* Mother? It shocked me to realize that she must be nearing forty. "She played in the very first performances of *The Cid,* Monsieur." There, I had said it, said it all. "She worships the work of the Great Corneille . . . as I do," I added, shy about revealing a matter so tender to my heart. "As does everyone, of course," I said, abashed now. (And flailing.)

"Which part did your mother play?" he asked, testing me.

"Leonora, the Infanta's lady-in-waiting, Monsieur. She talks of that performance often." Well—at least Father had.

"Then she would have known who played the Infanta, I should think."

I felt my cheeks and neck flush. "Mademoiselle Beau . . ." Something to do with a building. "Beauchâteau," I said, relieved when the name jumped into my head. (Thank you, Father!)

"And Rodrigue?"

What a question! "The great Montdory, Monsieur."

He pressed his thumb into the cleft in his chin. "What color is your mother's hair?"

"Red," I said uneasily; women with red hair were regarded with suspicion. "And my father played one of the minor nobles," I added. But which one—Don Arias, Sancho, or Alonzo?

"Are you certain of that?"

I could hear people laughing in the foyer, both men and women. "Don Sancho," I said, taking a wild guess. "He talked of the great crowds, all the benches and chairs that had to be put on the stage to accommodate them all, Monsieur Corneille applauding. It was the most wonderful moment of my father's life," I said, my voice catching. "He's passed on now."

"Nicolas de . . . *Vin*?"

I stared.

"But he changed his name . . . to something—" He twirled his right hand in the air. "Something flowery."

Was it possible this man *knew* my father?

There was a light tap at the door, which swung open. A dignified man with a neatly trimmed white beard divided into points stood holding a sheaf of papers. He was big-chested, his ancient embroidered doublet too small for him. "We're about ready, Monsieur Pierre." His voice was husky, loud.

"As you say, Monsieur la Roque," Monsieur Pierre said with a groan, struggling to his feet. I wondered if I should help him, but the bearded man stepped forward.

There were quite a few people in the entry now. Several followed Messieurs Pierre and La Roque through a door into the theater. A gong sounded three times and then everyone began to file in, finishing whatever crusts of pastry or mugs of hot wine they had in their hands.

"Coming?" the woman in the wig said.

trailed inconspicuously behind a group of men, stagehands and carpenters I guessed, by their dress. We filed into the rows of the amphitheater. I slid onto the bench behind them, as if I belonged.

The space under the roof let in a little light. A few candles in one of the hanging candelabras helped illuminate the parterre, which was partially full of trunks and sets. For fear of ruin by the flood, no doubt—yet miraculously untouched, it appeared. On the sides were the tiers of curtained loges for the wealthy. The empty stage was a dark, inviting presence. The floor appeared to be raked.

The bearded man named Monsieur la Roque strode to the center of the parterre and turned to address the assembly. He had a commanding presence. I decided that he must be the troupe's director. "Before we begin, I believe we should give thanks to the heavens that our theater was spared."

A murmur swept through the crowd. It *was* a large troupe. I would look for another showplace possibility, something smaller, more at the street level, perhaps in the fairgrounds I'd heard of. I'd been foolish to think we could start so grandly.

"I've set up a board in the entry. If you are in need, post a note. We are a family, we look after one another."

The woman who had been weeping outside let out a sob, but then laughed, apologizing.

Monsieur la Roque smiled gently, pulling on one point of his white beard. "I think you will all agree that the sooner we open our doors to the public, the better."

There was some applause and even a few cheers.

"The first fortnight of performances have been decided. We shall open with Brécourt's *False Death*—"

Everyone turned to smile at a blond young man, who I took to be the playwright. He grinned and tipped his hat. He was sitting beside an older woman, who gave him a kiss on the cheek.

"—then three others, all of which are staples of our repertory, so will require little in the way of rehearsal." Monsieur la Roque paused before saying: "But not long after we thought we should open with the Paris premiere of *The Golden Fleece*."

More applause, cheers, and a thunder of boots this time.

He smiled, waiting for everyone to quiet. "For those of you who are unfamiliar with the play, it's a rather amazing extravaganza, a tragedy about Medea—"

"Bravo!" several called out. I laughed along with all the others—the evil sorceress Medea was a popular subject.

"—a queen torn between erotic and political power."

Oh! people sighed.

But more important, Monsieur la Roque went on to explain, this was to be a "machine play," produced with special effects—players flying through the air on clouds, monsters coming alive. "However—" Monsieur la Roque waited patiently for a chance to be heard. One side of his beard was longer than the other, I noticed, from him pulling on it. "Such spectacles cost. We'll have to go into considerable debt." He threw up his hands. "It's a gamble."

"We like to live dangerously," a woman called out with enthusiasm, a sentiment that seemed to be shared.

"So long as we survive," Monsieur la Roque said. He had the look of a man who had endured. "As you no doubt know," he went on, "His Majesty has hired the Italian machinist Vigarani to construct a theater in the palace that will be capable of producing machine plays as well. But Vigarani is behind schedule, so if we work hard and keep on track, we will be the first company in Paris to offer a spectacle of this magnitude"—he held up his hand for silence—"made possible by our very own Keeper of Secrets." He gestured to a man sitting at the front. "The remarkable Denis Buffequin."

A burly, short man with a black patch over his left eye stood, made a perfunctory bow, and sat back down, flushing brightly. I wondered what a Keeper of Secrets did.

"There will be substantial work required to prepare," Monsieur la Roque continued. "Our scheduler will talk to you all, but first, the moment you've all been waiting for, the man who needs no introduction." He made a dramatic and fulsome bow. "Monsieur Pierre."

Two men carried in a throne chair—no doubt used as a stage prop—and placed it facing the group. Another man helped Monsieur Pierre to it and offered him an ear-trumpet to speak into, but he waved it off.

Vigorous applause fell away to an attentive silence. Monsieur Pierre began to speak, and then stopped to clear his throat. Someone jumped up to give him a jug of wine, which he theatrically raised in toast before pretending to down it.

"Well," he said, feigning to be drunk, "that's just what I needed."

It was a silly jest and he delivered it rather lamely, but I laughed along with all the others.

"Madame Babette?" He held out his hand. The old woman in the wig sprang (with surprising agility) from the bench with a stack of parchment secured at one corner with twine: a script.

"Since many of you are already familiar with *The Golden Fleece,* I'm just going to explain the highlights," Monsieur Pierre mumbled, looking over the pages. "It begins with a prologue, an allegory played out by War, Peace, and Victory. You can guess who wins."

A few people laughed. Monsieur Pierre was not a player, clearly—he was bumbling and spoke with a slight stutter—but might he possibly be the author of the play? I tapped the shoulder of the man sitting in front of me. "Excuse me, Monsieur, but . . . who is Monsieur Pierre?" I asked under my breath.

He glanced back at me with incredulity. "That's Pierre Corneille."

The *Great* Corneille?

I sat back, stunned. I did not believe it. Could not! For one thing, the great playwright was said to have retired. For another, this old man was endearingly humble, pathetically stooped, painfully awkward, tongue-tied, and stumbling. I'd been raised by his heroic, resounding words, learned to read from his scripts. He was, as my father had irreverently joked, our family saint.

I sat in a daze, unhearing, as the man who was, apparently, the *Great* Corneille, stuttered through a boring summary of *The Golden Fleece*. Everyone began to fidget.

How could a writer of such great lines mumble? It was difficult to hear half the words he spoke. There was polite but heartfelt applause as he finally described the closing scene.

"Thank you, Monsieur Pierre," Monsieur la Roque said, standing. "We are honored beyond measure to be the means by which you return to the Paris stage—and in *triumph*."

And with that, everyone jumped to their feet, applauding wildly, I among them. I could not believe what I was witnessing!

Monsieur Pierre carefully stood, and, one hand on the arm of his "throne," smiled gravely and tipped his hat.

I blinked back tears. If only Mother and my brother were with me now. I couldn't wait to tell them.

"Excusez-moi," a woman said, standing to get by. The meeting was over.

I stumbled down to the entry and pressed my way through the standing clusters of people toward the door. I felt dizzy and needed air.

But—stars!—*he* was standing at the door, clasping people's hands.

A quaking overtook me. I looked to see if there might be another way out.

"There she is," he said, spotting me.

I dipped into a deep curtsy, not daring to meet his eyes. I feared that my left leg was going to give out. "Monsieur Corneille," I said at last, managing to rise.

"I was hoping you'd still be here," he said amiably. He turned to Monsieur la Roque, who was standing near. "This is the young woman I was telling you about—the daughter of Alix des Oeillets."

Monsieur la Roque regarded me with interest. "And you are . . . ?"

I must not faint! I took a slow breath. "Claude des Oeillets." My cheeks were burning, my heart pounding, my mouth dry.

"I'd very much like to see your mother again," Monsieur Corneille said. "How long has it been? Twenty-three years?"

"And perhaps," added La Roque, "we might discuss the possibility of her playing the occasional minor role? We are in need of someone at the moment. It's only a walk-on, but . . ."

other pressed her hands to her throat, her eyes wide. "Claudette, I'm sorry—but I . . . *I can't.*"

I couldn't believe what she was saying! This was the most amazing opportunity! All our cares over, all our struggles—never to worry about the next meal. We'd be able to take Gaston to a healer who would know how to set him right. We'd hire him a tutor and eventually buy him an apprenticeship. I might even be able to save for a dowry—*marry*. "But, Maman, it's the Marais, *your* theater." I wouldn't have to scrub down tavern outhouses anymore. "The play is a new one by Corneille, and it's about the sorceress Medea, your favorite." The murderess Medea who kills her own children—as my mother was killing *me!*

She burst into tears. "You don't understand."

"You're right: I don't!" I slumped down beside her on the rushes. I felt at a loss when my mother wept. I should be the one to weep! "Monsieur Corneille asked for you himself." A prayer come true! But now it seemed it was all for naught. "He remembered you—you *and* Father. He remembered your names."

Mother made tight fists. "There's something you don't know." Her voice was reverent and tremulous. "I vowed to forsake the theater *on your father's grave.*"

"But Father wanted this, Maman," I said, pleading now. Never mind that he had no grave! "He said acting was your God-given gift."

The terrified look in my mother's eyes broke my heart. I put my arm around her thin shoulders, pressed my cheek against her frizzled red hair. "Those were his very words."

Mother wiped her eyes with the hem of her apron. "But it's been such a long time."

"I'll go with you—and Gaston too," I said. "We'll all go together. It's only to talk about a walk-on role. You won't have to do anything."

MOTHER HAD FRIGHTS in the morning, of course. I made her a calming lemon balm to take with her morning gruel. "I'm putting your little Virgin in my bag," I assured her, refreshing Gaston on proper etiquette: stand tall, at least *try* to lock eyes (he was so shy), dip with a sweep of his hat. "Monsieur Corneille looks like a clerk, but he's the greatest man in the land," I said. "Treat him as if he were king."

"Oh Mary!" Mother sighed, fanning herself with her chicken-feather fan (in spite of the bitter cold). The very mention of the Great Corneille stirred up her humors, put her in a state of profound disarray.

OUTSIDE, THE WORLD was frozen but bright. The sun was high, and everything seemed unearthly. Mother began dragging as we approached the theater, turning in a trance of memory. "I remember that shop. But oh, *that's* new. Look how this tree has grown."

I took advantage of her reverie to glide her through the theater doors, which had been propped open with a paving stone.

"This isn't it," she said, coming to a stop in the entry, her hands on her hips. "This isn't the theater of the Marais."

Now what? "Maman, this *is* the Marais."

"It's completely different, except for—" Mother gazed down at a star design set into the stone floor. "Except for this," she said, running the toe of her boot over the points of the star. "*This,* I remember. Gaston, Claudette, look! Your father, he proposed to me ... right here. My beloved Nicolas stood on this very spot." She blinked to keep back tears.

"It's all that is left of the old theater."

We turned, startled by a man's voice. The Great Corneille was plainly dressed: still looking like a weary accountant whose sums didn't add up.

I gestured to Gaston to wipe his chin as I sank into a curtsy.

"I'd raise my hat if I could." Monsieur Corneille held parcels in each hand. "Would you care for a beignet, Madame Alix . . . des Oeillets now, is that correct? I recall you had a fondness for them. These ones are cheese," he said, extending a hand.

"You know me too well, Monsieur Corneille," Mother said with a smile, accepting the offer.

"Monsieur *Pierre,* please."

"You've met my daughter?" Mother asked, biting into the treat with relish.

"And this must be your son," he said, insisting that Gaston take a beignet as well.

Only *one,* I motioned. And say *thanks.*

"I was saddened to learn that Nicolas is no longer with us, Alix," the great playwright added, helping Gaston get one out of the sack.

"I was just telling my children that he proposed marriage right on this spot." Mother glanced back down at the floor. "But everything else seems different," she said, pressing a finger against her quivering lower lip.

"Th-th-th-th-th-anks!" Gaston managed in a high, anxious voice. I smiled at him. *Well done.*

"The theater burned down and had to be rebuilt," Monsieur Corneille said, offering Gaston another beignet. I nodded: *Go ahead.* "This stone floor is all that remains. I'm grateful to have some remembrance of those days. Just this morning I was thinking of that opening performance of *The Cid.* I was so young, so nervous—"

"We all were!"

"—a failed lawyer from the provinces. Do you remember my little brother Thomas? The brat, I believe you players called him."

"Once he knotted my laces together. I almost missed a cue!"

"He's grown now, and a playwright himself—quite successful. Writes popular pieces, but I couldn't be more proud. He married my wife's sister—"

"Ah, so you married. We feared you'd be a bachelor forever."

"Oui, quite married, and settled in Rouen with a half-dozen children. I can hardly keep track of them all. I confess I don't mind my occasional trips into Paris. But allow me to show you the changes," he said, offering Mother his arm. "I doubt that you will be disappointed. We have good-sized dressing rooms—"

"*Dressing* rooms? Really?"

"And the stage is deeper than it was before, and raked, so that even the men standing in the pit can see."

"Doesn't that make the players dizzy?"

"They complain, but overall it has been a great success. As well, the troupe has recently invested in some machines—"

"For changing scenery?" Mother looked confused.

"That's only a fraction of what these new inventions can do: flying seraphim, monsters of every description, an entire cast descending from the clouds. It's witchcraft, some claim. No wonder the machinist is called Keeper of Secrets." He paused at the door. "I tried to retire, Alix—but I had to come back. These fantastical means of staging a play are simply too magical. I couldn't resist. And now, with peace here at last, it seems like the beginning of a new age."

"The glory days again," Mother said reverently.

"Ah! Do you remember when . . ."

Gaston and I followed after the great playwright and our mother, listening with wonder as they chattered on, like the best of old friends.

HOLDING A CANDLE aloft, Monsieur Corneille waved away cobwebs. Critters scurried at our approach. We were in the bowels of the theater. We passed by a series of rooms. "For the players," Monsieur Corneille said, but they were all locked. "Monsieur la Roque will be here soon. He'll have the keys."

A vast subterranean room was rigged with enormous logs, pulleys, and scaffoldings: the magical *machines* he'd mentioned. I kept Gaston near; they looked terrifying.

We climbed the worn wood stairs to the players' foyer.

"This is where the players wait until it's their turn to go onstage," Mother explained to Gaston.

To one side was a slate story board, so that the players could understand how the drama was unfolding. A chalk bag hung from a nail.

I followed Monsieur Corneille and my mother out onto the stage.

The *stage*.

In front: the parterre, where men stood to watch, and in the shadows at the back, stalls where beer and food could be bought. Along the walls on either side I could make out the tiers of curtained loges for the wealthy. Higher up, near the roof, was the Paradis, where servants and family of the players sat.

As Mother and Monsieur Corneille talked of the past, and Gaston stood slowly relishing the last of his beignet, I climbed up to the upper stage. Such height! I touched the rail and looked out over the empty theater. I tried to imagine what it would have been like, my mother and father dressed for their roles, the theater crowded with men (and even some women), the Knights of the Order of the Holy Ghost lined up on their special bench, Monsieur Corneille—the *Great* Corneille—pacing and applauding.

On this very stage, in this very place: the glory days.

CHAPTER 17

That night we celebrated, drinking weak beer and feasting on fried pig ears and a roasted turnip. We ate in a blissful stupor, Mother and I now and again recalling various moments: our chat with Monsieur la Roque about all the things we could do; the charming way he pulled on a point of his beard as he explained what was needed; that moment when he glanced at Monsieur Corneille, smiling: we were in!

We'd only be paid a few sous a day, but it was a beginning. "To the future," I said, raising my mug. We were to start at daybreak.

IN THE WEEKS that followed, all the members of the troupe frantically prepared for the ouverture, the play-day after Easter when theaters opened their doors to the public. Much of the time was spent in meetings, I discovered. The troupe did everything together, and by consensus: this required patience. Mother and I weren't voting members—these were the full-share players, the playwright and the director, who together made all the decisions—but even as part-time workers on the overhire list, we were allowed to observe. In this way we came to understand the workings of the troupe and got to know all the people involved, the players as well as baggage-men and wig-makers, dressers and scene-shifters, doorkeepers and stagehands, call-boys and prompters. I scratched their names on the back of an old playbill with a stick of burnt willow to help me remember.

Between watching Gaston (not always easy), trimming wicks and refilling oil lamps, finding props, mending costumes, and keeping loges tidy, there was a great deal to do. I watched over Mother to see how she was managing all this. She'd been in a dream world for a long time, a world of tears and shadow. Now suddenly she was surrounded by people—loud, expressive, sometimes rather eccentric people, people whose own humors were often out of balance. Amazingly, the world of the theater seemed to have restored her faculties to some extent. She was still charmingly witless, but now she seemed more her old self, lively and spunky. (Thank you, Father.)

As for Gaston, at first he was bewildered by all the commotion. I did my best to keep him close, watching what items he "took" for one of his curious trails of objects (watching that it wasn't a player's shoe or prop he borrowed). I tried over and over again to get him to understand that things belonged to people, and that just because an object—a hat, a feather, a valise—interested him, it was not acceptable to simply walk off with it. I explained his obsession to the players, who were fairly understanding, calling him Turnip and treating him as a pet.

Our first production, the play by Brécourt, drew only modest audiences. The young playwright was devastated, but the players assured him that it was not his play that was to blame—not at all! The problem was competition from a new troupe now performing in Paris, a troupe that had given a performance for the King and his new bride.

"New in town and they're *already* performing for His Majesty?" one of the players said with a groan.

"That's cause for concern."

"We have enough competition from the Bourgogne."

The Hôtel de Bourgogne, I gathered, was a long-established theatrical troupe that performed tragedies, serious fare.

"Ay, we don't need another rival company to contend with."

"Especially *now*—"

Now with the costly production of *The Golden Fleece*. In addition to supplying all their own costumes—no small expense!—the players had invested a great deal in this machine play.

"Don't worry about Monsieur Molière," Monsieur la Roque assured everyone, trying to alleviate concerns. "His troupe is good at farce, but not much else."

Even so, we fretted. A new machine play by the Great Corneille could be expected to be a success, but everything had to be perfect. It

didn't help that the flying system didn't seem to be working. Buffequin, the Keeper of Secrets, was constantly adjusting it, constantly testing. I looked on in horror one afternoon as Mother was being strapped
into the harness.

"Take me, instead," I said (but felt ill at the thought). Gaston
looked on, sucking his thumb.

Denis Buffequin regarded me with his one good eye. "Until I
know for sure that it's working, I need someone light in weight."

"Don't worry!" Mother said bravely, though I could see apprehension in her eyes.

I checked to make sure the buckles were secure and stepped back,
making a silent prayer to Father.

Without warning, Mother was jolted into the air and swung out
over the parterre. She went higher, higher, until—ye gods!—she was
level with the benches of the Paradis. Gaston grasped my hand. I
closed my eyes.

I heard a curse and the machinery came to a stop. Mother was
suspended up in the air. I feared I was going to lose my stomach and
make water at the same time.

"Just a moment, Madame des Oeillets," Buffequin assured her.
"We'll have you down in a moment."

"Must you?" Mother called down from above, spreading her arms
and extending a pointed toe. "This is glorious!"

The players applauded and Gaston, smiling hesitantly, brought his
hands together: once, twice.

I WAS FITTING Mother for her gown when I noticed Monsieur la
Roque run up to Monsieur Pierre, waving his hands in the air. I put
down my case of pins. Did it signify alarm or foolery? The troupe had
been working day and night in preparation for the opening of *The
Golden Fleece* and everyone was becoming teethy.

I watched as La Roque talked with Monsieur Pierre, who frowned
gravely, pulling on his chin tuft. Monsieur la Roque's big-chested voice
was often easy to hear, but there was a considerable clanging coming
from under the stage, where Buffequin was working on one of the
chariots that carried the side wing-flats.

"Is something going on?" Mother asked, turning to follow my gaze.

"I'm trying to hear." I watched over her shoulder as I gathered the thin gauze of her gown, securing the folds with pins. "La Roque said he's had word from Brécourt—something to do with Étiennette." Brécourt's wife, the actress who played Medea. "She won't be able to perform. She's with child—"

"That shouldn't stop her."

I nodded. "But she's bleeding, in danger."

"*Mercy.*"

"She must keep to her bed."

"A calamity," Mother hissed.

Indeed! Étiennette's understudy had quit two days before because she up-heaved whenever she rode the flying dragon, which was required in Act V.

And then I saw the disaster for what it really was. I put away my pins.

"THINK OF HOW much trouble it could save you," I argued. "Here you have a new Medea, ready to begin."

Monsieur la Roque and Monsieur Pierre exchanged a glance.

"Mademoiselle Claude," Monsieur Pierre began, not unkindly, "the casting of Medea is crucial to the success of this entire production."

"Maman did well in Brécourt's play—" I began.

"She played a maid," Monsieur la Roque cut in. "A walk-on—and in only two scenes."

Yet had garnered applause with only that! "All I ask is that you give her a chance. I promise it will be worth your time."

"But that's just it," Monsieur la Roque said with exasperation. "We don't have time. Alix would have to learn the lines and then if she can't perform—well . . . We will have lost days finding a replacement."

"One hour," I said. "Just give us the lines for one hour. Mother memorizes faster than anyone I've ever seen."

"But—" Monsieur la Roque was losing patience with this debate, I could see.

"Very well: one hour," Monsieur Pierre interjected. "Have her learn the second scene in Act Two. But are you sure you want to—"

"She will surprise you, Messieurs," I said. "Trust me."

I HAD TO tell Mother that the purpose of her reading was only to help Monsieur la Roque and Monsieur Pierre find someone to replace Medea. "They aren't certain which scene to have the actresses perform for them," I said, trying to sound casual. It was a half-lie, and not even a credible one at that, but it would be justified if my plan worked. "So it's important that you do it as well as you can . . ."

"This is for Monsieur Pierre?"

I nodded. "And Monsieur la Roque, to give them some idea of how challenging the scene is."

Mother looked confused, but nonetheless stepped into the empty dressing room I had claimed for us. *Father, we're going to need your help,* I thought, opening the stack of parchment: Medea's lines, with the cues inked in.

Mother worked with an intensity of focus that amazed me. She could hardly write her name, much less read, yet she had a profound ability to commit lines to heart. As I read the script to her, she used the memory techniques Father had taught us so long ago, tricks the ancients had developed to commit a script to memory. To memorize a line, she imagined a palace of many rooms, imagined the words within it. In no time at all, all I had to do was say the cue line and she would change into the evil Medea, her face contorted, her eyes bulging, the veins in her neck taut and throbbing.

"Bravo," I whispered, shocked at her transformation.

"Bravo, indeed," said a man's husky voice from behind me. I turned to see Monsieur Pierre in the doorway, Monsieur la Roque one step behind him, both of their faces filled with enchantment.

"OF COURSE, NOW that your mother is Medea," Monsieur la Roque told me the next morning, "you'll have to be Cupid."

Ay me. The flying machine! "Of course," I said, my palms damp.

CHAPTER 18

hortly before *The Golden Fleece* was scheduled to open, there was a fire at the Louvre. The blaze raged until a priest arrived with the Sacrament, at which point the fire immediately went out (which surprised me: I'm not *entirely* a believer). The Queen Mother's apartment had been saved, but the Petite Gallerie and the palace theater—still under construction—were destroyed. The theater for machines, which would have rivaled our own.

"And to think that we had nothing to do with it," Madame Babette said, but nobody laughed.

It was said that the blaze had started in the theater. Spectacle plays were risky, without a doubt. The machines themselves required a lot of light—a lot of candles. Monsieur la Roque held a special meeting to discuss our apprehension, and it was decided to double the number of Capuchins in the bucket brigade. But what about the concerns of the public, so close on the eve of the fire? The troupe considered postponing the opening, but that, too, would bring bad luck, so we opted to persevere, and entrust our fate to God.

Then—as if we weren't fretful enough!—Monsieur la Roque informed us that the King would be coming to see our production.

"Could you repeat that, Monsieur la Roque?" someone called out from the stage, where players had gathered for the first of the three rehearsals.

"You heard me," La Roque said with a grin.

The King? Players cheered and hooted; some even danced. Everything—*everything*—hinged on royal approval. If His Majesty enjoyed the show, we would be well rewarded.

Mother looked stricken. This was her first big role . . . and she was to play it before His Majesty?

THE DAYS THAT followed were lunatic with preparation. I ran from one task to another: making final alterations to Mother's gown; shaking out the chair covers in the loges; arranging flowers in vases here and there. It was said the King loved flowers.

The King!

AT THE FINAL rehearsal, everything—merci Dieu—went smoothly. I marveled at the effects. Thunder and lightning! Iris seated on a rainbow in a garden, Juno flying about. Hypsipyle floating on a river on a conch shell drawn by dolphins. In the fifth act, we all applauded as Medea (brave little Maman) appeared flying on the back of the dragon, and fought—in the *air*—with two winged Argonauts.

It awed me to see how a set could magically change—at *once*— from a palace of horrors into a wilderness, awed me to think that Buffequin and his hands managed this all from below stage. Setting the trolleys under the stage in motion, they were able to make all eight wing flats change in an instant—a palace into a garden, a garden into Heaven, Heaven into Hell.

No wonder players are accused of witchcraft, I thought, marveling at the effect. "You know it's not actually magic," I told Gaston.

TRUMPETS SOUNDED THE approach of the royal party. La Roque and a delegation of players rushed out to greet His Majesty at his carriage. They escorted the King and his entourage to their loges, torches in hand.

"His Majesty is comely," Madame Babette reported back. The braziers on either side of the parterre had been raging all morning, but even so, the theater was cold. "The attendants have taken up almost all of the third tier."

Mercy me. Only the loges in the first tier had been reserved for His Majesty. But of course the King traveled with an entourage—his courtiers, attendants, and guards, in addition to members of his family. (With the exception of his Spanish wife, who rarely attended such performances, likely because she did not understand French.)

I hated to think what condition the top tier would be in. Well, it was too late to do anything about it now, I thought, as people noisily filed into the pit. Hopefully, with the presence of His Majesty, there would be some semblance of order: no knife fights or muggings. Recently, an elderly porter had been killed in a tussle with an unruly drunk, a horrifying experience that had sobered us all.

Backstage, I listened nervously to the hum of the audience. As Mother prayed in her tiny dressing room, I stole to the stage gate. From this position I had an excellent view of the King in the first-tier loge, the one closest to the stage on the left. He was in the company of several young noblemen and attendants. I recognized a portly man with a florid, brutish face who often pressed himself upon young actresses, trying to bribe his way into their chambers. The son of Le Tellier, the Secretary of State for War, he seemed to think he had the right, boasting that he would inherit his father's powerful position one day. Louvois was his name, I recalled. La Roque had put us on notice not to allow him near. He was known to be ruthless, a young man of hasty temper, even given to violence if not accorded the favors he sought. It was rumored he'd snapped the neck of one young woman's cat when she refused him! I was somewhat surprised to see him in the familiar company of the King. I wondered if his sinister ways were known to his peers.

Broad-shouldered with curling long hair, His Majesty stood out from his companions, a striking young man, both graceful and manly. I could understand why he was often likened to Apollo, god of the sun. Although changed by kingship and maturity, I recognized in him the boy I had seen in Poitiers. He had that same poise, but now I saw self-consciousness in it, as if he were the one onstage.

I scanned the other loges to see who else I might recognize. Monsieur, the King's comely brother, and their cousin La Grande Mademoiselle in an enormous hat. It was only as the curtain started its slow creaking ascent that I glimpsed someone sitting with a group in a loge on the right. A young woman with blond curls and unusually big eyes.

"Claudette—it's time!" Madame Babette called out behind me, and I turned quickly away, my thoughts in disorder.

I FOUND MOTHER with all the other players, many of them pacing, murmuring their lines.

"What if I can't hear the prompter?" Her voice, normally deep, came out in a squeak.

It *was* a problem. The prompter's chair, usually set in a wing downstage, was now set way at the back because of all the machinery. "You know Medea's lines well," I assured her, adjusting her hairpiece.

I was nervous enough myself. I was worried about my own flight out over the audience as Cupid. My mother's gauzy gown was small on me. What if men could see my legs? I'd managed being in the flying machine through the three rehearsals—but over a crowd? I felt like up-heaving just thinking of it . . . and what if I did?

Monsieur la Roque came to the end of his director's greeting. I heard the fast twelve blows struck by his worn red-velvet-covered staff, followed by three slow ones, signaling that the play was about to begin.

"Here we go," young Brécourt said at the creaking ascent of the painted curtain. The audience cheered the magnificent set.

Mother looked up at me, her eyes wide with fright. For a heart-stopping moment, I feared she would not go on. "Tell me again what Nicolas said," she whispered.

"That you have a God-given talent, Maman."

She stared at me for a long moment. I nodded and gently nudged her forward.

She strode menacingly to the candles and shrieked, silencing the crowd.

CHAPTER 19

My flight as Cupid was to be the first "miraculous" sensation of the show; it was critical that it go perfectly. I double-checked my harness and discovered one buckle loose. *Ay me!* I was rechecking everything when Madame Babette gave me a deep-red rose. "Monsieur la Roque wants you to throw it down to the King."

"And manage the bow and arrow as well?" *All* while flying through the air?

She shrugged, straightened her wig, and rushed off.

A thorn cut into the palm of my hand. Zounds: now I was bleeding. At least I wasn't in my courses. Trembling, I bent my knees, waiting for the cymbals to sound—waiting for the machinery to hoist me up and out.

The cymbals sounded and I pushed off—but nothing happened. I fell forward, my knees dragging on the boards. Deus! I put the bow and rose in one hand, and was trying to pull down my skirts when I was jerked violently into the air.

Ah! the audience gasped.

Oh! I exclaimed as I was twirled out over the pit and around . . . once, twice, rising up ever higher, until I was level with the first-tier loges, swooping past the richly adorned courtiers. Ahead, coming on quickly, was the King. I grasped the rose with my right hand and tossed it neatly into his loge as I flew by. A cheer went up. Everyone was loving it!

On my next sweep by His Majesty's loge, a moustached valet held up the rose. Holding it to his heart, he winked at me as I flew by.

A wink!

Suspended, no longer circling, I set a tin arrow in my bow. My gaze settled on the young woman I'd briefly glimpsed before. She turned her face up to me, her blue eyes luminous. Deus! Cupid's arrow slipped from my grasp.

Someone in the pit grabbed it, triumphant. I was swirled away and down, landing with a thud. I quickly bowed out to laughter and applause, my heart pounding.

"What happened?" Monsieur la Roque demanded.

"I don't know," I said, unbuckling my harness. But I did. It was *her.*

SHAKEN, I QUICKLY got out of my costume and settled onto my perch beside the stage gate. Everyone's eyes were on His Majesty, but my eyes were on her. She was seated beside her father, the Duc de Morte-mart, the humorless man who had practically had us all arrested years before in Poitiers. I recognized him by his girth and thin moustache. With them was a young nobleman and several older men and women.

She was as lovely as I remembered, her hair arranged in locks that had been feathered, giving her a light, angelic look. She held her fan with the painted side facing out. Now and then she fluttered it quickly, charming the young nobleman with a languishing glance.

As the performance came to an end, the audience exploded with applause, hoots and cheers, a thunder of stomping boots. I watched as her party rose, noted the way she held up her skirts, turning out the inside of her wrists. The young man helped her adjust her shawl around her shoulders and she smiled up at him. Her father, at the door of the loge, waved his walking stick, motioning them to hurry. She dipped her head respectfully and, with an exquisitely graceful passing curtsy, preceded the young man out the door.

Madame Babette popped up behind me. "I can't take my eyes off of him either." She sighed.

"I know," I said, feigning to be enchanted by the King.

MOTHER FELL INTO my arms, wobbly with relief.

"I'll meet you down in your dressing room." There was a surprise for her there: a basket of beignets. "I need to let Gaston in backstage." He'd been sorting the door-take in the office. (Putting coins in order by size was something he could do well.)

Gaston was waiting for me at the gate. I let him in behind the curtain, where some of the players still lingered. "Mother's down below," I told him, but he stopped, dumbstruck, gazing somewhat fearfully at the sets, as if he might be swallowed up, struck by lightning. "Come," I said with a smile, nudging him out of his enchantment.

We found Mother sitting on a stool in her dressing room eating a beignet. She opened her arms wide to embrace us.

Oh, Gaston sang with a fearful vibrato, which made us laugh.

"That was my worst," she said, licking her fingers clean before taking off her wig and shaking out her sweat-soaked hair.

I clapped a fur hood on her to protect her from the cold. "You were excellent," I insisted, untying her laces and helping her into her red and yellow dressing gown. "It went well." Nothing had caught fire and no ushers had been murdered.

Monsieur Pierre appeared with sweetmeats. "You are a queen of the stage!" he told Mother, sweeping off his hat. "You must play tragedy—*real* tragedy," he said, lowering his voice conspiratorially. "I'm writing a new play, a tragedy that would be perfect for you to star in."

I looked from the playwright to my mother, not believing what Monsieur Pierre had just said. Zounds! If only Father could be here now.

"Monsieur Pierre!" someone called out, and he disappeared before we could even respond. *Well,* I sighed. What a day.

There was a peremptory rap on the door. Before we could say "Come in," a big, extravagantly ruffled man made a rude entrance.

"I wish to speak to Monsieur la Roque," he said with a frown. "Where might I find him?"

The Duc de Mortemart! I dropped into a respectful reverence.

Fortunately, the great man showed no sign of displeasure. Quite the contrary! "Madame des Oeillets," he said, addressing my mother, "His Majesty was entertained by your performance."

"I am honored," Mother said, pulling her wig back on. I slipped a fur cape on over her dressing gown for the sake of warmth (and modesty).

A young woman appeared behind the Duke: his *daughter.* "Monseigneur," she said, her voice soft, "His Majesty is speaking to Monsieur Corneille about it now."

"Is Monsieur la Roque with him?" the Duc de Mortemart demanded.

"The director?" she asked.

"Oui, he was," said a nobleman beside her. Tall and exactly proportioned, he was the young man who had been sitting with her in the loge. He was wearing bright silks, a lace collar, and high boots with the studied nonchalance of the young.

"He's to show us the machinery," the Duke said impatiently.

Appearing suddenly in the door was the brutish young Louvois. "His Majesty, I'm sure, would enjoy a private viewing. I will inform His Majesty now."

I was alarmed to see Louvois, knowing his nasty reputation. My princess gave her beau a mocking look, rolling her big eyes.

"It's Monsieur la Roque we await, Monsieur Louvois." The Duke regarded the florid-faced young man with impatience. "But he's in attendance on the King, who, you should know, showed no interest in the machinery when it was discussed."

"But—" Louvois's little eyes blinked. "If—"

"Leave it be, young man! Unless, of course, you wish to annoy His Majesty. Has your father not taught you anything?"

The princess turned her head away and smiled.

I wasn't sure what was going on; it appeared that young Louvois wished to court the King's favor, but was being held in check by his superior.

"No need for La Roque, Messieurs," Mother offered brightly. (As Medea, she'd become brazen!) "I'd be delighted to show you our secrets myself. The door to the understage is close by."

"Pathetic," I heard my princess say under her breath, watching as Louvois waddled after my mother and the two men. I wondered if she'd heard the stories I had; stories that portrayed Louvois not so much pathetic, as dangerous.

"You do not wish to join them, Mademoiselle? The machines are rather interesting," I added, folding Mother's shawl and placing it on the trunk, my hands trembling. "If grimy and forbidding," I prattled on, talking without purpose.

"Some other day, perhaps—when Monsieur Louvois is not of the party," she added with a smirk. She stepped into the room, pressing a scent ball to her nose. "For some reason I seem to know you."

"I am Claude des Oeillets. I played Cupid tonight."

"I *loved* that. No, from before, but I can't recall."

"We met . . . a very long time ago," I admitted with a curtsy. How was it possible to have such a perfect face? It was in the blood, surely, in the refinement and breeding of the noble race. "Mademoiselle," I added. I wasn't sure how I should address her; the Mortemarts were such high nobility. She was Mademoiselle de Tonnay-Charente, I recalled—but might she be titled now? "Near Poitiers—my family was camped by a cave."

"Ah! The magical cave in the fearsome wilds. I remember thinking it a fantastical adventure, like something out of a storybook." She laughed, a musical note that came from deep in her throat, charmingly trilling. "I also recall seeking a means to kill my loathsome governess."

I dipped my head. "And I failed to fulfill my promise."

"Indeed—you owe me," she said with a mocking frown.

She took off a fur-lined glove and ran her fingers over the decorative stitching on Mother's gown. Her nails were long, pointed, and tinged with gold. She wore a cluster of emeralds set into a gold band on her middle finger. "Is this your handiwork?" she asked. "I have urgent need of a seamstress."

It took only a moment to register what was being offered. "It would be an honor to serve you, Mademoiselle," I said, making a shaky but deep and heartfelt reverence.

CHAPTER 20

p by candle the next morning, I brushed out my hair with bran flour and, shivering with the unseasonable cold, braided it with a long yellow ribbon, coiling the braids tightly and covering them with a starched white cap.

By the thin light of dawn, I could see that it had snowed. Even so, I decided to wear my summer cloak, the only one that wasn't patched. I took up the carrying basket I'd prepared the night before. Lined with hemp, it held my precious tools—a bone case of brass pins and needles, silk and metal threads, iron scissors and long-bladed shears.

The Mortemart estate was on the other side of the river, in the parish of the Saint-Sulpice church. I would have liked to hire a litter, but I had only earned sixteen sous the night before—and the players nothing at all. The King had rewarded the troupe handsomely, but the debts were high and needed to be paid off first. I would call on Monsieur Martin that evening, explain that it would be a while yet before we would be able to pay him back for the money he'd so kindly advanced—money we'd needed to pay for Mother's rich costumes. I would give him two of her complimentary tickets to appease.

It took time to find the street the Mortemart residence was on, and once there I felt I was in another realm: the air was fresh after the frosting of snow, which made everything quiet. Above the high walls I could see the branches of great oak trees, the tips of dark pines cloaked in white.

I walked up and down the rue Saint-Guillaume several times before identifying the emblem with the coiled snake over a carriage gate entrance. The courtyard behind the ironwork gates was large: a six-horse carriage stood at the ready, the driver sitting atop smoking a pipe as two footmen in white livery brushed off the snow.

There seemed to be only one entrance. I pulled the bell rope. Three men in blue cloaks—the concierge and two guards—came to the gate.

"Mademoiselle de Tonnay-Charente is expecting me."

"For what purpose?" the concierge demanded, his breath billowing.

"I am a seamstress," I said, praying he wouldn't demand guild identification.

The concierge nodded to one of the guards, who sprinted across the courtyard toward the entrance.

I blew into my cupped hands to warm them. I feared I would be shown in with chattering teeth, my cheeks chapped and reddened, my eyes and nose running. Just as I was about to expire of the cold, one of the guards and a maid appeared. The guard fumbled with a big iron key and the creaking gate slowly opened. "You may enter," he said. Ushering me into the realm of the blessed.

The maid led me through a guardroom and down some stairs into the kitchens—a vast, warm, subterranean domain of enormous vats, emitting delicious (and some noxious) smells. Loaves of bread were being lifted out of the great ovens and gutted chickens draped over glowing embers. Five pies sat cooling.

I followed the maid past a buttery, a spicery, a chandlery, and into a narrow corridor which opened onto a dining hall for the servants of the house. Six men—a pantler (I guessed), two butlers, three yeomen of the kitchen—sat at a table covered with platters of grilled meats, boiled eggs, bread, bowls of thick soup.

Working for such a family would not be a hardship, I thought enviously. I imagined that the servants' living arrangements would not be shabby, either—beds of good straw, perhaps even comforters.

"This way," said the maid, heading up into a maze of narrow, dark stairs, the servants' side of the mansion. Finally we stepped through a door, emerging into a bright antechamber decorated with tapestries. Six richly upholstered chairs were lined up against one wall. Somewhere, canaries were singing and a cat mewled.

The maid stopped before a door. "Take off your cloak," she commanded imperiously, as if her own status had risen with each floor.

I passed her my humble wrap. The maid draped it over one arm and scratched at the door. I fluffed out my skirts, arranging the folds so that the stained parts didn't show. I felt like a beast in such a refined setting, like a pagan or wolf-child, one of the grotesque and wild creatures displayed at country fairs.

Mademoiselle de Tonnay-Charente opened the door herself, dressed in a charmingly laced confection. Behind her were the bent-over figures of three aged serving women, one of them her governess (*still* alive).

"You're early," Mademoiselle de Tonnay-Charente said, firmly shooing the shuffling old women out.

"I'm sorry."

She closed the door and fixed the latch. "Be gone, ye witches!" she hissed with a comic flourish. "Welcome to *my* cave, Mademoiselle." She put out her arms. "I can't claim that it's enchanted, however."

The majestic room was warm, adorned with great paintings, tapestries, carpets from Turkey (worn thin in spots), and a candleholder of many branches. A fire burned brightly, giving off heat. Two latticed windows faced onto the courtyard. The air smelled strongly of cat, woodsmoke, and lavender—this last from a brass perfume burner set by the door. Everywhere I looked there were piles of leather-bound books, plates of artfully arranged sweetmeats. A gray parrot rattled a chain that was secured to a brass stand.

So, I thought. This is the lair of a princess.

I was startled out of my reverie by a shriek. I turned to see Mademoiselle de Tonnay-Charente pulling her skirts up to her knees. "Ugly Thing!"

A monkey dressed in a quilted velvet jacket and cap was grasping her calf. She pulled the creature off and handed him to me.

I cradled him like a baby, trying to appear at ease holding this strange animal. The monkey hissed, but I hissed back, and that made him stare.

"He's not hard to amuse," Mademoiselle de Tonnay-Charente said, tickling him under his ribs. The monkey squirmed free, climbing on top of my head. I didn't like the feel of his little fingers. I reached up, but he bared his teeth, chattering angrily.

At that Mademoiselle de Tonnay-Charente and I both began to giggle: the absurdity of it!

I bent my knees to put the monkey within her reach, but he jumped over the top of a chair and made a flying leap onto a tapestry and up onto a hanging rod.

"Curses. He's not to be on the hangings. The ancients will scold," Mademoiselle de Tonnay-Charente said, opening a cabinet and withdrawing a bowl. "Nuts for Ugly," she said brightly, "and a little something for me and my guest," she added, filling two mugs from a jug.

I was a *guest*?

ay I?" I dared to suggest. "I think I know how to tempt Ugly." I'd had a lifetime of experience luring animals (in order to eat them). I moved the bowl onto a low table and made a trail of nuts leading up to it. "We need to pretend we're not watching," I told her, stepping well back.

We turned our backs to the monkey and stood talking by the sideboard. "Are you a player, as well as your mother?" Mademoiselle de Tonnay-Charente asked in a hushed voice. "I love theater so much, but I was lucky to even get to go. The ancients claim it stirs a girl's emotions in an unnatural way."

I gathered that the "ancients" were her old serving women. "I'm not really a player," I said. "I'm too tall to play female roles, but I do perform parts in crowd scenes from time to time." And most often in travesty, as a man.

"I've never met a woman as tall as you—other than the King's cousin La Grande Mademoiselle."

"Damnation!" the parrot screeched, making me jump.

"Silence, Jolie!" she commanded, and the parrot obediently quieted.

"I believe La Grande Mademoiselle is even taller than I am."

"She only looks taller because of the stupid hats she wears."

We smiled to hear the monkey chattering happily at the table behind us. He was on the floor in front of his bowl of nuts, picking them out one by one with great delicacy.

"Your trick worked," she whispered, handing me one of the mugs.

"It's called coffey, a hot Turkish liqueur." She lowered herself onto a chair. "Sit, please."

I stood without moving, holding the warm mug in my hands. "Mademoiselle, I—"

"I insist," she said brightly. "The ancients would never allow it, but I am *moderne*."

I wasn't sure what being "moderne" meant, but I did as instructed and perched on the edge of a footstool.

"Just because you're of the theater, Mademoiselle, doesn't mean I'll treat you like a peasant—or worse—no matter what *they* say. The ancients go on and on about how going to the theater causes a disorder of the senses, that young women are especially in danger of becoming *inflamed*." She laughed with delight. "They say it detaches the soul into an imaginary world, unregulated by 'the laws of nature.' Imagine if they had seen you flying! It must have been wonderful to go through the air like that. Were you scared?"

"At first," I admitted. The mug was filled with a vile-looking brown liquid. I took a cautious sip. At least it was sweet.

"What animals do *you* keep?" she asked, caressing Ugly's head.

"I love animals," I lied, "but we don't keep any." The pigeons hardly counted.

"Not even a horse?"

"We used to have a donkey named Bravo." Speaking his name made me feel sad. The steadfast creature had died not long after Father.

"Frankly, I prefer animals to people," she said, pouring what I thought might be spirits into our mugs. "Coffey is best this way," she said in a staged whisper. "It's my little secret."

I sniffed it. It *was* spirits. How daring! "Why do you prefer animals?" There seemed to be a number. I glimpsed two cats skulking behind the close stool and realized that the mound by the fire was a sleeping pug with a litter of pups.

"Because they never lie."

I didn't care for the coffey—with or without spirits—but I finished it to be polite. Then she filled my mug again. It was discomforting to be seated in a noblewoman's presence, and even more so to be served by her. It felt like Mardi Gras, the day everything went topsy-turvy. I wondered if the coffey was affecting my wits.

"My father lies," Mademoiselle de Tonnay-Charente went on, leaning forward, her full breasts bulging out over her stays. I adjusted my fichu to make sure I was covered, as was proper for a servant. "He says he's going to the theater or to the gaming tables, when really he's going to see his concubine."

I'd been taught that it wasn't appropriate to speak of such things. Apparently it was different for nobility. "Oh," I said again (stupidly).

"His harlot is the wife of a commoner," she said, "so of course he's ashamed. My mother lies too—she says she's going to visit a friend, when she's really going to a convent to pray . . . for *hours*. Do you lie?"

"Sometimes," I admitted. Why had I said that? No one would hire a dishonest seamstress.

"Yet you didn't lie to me just now," she observed, running the pearls of her necklace through her fingers.

"I was tempted." I could feel the heat in my cheeks.

"Do you have secrets?"

"Of course." I felt lively, *tingly*. "How do you know that your parents are lying?" It was brazen of me to ask!

"I spy on them," she gloated.

I mimed a skulk and she laughed with delight. "Truly. My mother keeps a journal. Her spiritual notes, she calls them, but it's full of fury—at my *father*. And as for my father—well, all of Paris knows his so-called secret vice. What's yours?"

"I have big feet."

"That doesn't count," she said, but exclaimed at their size when I showed her. "Answer my question," she said in the voice of a tutor, pouring out yet more spirits.

Should I tell her the truth? "I aspire to be among the blessed."

She snorted with amusement. "*I* aspire to be queen."

"And sometimes I steal," I added. The spirit of intimate disclosure had made me reckless. Or perhaps it was the coffey. And spirits.

"Ah, I remember. I caught you stealing a fritter."

"Four beignets."

"Why so many?"

"We were hungry."

"Were you *poor*?" She spoke the word as if it were a foreign tongue. "I've read about people like you in books."

Did she think it an imaginary world? There was talk of starvation in the provinces, entire families perishing. "And I've read about people like you," I said.

"You read? I adore stories. I've changed my name to Athénaïs, the virgin goddess of war."

Bright-eyed Athena. How apt, I thought.

"My father and mother don't approve—" She flicked her hand, her nails sharp. "But soon I will be married and may do as I wish."

My head was buzzing pleasantly. I wished she would offer to refill my mug. "In the theater, people often change their name, Mademoiselle de—"

"You're to address me as Athénaïs," she chided.

"Mademoiselle . . . Athénaïs?" To speak to her so familiarly felt dangerous.

She laughed at my droll face. "*Queen* Athénaïs, if you insist. Tell me about magic. You practice it, do you not?"

But before I could respond, chimes sounded and Mademoiselle de Tonnay-Charente—Athénaïs—jumped up. "Mort Dieu, we don't have much time. Quick: unlace me," she commanded. "I need a gown for a ball at the Palais-Royal. The Marquis Alexandre de Noirmoutier—my *betrothed*—will be attending, so it must be special, but my father doesn't give me any coin, so . . ."

"So perhaps we should have a look in your wardrobe chests," I suggested.

SUCH GOWNS! I'd never seen—much less touched—such luxury. A laced silk with a skirt of scarlet brocade, its fine knife pleats making it narrow at the hip; a black velvet ensemble; a white taffeta underskirt with ermine trim; a sable snug. I felt breathless with the feel of the billowing silks, the crusty, shimmering silver embroidery.

I held up a skirt embroidered with tiny pearls, fingering the tiny gems. Could they possibly be real?

"But that skirt is so heavy it can stand by itself," Athénaïs said derisively. "I certainly couldn't dance in it."

I studied the black velvet. "This would look lovely over the white taffeta," I suggested. "I could change the folds to make it lighter." I held the two up together.

"Perfect. Have it ready for a fitting tomorrow."

"Certainly," I said lightly, knowing I would have to be up all night. Could I even afford the candles? There had been no mention of a fee, but I was confident that serving Mademoiselle *Athénaïs* would prove lucrative.

And in any case, I couldn't resist.

CHAPTER 22

thénaïs twirled, kicking back the black velvet overskirt. She was enormously pleased with my creation, exclaiming over it effusively. "It's so light yet perfectly weighted. Watch." She twirled and dropped to the floor, her skirts forming a circle around her. "That's the third perfect one so far," she said, rising, twirling, and dropping again, but this time scowling at the imperfect formation. It amused and surprised me to see her playing Mushrooms, a game I associated with young girls, who were content to twirl and drop for hours, seeking those rare moments when their skirts formed a perfect circle around them.

"I want you there as my attendant," she said, standing and shaking out her gown.

"At the . . . ball, Mademoiselle?" Surely not. I puffed out her sleeves, which were full above the elbow. I had used a running stitch to gather the top of the sleeve and then sewn each fold flat lengthwise before mounting it into the armhole. I was pleased with the effect. The pointed satin bodice emphasized her voluptuous figure.

"In case a ribbon comes untied or I step on the hem."

"Certainly," I said, as if it were the type of thing I did all the time. The ball was this evening!

"There will be seamstresses provided," Athénaïs explained, "but I don't trust them. They work in the Cimetière des Innocents, next to the scribes there, and have both ink and disease under their fingernails, ruining everything they touch." She scratched out a note with a peacock quill pen, dusted it, then held a stick of sealing wax to a candle flame. She rummaged in a box before finding a gold signet ring and pressed it into the wax. "You'll need this to get in."

I curtsied, holding the paper to my heart. A royal ball! "Certainly, Mademoiselle," I repeated, but once again she was twirling and dropping, twirling and dropping, absorbed in her childish game.

I ARRIVED AT the service entrance of the Palais-Royal before six, earlier than instructed, my cloak and boots somewhat mud-splattered. I was directed through a series of dark, cold corridors to a door that opened onto an antechamber, separated from the ballroom by a heavy brocade curtain. Three bone-thin women muffled in layers sat working: the cemetery seamstresses, I gathered, mending what I suspected were winding sheets by the flickering flame of only two candles. There was a fire burning, but they had encircled it, murmuring amongst themselves in a language I could not identify. I sat on a stool by the drapes, listening to the musicians tune their instruments.

A footman parted the curtains and looked in to see if all was in order. "It's dark," I said.

"I'll have more candles brought in," he said with a frown.

At last came the sounds of women laughing, men coughing. The violins and lutes began playing a courante. The curtains parted again: Athénaïs, cloaked in fur, her cheeks rosy. "It's dark in here."

I jumped to my feet and made a reverence. "A footman is bringing more candles."

She threw off her cape and lowered herself onto a stool. She was glowing and vibrant. "It's snowing *again*. My father took forever! Quick, change me out of my boots. Do I look a fright?"

How could she even think such a word? "Not at all!" She looked lovesome and sumptuous. I unlaced her wet boots and slipped on her gold-embroidered mules. "Wait, Mademoiselle," I said as she jumped up, eager to go. I checked the fall of her train.

"Do I pass inspection?" She stood on tiptoe to playfully peck my cheek.

"You do," I stuttered, flushing. I held back the curtain and stood watching as she disappeared into the glittering assembly.

I let the cloth drop, but held a length of it slightly open so that I could take it all in—the room ablaze with sweetly scented beeswax candles, the tables in a room beyond laden with roast pheasant and other succulents. Richly liveried servants moved through the crowd offering spirits. It was all so exquisitely refined, so *pure*.

The King and his little Spanish Queen entered to great fanfare, and were seated on a carpet-covered podium. The musicians struck up a pavane, a slow and stately walking dance. Nearing the end of the procession, I finally spotted Athénaïs and the young man who had accompanied her at the theater: the Marquis Alexandre de Noirmoutier—her intended, her betrothed. Her *beloved*.

The next dance was a minuet, opened by the King's brother and his wife, and followed by the most important couples. Athénaïs and her betrothed stood with her father on the far side of the ballroom, watching.

A courante was announced by a prelude, and a number of couples formed a line, including—this time—Athénaïs and her betrothed. I watched the progression of the steps, the music filling me with a feeling of longing and expectation. Elegant in scarlet petticoat breeches, Alexandre held out his hand with a dip of his feathered hat. Athénaïs curtsied, rose up on tiptoe, and turned to the music, her beau watching her steadily. The swirl of white taffeta at her hem revealed just a hint of her embroidered slippers, which caught the light as she turned.

Alexandre and Athénaïs. Athénaïs and Alexandre. I caught a glimpse of her face, her radiant eyes. She was the most beautiful woman in the room, without a doubt, and he the most handsome man.

A servant arrived with more candles and made a point of closing the curtains. No more peeking for me. Reluctantly, I returned to my stool. Now and then a countess or marquise would sweep in with a torn sleeve or a ribbon undone, and the cemetery seamstresses would descend on her in a swarm—deftly slipping things into a bodice or sleeve (a pearl ornament, a bit of gold lace). Repaired, the noblewoman would use a hand cloth to wipe the perspiration from between her breasts, then press the damp cloth to her brow before dashing back out.

In that moment, the curtain opened once again onto a magical world of swirling silk brocade and velvet, gems set aglow. I recalled—in a swoon of reverie—dancing in the moonlight with a worn lilac gown in my hands, imagining *this*. It was an entrancing spectacle, but, unlike my fantasy, unlike the world of the theater, it was *real*.

BELLS RANG AND trumpets sounded: the King and Queen were leaving. The ball, it appeared, was over. The graveyard seamstresses blew out the candles and pocketed the stubs, leaving me in the dark. The fire had long since burned down to embers.

I drew aside the heavy curtain. Across the room, I saw Athénaïs standing with her father and three other noblemen. She turned and, lifting her skirts, approached. I scooped up her fur cloak and her tooled leather boots, now dry, clean, and polished.

"The vultures took the candles," I said, tying back the curtain so that there would be enough light to see. Sometimes I felt like a queen of shadow realms, forever peering out onto glittering worlds—watching my mother perform from the dark wings, watching Athénaïs from this gloomy room.

"I'm in love," she said with a frown, as if it were a disease.

I knelt before her and slipped off her dancing shoes. "How do you know?" I said teasingly. "Maybe you're ill." I slipped on one boot and then the other. "Maybe it's the vapors." I laced her boots tight, my cheeks burning. Athénaïs brought out a dangerous recklessness in me. I must learn to hold my tongue!

"You *are* a clown," she said, laughing. "No doubt you know a cure? Some sort of disenchantment, a protective spell?"

"Do you want to be cured?"

"Mort Dieu, non!" she exclaimed earnestly, her hands over her heart.

"Are you going to faint?" I wasn't joking this time.

"Claude, truly, you are *so* droll. Oh! I almost forgot." She slipped her hand into her skirts, pulling out coins.

"Merci, Mademoiselle," I said, slipping them into the top of my boots. By their weight and size, I guessed (and hoped) they might be écus. I draped the lush fur cloak over her bare shoulders. She turned and, like an obedient child, tipped up her chin so that I could fasten the clasp at the neck.

"Au revoir, my funny Claudette."

I stood, heart aching, somewhat overcome. She had addressed me familiarly, by the affectionate name my mother called me. This, I feared, was the end of my employment. "If you are ever in need, Mademoiselle—of anything at all—you can always reach me at the theater." Then I added, on impulse, and without quite knowing what I meant by it: "I can be trusted."

CHAPTER 23

The snow had stopped falling and the stars were bright. Heading east along the rue Saint-Honoré, I made my way through the congested courtyard. I heard angry voices, and in the flickering torchlight saw what looked like a fight brewing: two noblemen were standing facing each other on the stairs, hands on the hilts of their swords.

The coachmen became watchful, like spectators at a cockfight.

I recognized the man at the right: the swarthy Marquis de la Frette. He often purchased showy seats onstage. He had caused trouble at the theater on three occasions, once even injuring Monsieur la Roque. He was a mean drunk, and although of noble blood, he was no gentleman.

The little man opposite him was a prince of some kind. I started to hurry past, but then I recognized the tall, slender man standing behind him: it was Alexandre, Marquis de Noirmoutier—Athénaïs's betrothed.

Harsh words were spoken and the little Prince slapped La Frette full across the cheek. The valets and drivers exclaimed. The sound was sharp, the blow hard, but La Frette didn't even turn his head.

My heart sank. *A slap:* there could be no greater offense. A slap challenged a nobleman's honor. A slap announced to the world: *You are not worthy.*

Then came the inevitable blows. A footman with a massive staff jumped in to break up the fight. It took three to hold back La Frette. Swaying on his heels he slurred, loud enough for me to hear: "I demand satisfaction!" He turned to the gawkers. "Satisfaction!" he cried out again, shaking off the men who held him.

"He's calling a *duel*," a valet near me said.

"Ay—but they'll both lose their heads," said another.

It's true, I thought, with horror. Dueling was punishable by decapitation now. His Majesty was determined to put a stop to the ancient practice.

The Prince and his supporters retreated to a tight cluster by some columns. I stepped into the shadows. *Pré-aux-Clercs,* I overheard, *rapiers, dawn.* Athénaïs's betrothed—the Marquis de Noirmoutier—was to be the prince's second.

I had to alert Athénaïs! I dared not cross the bridge on foot, not at this time, not when the cutpurses were out. I pulled the coins out of my boot—the money Athénaïs had given me for my labor. Three silver écus and seven sous—not as much as I had hoped, but enough to hire a coach or litter—*if* I could find one.

Luck was with me: a footman pointed out a coach for hire, its blanketed horse asleep on its feet. The driver demanded all seven sous because of the bridge toll. I agreed without a quarrel.

The reluctant horse ambled slowly toward the rickety Pont Rouge and up the deserted rue du Bac. Snow-covered streets are often empty, especially during the dark hours, but the silence seemed especially ominous.

This night, approaching the rue Saint-Dominique, I tapped on the window for the driver to turn left, and left again just after the Jacobin monastery. I commanded him to stop in front of the Mortemart mansion. I was relieved to see a sliver of light through one of Athénaïs's shuttered windows overlooking the courtyard.

I climbed down, retrieving one of the silver écus out of my boot. "Yours if you wait," I told the driver, then stepped to the coach gate and pulled the bell rope. The gates swung open and the coach turned into the courtyard.

A half-asleep concierge came lurching out. "I must talk to Mademoiselle de Tonnay-Charente," I said.

"She's retired."

"Her lantern is on."

"Her lantern is always on. She's afraid of the dark," he said with a hint of derision.

"It's a matter of life and death."

"Aye, *my* death, were I to rouse her."

I withdrew another silver écu.

ATHÉNAÏS SLIPPED DOWN the grand curving stairs, following a maid holding a lantern. She was still in her cape and ballgown, her pearls at her neck. "Didn't I already pay you?" she asked, a little annoyed.

"It's not that, Mademoiselle," I said, taken aback. "I'm sorry to disturb you, but something has happened . . . Something I think you should know." I glanced at the maid standing shivering behind her. I paused, uneasy about being overheard. "It involves your . . . dance partner."

Athénaïs looked confused for only a moment. She took the lantern from the maid and led me into a small chamber off the main entrance. She set the lantern down on a cluttered shelf, closed the door, and turned up the oil. Hats, boots, wraps, and capes were piled up everywhere. A black cat with a litter of nursing kittens was curled into a fur wrap thrown down on the floor. Three swords were propped in a corner.

"Does Alexandre want me to meet him?" Athénaïs asked, whispering in spite of our seclusion. Her breath misted in the faint light.

"It's nothing like that. There's going to be a duel."

"Over me?" Her eyes were bright, like those of a child. There was recklessness in her passion.

"No—over an insult," I began, surprised by her romantic notion. Men rarely dueled over a woman! "Your betrothed is to be second for a short young man who was wearing purple velvet and red heels tonight." I held out my hand to indicate height. "A prince, I think."

"Prince de Chalais—Alexandre's sister's husband. Alexandre and his sister are twins. Did you know?"

"I didn't," I said, disconcerted. I pressed on, relating that the Marquis de la Frette had pushed the Prince de Chalais on the stairs coming out of the Palais, and that La Frette had called Chalais a sodomite, that Chalais had slapped him—

"Slapped his *face*?" The shadows from the lantern concealed her eyes.

"Oui. And then La Frette threw a punch, and then Chalais, and that's when your betrothed and some footmen jumped in to pull them apart." And to throw some punches as well. "And that's when La Frette demanded satisfaction."

"He's a beast."

No one would argue that. "They're meeting at the Pré-aux-Clercs, that marshy field behind the Abbaye de Saint-Germain-des-Prés."

"That's not far from here."

I nodded—not far, but another world, nonetheless, a wild and marshy realm, a realm where spirits gathered. "They're meeting at daybreak, fighting with rapiers." I took a shaky breath. Rapiers were traditional, but pistols would have been a wiser choice. La Frette was taller and would therefore carry a longer blade, possibly as long as four feet—giving him a deadly advantage. But then, La Frette would be drunk, and Chalais, judging from his appearance, would likely be nimble and quick. A shorter rapier could be used to advantage if he could duck under the long blade of his opponent, close in for a kill. But then, too, Chalais didn't seem the killing type, and La Frette did.

It made me queasy to think of it. The situation was urgent and I had to be clear. "Your father would know how to get word to His Majesty, put a stop to it."

Athénaïs snorted.

I could hear the mother cat purring. "Dueling is against the law!"

"Not *really*."

Really! Perhaps she simply didn't know. "The punishment is—" I sliced my finger across my neck.

"That's only for when an unblood challenges a noble." Her tone was condescending. "It would be dishonorable for Alexandre not to defend his brother-in-law."

I thought my mission would be an easy one, assumed that Athénaïs would leap at the chance to save a life, prevent disaster. I cautioned myself to be calm; it was impolite to press someone above one's station. No doubt the King had already been informed: there were so many witnesses. It wasn't my concern, after all. I'd done my duty and that was that.

"I must go," Athénaïs said, taking up the lantern.

"Good night. I'm sorry to have disturbed you."

"No, I mean I must be there when they duel."

"Mademoiselle—" I sputtered. Every night men were robbed and murdered. Women who dared to venture out in the dark hours unescorted were molested and raped. "You must not—"

"You don't understand," she said. "I *must*."

"It wouldn't be safe," I argued with some urgency. She had named herself for a virgin goddess of war, but she was an innocent in so many ways. Perhaps that was what being noble meant, to not be part of the oft-ugly world, to not even know it existed.

She gently squeezed my hand. "But you will be with me, my dear Claudette," she said with a flitting smile. Her skin was warm and silken smooth. "After all, you still owe me."

he night watchman called out five of the clock. Taking care not to disturb my sleeping mother, I groped through the room feeling for my travesty ensemble, which I'd set out the night before: my high boots, breeches, waistcoat, and quilted cloak. A wig, a hat.

The moon was full; I had no need of a lantern. I grabbed a dagger, for protection. A rosary, likewise.

It was wrong, I knew. I should have nothing to do with an illegal duel. If foolish young noblemen wanted to risk their lives, tant pis! It wasn't my affair. Yet I could not let it go—could not let *her* go, could not bear the thought of the danger she would be in.

I set out. The streets were deserted. Who but a madman would venture out at such a time? Who but villains, rapists, murderers, and thieves? Not even women selling relief came out at such an hour.

I marched along, my boot heels making echoes on the cobbles, a secure, fearless staccato. I was frustrated by what Athénaïs's madcap demand was forcing me to do.

I headed toward the Cimetière des Innocents. There was often a fête going on there at full moon, common folk communing with spirits, dancing around fires in the bright night. Several times I'd seen a cab for hire on the rue de la Ferronnerie.

It was there again, but the driver was asleep, locked inside his shabby carriage. I had to bang on the shutter four times before he called out, "Leave off! I'm armed! Go away!" A church-dog, one of the wush-hounds that haunted graveyards, sniffed at my boots and slinked by.

In frustration I took the mare's bridle and pulled, rocking the carriage forward. The driver, a one-eyed dwarf, emerged cursing, waving his whip.

"I need to go to the Abbaye de Saint-Germain," I told him. Jumping out of the whip's range wasn't hard: I wondered how well the little man could see. I dared not tell him I needed to go to the Pré-aux-Clercs. The Abbaye was close enough. "I know the way." More or less.

"You're a woman," he said, looking at me squint-eyed.

"I will make it worth your while." I held up the remaining écu—the last of my earnings. Working for Athénaïs was proving not only dangerous but costful.

The driver insisted I clean my boots before he would let down the step. The interior of the coach was surprisingly tidy . . . and thankfully warmed by a burner, which threw off a flickering light. Clearly, this was the little man's home: there was even a paper flower stuck in a wall bracket. A rosary and several saints' medals swung from a shutter socket. "But first, I must collect someone," I told him.

ATHÉNAÏS WAS STANDING at the corner of her house, bundled in fur. She seemed entirely unaware of the menacing shadows, the two men watching her from across the road.

"You look a proper gentleman, Monsieur." She batted her eyelashes at my get-up. "It's hot as Hades in here," she said, slipping down her hood, her golden curls falling about her face. In the lantern light she looked like an angel—an impetuous, headstrong, but heartbreakingly beautiful angel.

I gave the driver instructions and secured the doors.

"I hardly slept at all," she said. "I doped the ancients, but then they snored." She smelled strongly of spirits herself. "Did you sleep?"

"A little," I lied, watching to make sure that we were going in the right direction. I would have the driver let us down at the monastery and ask him to wait: he would assume that we were on a spiritual mission. It would be a bit of a walk from there to the Pré-aux-Clercs field behind, but otherwise we might be detected.

"I'm *so* tired," she said, laying her head on my shoulder. And then she was asleep.

I sat frozen, warmed by her body next to mine. I breathed in her scent, a tantalizing mix of lavender and musk. As I listened to the dwarf's whistling tune, the nag's slow progress through the echoing silence, it seemed a moment stopped in time. I laid my mittened hand over hers: I'd been charged with her safety. *Handfasted.* I was her knight.

THE OPEN COUNTRY behind the Abbaye de Saint-Germain was ghostly in the moonlight. The snow-dusted marsh was encircled by woods that hid it from the roadway; hence its popularity for duels. The still-frozen ground was brittle under my feet.

Athénaïs was silent behind me. "I didn't know there were such places."

I cracked through in one boggy spot. "The city has many secrets," I said, my eyes slowly adjusting. I looked for a path.

"Secret vices?" she joked, but I didn't laugh. Many a vice had occurred in this place, no doubt, vices she'd never even heard of.

I stopped. Something smelled foul in spite of the cold. I scanned the bushes and grasses as I felt my way along—looking out for something dead, but also for something moving, the wild dogs and werewolves that haunted such spheres. A sense came back to me from my childhood, a certain way of moving in the night, wary and alert.

"How far do we have to go?" Her face was deathly gray in the moonlight.

She *is* afraid of the dark, I realized. "Not far. We'll hide in the evergreens over there," I said, pointing. From there, we would have a view of the field.

IN THE HALF-LIGHT of dawn, two horsemen appeared. La Frette and his younger brother Ovart ("his *bastard* half brother," Athénaïs whispered). They walked their horses over the turf—looking for level ground, I guessed. They dismounted not far from where we were hiding.

The brothers took off their spurs and set to cutting away the timber-heels of their boots. (Smart: they would more securely stand their ground.) Then they paced in the chill air, slapping their arms for warmth. I could make out the long rapiers under their heavy cloaks.

La Frette didn't look drunk anymore. He had the walk of a victor. He said something to his half brother, but I couldn't make out the words.

"Where are the others?" Athénaïs whispered.

Maybe they aren't coming, I thought hopefully. Maybe the King had been notified and had laid down the law. I prayed that it was so, but one of the horses, a big black, raised its head and whinnied as four men on horseback trotted onto the field. The sun was more fully up now; I could see the feathers in their hats.

"*Our* men," Athénaïs whispered with a smile: her betrothed and his brother-in-law—the Prince de Chalais—together with two others.

They were all carrying rapiers.

"The one in the white hat is the Marquis de Flamarens—"

I recognized him from the Palais-Royal ball.

"—and the plump one is Henri, Marquis d'Antin, the Bishop de Sens's nephew."

Zounds. The Bishop de Sens was nigh on king in Paris.

"Henri is a very good friend of Alexandre's—his closest friend, really."

The four men dismounted opposite La Frette and tied their reins to some bushes. There was a slight difficulty with this minor matter, one horse kicking out at another, so the men tied them farther apart, making uneasy laughter.

Alexandre stood surveying the field, his gloved hand on the hilt of his rapier. He was tall, but a slight-built man, thin as a wafer—which worried me. Even with rapiers, strength was important. He walked over to his brother-in-law and put his hand on his shoulder. Chalais shook his head.

Athénaïs moved a branch, the better to see.

"It looks like the Marquis wants to attempt a reconciliation," I whispered.

"Really?" Her tone was disapproving.

Alexandre threw open his hands to the La Frette brothers as if to say, Well, can't we talk?

My heart sank as the younger Ovart made a rude gesture and his brother scoffed.

The horses stilled, pricking their ears. "Here come the rest of them," I said.

here were eight young men in all: Prince de Chalais and his three, La Frette with his. La Frette stood opposite Chalais, gesturing to his half brother and the others to form a line. His half brother Ovart positioned himself opposite Alexandre.

"A bastard like Ovart should never duel a man of Alexandre's nobility," Athénaïs said, indignant.

True, it wasn't correct, but I was more concerned by the way they were pairing off. Did they intend to fight all at once? Surely not. "They're going four-on-four," I whispered. A horror, in my mind, an ancient rite of honor performed without any constraint or dignity, just a parcel of hotheaded young nobles with nothing better to do than run each other through with their grandfathers' rapiers. There wasn't even a doctor or an attendant present. "Mademoiselle," I began, hesitantly, "you have the power to stop this. Step out, speak up. They will listen to you."

She scoffed. "You must be mad! Were I to meddle, Alexandre would have nothing more to do with me," she hissed.

"Then I will speak—"

"Claude, don't be ridiculous. You're an unblood. They will laugh at you—as they should."

La Frette threw off his cloak and doublet. "Count down," he said, loud enough for us to hear.

La Frette was going to count down?

"Wait," Alexandre called out, helping the Prince de Chalais struggle out of his doublet.

"Ready," the Prince de Chalais said, drawing his blade. There was a tremor in his voice. His rapier was of an antique style, flatter and wider than most, with an elaborately carved hilt. It would be cumbersome and heavy. "We'll both count."

Un . . . deux . . . trois . . .

"Close your eyes," I told Athénaïs as the air filled with the sound of clanging steel, grunts, threats, and curses.

"I'm not a child," she protested angrily.

I opened my eyes at one crazed peal of laughter. It was a macabre dance I saw, the combating pairs clashing, thrusting, jabbing, and feinting—advancing and retreating, advancing and retreating.

The Prince de Chalais had been slashed across his cheek. He was bloodied, falling back, losing ground. The man fighting the Marquis de Flamarens had him in a chokehold and was ignobly hitting him over the head with the heavy hilt of his rapier.

Only Alexandre seemed to be holding his own against his opponent. He deflected a blow against the hilt of Ovart's weapon. "Cock's bones," he cursed when the razor-thin tip of his rapier snapped off.

I gasped, dumbstruck, as Alexandre fell. I hadn't even seen Ovart's thrust. "He's alive," I said, swallowing. Bloodied, moaning, writhing in pain—but alive.

And then I heard something that made my heart stop: three sharp cries followed by a chilling silence. The men stood back, panting.

I could make out a still shape sprawled in the tall grass: it was Alexandre's good friend, plump Henri d'Antin—with a rapier in his chest.

One of La Frette's men got to his feet, wiping his eyes with his sleeve. He bent over d'Antin, withdrawing his rapier. He stood over his victim for a moment and then picked up d'Antin's weapon in the grass as well, and hurried after La Frette, who'd already mounted his horse. Soon they'd all cantered off, whooping: the victors.

The monastery bells began to ring for early morning prayer.

Athénaïs said something, but she was drowned out. I leaned into her. "Alexandre's hurt," she said faintly.

Badly, I feared. I was relieved to see him start moving, crawling toward d'Antin's still body.

The bells ceased. Alexandre collapsed over the body of his friend, his cries piercing the silence. He slumped as Chalais and Flamarens pried him off and dragged the body into a thicket.

"Henri's dead?" Athénaïs whispered.

I should have brought salts, I thought.

THE THREE MEN stared dumbfounded as we emerged from the woods.

Mon Dieu, I heard Alexandre gasp. Athénaïs broke into a run and fell down on her knees beside him, gasping convulsively.

"I took you for a man," the Prince de Chalais told me, pressing a bloody kerchief to his cheek.

I could hear a wagon rumbling on the road, a cock crowing, a goat bleating. I glanced at the bushes. I could see the soles of d'Antin's boots—they had high red heels, like the boots the cobbler had given me long before. The strong scent of blood brought on a moment of nausea; I pressed my nose into the crook of my elbow.

"Flamarens, Chalais, make for the frontiers," Alexandre said weakly, his teeth chattering. He was weeping still. "The King will have your heads if he finds you."

"We can't leave you like this," the Prince de Chalais protested.

"Messieurs, we have a coach waiting at the monastery," I managed to say, tilting my head in the direction of the Abbaye de Saint-Germain. "We could take the Marquis." They regarded my offer with stunned relief.

I stooped to examine Alexandre's wound. It wasn't my place, but someone had to act. It was a slash across his thigh. That was better—far better—than a thrust wound, although it looked deep, possibly to the bone. "We need a linen," I told the Prince de Chalais. "Your sleeve?"

The boy—for he was hardly more—shed his layers. He was white and thin, shivering in the cold, his ribs showing. That he had survived against big La Frette was a miracle. He tossed me his chemise and quickly put his doublet and cloak back on, his movements stiff and clumsy.

I ripped the lace off with my teeth and tore the cloth down the seam. "This will hurt," I warned. But in truth, I didn't care. I was furious at them all.

Alexandre clasped the saint's medal hanging from his neck and pressed his face into Athénaïs's bosom. "Don't worry about me, lads," he said gamely, but nobody laughed.

I wound the linen tight around his thigh. Quickly, it bloomed bright. I tore off another sleeve, which slowed the stain. Merci Dieu— but how to move him across the field?

"I refuse to go anywhere until you two are on your way," Alexandre told his compatriots.

"Heft him onto his horse before you go," I suggested curtly. It was too far for me to carry him—and Athénaïs would certainly be no help.

Alexandre groaned as Chalais and Flamarens lifted him into the saddle.

"We're just going to leave Henri?" Athénaïs looked dangerously pale.

"Breathe!" I commanded, shaking her to keep her from fainting.

"Be gone!" Alexandre gasped. "Athénaïs will get word to your families."

The convent bells rang for morning Mass as the two men cantered off.

I glanced back at the boots. How long would it be before the buzzards started circling? How long before the body of the mighty Bishop de Sens's nephew was discovered hidden in the bushes of a frozen marsh? Holding the reins of Alexandre's horse, I set out across the field, Athénaïs trailing behind. My thoughts were sluggish, spent. I felt numb with it all, exhausted.

What were we going to do with Alexandre?

Don't die, I thought furiously. Just don't *die.*

CHAPTER 26

aston was at the little platform table by the shuttered window eating from a pot of gruel. He looked up, surprised to see me. He made a gesture of worry, his forehead wrinkled up. I could tell from his tremulous singsong that he'd been fretful.

"I'm sorry," I said, pushing Gaston's line of objects out of the way of the door with one foot. The wounded aristocrat was in the coach below. I'd rashly offered to hide him until Athénaïs could find a suitable place. *You're my guardian angel,* she'd told me, weeping—but I was still angry. They'd brought it on themselves. "Where's Mother?" The fire was blazing; I was thankful for the heat, thankful that there was still wood stacked—we were going to need it.

"Play," he said with a stutter.

Of course. Monsieur Pierre was introducing his new play to the troupe.

"I. Go." He wrinkled up his forehead again. "She—"

"Stay. I need your help," I said with some urgency, relieved that Mother would not be present.

Gaston was young, but he had strength. Between us, we managed to carry the moaning nobleman up the narrow stairs (fortunately unobserved). We laid him out on Gaston's straw mattress, his booted feet hanging off the end. I tossed Gaston the rag doll he slept with, which he pressed to his heart.

The Marquis looked like death. I'd been foolish to offer to hide him, foolish to expose my family to the King's ire. Cursing at what I'd gotten myself into, I pulled a threadbare blanket from the bottom of a storage trunk. It was rough and patched—a rag to most—but it was all we had. Tant pis. Soon it would be bloodied.

I started to unlace the high boot on Alexandre's injured leg. "Don't watch," I told Gaston. As I feared, the boot was full of blood. I closed my eyes, suddenly light-headed. What would we do if he died? What would we do with his *body*? I broke into a sweat just thinking of it. I wished I could send for a surgeon—but the nature of the wound would be obvious, and who wouldn't profit by going to the King? I dared not take the risk.

"Go boil some water and fetch me some clean rags," I told Gaston, who seemed frozen, sucking on his thumb and staring.

I peeled off the Marquis's knit sock. It was a terrible gash, long and deep. "Vinegar too," I said, pressing my fingers into the wound to stanch the bleeding. Finally, Gaston moved. "And my sewing basket," I called out. Like it or not, I was going to have to stitch him.

Gaston returned with the rags and steaming water in the cast-iron pot.

"Not a hint of this to anyone, do you hear?" I told him sternly, using a steaming rag to wipe my hands clean. Not that Gaston could even talk! I dipped the sharpest needle into the hot water and then laced it with the linen thread. "Leave, Turnip," I said.

ATHÉNAÏS'S ROOM WAS in a state of disarray, gowns and shawls flung everywhere. A mess of jeweled necklaces had been unceremoniously dumped on the marble-topped table. The parrot was perched atop a candlestick holder, watching me with one eye. The monkey grinned at me ghoulishly from its stand and rattled its chain.

Athénaïs emerged from behind a screen wearing only a chemise. She, too, looked disordered, her hair undressed, her face unpowdered.

"He's doing well," I told her. I wasn't sure I could mention him by name. Who might be listening behind closed doors? I gently set down my basket. The wound had closed and the inflammation was down. Noble blood healed fast.

"Yet his life is over," Athénaïs said tremulously, through tears. "The King—"

I held silent. The news was everywhere. His Majesty was enraged! He took dueling seriously. (*That* I knew too well.)

"He might as well be dead," she said.

I handed her my nose cloth. She looked at it askance. "It's clean," I assured her.

She patted her cheeks with it. "His Majesty has ordered guards posted all over Paris," she whispered, handing the kerchief back, her voice strangled. "He's intent on arresting them: *all* of them." She scratched at her breast with her long nails, drawing blood lines on her flesh. "How can the King be so . . . so *base*! Dueling is a noble tradition—an *honorable* tradition."

As if honor were a luxury reserved exclusively for the blessed. I thought of the line from *The Cid* I'd scratched on my father's pile of stones: *Men may reduce me to live without happiness, but they cannot compel me to live without honor.*

I heard footsteps, the creak of floorboards. "You have need of a costume, Mademoiselle?" I said in a carrying voice.

"Oui, I'm to perform at a ball, His Majesty insists," Athénaïs said, daring to refer to the King in a mocking tone. "Any gown will do, so long as it is gold. The King is to be the sun, and *we're* to reflect his light," she added with spite. She fell back onto her bed, kicking pillows and gowns fitfully onto the floor. "Everyone is in a state of terror over the duel," she hissed. "It's going to be impossible to find somewhere suitable to hide him. I dare not even ask."

I stepped closer. "He's safe at our place, Mademoiselle," I whispered. "No one would ever suspect." Or so I prayed, knowing the risk to my family.

I TOOK A long, circuitous route back to our humble room, lest I was being followed. I paused outside our door, listening to the voices within. I could hear Gaston humming.

"Hush, Gaston—we're working," I heard Mother say, and he quieted. "Give me that cue line again, Monsieur."

Who is here? I thought with alarm. It had been agreed that there would be no callers—not so long as we were harboring Alexandre.

"Madame, your love for him surprises me," a man said.

I recognized the line from Monsieur Pierre's newest play, *Sertorius*.

"It is unusual for a man of his age to attract a young woman," the man continued.

Alexandre?

"What I love is his greatness in war," Mother said with fervor. *Sertorius* wouldn't be peformed for some time, but already she'd begun to commit it to memory.

"Before that, there's a line about passion . . ."

I stepped in, surprising them all. "I hate passion, the impetuous tumult," I recited.

Alexandre was seated on the wood chair next to the plank table, the play-script of Mother's lines on his lap. Gaston was on the stool, the stones for a game of Mill set out between them. "I'm pleased to see you up and about, Monsieur le Marquis," I said, dropping a pert curtsy. The heat from the coals made my frozen cheeks tingle and the smell of bean soup and baked bread sharpened my appetite. I hung my damp cloak on a peg. When I'd left that morning, Alexandre had been in bed. During the hours I'd been away, he'd clearly been transformed. "I see that my mother lost no time putting you to work."

"The Marquis loves theater," Mother said, stirring the beans. She'd pulled her long hair back into a bun, but wisps had escaped, making her look charmingly disheveled.

"Oh?" I was amazed (and not a little jealous) at her tone of familiarity.

"He knows Monsieur Corneille's plays well," she said, "even *La Suivante*. He is delighted to learn of this new work."

"It's extraordinary, Madame des Oeillets," Alexandre said, making a move on the Mill board (and then groaning as Gaston deftly took one of his pieces). "Especially your role, Queen Viriate—"

Viriate: it *was* a thrillingly evil part Mother was to play. Lusting, ambitious—and yet profoundly heroic—she is wooed by Sertorius, the man who murdered her lover—the man she marries just to avenge her lover's death. It was hard for me to believe that Monsieur Pierre had cast my gentle, feckless mother in such an evil role.

"The Marquis has been explaining to me how a queen must act,"

Mother said. "He knows both the Queen Mother and the Queen, and I'm far too kind, he says."

Alexandre glanced at me and shrugged. "She is." He groaned again as Gaston took another of his pieces.

"You look fatigued, my dear," Mother said. "Have some soup."

"I have a letter for you, Monsieur le Marquis," I said, sitting down. I felt uncomfortable sitting at a table with a nobleman—it wasn't proper—but I felt even more uncomfortable standing in my own home. I reached into my skirts and withdrew the scented packet, the ink splotched "with tears." (White wine, in fact—my idea.) Within was a tiny locket containing a golden hair from Athénaïs's pubis. (Her idea.)

Alexandre smiled fondly at the inscription—*For my Beloved*—and struggled to stand. "Adieu et merci, mes amis. I must now retire," he said, leaning on the table. Gaston jumped to his feet to help him limp back into the closet.

"I should spend the morning out more often," I told Mother, holding the warm bowl of bean soup in both hands.

"What you should do," she said, taking Alexandre's chair, "is find a way to get that good young man out of the country. The town criers—"

"I know, Maman." *I know.* The King had condemned the duelists to decapitation should they be apprehended. All the others had scattered far and wide—some fleeing to England, others to Spain or Portugal. Alexandre was the only one still in the city, still in hiding. "I have an idea," I said.

CHAPTER 27

I've found a way out for you," I told Alexandre. Mother and Gaston were at the theater. I could speak openly.

He was leaning on the crutch I had made for him. In the month he'd been with us, he'd rapidly improved. "Out of France?" he asked and I nodded. He leaned the crutch against the windowsill and eased himself onto the stool by the trestle table. We'd taken to having talks there, over bowls of warm gruel. "It's the only way, I guess." He looked sad but also relieved.

"You'll be part of a traveling group of players—they're on their way to Portugal." The sooner he was gone, the better. There were still guards everywhere. I'd heard of searches, the prestigious families of the duelists grilled and even threatened. At any time, Athénaïs could be questioned. "I have a costume you can use, and you already know how to juggle." I'd been teaching him.

He combed his long hair with his fingers, pushing it up off his forehead. "Portugal might not be so bad . . ."

He looked a little lost, in truth. His life had been perfectly plotted, up until now. The eldest son of a wealthy nobleman, engaged to marry an aristocratic woman—a woman he sincerely loved: all was in place for a happy and fulfilling future. Now he was cast to the winds.

"How shall I ever thank you?" he said.

I stood, looking about our shabby room: the cracks in the plaster, the smoky fire pit. "I regret that we couldn't have looked after you more comfortably."

"You saved my life."

"I'll help you with your things. I told them you'd meet them on the

Pont Neuf at midday." I wanted him gone before Mother and Gaston returned.

He took out his sundial and held it to the window. "That's fairly soon."

"I've already arranged for a litter." I didn't like prolonged farewells. "I'd not show that sundial once you're out." It was gold, intricately tooled. "Just a word of caution."

He held it out to me.

I hesitated. A knight expected no reward.

"Give it to Athénaïs," he said. "To remember me by."

Of course, *Athénaïs*.

It didn't take Alexandre long to change and pack up his things. He even helped me pull up the bed linens (which surprised me). "Thank your brother for the use of his closet," he said.

I nodded but said nothing.

"Tell him I intend to return and beat him at Mill." He looked comically charming in his rags, his bundle of clothes tied up on a stick, like any homeless itinerant. I blinked back stinging tears.

"You'll tell your mother farewell for me? I wish I could be here to see her perform Queen Viriate. She's going to be magnificent, I know."

I nodded, my hand on the door: the litter carriers would be waiting. I handed him his crutch. "You will need it."

"This is for Athénaïs as well," he said, handing me a tightly scrolled paper.

A letter? Where had he found the paper, the ink, a quill?

He kissed my cheek. His beard was prickly but soft. "Au revoir, Claudette," he said, using the tender name Mother called me. "Et merci."

I LAY ON the neatly made-up bed, listening to the sounds of Alexandre's uneven steps on the winding stairs. What if the litter carriers weren't there? What if the players failed to meet him? What if he was recognized?

I started to get up—to follow after him—but stopped, looking at the paper I had clutched in my fist. It was not sealed, merely tied with a length of ribbon.

Mademoiselle de Tonnay-Charente, my beloved Athénaïs, my love, my life, forgive me. I pray for a miracle, pray that His Majesty will allow me to return to your arms, but we both know that is not likely. His Majesty will remain firm: I know him well.

With great sadness and regret, I release you from our vows, our tender promises, given in love. (Such love!)

I depart burdened with the knowledge that I have ruined several lives—my own, certainly—as well as ended the life of my dearest friend, Henri, whom I roused from a peaceful sleep in order to persuade him to take part in that loathsome duel.

I, therefore, stand guilty and condemn myself, even were I to be pardoned.

I beg you to assuage his family's sorrow, in any way possible.

Pray for me, as I will pray for you.

I remain yours forever.
Alexandre de La Trémoille, Marquis de Noirmoutier

I rolled the letter back up tightly, then wound the ribbon and knotted it.

I remain yours forever.

Yet he owed *me* his life.

I lay for some time with my confused and angry thoughts. I felt lumpish and ugly, a tall freak in shabby rags.

ATHÉNAÏS THREW ALEXANDRE'S letter into the fire. "You didn't warn me!"

"Leaving the country saves his life." I trembled, but not at my presumption (which was great). I'd risked everything—

"And ruins *mine*." She spat into the flames, convulsed.

I was caught in a web of confusion. I had tried to prevent the duel, but had been ignored. I'd sheltered Alexandre at grave risk to me and my family. And now *I* was blamed! Like winged Icarus, I had flown too close to the sun, and like him, I had been burned.

"Au revoir, Mademoiselle," I said coldly, my heart twisted. She had resolved to forget Alexandre, and I resolved to forget them both. I didn't belong in their world. My "princess" had been a fantasy of my childhood, a talisman against my own bleak world, a treasured fable of a perfect life. But there was no such thing, I now knew.

She cursed me as I left.

I walked all the way back to our meager room, past the gates of the wealthy, past the Abbaye de Saint-Germain-des-Prés, only glancing at the trees that concealed the dueling field. I picked up my pace nearing the river, stomping carelessly through puddles of refuse, fuming and chafed—but also, inexplicably, bereft.

Crossing the Pont Neuf, I ignored the whores, the pleading children, the evil Bird Catcher with his clutch of sad and pretty boys. I paused for breath at the statue of Henri IV—at the very spot where Alexandre was to meet the traveling players only the day before.

Nearby, a small crowd surrounded a man with a pockmarked face, hovering over a fire on a grate. I'd seen him several times before. "Ask a spirit," he called out. "Ask it anything!" A woman handed him a coin. She wanted to know where her husband had gone. The pocked man wrote her question on a note, enclosed it in a ball of wax, and threw it on the fire. Then a note appeared in his hand. "The spirit says he's in a tavern, Madame," he told her, and everyone laughed.

A cutting wind blew across the gray water. I blinked back tears and pulled my hood down over my eyes. Shivering, I walked on, plunging my hands under my cloak, where I suddenly felt—with some satisfaction, I confess—the hard weight of Alexandre's timepiece. I'd not given it to Athénaïs, as I'd intended.

I checked to make sure nobody was close—thieves on the Pont Neuf were thick as stars—and took it out of my poke, weighing the object in my mittened hand, calculating its worth.

I SOLD ALEXANDRE'S timepiece for a handsome sum and found Gaston a helper, someone who actually began to have some success teaching him things. I considered paying for a healer like the one Madame Catherine had mentioned, as well, but Gaston proved mysteriously fearful. In any case, his ever-patient helper was making progress: he could do up a button! Her fee—a livre a week—was considerable, but it was worth it, and it freed Mother and me to work with the troupe.

In spite of my resolve and the demands of my life, I would now and again be irresistibly moved to go back over the river, making the long trek to Athénaïs's home. I never lingered, or even slowed: I didn't want to arouse the suspicion of the guards at the gate. I would just walk by as if going about my business, my eyes darting through the iron gate. Once I saw one of her little dogs doing his business in the gravel, attended by a frowning maid. Another time I saw a delivery of an entire cow carcass, skinned, befooted, and beheaded. But never Athénaïs herself.

My compulsion shamed me. I feared I was under an enchantment. I paid a cunning woman to make an amulet for me to wear, to break the spell. For a time this seemed to help. It helped, too, that events conspired to capture my attention. We were—without knowing it at the time—in the early stages of that great disruption: the War of the Theaters.

Act III

War of the Theaters

(1662, Paris)

CHAPTER 28

eading out to a meeting at the Marais, Mother and I stopped to borrow Monsieur Martin's copy of the weekly verse gazette, *La Muze historique*. We arrived at the theater flush with excitement. The editor Loret had written about *Sertorius* in glowing terms—"You can't praise the actors too highly," he'd written, with a special mention of Mother's wonderful performance!

"Did you see what Loret said?" I asked Madame Babette on entering. She was leaning on a sweep, staring into the pit. Monsieur la Roque and some of the players had pulled benches around the coal brazier for warmth. It looked like they'd opened the liquor case. They were sharing a jug, yet they did not seem to have a festive manner. "In *La Muze*?" I said, showing her the news sheet. I had scanned it for mention of the duelists, but there was nothing.

Madame Babette nodded dolefully. "Molière's troupe is going to produce *Sertorius* as well," she said with a tone of defeat.

I glanced at Mother and then back at Madame Babette, more confused than alarmed. "But the play hasn't been published yet." Once in print, a play was public property, available for any troupe to stage—but not before. This was not a written law, but it was respected nonetheless.

"Monsieur Molière is the King's favorite these days. He seems to think he can do anything."

"But how could he even get the script?" There was only one complete copy, and the prompter locked it away safely each night. The players were given only their lines and cues, no more.

Madame Babette screwed up her face. "Well—Brécourt and La Thorillière . . ."

I took note of the players present: Brécourt, La Thorillière, and their wives were usually the first to arrive at meetings, blaze the fire, and set out the benches—but I didn't see them.

"*They've* signed with Molière," Madame Babette said.

Mother let out a yelp.

"Their wives too?" Sacré coeur. It would be a challenge to perform *Sertorius* without them—and then it struck me. "You think they *stole* the prompt copy?"

"Monsieur la Roque checked. It's still locked away." Madame Babette shrugged her shoulders. "But they could have committed it to memory."

"In this short time?"

"Well—there are four of them."

A betrayal! "How is Monsieur la Roque taking it?" La Thorillière's wife, Marie, was his daughter.

"*Hard.*"

I felt sickened. The troupe was like a family. Were we to be torn apart?

"Not that *I* would mind getting paid," Madame Babette added as Monsieur la Roque gestured us forward.

THE MEETING WAS adjourned shortly after, everyone dazed. The wonderful notice in *La Muze historique* only made us feel worse.

Breath misting, Mother and I walked back to our room.

"I have faith," she whispered to her little Virgin, stringing her up on a hook.

I wish I did, I thought, building up the fire and filling the cauldron. Had I heard a knock? I went to the door, the iron skimmer in my hand.

"That's quite a climb up your stairs," Monsieur Pierre said, leaning against the wall, catching his breath.

"We've something outrageous to tell you," Mother said, joining me at the door.

"It *has* been a day," he said, stepping into the room.

Did he know? I lit a pine-scented taper, uncomfortably aware of the stench of the communal latrine. "Please, have a seat, Monsieur," I said, pulling a wood chair away from the wall. I noticed mouse droppings in the corner and made a note to set out traps.

"You aren't going to believe it," Mother said, flinging a tattered shawl around her shoulders and sitting down beside the great playwright.

I perched on the windowsill. I could feel a cold draft coming through. I wished I could talk to Monsieur Pierre privately, without my mother's emotional exclamations.

"Molière stole Brécourt and Étiennette, *and* La Thorillière and Marie," she went on. "All four of them."

Monsieur Pierre raised one bushy brow.

"And he's going to produce *Sertorius*—with *them.*"

Monsieur Pierre cleared his throat, pulling on the patch of hair under his lower lip. "I know. I've been talking to Josias Floridor."

This puzzled me. Floridor was the leader of another rival troupe, the Bourgogne. What did *he* have to do with it?

Monsieur Pierre put his hand over Mother's. "One of their leading players wishes to retire and they are in need of a replacement. I've been asked to inquire."

"But surely you wouldn't want me to leave the Marais—"

"For your own sake, Alix, you must seriously give it thought. Floridor is a remarkable tragic actor."

Indeed. He'd even traveled to London and been a success there, I'd heard. Nonetheless, it was said he remained a perfect gentleman, without the blunt manners of the English. His gestures, manner, and posture were said to be natural and unstudied; some claimed he was the best player in the entire world.

"Floridor and I first worked together . . . oh, mon Dieu, fifteen years ago? Where does the time go? It was the year I joined the Académie Française, so, oui, fifteen. We're very close—he's godfather to one of my sons, in fact. He leads a fine company and you would learn from them . . . and they're going to produce *Sertorius* as well—"

The Bourgogne *and* Molière's troupe? In addition to the Marais? *Three* troupes performing the same play? I was dumbfounded.

Monsieur Pierre put up his hands. "To tell you the truth, I think the Bourgogne production might be the finest of the three—but only if you are in it, Alix."

"Monsieur Pierre, if I were to leave the Marais, what would happen to our beautiful production?"

He let out a long, sputtering breath. "With the loss of four players and the two rival enactments, the Marais is going to have to reconsider its repertoire."

"Do you think they will close down *Sertorius?*"

He shrugged. "Likely."

I pressed my hand to my forehead, feeling suddenly faint. We'd invested so much. Would we ever recover the loss?

Mother stood and paced. "I couldn't leave the Marais."

"Alix! You must consider! They'll be reduced to performing farces again, just to survive. Your talent—your *great* talent—will be wasted."

Plus there would be no money in it. I would have to let Gaston's tutor go—just when he was starting to make progress.

"I met Nicolas on that stage," Mother protested. "His spirit is there."

"The spirit of Nicolas is with *you*," Monsieur Pierre said (surprising me).

"Maman, he's right," I said, taking advantage. The Bourgogne was considered the best troupe in the land for tragedy. "About joining Floridor's company," I added, to clarify. The geography of the afterlife and the whereabouts of my father's spirit were not subjects I wished to delve into.

Mother sat back down, deflated.

"One other thing," the great playwright said, his big hands flat on the table. "As you know, I've been thinking of writing another tragedy—this one about Sophonisbe."

"The warrior queen," Mother said with a glint of a smile.

We had talked of Sophonisbe's story before, the three of us, talked of its rich potential. There had been other plays about the African queen, but none that had portrayed her accurately: none that showed her cruel nature.

"The heartless queen," I said, recalling telling Sophonisbe's story to Athénaïs, remembering her glee at the Queen's wickedness, her big eyes alight. I clasped the amulet. The memory pierced me.

"I intend to write her story this winter in Rouen," Monsieur Pierre said. "I told Josias that I would offer it to the Bourgogne—and that I had you, Alix, in mind for the title role."

An honor, truly! "Would the Bourgogne give Maman a full share?" I asked. In spite of her major roles, Mother still had only a half share at the Marais.

"Absolutely," Monsieur Pierre said, standing. "Perhaps you should go and discuss things with Floridor. Why not tomorrow?"

CHAPTER 29

The Bourgogne was an old building, built nearly a hundred years before the Marais. It claimed to be the first public playhouse in the country, in fact. It was less well located than the Marais, near the meat and vegetable markets at the junction of the rue Mauconseil and the rue Neuve de Bourgogne, two horribly congested and noisy streets. Even so, it was closer to the Court and attracted a better class of clientele.

"We are flattered that you should wish to join our company," Floridor said, bowing over Mother's hand. He had a flexible carrying voice and the fluid, dignified presence one expected in a tragic actor.

Mother glanced at me, perplexed.

"My mother is undecided, Monsieur," I said, somewhat disarmed by his noble air and the unexpected sweetness of his manner. He was a man of birth and quality, yet he wasn't pompous in the least. Indeed, he looked somewhat comical in an ancient ruff and sagging breeches.

"Of *course*," he said, gracefully bowing us through to the grande salle. In spite of his advanced years, he had a superb physique and excellent carriage. "Have you ever been to our theater, Mesdames?"

I admitted we had not. (Not that I hadn't tried, but the Bourgogne was more carefully controlled than most theaters; it was difficult to sneak into the pit without paying.)

There were twelve full-share members in all, he explained, leading us up to the first-tier loges. "And we are intent on holding it to that number."

(Good, I thought: the fewer the shares, the greater the take.)

He unlocked a door to a loge. I took in the gilded balustrade, the tasseled cushions on the cane chairs (not too worn). Although the theater was empty, the candles in a couple of the forestage candelabras had been lit—in anticipation of Mother's visit, I suspected; an expensive welcome, if so.

"I understand you know Monsieur Montfleury," Floridor said, leading us out of the theater and back around to the door to the parterre.

"Zacharie?" Mother said.

"Didn't he play in *The Cid?*" I asked them both. Father had described the tragic actor's sonorous voice and bombastic style. Of enormous heft, he required a corset of metal.

"He's been with us for years," Floridor said, helping us up onto the stage, which was somewhat smaller than that of the Marais.

We were then shown what would be Mother's own dressing room. It was impressively large with a long toilette table, a polished metal mirror, and two wardrobe chests. A brass candlestick of six branches was set into the wall. A brazier in the corner gave off heat.

I glanced at Mother. Wasn't she impressed?

Floridor must also have wondered, for he rushed to assure her that she would have a garçon de théâtre to run errands for her.

"I have my children for that," Mother said.

I smiled, relieved: it had been decided.

IN THE FALL, with the first icy drizzle, the Bourgogne staged their own production of *Sertorius*. It was a relief for Mother to return to a role she already knew well. During her initial months with the troupe, I'd had to coach her through many of the new parts in the Bourgogne's extensive repertoire. In any single month, they put on as many as eight different plays, changing them constantly.

One chilly afternoon, on a day when we were not giving a performance, Monsieur Pierre appeared at our door again, his shoulders dusted with snow. "Your stairs are still steep."

"We hope to move," I said, taking his damp woolen cape. "Closer to the Bourgogne." Our long walks back and forth to the theater were rigorous, the more so now with winter upon us. "I thought you were with your family in Rouen."

"You didn't think I'd miss seeing Queen Viriate onstage again, did you?" He held his black felt hat with one hand; in the other he was carrying a worn leather portmanteau.

"You're looking thin, Monsieur," Mother said, drying her hands on her apron. "We need to fatten you up."

"You're sounding like my wife," he grumbled, but with the usual tone of affection he used when speaking of the saintly Marie de Lampérière, mother of their six children. He brushed the snow off his thick moustache.

"We're in league, you see," Mother said, "we women."

"And you're outnumbered," I said, taking up my sewing basket. The work at the Bourgogne mostly entailed keeping the costumes of the walk-on parts in repair. It was not very interesting, and the pay was meager, but I'd been too busy looking after Mother and Gaston to seek additional work elsewhere.

"You're cruel and heartless, every one of you," Monsieur Pierre said, removing a packet wrapped in linen from his portmanteau. "Hence . . ." He loosened the cloth to reveal the title: *Sophonisbe*.

"You did it," Mother said, smiling broadly.

"A cruel and heartless heroine, written just for you, Alix. True to life, to history. Floridor paid me for it without even reading it."

"Well, of course," Mother said, adding, with a flourish, "You are, after all, the Great Corneille."

"Sometimes," Monsieur Pierre said with a downturned grimace. "He caught me up on the Paris news. I understand Molière's group performed *Sertorius* a number of times—"

"Performed it poorly," I said.

"—and that the Marais has performed not a thing."

"Except for a few farces." One was about the new five-sou coach lines, very light fare.

"May they rest in peace," Mother said, signing herself.

"May they pay us what is owed," Monsieur Pierre said humorlessly.

"Amen!" I exclaimed, and then reddened. Although Mother was a full partner in the Bourgogne, we had yet to recover what we'd invested in the Marais.

"I miss the machines, I confess," Mother said. "All that lovely flying through the air."

"Oui, there is rather less gaiety at the Bourgogne," Monsieur Pierre said in a mock scolding manner, which made us laugh.

"But potentially more profit," I remarked. The sets were not as complex and there were fewer of them for each performance. The troupe relied on acting to create the drama (and succeeded magnificently).

"I gather the competition from Molière's comic productions is a concern," Monsieur Pierre said, pulling on the tuft of hair above his chin.

"His *School for Husbands* is said to be an amusing farce," Mother said, "for those who care for that type of thing." Her tone indicated those of a lower literary sensibility.

"They're in rehearsal for another 'school' play now," I said, not admitting that I had found *School for Husbands* delightful. Madame Babette was now working cleanup for the rival troupe. She'd become a good source of information—as well as the occasional free pass. "This one about a school for wives."

"I doubt that the Bourgogne need worry: Molière's players are simply not up to the standard of our Queen Viriate here," Monsieur Pierre said, tipping his hand to Mother.

After Monsieur Pierre left, I read the new play to Mother. (He'd been kind enough to entrust the precious script to us for one night.) We broke after the second act when Gaston clambered home from putting up announcements with the bill-poster crew, ravenous and cold. We returned to the play-script as soon as the soup pot was empty, anxious to finish before the candles guttered.

With the last line, Mother put her hands over her heart. "Who but Monsieur Pierre creates such powerful women?"

Powerful and thrillingly wicked. I could not help but wonder if Athénaïs would come to see it.

"WELL DONE, MONSIEUR PIERRE!" Floridor's sonorous voice boomed out over the theater. Behind him players had gathered on the stage, their *Sophonisbe* lines in hand, preparing to go through the first of the three group rehearsals. Monsieur Pierre's newest play was scheduled to open in only nine days.

Monsieur Pierre climbed up, holding onto a railing for support.
"What have I done now?"

"You've trumped Monsieur Molière."

I looked up from the basket of costumes I was sorting for the
walk-on parts. "I should hope so," I said, but indifferently. I'd been
distracted of late, overcome once again with urges to walk by Athénaïs's home. The amulet I wore seemed to have lost its power; I was
considering buying another, but they were dear.

"I'd like to kill him, not trump him." Monsieur Pierre had been
enraged by Molière's *School for Wives,* in which the fool of a main character exclaims a line from his *Sertorius,* Corneille's beautiful text ridiculed. "If only duels were allowed."

"Tsk!" Floridor said. "In our enlightened times, honor means
nothing. The only important thing today is earning the King's favor."
He held out a paper. "And that's a duel you're winning."

"The pensions list?" Monsieur Pierre asked, fumbling for his thick
spectacles.

"The Crown awarded Molière one thousand this year. You, however, double it."

"Molière shouldn't get a penny," Monsieur Pierre grumbled, looking over the document. "Nor that youngster Racine."

I looked up. I'd been hearing about Jean Racine. Madame Babette
reported that Molière saw talent in the young man's work and was
encouraging him to write tragedy.

"Interesting," Floridor said, looking over Monsieur Pierre's shoulder. "A complete unknown and he's right on the tail of his mentor with
a royal pension of eight hundred."

Monsieur Pierre grunted. "If I were Molière, I'd be watching."

A WEEK LATER, *Sophonisbe* opened to faint praise. The audience
was sparse, and strangely silent.

"They simply don't care for a ruthless heroine," Monsieur Pierre
said, pacing.

"It's not that. It's the *Wives,*" I said. Molière's *School for Wives* had
been causing such a scandal that people were flocking to it in droves.
Madame Babette told me that one night they took in more than fifteen

hundred livres. "I'm going to mingle," I told him. Eavesdrop. I couldn't understand why the tragedy was not more of a success.

I groped my way through the dark corridor to the door to the pit. The crowds at the Bourgogne were less rowdy than those at the Marais. The violence was of a different sort: servants in livery threatening duels, drunken merchants of the rue Saint-Denis falling over each other. I found a seat on a side bench, close to the stove: in a gown, I dared not venture into the crowd of men.

I watched with pride as Mother moved to the foot-candles, her deep dramatic voice silencing the chatter. She was not a handsome woman, so I was always surprised how attractive she looked under candlelight (more attractive, certainly, than in daylight). An uncanny power came over her when she stepped onto a stage.

The first act ended and three musicians started up. Five male dancers came onto the stage to perform during the interlude. Men in the pit made catcalls at the two dressed in travesty. Everyone was jostling about, the men of the pit leaving to relieve themselves, or to get ale and macarons from the vendors at the back.

I was startled by a light touch on my shoulder. A parterre attendant pointed to one of the loges in the second tier, where a young woman was leaning out, waving a fur muff.

Athénaïs, seated beside a man in a puce cloak.

In spite of myself, my heart gladdened to see her.

Come up here, she gestured.

CHAPTER 30

To go from the parterre to the exclusive velvet-draped loges was not easy. I had to leave the theater and go around to the entrance for the nobility, ascending into another realm: wafts of floral scent and Hungary Water diffused the more odiferous and common smells. The voices were hushed, accented now and again by a muted cough.

An attendant opened the door to the loge. I touched the amulet that hung from my neck and stepped in.

Athénaïs was seated beside a tall, gawky man with big, transparent ears. I curtsied. He touched his gloved hand to his forehead: a measured and somewhat reluctant response due to someone he obviously considered well beneath his station.

"My dear Claudette," Athénaïs exclaimed affectionately, effusively welcoming. (As if she had never cursed me!) She introduced her companion with a sweep of her hand: "My betrothed, the Marquis de Montespan." Her knees were high; her feet no doubt perched on a coal foot warmer under her skirts.

"Honored to meet you." I admit I was shocked by his ugliness. I thought of dear Alexandre, who'd been so comely and charming.

"Mademoiselle Claude is the daughter of Madame Alix des Oeillets, the woman playing the lead," Athénaïs explained brightly to the Marquis, one hand fisted.

He leaned into her, lowering his voice, but I could make out what he said. "You've summoned the daughter of a *player*?"

"And she's a player as well. She flies—!"

"Mademoiselle, you must know—" the Marquis de Montespan

began, but then collected himself, looking away, his mouth down-turned. "We will discuss this anon—privately."

"Certainly, Monsieur. The ceremony is in two weeks," Athénaïs informed me with feigned cheer, "and I need some alterations made to my gown."

The Marquis de Montespan clasped her wrist.

"Claude's work is excellent," Athénaïs protested, tugging her hand free. "I assure you."

"As are the seamstresses my tailor employs."

She dipped her head. "Once we are married, certainly." She glanced at the stage, her lower lip trembling. "Tomorrow afternoon would be best, Claude."

I lowered my eyes. I had vowed to forsake her.

"Two of the clock?"

I paused only a moment before saying: "Oui, Mademoiselle."

I FOUND ATHÉNAÏS collapsed on her bed in a chemise, staring at the flickering candles. Parts of a gown ensemble were hung over various chairs: skirts, a boned bodice, tie-on sleeves, a train. The parrot stared from its perch and the monkey—Ugly Thing—was grooming an angry black cat. A puppy with a pushed-in nose dozed by the embers, curled in a basket of scarves. There were shoes and boots everywhere. One of the ancients was leaning tiredly against the wall.

"It's my gown," Athénaïs said, rising slowly to her feet. "My wedding gown," she added with a hint of derision. "I had it made long ago." She had the thick manner of someone half asleep. "I was going to wear it to marry Alexandre."

My heart ached for her. "It's beautiful," I said, stooping to feel the fabric of the overskirt, a lush pink satin trimmed with point lace.

"But the train is too long," she said as the ancient helped her slip the underskirt on over her head.

She had summoned me just to take up the hem of a train? Any tailor or seamstress could do as much.

"My father told me not to go over one foot," she said, "but he gets all his information from his whore of a mistress."

I glanced at the maid.

"Don't worry. She's deaf."

Indeed. The old woman seemed oblivious. "What does your mother recommend?" I asked, looking around for something for Athénaïs to stand on. Usually it was a girl's mother who saw to all the details of her daughter's marriage, considered the most important day in both their lives.

"She's shut herself up in a convent. I can't even talk to her."

"Hold still," the ancient hissed, trying—with fumbling difficulty—to tie the skirt on over Athénaïs's underskirt.

Athénaïs dismissed the woman with an impatient wave. "Heaven help me," she said, bolting the door. "My father threatened to send all three of my old maids along with me after I'm married, but my intended forbade it. It was the only thing the Marquis de Montespan had done that in any way pleased me—until I met the staff *he's* hired to attend me. They're even worse than the ancients! Mort Dieu, my life is a living hell."

I felt wary of the affection I still felt for her, wary of the seductive comfort of her warm room, so full of luxuriant beauty. "I need you to stand on something," I said, looking around. Hers was an enchanting, intoxicating world, a world of ease and privilege I dreamt of—but it was more than that, I knew. She was high, high nobility, yet she'd honored me with her confidence, her secret confessions. She'd even called me her guardian angel. There was passionate recklessness in her that was frightening, true, but also dangerously entrancing. In truth I felt blessed in her company—one of the blessed.

Scooping up her train, Athénaïs shuffled over to the bed and kicked a little stool out from under it. I placed it in the middle of the room. She slipped her feet into a pair of heeled mules and stepped onto it. "You're not married, Claude," she said, turning slowly as I directed. "How did you manage that?"

I winced, a pin piercing my thumb. I sucked it clean of blood, then dipped it in pooled candle wax. "I have my family to look after."

She made a clucking sound, which the parrot echoed. "Your mother is a queen of the stage and your brother practically a grown man."

"But he's a child at heart."

"There are places that take in people like that," I heard her say from above. "You can't look after him forever."

I remained silent. Gaston *had* been a trial of late. Some of the players were furious with him, upset about props disappearing. There were times when I longed to be free, longed for a life of my own. Who could I talk to about such things? It was a betrayal even to think such thoughts. "The lace of your chemise should be showing at the hem in the front," I said, sitting back, "but as to the length of the train . . . That depends on your title."

"When I marry, I'll be a marquise—" She made a mocking *la de da* look that made me smile. In spite of everything, there was still a feeling of intimacy between us.

"It's two feet for a marquise," I said. The rules on this were exact. "We have to know these things for the stage."

"Ah, the *stage*! You don't know how lucky you are to live without restriction. I sometimes dream of running away, becoming an actress."

How curious, I thought. She lived a life I could only dream of, and I, in turn, lived a life she longed for. I unfolded my measuring stick. "But you'll not be a marquise until after you marry, so your father is right. I could leave plenty of hem so that you could have it let out after."

She looked down at me. "I've had word," she said quietly.

My heart skipped. *Alexandre.* So that's why I'd been summoned.

"He's safely in Portugal," she said.

"Merci Dieu," I breathed, then bit my lips. My tender feelings were inappropriate.

"Remember the Marquis Henri d'Antin?" she asked.

How could I ever forget the sight of that young man with a rapier in his chest? How could I ever forget the sight of the soles of his boots sticking out of the bushes?

"The man I'm to marry . . . is his brother."

Non! I caught my breath. But of course: they had the same sticking-out ears.

And then I recalled Alexandre's letter to Athénaïs: *I beg you to assuage his family's sorrow.*

I sat back on my heels, my hands clasped as if in prayer. "It's what Alexandre would have wanted," I offered with feeling. "To atone for the death of his friend." And then I felt terrible. I'd been looking for tragic redemption, as if Athénaïs's life were a play being performed on a stage. "Forgive me!"

"But that's it exactly," Athénaïs said, her huge eyes brimming. "*You* understand, Claudette. And you're the only one."

CHAPTER 31

On the day of Athénaïs's wedding, I hovered outside the church of Saint-Sulpice, part of a gawking crowd.

I watched as the carriages slowly pulled up, one by one. Liveried footmen offered gloved hands to the bride, the groom, the members of the family. Athénaïs looked exquisite in her gown, but her eyes were red and her cheeks blotchy, even under powder.

The enormous church doors closed. I waited until the bells pealed in celebration, then turned away. She was a married woman now, the Marquise de Montespan, whose husband forbade her to have anything to do with me. I found myself inexplicably close to tears. I threw the amulet in a cesspool: clearly, it wasn't working.

IT WAS A busy time at the theater—and I was thankful for that. The Bourgogne was at war with Molière. In response to the outpouring of jealous criticism of *School for Wives* (which was, without a doubt, a triumph), Molière staged a satirical piece, *The Critique of School for Wives*. In turn, we staged *The Counter-critique of School for Wives*, followed by a short piece, *The Husband Without a Wife*. Written by Montfleury, it hinted that Molière's new young wife was unfaithful. Molière, in turn, ridiculed some of our players (*not* Mother, merci Dieu) in a performance before the King, singling out Montfleury, mocking him as fat and pompous.

How to fight back? The answer came in an unexpected way.

. . .

MOTHER AND I arrived for a theater meeting just as someone was being introduced. He was a slight young man in his mid-twenties, yet wearing a fusty wig. There was both terror and arrogance in his wide-set eyes.

"That's Jean Racine, I think," Mother whispered.

"Molière's protégé?" My mind was on other things. Earlier that morning, I had glimpsed Athénaïs and her husband entering the church of Saint-Eustache. Her husband's smug face, long as a fiddle, shot daggers at the beggars at the door. He raised his silver-tipped cane at them in warning. Athénaïs, who followed behind him, looked drawn—and my heart beat high in sympathy. I'd been plagued by ominous dreams in which she screamed out to me for help.

Floridor signaled for silence and then introduced the playwright. "Monsieur Racine has proposed that we produce his tragedy, *Alexandre the Great.*"

Several of the players gasped.

I was confounded. Racine's *Alexandre the Great* was soon to be pre-miered by Molière's troupe at the Palais-Royal.

"He wishes it prepared quickly—and, needless to say, under the circumstances, secretly."

How was that even possible?

"There are a number of things to be considered," Floridor went on, squinting down at his notes, "not the least of which is the schedul-ing. We would have to have it mastered in a matter of weeks—"

Someone close to me groaned. As it was, the players had just begun to commit Monsieur Pierre's newest play, *Agésilas,* to memory. An experiment in irregular verse—eight-syllable lines mixed with alexan-drines and other rhyme schemes—it was proving to be a challenge—even for Mother.

"So we'll need to talk it over." Floridor paused, letting out an exhale. "Do you wish to address the troupe before you go?" he asked the young playwright.

Jean Racine stood, clasping and unclasping his hands. His mouth was small, almost prim, a hint of moustache above his upper lip. He shrugged his thin shoulders. "Do you have any questions?" His accent was refined, educated, but his voice hard to hear.

"Do you have any questions?" Floridor repeated in his carrying voice.

Why didn't anybody speak up? My heart pounding, I stood. "Monsieur Racine, please explain: *Alexandre the Great* is in rehearsal with Molière's troupe."

"I'm not happy with their approach," Racine said.

"Of course not!" Montfleury jumped up. "Monsieur Racine wishes his masterpiece produced by *real* players of tragedy."

"We're better, it's true," Mother whispered.

"That's not the point!" I said, heated. Molière had taken a chance on young Jean Racine, producing his first play. It had not done well, yet even so Molière had encouraged him to write another tragedy: *this* one, about Alexandre the Great. From what I'd heard, Molière had invested a small fortune in what was going to be a lavish production. And now Racine was offering it to *us,* just as it was about to be premiered?

"In a natural cadence, the poetry of the lines is lost," Racine went on, straining his voice so that he might be heard.

"Forsooth! What do comedians know about dramatic declamation?" Montfleury was obviously still furious over the way Molière had ridiculed him before the King. I wondered if he'd gone so far as to lure the young playwright away from Molière.

"It is here that I would have my verses spoken," Racine concluded, the twelve syllables constituting an inelegant alexandrine. "This is the true home of tragedy."

"Hear, hear!" Montfleury cried out, accompanying the playwright to the door, patting him heartily on the back (very nearly knocking the slight young man over).

Floridor frowned down at his notes, pulling at his ruff. "Well?" he said, once the chatter following Jean Racine's departure had died down.

"It depends on the principal players," someone spoke up. "They would have the most lines to learn, and quickly."

"I'd need two weeks to master Alexandre's lines," Floridor said. "Montfleury would play Porus, of course, and Alix, Axiane. Could you two commit a major part to memory in that time?"

"Easily," Montfleury said.

"Alix could have it mastered in days," a player at the back called out and several clapped.

"So long as it's not irregular verse," Mother said, and a number of the players moaned.

"What about the sets?"

"Could we use the ones made for Boyer's *Alexandre*?" someone asked. Not long before, we had produced a play about Alexandre the Great as well, but it was a listless script and the production had closed after only a few nights.

"Monsieur Racine thinks Molière's backdrops are unoriginal, but our Boyer sets are not much better," Floridor admitted. "So no: I think we would have to move quickly on that, and give some consideration to the expense involved. As for costumes . . . I suspect that with enhancements, your Boyer costumes might do."

There was a murmur of relief. The elaborate costumes required for serious tragedy cost each player a great deal.

"There are other things to consider, however." I raised my voice so that I would be better heard. I wasn't a shareholder like my mother, so I couldn't vote, but the members of the troupe allowed me to speak in meetings. "I'm told that Monsieur Racine is demanding and temperamental: some of Molière's players wept at their first rehearsal."

"They deserve to be miserable!" Montfleury roared.

"One other thing," I persisted. "Monsieur Molière has been like a mentor to Racine—and now Racine is stabbing him in the back. How can we trust such a man?"

"Molière's no innocent," someone observed. "He produced *Sertorius* before it was published."

"He married his own daughter!" Montfleury exclaimed.

"That's not true," I protested.

"Are you defending Molière?"

"He mocked us to the Court."

"He mocked the Great Corneille!"

"And now he's putting *us* out of business."

Ultimately, it was no use. The arguments in favor of revenge won the day. All was fair in the War of the Theaters.

onsieur Pierre stood to one side as Gaston hefted a crate of our belongings into our new apartment close to the Bourgogne theater. Monsieur Martin and his wife had been sorry to see us go, but with Mother's success, we could finally afford something more than a dingy little room and a closet.

I hadn't seen the playwright for months, not since the wild success of Racine's *Alexandre the Great*.

Mother stuck her head out of a door, her head wrapped in a cloth like a Turk. "Welcome to our palace, Monsieur Pierre." We had three rooms and a necessary all our own in the courtyard.

He held out a bouquet of flowers.

Signs of spring were most welcome. It had been a grim winter, with constant prayer vigils for the Queen Mother, who had died of a cancer in her breast in January. "I'll put them in a vase." I hoped he hadn't brought them thinking to mask the odors of our place.

"Sit, please sit," Mother said. "You're nobility now." Corneille's family had long ago been awarded noble status following the initial success of *The Cid*. It had taken all these years for the legal certification to come through.

"Thank you, Alix, but I can't be long."

"You'll have to excuse the mess," I said, digging out a small vase and making a space for it on the table. I stuck the flowers in and arranged them roughly. Water would have to wait.

The playwright had an air of gloom. "Is something wrong, Pierre?" Mother asked tenderly, pulling up a stool.

He opened his hands in a gesture of futility. "The troupe doesn't want my new play."

"We turned down *Attila*?" Mother and I had been so busy with the move, we'd missed the weekly business meeting.

"That can't be," Mother said, her hands on her flour-powdered cheeks.

"Turned it down flat. The Bourgogne lost money on my last play—as you know."

Agésilas had been an interesting experiment in irregular verse, but it had not gone over well with the public. The players hadn't earned a sou. "But *Attila* is a completely different sort of play," I protested.

"I tried to tell Floridor that, but . . ." He shook his head. "We used to care about art; now all that matters is the door take."

"It's because of the competition from Monsieur Molière," I said, stopping Gaston at the door. "Would you like something to eat before you go back for another load?" He had been working so hard.

"Oui, sit here," Monsieur Pierre said, standing.

"Please, Monsieur Pierre, stay. It's such a pleasure to see you," I said, pulling up a bench.

"Stay, do," Mother said. "We'll talk of art and be restored."

Monsieur Pierre sat back down. "Sit beside me then, Gaston. I've yet to hear your news. I have a boy about your age. Are you in an apprenticeship yet?"

Gaston looked at me, bewildered.

"Not yet," I said, chagrined. If ever.

RACINE WAS PRESENT at the first business meeting of the Easter break. He was smiling, which made me uneasy. My suspicions were confirmed when Floridor announced that the wildly popular actress Thérèse du Parc—the so-called "Marquise"—would agree to leave Molière's troupe if she could join us.

The players responded dubiously. Thérèse du Parc had learned her trade as a rope dancer on the streets of Lyon. She was alluring—a draw, no doubt—but mainly because of her legs, which she allowed the audience to glimpse when making her famous leaps. The players of the Bourgogne were respected for serious tragedy, not acrobatics.

"At full share?" one of the players asked.

Floridor glanced down at his notes. "And with an advance of five hundred livres."

Five hundred!

"I intend for her to perform one of the lead roles in the play I'm writing now." Racine's voice could hardly be heard.

I exchanged a concerned look with my mother. *Alix* was the troupe's lead actress. Did we really need another?

"*Andromaque,*" Floridor said, clarifying, "which we're to perform this autumn."

"I'm in favor," big Montfleury said with passion. "It will be another blow to Molière."

"SHE CAN'T PERFORM tragedy," I assured Mother, walking home through the spring slush. "I don't think you have to worry."

"She's young and beautiful—and I'm neither."

"She's thirty-four, Maman." Privately, I thought it wasn't a bad notion to introduce a younger player into the Bourgogne. Mother, at forty-seven, was younger by far than Floridor, who was fifty-nine, and Montfleury, who was an astonishing sixty-eight. The Bourgogne was an aging company (despite which young Racine drove the players hard, disdainful of their frailties).

"That's young," Mother said, touching her cheek. She'd recently resorted to using a much-touted face cream in hope of a fair-as-lilies complexion. Fortunately, she stopped using it because it made her skin raw. (I'd since learned that people who used the cream were being called Les Écorchées, skinned alive!) "Men go crazy over her," she said.

"And now, apparently, Racine," I said.

Mother stopped. *Non.*

I made wide eyes. *Oui!* Why else would he cast her in a lead role?

"She's so much older than he is."

"But wealthy," I said with a smirk, ever suspicious of Jean Racine's motives.

he great exodus of the King and Court began toward the end of May, riding to war in Flanders. Leading an army of thirty-five thousand, His Majesty's intention was to lay claim to the northern lands that had been legally promised him by the King of Spain when he married the King of Spain's daughter—lands Spain was now not willing to give up. The Righteous War, it was called.

"I've never seen anything so fine," Thérèse du Parc exclaimed in Mother's dressing room. She'd glimpsed the King's glass coach "filled with women," escorted by hundreds "and *hundreds*" of horsemen, the King himself riding—

"Sword in hand," I recited drearily—for Thérèse had already told the story three times.

"Seeing His Majesty up close makes me faint," Thérèse said, feigning a swoon.

Like all women, it seemed.

"Without the Court, Paris is a desert." She missed her fanatics, the ardent noblemen who bought expensive seats on the stage so they could gaze at her heaving bosom and fine legs. Now the only noblemen in Paris were gray-bearded and stooped.

In spite of Thérèse's tiresome airs, I'd come to rather admire her: she had a wonderful singing voice and she worked hard at her craft.

Or, rather, was pushed by Jean Racine to work hard. "Du Parc!" I heard him call out imperiously. "Get up here!"

. . .

THE COURTIERS' RETURN enlivened the city once again. Much to Mother's intense displeasure, Thérèse du Parc proved to be a popular draw (and not a bad actress, in fact); she was clearly a profitable addition to the troupe. Our hard times were far from over, however. Just after we began to see a return on Racine's *Andromaque,* disaster struck. In the second week of December, big Montfleury, vigorously proclaiming his lines during the mad scene in Act V, ruptured a blood vessel in his neck and collapsed on the stage, the men in the pit jeering at him to rise. I led Mother and Gaston quickly away, shielding them from the tragic sight, but even from below we could hear the big man's dying gasps.

Floridor canceled our next performances, the troupe too stunned to perform.

"The play is cursed," Mother said. Rumor was that Molière had paid a witch to cast an evil spell on *Andromaque* because we'd stolen Thérèse du Parc away from his troupe.

"Yes, but cursed by Racine," I said, finding the pincushion I was looking for in Gaston's line of objects. He cried out in protest as I retrieved it; I gave him a cross look. "He pushed Montfleury far too hard." Proclaiming Racine's intensely emotional verse had brought on Montfleury's death. (Ironic, I thought, considering that Montfleury had been the one to so ardently champion Racine's work.)

No sooner had the Bourgogne regained momentum in the new year than we suffered yet another blow: Thérèse du Parc announced that she wouldn't be performing for a period of time. "I need to be away a spell," she said, mumbling something about her health.

"There's nothing wrong with her health!" Mother later scoffed.

I knew better. "She's with child." As the one who had to keep letting out her costumes (richly adorned gowns given to her by noble admirers—gowns that eclipsed the ones I could provide Mother), I had suspected for some time. "And my guess is by you-know-who." Racine was often in her dressing room. I couldn't understand what Thérèse saw in him—she had her pick of suitors, and noble ones at that.

Having suffered through such calamities, the troupe was greatly cheered to be invited to perform for the King at Saint-Germain-en-Laye. It was only a one-performance engagement, but His Majesty paid handsomely, covering costs and feeding players in style. To be commanded to make what players called "a voyage" to play for the King was the answer to every troupe's prayers. This had been an especially enjoyable excursion, even if I did have to play the part of the dog. (I was both relieved and disappointed not to have glimpsed Athénaïs in the audience.)

The troupe met back in Paris the next morning, groggy, boisterous, some ill and others still drunk from celebrating the King's approval of the play. Floridor stood to address us. There was something serious in his demeanor, his face dark with shadow as he waited for silence. He arranged his ruff, pausing gravely before informing us that he had sad news: "Thérèse du Parc will not be coming back—"

There were a few muted exclamations. Had she decided to return to Molière's troupe?

"I am grieved to inform you that she died last night."

There was a stir, and then gasps.

My mouth dropped open in incredulity.

"We're closing down until further notice," I heard Floridor say. "Even Molière's troupe has canceled performances, out of respect."

There was a hum of surprise.

"Fortunately," he continued, "she was able to renounce the stage before passing."

"Merci Dieu!" someone cried out in the silence that followed.

The next morning, Thérèse's body was displayed in her rooms on the rue de Richelieu. She looked like a girl in her big, expensive coffin, dressed in one of her gaud-glorious theatrical costumes. She'd died giving birth, it was whispered. Leaving, I glanced across the street at the door opposite, wreathed in black: Racine's modest abode.

The procession to the cemetery the next day turned into a mob scene. Racine was almost unrecognizable, his face puffy. As the coffin was lowered into the ground, he let out a heart-wrenching cry, causing even me to weep.

IN THE DAYS that followed, I went about my chores in a daze. It was a relief not to have to rush off to the theater for meetings, rehearsals, and performances every day, but at the same time I felt at a loss. Even the diversion of walking the newly cobbled streets of Paris by night—ablaze now with the light of three thousand lanterns—failed to cheer. Mother took up knitting her hideous shawl and I resumed pacing the creaking floorboards, worrying about how we would manage, worrying (as always) about money. To keep Mother in spangles and feathers, to keep our rooms heated, I took whatever jobs I could find: cleaning out a charnel house, hiring on as a professional mourner following funeral processions, tending a stinking tavern in the late-late hours—fending off drunken customers on more than one occasion. We'd been years in the theater. Mother was a great success, and yet we seemed not much further along than before.

The magical transition from sordid to grand was, in truth, a meager living. Repairing costumes and performing the occasional walk-on part in travesty earned me little. There were times when I longed, in truth, for a *respectable* life, like those of the blessed who sat in the loges. A life where it would not be assumed I was a whore just because I worked for the theater. A life where I would not have to carry a dagger in my skirts to ward off attackers, coming and going from the theater at all hours. I was weary of working long hours for only a few sous, weary of juggling debts, making do with a cup of parsnip soup and a trencher of bean-flour bread for a meal.

Was this to be my life? Forever scrambling to make ends meet, looking after Mother and my helpless brother, only to die an old maid?

ON THE SEVENTEENTH of January, a gloomy Thursday, Gaston climbed the stairs laden with buckets of water from the river. He put down his load and handed me a folded piece of paper. "For." He pointed at me.

I examined the sealed envelope. The handwriting—which spelled out my name—was schooled, feminine.

Inside, was a gold louis (heavens!), folded up in a scrap of paper. It wasn't a letter; it was a map, awkwardly drawn, indicating a place on the rue l'Échelle, next to a lace shop not far from the Louvre. Two blunt sentences were written below the sketch:

Do not fail me.
Do not speak my name.

And no signature whatsoever.

CHAPTER 34

he house on the rue l'Échelle was modest. At one time the ground-floor rooms had been a lace shop, but now the shop sign listed, attached only at one corner. Soot-covered snow was piled at the door. I looked to find a bell, but there was only a tarnished brass knocker. I dusted snow off the lion's head and let it drop: once, twice, three times. I looked up at the windows above. Surely there had been a mistake.

The shutters opened and an old woman peered down. I slipped back the hood of my cloak to reveal my face. *I am wanted here.* (But why?)

The shutters closed. I was almost through my second Ave Maria when I heard the sound of bolts and latches. The door creaked open. It was the old woman, a bent-over hag with whiskers hanging from her chin. Her withered hands hung in front of her crisp linen apron.

"I am Mademoiselle des Oeillets. I was sent for."

She lifted her thin upper lip to reveal one long but surprisingly white tooth. She drew the door back, and I entered a dark corridor. I followed her up a narrow set of stairs and down a dark hall to a door, which opened onto a large room of surprising opulence. A Turkey carpet, two Japon cabinets, a massive pendulum clock: everything conveyed luxury.

The woman motioned me to wait and went shuffling off.

I stood by the fire, warming my hands. I heard pricking sounds and looked behind me. A black cat was pulling its nails on the carpet.

I heard a woman's scolding voice. "You fool! Why didn't you tell me?"

"Madame de Sconin, you were—"

A masked woman entered the room wearing a fur-lined morning robe over a chemise. It was clear she was heavy with child. Her golden hair was loose, hanging down over her shoulders.

I curtsied, perplexed. Athénaïs?

"Go, in heaven's name," the woman commanded the hag, who slouched out of the room. "And close the damn door!" she cursed, throwing the bolt. "Mort Dieu." She took off her mask.

It *was* her.

I was struck by her fatigue, the lines in her extraordinarily perfect face. She was younger than I was, not yet even thirty—but she looked older than that, worn. And out of humor, certainly, scowling as she reached for a chair.

I stepped forward to lend a hand. "I can manage it," she said crossly, using the back of the chair for support. "I feel like an upturned turtle most days." She sat down, pulling her shawl around her shoulders. "It's not the first time, but I can never get used to it."

She'd married years ago. Of course she would have children.

"This one poses a problem, however, which is why I've summoned you." She frowned up at me. "Sit, Claude, for God's sake. I've a rather shocking proposition to make, and I think it best you not be standing."

I lowered myself onto a tapestry-covered footrest. I wondered if I could take off my gloves, which were damp from the snow. I felt light-headed. I had never expected to be summoned again.

"You no doubt wonder why I sent you a cryptic note, why you've been asked to come here, and why, for that matter, that crow of a maid addresses me as Madame de Sconin, when she deigns to address me at all."

"You are a woman of mystery," I said, and was relieved to hear her chuckle. We'd been jocular with each other in the past—in our youth, our foolish youth—but things were different now.

"Obviously, I am going to have a baby—soon, I hope, for I am weary of this burden. The child, however, is not my husband's." Her azure eyes were teasing.

"This happens, Madame." I was hot now, too close to the fire. I wished I could slip off my cloak.

"More often than one would guess," she said, touching a silver key hanging from a chain around her neck. "But most of the time it is easy enough to fob it off as the husband's. *My* husband, however, was unfortunately many leagues away at the time of . . . conception, let us say? He has been banished—"

Banished? I was startled to hear this.

"—for publicly casting judgment on the King's choice of a tutor for the Dauphin. That he tried to throw the tutor's wife and then me out a window had little to do with his punishment, apparently." This with a wry tone. "It's something of a relief to have him out of the country, to tell you the truth—although he took my two babies with him." She stroked the cat, her hands trembling. "He's a lunatic. *Verily.* But by law he has a right to do whatever he pleases with my children—as well as the child I'm carrying now. I have reason to fear what he might do were he to find out." She looked at me, her eyes impossibly large. "Curious—isn't it?—how life plays out?" She threaded a long strand of the fringe of her shawl through her fingers, twisting it. "I've had word that Alexandre is dead."

Non!

"In battle in Portugal apparently—" This with a weary tone.

I felt robbed: angry even. I had risked so much to save his life. How could he die?

Athénaïs shrugged with a show of indifference, but I recognized fragility in her gesture. "In any case: *now.*" She put her hands on her belly. "Not only do I have a lunatic husband to hide from, but there's also the problem of my lover's wife—as well as his *other* mistress," she added with amusement, removing the silver key from the chain around her neck and using it to open a black enamel cabinet. "Monsieur Mysterious, let's call him, would rather *they* not discover my present predicament." She slid out a shelf and withdrew a small velvet bag. "Hence, this curious abode, my false name." She looked at me, her eyes so alluring I had to glance away. "Claudette," I heard her say, "I have dire need of someone I can trust."

I stared into the fire as she spoke. The proposition was a simple one. I would move in for a few months, tend to the birth, the baby. It would be a temporary position until she found a suitable governess (someone from the aristocracy it was implied, but not said).

"But confidentiality is key," she said. "Nobody—and I mean that rather literally, I'm afraid—nobody must know."

The cat meowed plaintively at the door.

"I'm honored, Madame," I said, sitting back. I put my gloved hands to my throat. "But . . ." But I'd vowed to forsake her! I'd worn an amulet to break her spell over me, vowed to put her memory behind me, forsake my longings for her world. My longing for *her*. "The Bourgogne is about to get back into full production. I have commitments."

"I've neglected to mention one thing," she said with a smile, tossing the bag from one hand to the other. "Well, *two*—" She spilled out the contents of the little pouch onto one hand. Two gems sparkled in her palm. "I'm now in a position to reward you rather well."

I had never seen such stones. They were clear, yet threw out shards of light.

"They're Indian stones called diamonds." Her voice was reverent. "These are worth quite a lot, I'm told—two, three thousand livres? Yours, should you accept."

Sacré coeur. With that much money . . . ! "You know you can trust me, Madame," I said, sitting forward.

"DON'T LOOK SO MOROSE," I told Mother and Gaston. I'd been able to sell the diamonds, but only for a little over one thousand livres, a third of what Athénaïs had estimated. Even so, it was a very great deal. I'd *finally* paid off our debt to Monsieur Martin, paid the back rent owed, and still had enough to hire back Gaston's tutor. "It's only temporary, and it's not as if I won't be visiting often."

Still, it *was* a big step. In all my years, I'd never slept apart from them. "Kiss me now," I said gruffly, taking up my worn portmanteau. The gray wool gown I'd scrabbled together—a respectable sort of ensemble suitable for one in service—felt like a costume.

Gaston, ever the boy, embraced me.

"Remember . . . ?" I'd had a long talk with them both the night before about all the things that needed to be looked after.

Gaston nodded, but the expression in his eyes lacked confidence.

I turned to my weeping mother. My heart ached with how unhappy

I was making them both. "Maman, dear Maman," I said, rocking her in my arms, "remember that you can simply send Gaston for me if ever you need." But not just because you can't find your lace mantilla! Not just because you can't get off your white-face and rouge!

I stepped back, my eyes overspilling.

And then, with wrenching last embraces, I began down the winding stone stairs, my free hand on the splintered rail. I stopped at the ground floor to wipe my cheeks dry with my knit mitt, then set off through the slush, heading toward the river.

put down my bag: a room of my own—a *bed* of my own. I pried open the shutter and looked out the window: between two buildings, I could see the glittering river.

Already I wanted to go home, hear Gaston's infectious giggle, Mother murmuring her lines. I was thirty now—an old maid by any account—and for the first time in my very long life, I was alone.

I turned at the sound of the door opening. The hag tossed a skirt, apron, bodice, and cap onto the narrow bed and slammed the plank door shut.

I held the bodice to my chest. The fabric was an ugly shade of brown. It looked to fit a girl, certainly not a woman, not even a small-breasted one. The tips of two of the bones—made of crude wood slats, not whalebone—had worn through. I picked up the skirt, which was stained at the hem. Even with the laces fully out, I couldn't get it on over my hips. I felt like a giant in a circus show.

The apron was ridiculously frilly and not perfectly clean, but at least it had a patch pocket. I emptied it of its contents: lint, a soiled nose cloth, a small, rusty nail. I examined the enormous cap for vermin before slipping it on over my coiled braids and pulling the ties. If this were a play, I would be the clownish servant, the one everyone mocked.

Athénaïs burst into unrestrained laughter when I entered the room. "Mort Dieu," she gasped, bolting the door and taking off her mask. "You look like a half-wit." She could hardly speak for laughing.

"Damnation!" the parrot squawked.

"Take that apron off . . . and the cap too. Was this the wench's idea?" She wiped tears from her cheeks with her sleeve.

"I'm relieved, I confess," I said, smiling now myself. The brocade drapes had been drawn back to let in light, but even so, ten scented beeswax candles were alight. (Such extravagance!) "I was preparing to run away."

"Over an apron and cap? That will never do. Come, sit, join me for some wine and sweetmeats. I promised my confessor I would not imbibe spirits—at least not alone."

Served in a crystal goblet, the pale pink liquid had bubbles in it, which alarmed me.

"It won't hurt you," Athénaïs said, perceiving my concern. "Dom Pérignon, the Benedictine monk I order it from, keeps trying to get rid of the bubbles, but I rather like it this way," she said, taking one of the little cakes that circled a pyramid of bonbons set on a gilded platter. "He gives me an excellent price because of the flaw." She pushed the plate across to me.

"Thank you." My mouth watered at the sight of the delicacies, but my rough hands shamed me.

After three goblets of the strange wine, I felt more at ease. Athénaïs liked to chatter, and it was easy enough to be a good listener. Her father had recently sold his post as First Gentleman of the King's Chamber for a million livres (a million!), four hundred thousand of that going to buy her brother Vivonne the post of Generalship of the Galleys. The King's ministers Colbert and Louvois were at each other's throats, vying for His Majesty's favor. When Colbert got ill recently, it was whispered that Louvois had tried to poison him. (The awful Louvois! The cat man.) Her friend the Duc de Lauzun lost his prized stud at the game tables, Athénaïs chatted on. She'd advised him to go to a witch for charms to improve his chances, as so many others had been doing—with success. "Do you go to witches?" Players knew all about such things: I must know of a good one.

"I've heard tell of several," I said. Players were fond of good-luck charms, enchantments to ensure a good performance. I thought of the cunning woman who had sold me the amulet. (Money wasted, considering.)

She plied me for tittle-tattle on players, particularly Thérèse du Parc, whose father had been a witch, she'd heard. A charlatan, I told her—not quite the same thing. Was Du Parc really thirty-five when she died? How many lovers had she had? Athénaïs suspected her father and even her brother might have been of their number. Did I know that the actress's stepsisters—who worked at the Hôtel de Soissons—were proclaiming that she'd been poisoned by the playwright Racine?

"That's not possible," I protested. Jean Racine had been grief-stricken at Thérèse's funeral. Even I had been moved.

"Word is that the child she was carrying was not his—but that of the Chevalier de Rohan."

Heavens. Rohan had been one of the many noblemen who had courted Thérèse. I recalled his painted cheeks. He'd been more persistent than all the others, reserving a chair on the stage every time she performed. It was said he'd wanted to marry her, but his family forbade it. Still, I could not credit the rumor.

When eventually Athénaïs's stream of gossip ran dry—"Cloistered like this, I hear nothing," she lamented—we got down to work, fortified by yet another goblet of faulty wine.

I was to begin my search on the morrow for a wet-nurse, someone who wasn't nursing children of her own, Athénaïs emphasized—*her* baby must not be obliged to share milk.

I was accustomed to working hard, used to the constant demands of theater life—scheduling rehearsals, mending costumes, counting out office receipts—but this was an entirely different realm. Instead of searching out lengths of worn fabric in the used-clothing stalls, I was to assemble tailclouts, swaddling bands, biggins, and bibs. Instead of prompting players with their lines, I would be sitting in a luxurious room, eating rich delicacies, drinking Turkish liqueur and bubbly wine while listening to tales of Court life—tales from the Land of the Blessed.

January 25, 1669

Dear Claudette,

Thank you for your letter. However, you need not worry. Your mother and dear brother seem to be managing. My wife and I will alert you if there are any problems.

Alix claims the new prompter reads too softly, yet I can hear him from the parterre. You are greatly missed.

The world of the theater carries on apace, with all the usual uproar. As you know, Molière near died of vexation over the Company forcing His Majesty to forbid his play Tartuffe *from being performed. Now there is talk that the King is going to allow him to stage it again, which will have the bigots in a lathering fury, no doubt. One must be so careful. I have to admire Molière for persevering.*

We did not earn out on Marius, *unfortunately, but we've begun to prepare for a new tragedy by Racine, which we anticipate will be well received. He is being hailed as the new King of Tragedy—which irks dear old Pierre, of course.*

The rivalry between the Racine and Corneille factions has become bitter, in fact. Racine supporters openly attack Corneille's work as archaic, and Corneille supporters denounce works by Racine as unheroic. Such rivalry is not bad for the door take, frankly, but it's hard on the players when confronted with one or the other faction's noisy claque, whistling disapproval. You will be pleased to know that the claques remain silent whenever your mother performs.
Believe me yours faithfully,
Monsieur Josias de Floridor, Theater of the Bourgogne

Note: The rumor about the cause of Thérèse du Parc's death is outrageous. It is impossible for there to be any truth in it. Fortunately, Racine seems unaware of the accusations.

BEFORE LONG I had taken charge of managing Athénaïs's household, the baby to come, and everything in between. I fired the old hag—curtly, without remorse, throwing her rags after her, fair riddance!—and hired an energetic girl to do the cleaning. I found a violinist to help soothe "Madame de Sconin's" frayed nerves, and lined up an excellent wet-nurse in the country, where the air would be beneficial to a newborn. The woman, a peasant (but clean, I checked), was due to wean her own infant in a week. I made her husband vow on a Bible not to have relations during the years of nursing.

The baby was to be delivered not by a midwife, but by Monsieur Blucher, a surgeon. It seemed strange that a man would be involved in such an intimate matter, but Athénaïs said that the father of the child—"Monsieur Mysterious"—insisted. A surgeon was permitted to use surgical instruments, should such be needed, and instruments were forbidden to midwives. "He's promised I'll stay nice and tight."

I met with Monsieur Blucher at his office on the rue Saint-Honoré. He is short, with hair on his knuckles. He agreed to be brought to the residence blindfolded—for a fee.

"He's expensive," I told Athénaïs, presenting her with Blucher's account—eleven livres, and this only for a consultation.

She waved the note away. Monsieur Mysterious would pay.

It was obvious that Athénaïs no longer had any problems with respect to finances. Since selling his position in the King's Chamber, her father had been made Governor of Paris, a prestigious position that paid richly. I suspected that such good family fortune had something to do with Monsieur Mysterious, who must have influence at Court, I deduced. No doubt he was both rich and powerful.

I recalled—with revulsion—the unctuous man who had barged into Mother's dressing room the night she performed as Medea. Could Monsieur Mysterious possibly be the Marquis de Louvois, now the Secretary of State for War? Athénaïs often mocked him, but who else had such power?

IN EARLY MARCH—two days before the dissolute unruliness of Mardi Gras—Monsieur Blucher was brought blindfolded into the house and led groping to "Madame de Sconin's" chamber, where, masked herself, Athénaïs screamed the all-too-real agonies of a woman in labor.

It was a long night, a long day, and another long night. I resorted to prayer. Finally, after Athénaïs had fallen senseless (thanks to opium pills), twins were delivered: first a beautiful blue boy, strangled on the cord, and then a girl with a strangely large head.

Dazed from lack of sleep and the trauma of birthing, I paid Monsieur Blucher, tipping him well. I instructed the maid to sew the body of the boy into a shroud and take it to the Cimetière des Innocents, to be dumped into the open pit for the bodies of bastard babies. As for the girl, such a misshapen baby would normally be exposed to weather, left to die, but I wasn't sure if that was the custom for nobility. I wished I could rouse Athénaïs from her deep sleep, ask her what I should do, but I couldn't—and at any rate the thought sickened me. Many, if they had known how Gaston would come to be, would have left him to this same fate.

Masked, in an unmarked carriage, I wended my way through streets congested with revelers in Mardi Gras costume, the mewling baby girl in my arms. All the way to the wet-nurse's abode in the country, I coddled her, a nagging sadness weighing down my heart. I would never hold a child of my own.

ATHÉNAÏS RECOVERED SLOWLY. I entertained her through the long hours by playing piquet and reading to her out loud. Secluded as we were day and night, invariably sipping bubbly wine, we became almost familiar. I was her maid, certainly, but my relationship with her was intimate. I bound her breasts, cleaned her small linens, and applied fine flour to her face. She was still afraid of the dark and when she woke in the night, I soothed her. By day, I learned to amuse and intrigue her, bring a smile to her luminous eyes.

She was fascinated by the world of the theater, drawn to the practice of what she called "the magical arts." Her interest in me, my world, was as heady as the potent wine. Playfully enigmatic, I alluded to a knowledge of charms, hinting at powers of enchantment.

Once, feigning to have access to the occult, I called on "spirits" to reveal the identity of Monsieur Mysterious. This had become a teasing game between us. "Marquis de Louvois!" I whispered dramatically.

She laughed at my ploy. "I wouldn't let that guttersnipe lay a finger on me," I was relieved to hear her say. The Secretary of State had the manners of a servant, she said with mocking scorn. He was so desperate to be accepted as a member of the high nobility, he spent hours each day just trying to get his ribbons right. "As if nobility has anything to do with ribbons."

"Then who?" I asked evenly, dealing out the cards facedown, two at a time.

Athénaïs turned over a king. "Keep guessing," she said, smiling impishly.

I stared at her in astonishment: the *King*?

he thirteenth of December, an unlucky Friday, was the premiere of Racine's newest play *Britannicus,* and Mother had been cast in the lead. I arrived at my family's rooms laden with scarves, shawls, and even a few (glass) jewels. Shortly before, Athénaïs had returned to Saint-Germain-en-Laye—to Court—and no longer considered these items suitable.

"From Madame de Sconin," I explained. I myself was wearing a lovely gown from "Madame de Sconin's" charity basket.

"This shawl could easily be mended," Mother said, running the fine fabric through her fingers. "You'll do it, won't you, Claudette?" She held it to the light. "Now that you'll be back home."

The window was open. Street vendors below called out their wares: secondhand clothes, lice bags, tin toys.

"Of course, Maman," I said, ruffling Gaston's long hair (in need of a trim). His beard had grown! My throat tightened at the thought of what I was going to have to tell them. "I will mend it—but there has been a change of plan." Athénaïs was already with child again, but this time she did not need to retreat to a hideaway for her confinement. The King's "official mistress," the Duchesse de la Vallière, had agreed—under coercion, I did not doubt—to accept Athénaïs's existence, and even to cooperate in keeping the nature of the illicit relationship a secret. As for the Queen, she apparently was easily duped.

"Ah, the dramatic pause," Mother said after an uncomfortable silence, her penciled brows lifted. She had thrown the shawl over her "good luck" red and yellow dressing gown. The old gown was worn to threads at the cuffs and elbows, yet she superstitiously insisted on wearing it before every new performance.

"Do you remember the Duc de Mortemart's daughter?" I began.

"She visited my dressing room once," Mother said.

"Oui. She's with the Court now . . . and she wants me to work for her." *You're the only one I can trust,* Athénaïs had told me. I was to be her suivante, her confidential maid: the person with whom she could speak openly, the person she entrusted with her secrets. "Madame de Sconin arranged it." My lies were a shadow of the truth. "But I'll have to live in Saint-Germain-en-Laye." In truth, I felt a little hiddy-giddy about it, an emotion I took care to conceal. Life at Court! "I'm to begin tomorrow," I admitted apologetically. *Your mother and brother will be fine,* Athénaïs insisted. *I need you more.*

Gaston stared at the floor. The silence was unnerving. Why was my mother not speaking?

"I'll earn money," I added. Not as much as one would think, but more than at the theater. "We'll be able to put Gaston into an apprenticeship." Eventually. God willing. "And I will be coming to Paris often." I was to be the go-between—the *internunce,* Athénaïs called my role, using the Latin term—the one to make sure all was in order with the new governess and the soon-to-be two bastard babies.

"Then tonight is a farewell," Mother said finally, her voice husky.

"Non," I said, taking her hands. (Mort Dieu, so cold.) "Tonight is to applaud *you.*"

IT FELT BOTH familiar and strange to be backstage at the theater again: back in shabby rooms hung with sweat-stained costumes, listening to the murmurs of players going over their lines, the sound of Floridor pacing.

After helping Gaston into his usher's coat and settling Mother in her dressing room—after helping her review her lines and dressing her hair in a new style I'd learned from Athénaïs—I went out front. I listened with anticipation as the loges began to fill, people talking amongst themselves, greeting one another.

Going around to the entrance for the nobility, I was rather alarmed to encounter Monsieur Pierre at the foot of the stairs to the second-tier loges. "I'm surprised to see you here!" I whispered. Racine and his supporters would be rabid with suspicion.

"I'm in disguise," he said, holding up a cane.

I smiled. It hardly masked the great man.

"I thought it time I regarded the work of the young playwright who is said to have bested me."

"Nobody could do that."

"Care to join me?"

"You have room?" I didn't really care for the Paradis, where the family of players were permitted to sit. The railing was low, the benches hard, and the servants of the nobility who sat there tended to be rowdy.

"My brother Thomas and I reserved an entire loge, but he and his companions can't make it. I have it all to myself."

Seated beside Monsieur Pierre in the comfort of his private loge—sipping the cordials the loge attendant brought—we caught up on news: his wife was doing "not badly"; his brother's play *The Death of Hannibal* had been a moderate success; the death of the Queen of England had not been a surprise, but rumor had it that it was the opium prescribed for her sleeplessness that had killed her; an Armenian had opened a bar just for serving a hot Turkish liqueur—

"Coffey?"

"Have you tried it? They say it perks one up."

"It does," I confessed, looking out over the audience. I was concerned to see so many empty seats. The theater was only half full, if that. Normally the parterre would be bursting with shopkeepers from the rue Saint-Denis.

"Thomas and his friends went to see the Marquis de Courboyer beheaded instead," Monsieur Pierre said as Floridor ended his oration.

Ah, that would explain the poor attendance, I thought, applauding as the first set was revealed. Courboyer was a Huguenot and had been convicted of treason.

"He refused to renounce his religion, in spite of priests proclaiming his eternal damnation if he didn't."

I had sympathy for such resistance, in truth.

There was a scattering of weak applause as Mother stepped into the light of the foot candles. It had been some time since I'd seen her onstage. She seemed to lack her usual confidence, and on her second verse, she faltered. I sat forward, concerned.

The audience became restless. Racine's play was challenging, penetrating, but without movement. I was relieved that there weren't whistlers, no sign of a claque, but chagrined to hear snores from several of the loges. I felt compassion for the players, but especially for my mother, who was clearly struggling, her magnificent voice gradually becoming hoarse.

"I admit Racine's verse is refined," Monsieur Pierre observed at the close of the final act.

"That's generous of you," I said, helping him to his feet. Refined . . . and emotionally intense. After a performance of a play by Racine, Mother invariably collapsed. "I thought my mother's enactment was . . . well, weak, I'm afraid."

Monsieur Pierre took up his cane. "Certainly we've seen her stronger."

"I'm worried about her. I've taken a job at Court," I blurted out, my voice breaking.

He looked horrified. "Why would you do that?"

"I'm to be an attendant to Madame la Marquise de Montespan," I said, hoping that that would explain. It was, without a doubt, a prestigious position, especially for someone from the theater.

He pulled on the little patch of hair beneath his lip. "Well, she's better than most—an active supporter of the arts and all that. I gather the bigots aren't too happy with her. She's a power now, I understand. She's got the King's ear."

And more. "I'll put in a good word for you," I joked.

"Do," he said, taking me seriously. "She's a patron of both Molière and Racine, but I never could manage the courtier role—all that waiting around, all that bowing."

"I made the mistake of telling Maman tonight," I confessed. I should have known better. I should have waited until after the performance.

"Tell Alix she was excellent." He touched the rim of his worn leather hat. "But whatever you do, don't tell Racine I was impressed."

.   .   .

I FOUND MOTHER slumped on the bench in her dressing room, Gaston looking on with concern. Usually the room was filled with admirers, but tonight it was empty.

"I'm *fine,*" she insisted, coughing into her hideous shawl, which she'd finally finished.

"Attendance will be better tomorrow," I said, giving her a nose cloth of my own, a fine embroidered linen from Athénaïs's offcasts, only slightly stained. "There was a beheading tonight—all of Paris was there, no doubt. You were wonderful, Maman. Monsieur Pierre said to tell you so."

She coughed again, a nasty rattle. "Monsieur Pierre was *here?*" she asked once she'd caught her breath, handing back the linen.

Quiet, I gestured, hearing Racine's voice in the hallway outside. I frowned down at the specks on the cloth: *blood?*

Act IV

In the Service of the Shadow Queen

(1669, Saint-Germain-en-Laye)

CHAPTER 37

he turrets of the castle at Saint-Germain-en-Laye glittered with ice, sparkling in the bright winter sun. Mist rose from the breath of all the horses. Courtiers walked briskly, cocooned in furs.

Shivering, I followed after the porter, who carried my shabby wardrobe chest on his shoulder. It had scribbles all over it, made by Gaston on scraps of pasted-on theatrical playbills: *Music & Lofty Tumbling! A Juggling Clown! Last Chance!*

I could feel the appraising glances of the other servants. I boldly met their eyes. I was, I reminded myself, confidential maid to the mighty Athénaïs, the Marquise de Montespan. I was not an interloper; I belonged.

The porter led me to a door on the second floor of the castle. It opened onto a room with a high vaulted ceiling. A silver brazier gave off a sweet perfume, only slightly covering the strong scent of a male cat.

Pale blue drapes framed three narrow windows which opened onto the river valley. The frozen Seine unfurled like a silver ribbon in and around the gentle hills, clouded at times by wreaths of smoke. Below, at the river's edge, was the sprawling new château where the King, his family, and attendants lived. This older castle was on a rise well above the river, safe from flood.

I turned from the window, taking it all in. The walls were covered in cut velvet. Turkey carpets covered a polished mosaic floor. A lovely alabaster lamp in the form of a lotus graced a marble table. Even the ceiling was artful, a painting of Flora scattering flowers.

This was my new home? I could hardly believe my good fortune. Somewhere, a Keeper of Secrets had set a machine in motion, changing the set in an instant, delivering me into another world.

"There you are."

I turned to face Athénaïs, accompanied by a footman and three maids. She was wearing a gown that padded out her already abundant bosom—a voluminous gown I had designed for her, in fact, one that helped disguise her condition.

She dismissed the attendants, then kicked forward a low stool. "Your taboret," she said with a hint of a slur. It was not yet midday.

I removed my cloak and, draping it over my right arm, lowered myself onto the stool, my knees at my chest. I sat forward to keep from toppling. "A pleasure to serve you, Madame."

Athénaïs rapped me on the head with her fan. "Let's not get into that 'serve you' nonsense."

"As you wish, Madame," I said with a smile. Here, at Court, I felt like a country bumpkin paying homage to a queen.

"I had planned to introduce you to the staff today, but that will have to wait. I've already informed them that you are to be my personal attendant—answering only to me. You will be provided with a room on this floor. I will ring for you when I'm in need of assistance. Unless I am entertaining, you will take your meals with me—as was our custom in Paris."

An oak longcase clock, gilded and silvered with intricate bone marquetry panels, softly chimed the hour.

"Four of the clock . . . *already*? We've a great deal to do. This evening we'll be seeing a new play by Monsieur Molière—"

Court entertainments were often held after dark; the King could afford the copious candles required. Even so, it seemed unnatural to me.

"It's titled *The Magnificent Lovers,* and no: it's not about me and the King, as I'm sure all the gossips assume. But it *will* be your introduction to the Court as my suivante, and your gown, I must be frank, is a problem."

A simple ensemble of gray wool, it was one I'd worn when I served her in Paris. I had assumed it appropriate for an attendant.

Athénaïs rang a brass bell and a maid appeared. "Bring the gowns I set out yesterday." The girl returned laden with clothing.

"These are old ones of mine," Athénaïs said, "but I had them lengthened. All they required was another tier of lace, which a seamstress was able to do overnight." She examined one hem. "Somewhat hastily," she said with downturned mouth.

She chose a bodice and overskirt of ruby brocade and an ivory silk underskirt with an embroidered black hem. The maid helped me out of my wools and into the shimmering layers.

"That's better," Athénaïs said, stroking a cat that had jumped onto the chaise beside her.

Surprisingly, the fit was good. I felt like a proper lady but for my ill-shod feet, which the hems fortunately covered. It was the most magnificent costume I'd ever worn.

"I've some pearls you can use and I'll have a maid do your hair." She took my hands and examined my fingers. "And nails," she added, clucking. "Deus!" she exclaimed, scowling at the sudden sound of a woman singing in another room, plaintive and angelic. "It's the Duchesse de la Vallière . . . or, as we call her *chez moi,* the Limping One. She's forever going on."

"The King's mistress? His former mistress," I added, cringing at my faux pas.

Athénaïs laughed, but not gaily. "Verily—but until my lunatic husband agrees to a legal separation, the Limping One must *appear* to be His Majesty's 'official' mistress." And thus, she explained, the two of them had to live side by side, and act as if they were the best of friends. She pointed to a green door. "It connects to the Limping One's rooms. When His Majesty comes to call, he arrives through that door, so people assume he's really with her."

"I've seen that done in a play," I said, trying to recall the title of the piece that had used a similar device.

Athénaïs looked amused. "You will discover, my dear Claudette, that Court is in fact very much like a stage. You should feel quite at home here."

I didn't think this world could be more different from the one I'd left behind. Onstage, every candlestick, every crown was false, a cheap imitation. Here at Court everything was real—and of unimaginable luxury.

"Speaking of the stage," Athénaïs said, "I've informed my staff

that if any of them object to working with you, they will be dismissed.
Do inform me if you are abused in any way. I should warn you, as well,
that there are bigots here at Court who have already objected to my
hiring a woman of the theater."

"Why?" I asked, although I knew. Always *this*. Would I ever be
free of it?

"Idiots! They go on and *on* about the sins of the theater, claim-
ing that anyone who is in any way part of that world is tainted by the
Devil." She raised her hands, her long nails like claws, in mock attack.
"They are in the thrall of that group of extreme devouts, the Company
of the Blessed Sacrament. I've even been warned that you will corrupt
my staff, that as an outlaw of the Church you are forbidden from partaking of the sacraments! Fortunately, His Majesty finds such attitudes
ludicrous, archaic remnants of an unenlightened age. Their ignorance
would be frightening if it weren't so laughable. I intend to make a show
of devotion. You are to accompany me to Mass in the morning: *every*
morning."

I tried with difficulty to swallow. "Madame, one thing they say
is true," I offered hesitantly, my heart thumping like a fish caught in
a net. "I may not take Communion," I admitted. A sick feeling came
over me recalling the shadows on the narrow street in Poitiers, the
hooded men attacking my mother and father, their pious hate.

"Really? You've never received the Eucharist?"

I shook my head, very slightly. According to the Church, I was in
a state of mortal sin. "But I observe fasts," I said in my defense, "and
pray, of course." I thought of Mother's little Virgin, who went with her
everywhere. "And I was baptized." Father had found a country priest
who agreed to do so—for a price.

"But you've never made confession?" This with a tone of incredulity.

"It's the same for all players," I said, my voice betraying my attempt
at calm. "That's why we may not be buried in hallowed ground." I
thought of my father's body, abandoned in a shepherd's hut—no doubt
ravaged long ago. I'd carried the weight of my sorrow for all these
years. If only I had gone back to face that awful village priest, *begged*
him to hear Father's formal renunciation.

"And this is Church *policy*?" Athénaïs asked.

I nodded dumbly. How could she not know? "Unless, of course, one were to make a formal renunciation of the stage."

"And then you'd be permitted the sacraments?"

"Oui." A simple vow was all that stood between the community of players and the world of the blessed. All that stood between an eternity in Hell, or in Heaven.

She looked relieved. "Then that's rather easily resolved."

Easy, certainly, to sign an oath before a priest. It would take all of a moment to make the vow—vow to have nothing more to do with the theater, forever and ever.

"Is it not?" Athénaïs asked, sensing my resistance.

I swallowed before speaking: "It's not easy to forsake one's family."

Athénaïs sat back. "You're a practical woman: consider the advantages. But more to the point—why allow bigots to deprive you? One can't simply give way to them. They call themselves Christian, yet they are fueled by hate. They even dare to threaten His Majesty! Some say their aim is to rule this country. Imagine! In all sorts of devious ways, they made it difficult for me to even hire a woman of the theater. I was determined not to be cowed, but for you to be a heathen as well? That gives them far too much ammunition. Frankly, if I had known—"

"I am willing to renounce," I said, exhaling. I pressed my hands together, my palms damp.

"Excellent. I'll send for the priest," Athénaïs said, reaching for a bell.

Ay me. Now?

THE PRIEST WAS a plump little man with an eye tic. "You wish to renounce the theater?" he said with an unctuous smile, waving a document as if it were a victory flag.

I ran my hands over my skirt. I wanted this over with quickly.

"I will read it to you," he said (assuming that I couldn't).

"That will not be necessary." I knew the words, as every player did.

With all my heart, I freely promise God to not perform on the stage for the rest of my life . . .

I took up the goose quill and dipped it into the ink, concentrating on making a steady line.

thought we should celebrate," Athénaïs said, inviting me to join her for a tumbler of her strange wine. A table had been spread with an assortment of food: stewed trout, gammon pie, fritters, quince cream and curd-cakes, pickled cowcumbers, a plate of candied flowers, and fruit. Two dogs, three cats, and the monkey all stared at it expectantly. "Welcome you into the arms of the One True Faith and all that. Didn't you find Père d'Ossat droll? He thinks nobody notices how he pads out the shoulders of his cassock. But he's agreeable. A sweet-water confessor, he forgives everything—very convenient."

I poured a glass from a crystal decanter and handed it to her. It was a familiar ritual from our days in seclusion, yet my hand was not steady.

"To your future here with me at Court, my dear Claudette: may the Company be damned," she hissed as a valet announced a caller. "Don't stand," she said, reading the calling card proffered on a brass tray. "It's only Monsieur Molière."

Molière! I hadn't expected my worlds to collide so immediately.

The comic playwright entered the room, a sheaf of papers in his hand. He removed his hat and pressed it to his heart, making a smooth bow. He seemed at ease in the world of the Court—or was he simply well rehearsed? For a time, I knew, he'd had the role of making up the foot of the King's bed every morning, an upholsterer's privilege he'd inherited from his father. It was even said he'd once been invited to *sit* with the King.

"The incomparable Marquise," Monsieur Molière said, kneeling to kiss the hem of Athénaïs's gown.

He was playing a part, I knew—giving homage to someone who could influence his standing with the King. It made me a little sad to see him thus humbled. I was reminded, painfully, of my father bowing in front of Athénaïs's father so many decades before in Poitiers.

"Monsieur, why are you here?" Athénaïs demanded. "Should you not be preparing *The Magnificent Lovers*?"

I must have rustled my gown, for Molière glanced over at me . . . and blanched. He recognized me—but the setting didn't fit. Nor the gown. Nor my sitting so intimately with the lofty Marquise, "secretly" known to be the King's chosen.

"Madame," he said, recovering, "we have a problem. His Majesty has expressed a reluctance to dance."

Athénaïs snapped open her ivory fan. "Impossible."

"Oui! The play is all about him, his glory! His parts convey an important message—the formidable power of his navy—but what will the ambassadors in attendance conclude if some weakling dances his role? We begin in two hours: I'm at my wit's end."

Athénaïs sat back, fanning herself lazily. "Why do you suppose His Majesty has declined, Monsieur?"

Molière exhaled. "One does not ask His Majesty for reasons; one can only conjecture."

"Is it possibly because the two princes in the piece resemble the King and his brother?"

I'd heard that the King's brother, Philippe, had left Court in a huff because the King had sent his male lover, the fetching Chevalier de Lorraine, into exile.

"And that the two princes are portrayed as *equals*?" Athénaïs continued, her voice cajoling.

"I suppose it might offend, if interpreted as such," Monsieur Molière suggested timorously.

"Of *course* it would offend!" Athénaïs exploded, causing me to nearly spill wine on my gown. "And what of the general's part? I told you days ago that it's outrageous for a modest military man to be portrayed as the hero. And to suggest that all nobles are of equally honorable birth? Mort Dieu."

Molière worked the brim of his hat in his hands. "His Majesty approved the script, Madame."

"But then you worked in a scene with Venus descending, telling the lovers to forget their differences in rank and marry for love. What kind of chaos are you aiming to provoke?" Her eyes sparked with fury.

I sat motionless, as still as the guards at the door. I'd never seen Athénaïs in this role: queen-like, haughty, and judgmental. I was amazed by her display of power. I recognized something of my mother's roles as Medea, Viriate, and Sophonisbe. (Might Athénaïs have taken a few lessons from the performances she attended? The thought awed me.)

"Madame, forgive me," Molière said, his brow glistening with perspiration, "but I showed that change to His Majesty, and he found it charming."

She scoffed.

Monsieur Molière persisted. "Is it possible His Majesty may simply be finding this dancing role a little demanding? He hasn't performed since the *Ballet de Flore* a year ago."

"You question His Majesty's prowess? The King is thirty-two, and—I can personally assure you—a vigorous thirty-two at that. I believe *you* are the one who appears frail, working yourself unto death. Morbidity does not become a clown." Athénaïs smiled coldly. "Inform His Majesty that you will make those changes and I'm confident all will be well. My maid will see you out."

I started: did that mean me? I stood and proceeded through the rooms to the entry. "Monsieur Molière," I said, turning at the door and making a deep curtsy, "we have not been introduced, not formerly, but I am Claude des Oeillets, daughter of Alix des Oeillets."

"*La* des Oeillets?" Molière touched his chin.

Athénaïs was right: the comedian did not look well. "I joined Madame la Marquise's household staff today."

He made a sweeping bow.

"Please," I said, embarrassed. "I am looking forward to this performance."

He pressed his hat against his heart. "It is not what I usually . . ." He sounded almost apologetic. "His Majesty and the Marquise wished a comedy-ballet in the classical and pastoral style. I aim only to please."

"As do we all," I said, recalling what Monsieur Pierre had said to me only the day before about playing the role of a courtier: *All that waiting around, all that bowing.* What would he think of me now? I wondered, adorned in a borrowed costume of ruby brocade and pearls. What would he say of the document I had just signed, renouncing forever the only world in which I'd ever truly belonged?

owdered and scented, I walked behind Athénaïs, followed by four (glaring) attendants—three waiting maids and a valet. Two big footmen preceded us.

Carrying Athénaïs's wraps, her fan, and other necessities, I kept my eyes steadily on her, both anxious and glowing. It amazed me to see the way the throngs parted at her approach. I was overcome with pride to be a member of her entourage.

At the foot of the great stairwell, Athénaïs made a show of greeting Louise de la Vallière, who was likewise attended (although not nearly as grandly). The two women made public gestures of friendship and proceeded on together, linked arm in arm. The King's "official" mistress was a surprisingly plain woman, almost boyish in her gait. She smelled of the stable and walked with a limp. Clearly timid, she lacked Athénaïs's intimidating regality.

The great hall of the ancient castle had been lavishly decorated, the walls covered with tapestries, illuminated by the countless candles burning. A fire roared in the massive stone hearth. A banquet table had been set up in an adjoining hall: the smoky scent of roast meat and other succulents filled the air. Musicians played as courtiers entered, their divine music resonating off the stone walls. (*This* is Heaven, I thought.)

The maids, valet, and footmen disappeared up a stone stairway to the humble Paradis, leaving me and La Vallière's bucktoothed attendant following behind Athénaïs and the Limping One into the tiers for the privileged. Courtiers bowed low as the two women approached, as if they were queens. I stood tall, imagining I was walking onto a stage.

The loge was luxurious, well furnished, and bedecked with flowers. I helped Athénaïs get seated and arranged her gown becomingly. I stood back against the wall, but she frowned, indicating that I was to sit on the bench behind her. I glanced uneasily at La Vallière's attendant standing by the entry, but did as Athénaïs commanded.

The Queen—the *real* queen—sat in a loge opposite, surrounded by her attendants and dwarfs. The few times I'd seen her, I'd been surprised by how tiny she was; one could take her for a child playing in adult garb of rich fabrics. I wondered if she suspected Athénaïs's relationship with the King. (Athénaïs herself doubted it. "She's not very bright," she'd once told me.)

On each side of the stage were tall columns. Enormous candelabras lit up the room, which buzzed with anticipation. I felt strange being part of such a regal gathering. I knew that some of the players behind the curtain would be scanning the crowd, looking for the royal family. Not long before, I had been that person—dressed in the costume of a dog, peaking out at the regal assembly looking for a glimpse of Athénaïs—and now here I was, seated in one of the finest loges, and in attendance on her.

The courtiers hushed as the candles were raised. Jean-Baptiste de Lully, the gifted and temperamental Italian composer, banged his long staff against the floor. The orchestra sounded and the performance began, a moment that always thrilled me.

In spite of the rich trappings, *The Magnificent Lovers* was, I thought, a disappointment. A mythological ballet laced with romantic burlesque, it was a somewhat insipid comédie galante. And tiring, certainly: five acts, with intermèdes at every turn. The noise of the audience milling was so loud it was difficult to hear the singing.

Only when the King performed was there silence—and then, I had to admit, it was riveting. The changes that Molière had hastily made to the script had clearly appeased His Majesty, for he danced like the supreme being that he was, leaping and twirling with breathless grace.

"So, Mademoiselle Claude," Athénaïs said, turning to me during the final intermède, "what is your intellection concerning this performance?"

"The effects are spectacular," I offered charitably. Venus flying down on a cloud? I'd seen it many times before. "And the costumes stunning."

"The heroine's cost three hundred fifty livres I'm told," Athénaïs said, fanning herself.

A very great deal! The advantage of performing for His Majesty, of course, was that the costume costs were covered by the King's purse. (I hoped to help the Bourgogne get invited more often.)

"With a few exceptions, the unities were respected in the central drama," La Vallière observed primly. "One main action, in one place, and everything happening in a day or less."

Deus, the *unities*. I was sick to death of debates about the unities, Aristotle's three rules for drama. "Certainly," I said. La Vallière's attendant had fallen asleep, propped up and snoring softly in the corner.

"But overall?" Athénaïs persisted. "You didn't find it dreary?"

"Perhaps in parts," I admitted, smiling at Athénaïs's candid assessment. She was so different from La Vallière. It was hard to imagine the same man loving both women.

"I find it an interesting artistic experiment," Louise de la Vallière offered quietly. "The intermèdes especially. His Majesty calls it *opera*."

I recalled Mother and Monsieur Pierre discussing the new form. Monsieur Pierre had said he didn't like combining singing with drama, and preferred music only between acts. The memory made me sad. I wondered what my mother was doing now. On a Wednesday, a jour extraordinaire, she would likely be in rehearsal, preparing for the show to play on Friday. I hoped her health was better and that Gaston was staying out of trouble.

The doors opened and a man wearing an abundance of ribbons stepped into the loge, wafting a strong scent of sweat.

"Bienvenue, Monsieur le Marquis de Louvois," Athénaïs said with a cough.

Zounds. The Secretary of State for War. I hardly recognized him. He was now the size of an ox, but resembled a pig, his small eyes beady.

La Vallière's attendant woke with a start. I stood and joined her against the wall, keeping my eyes down.

Louvois bowed gracelessly. "Madame la Marquise de Montespan. Mademoiselle la Duchesse de la Vallière." His voice was high for such a large man.

"Please join us," offered La Vallière.

"I'm just stopping by." He blew his nose into a kerchief and examined the result before folding it carefully in fours and putting it back in his vest.

"Are you enjoying the performance, Monsieur le Marquis?" Athénaïs asked with little enthusiasm.

"His Majesty is magnificent, as always. Au revoir," he said, retreating, bumping into a chair.

"Charmed," Athénaïs said to his back. "Can you believe that he actually *boasts* of never having read a book," she hissed with disgust once the loge door had closed behind him.

"Yet he's efficient and devoted to His Majesty," La Vallière noted.

I blanched. The "efficiency" of Louvois's armies was credited to unrestrained violence. It was said he actually encouraged his soldiers to rape, murder, and plunder.

People in the audience began to laugh. We turned to the stage, where Molière, playing the jester, was staggering, very nearly falling, catching himself, then teetering again. The final act had begun—at last.

The royal entertainment came to an end with a ballet of six executioners with axes. (Odd.) Athénaïs struggled to rise up out of her armchair. La Vallière moved to help her, but Athénaïs signaled impatiently and I slipped a hand under her elbow instead.

"There will be dancing into the small hours, but we must not dally," she told me in the corridor leading to the stairs. "His Majesty will be calling," she whispered.

he entry to Athénaïs's apartment was crowded: four armed guards ("the King's, but they practically live here"), two footmen, and three maids. Athénaïs ordered the guards to prepare for His Majesty's arrival, dismissed the footmen, and commanded the maids to set out orange water, sweetmeats, and flowers.

I followed Athénaïs into her bedchamber, already ablaze with candlelight. I recognized some of the things from our hideaway in the rue l'Échelle: the little black enamel cabinet, her India shawls, and Turkey carpet. The massive silvered bed and toilette table were new. Everything was red and glittery. It was a room such as only Athénaïs could create, a room where one was invited to give way to sensual reverie. A stage set for a queen of seduction.

A fire crackled in the fireplace, making the room comfortably warm. Athénaïs stood in front of an enormous mirror—a Venice reflecting glass of such clarity I wanted to touch it, test it to see if what I saw *was* an image, not a door into another world.

"Unlace me, Claude." I pulled on her bodice strings to release her stays. "I'm not going to be able to wear Court dress much longer," she moaned as the laces gave way. As full and loose as the gown was, it was heavy. I untied the train.

"Thank God it will be Lent soon." She held onto my shoulder as she stepped out of her skirts. "It's wearisome having to entertain His Majesty in my condition."

I wasn't sure where I should put the train, skirt, and bodice.

"Just hang them over that chair. His Majesty likes a certain disarray, an erotic aura of having come *undone*." This with a twisted smile.

"My chemises are in that chest over there," she said, pulling off the last of her layers. Her pubis was golden, like her hair, her breasts and belly full.

I tugged on the lid to open it. It was filled with tangled silk and fine linens. "Will any one do?"

"Oui, oui," she said impatiently, slipping her feet into mules.

I pulled a laced chemise out by its sleeve and helped her get it on over her head, then draped an ermine-lined dressing gown over her shoulders.

She opened the door of a carved court cupboard. "Want some?" she offered, pouring out a tumbler of wine.

"No, merci." I needed my wits.

"Allow me to introduce you to *my* magical arts." She held up a small green jar-glass stoppered with cork and a bone salt spoon. "Add one spoon of this liquid to His Majesty's wine." She measured in the fluid, which was brown and smelled noxious, even at a distance. "It's to help him relax," she explained, adding wine from a pitcher and then sipping from the glass herself. She placed the glass on a round silver tray with a gold floral design around the edge.

I was to serve the King?

"His Majesty comes here to be at his ease, to escape the rigors of his world. This is his sanctuary. If he speaks to you, you may respond, but otherwise remain silent." She stood back and appraised me. Her eyes were dark, her pupils dilated. "Take off your fichu." Her voice had a dreamy quality.

Puzzled, I untied the large linen kerchief that covered my shoulders. It was one of my own, but I'd embroidered it nicely, disguising the rents in the fabric.

"That's better." Athénaïs tugged on my bodice and pulled the sleeves farther down my shoulders. "Although small, you have lovely breasts, well shaped."

I pressed my hands to my chest, flushing at such immodesty.

Athénaïs pulled my hands away, smiling. "Don't be shy. Everything chez moi must be pleasing to His Majesty. What pleases him, pleases God."

I hadn't expected a spiritual connection—not in this circumstance, certainly.

"But more to the point," she added with the look of a coquette, "what pleases His Majesty, *profits* me." She raised her brows conspiratorially. "Understand?"

I nodded. I was beginning to understand that she was setting the stage for a scene in a sultan's harem. Very well: I knew how to play a part.

There was the sound of commotion: men's deep voices, the clanking of swords and clinking of spurs. "Ready?" Athénaïs said over her shoulder. I followed her out, concentrating on holding the silver tray steady. How like a stage this was.

My heart jumped as the King entered the salon, attended only by a valet. Athénaïs "swooned" into a reverence.

I stepped back to stand beside the King's valet, my eyes lowered, my heart beating violently. His Majesty was taller than most, almost as tall as I was—a handsome, well-made man. He still had traces of stage grease and powder on his brow.

"I'm afraid I'm getting too old for this, my love," I heard him say.

I glanced up to see Athénaïs in his embrace.

"You were magnificent. You were in your *glory*." Athénaïs's words were modulated, soft, and caressing. She gazed up at the King with a worshipping look I thought just a bit overplayed.

The King's valet caught my eyes and I looked away, ashamed to have been caught staring. He was a sturdy man with round cheeks and a bushy moustache. I had seen him before—I was sure of it—but I couldn't place where.

"Mademoiselle, you have something for His Majesty?" Athénaïs asked.

I presented the laced wine on the silver tray with a slow, controlled curtsy. I had to concentrate lest the stemmed goblet tip.

"Your Majesty, this is Mademoiselle Claude des Oeillets, my new suivante. She attended me in Paris, on the rue l'Échelle. She can be trusted," Athénaïs added in a low voice, slipping her hand under the King's doublet.

I stumbled back, the tray clattering.

The doors closed behind Athénaïs and the King.

"I'm Xavier," the valet said in the awkward silence that followed. "Xavier Breton. Go ahead and sit," he said. "I won't tell."

"Thank you, but no." He was manful, handsome in a fashion. I wondered how old he was. Possibly forty? His hair was black, but his moustache had some gray.

"His Majesty won't return for at least ten minutes."

"You know the routine well." I felt flushed. "Do I know you?" I asked, leaning against a side table for support.

"I was wondering that myself."

His lips were full and soft, protruding from under his bushy moustache. I wondered what it would be like to lick them. (What had come over me!)

"Des Oeillets is a lovely name, but uncommon. Are you related to the actress?"

"She's my mother," I said, bracing myself for the inevitable scorn. Royal attendants could be the worst, fancying themselves above the world.

But his reaction was precluded by a male yelp of pleasure from behind the doors, followed by a low groan.

Oh dear, I thought.

He winked at me. "His Majesty is ahead of schedule," he said, glancing at the clock.

That wink. And then it came back to me: swooping through the air in my flimsy gown . . . "I threw you a flower," I stammered, recalling.

He laughed. "You're *Cupid*!"

Pleased and proud, I put out my arms as if flying.

He shook his head in disbelief. "I still have that rose," he confessed.

laude?" Athénaïs turned from her toilette table to look up at me. "Are you dreaming again? Didn't you hear what I said?"

"I'm sorry, Madame!" I said with a start, working a bit more bear grease into her scalp. I was exhausted, in truth. My position at Court hadn't been easy to adjust to. The rhythm of each day felt off. Other than morning Mass and the King's afternoon visit, nothing was consistent. We ate all the time—drank all the time. I was either frantically busy or required to stand invisibly, doing nothing. (That was the hardest part, by far.)

And, too, I had to admit, I'd found it unsettling having to stand side by side every afternoon with the King's valet—the kindly Xavier Breton—making whispered conversation to the sounds of ardent passion coming from the other room. Athénaïs and the King were noisy lovers.

"Forgive me," I said with an obliging inflection, smiling winsomely (stagecraft) at Athénaïs's reflection in the looking glass. She was all sugar water now, but I was wary of her temper, which could blaze up in a moment like dry tinder. Most of her vexation was caused by Louise de la Vallière, I knew. The King's obvious respect for the "official" mistress was driving her mad. Athénaïs inflamed the King's passion, but Louise, mother of two of his children, remained his frequent companion (especially out riding, which His Majesty did religiously with her every day, even in inclement weather).

As a result, Athénaïs was tightly wound, even in repose. She did not sleep well, in spite of opium pills. Her fears of the dark were morbid, and she often asked me to share her bed. "Kiss me, Claudette," she said sleepily to me one night, her voice thick from the pills. "What? Aren't you curious? Come here, my pet . . . ," she murmured as she drifted back into dreams.

"You were saying, Madame?" I asked, gently working out a snarl.

"I need you to go to Paris."

Gladly! I thought, resuming brushing. One hundred vigorous strokes with the boar-bristle hairbrush, then twenty with the softer one of horsehair. Almost done. "When, Madame?" I longed to see Mother and Gaston; I'd bring them tasty treats for Easter. I hadn't had news of them and hoped that meant all was well.

"Tomorrow," she said, pulling a folded-up paper from her bosom. "We're running low on my amatory assistant."

I smiled. Her "amatory assistant" was what she called the liquid I put in His Majesty's wine.

"God forbid I should run out. You're to deliver this note to the woman who lives next to Notre-Dame de Bonne Nouvelle, a little church just outside the old city wall. Her name is Madame Voisin, although sometimes she goes by Monvoisin, or even Deshayes. You'll be given a parcel to bring back, so you'll need this as well." She handed me a beaded bag. "A gold louis and two silver écus, plus extra for a driver and some money for the Widow." The Widow Scarron, the woman Athénaïs had hired to supervise the care of the babies—one now, soon to be two. "You will have to go in a rented coach. I can't send you in one of mine, lest it be recognized."

I cocked my head. There was something curious about this arrangement.

"The woman you're to call on is a 'seer,' well known for her spells, powders, and love potions, all manner of things. All the ladies at Court send their maids to her—in disguise, of course. I suggest you go as your charming Monsieur."

I SET OUT early the next morning in pouring rain, dressed in bucket-top boots, breeches, and doublet, topped by a wig, a hat, and wearing a bushy moustache. I had a lot to accomplish in one day: pick up the parcel from the seer, check on my family, and deliver money to the Widow.

Finding the seer's house was not easy. It was not far from where my mother and brother lived, but in the uncharted realm beyond the old city walls. The streets—if you could call them that—were uncobbled, pitted with sewage-filled holes. Barefoot children and mangy dogs stood staring from the doors of wattle-and-daub shanties. The area was ungoverned, known to be inhabited by criminals who could live there without harassment. I was thankful that it was midday, thankful that the sun was bright, thankful to be armed and dressed as a man.

"I won't be long," I assured the coach driver, who had laid a fire-arm across his knees.

The seer's house abutted a small village church, just as Athé-naïs had said. It was a modest abode, the shutters in need of repair. I knocked on the splintered plank door.

A round little woman in an apron and cap came to greet me. The skirt under her stained apron was of velvet. There was even a train attached, which she'd tucked up into a bustle. Bright glass beads adorned the folds of her neck. "Come in, come in, Monsieur."

There was something familiar about her. "I wish to speak to Madame Voisin." The room beyond was crammed with broken-down furnishings. An enormous Easter altar had been set up over the fire-place.

"I am she." She grinned. She smelled of ale and tobacco.

A girl peeked in from another room, then ducked back out of sight. I could hear a man's voice.

"The woman I serve wishes me to give you this." I handed her the folded paper.

"Oh, bless," she said, squinting at it. "Where have I put it?" She frowned at a table stacked with boxes, books, and baskets. "Saints help me. Wait here. You're not overheated, are you? Would you like an ale?"

"No. No, thank you."

Humming cheerily, she sorted through the heaps on the table.

Stars! It came to me: she was the fortune-teller on the bridge, the woman who had a booth on the Pont Marie. Madame *Catherine*. She hadn't died in the flood, as I'd thought!

"Ah, here we are." Two baskets spilled onto the floor as she reached for a box. She stepped over the wreckage. "I've vowed to my confessor to clean all this up before Easter." This with a sweep of her hands. "As soon as I can get my lazy husband to make me some trunks," she confided with a look of impatience.

"My mistress also seeks a cure for a simpleton," I dared to ask, my heart pounding. "Would you happen to know someone who does that type of work?" She had spoken to me before of such a woman, someone who performed miracles.

She stared at me, and for a moment I feared she could see through my disguise. "I used to know a woman who claimed to do that sort of thing," she said, "but she's in an asylum now herself." She laughed with a shrug. "If you like, I could make inquiries. But I would have to see the simple first."

"I will let her know." Bringing Gaston was out of the question. There would be no way to disguise him.

There was a commotion in the back room: a crow squawking, a dog barking. "So your mistress knows how to use this?" She held up a bottle similar to the one Athénaïs kept in her locked chest. "One salt spoon in a glass of wine. No more."

I gave her the gold louis.

"Merci. God bless, Monsieur!" she said, pocketing the heavy coin. "Money back if your lady doesn't get results."

CHAPTER 42

rapped on the door of my mother's rooms, but there was no answer. I creaked open the door and called out. "Maman? Gaston? It's me, Claudette." A faint light shone through the begrimed window. Our familiar things looked sordid and worn in the dimness. The fire had gone out: I could see my breath. The stench from the necessary was strong. "Maman?"

I heard a squeak from Mother's bedroom and quickly crossed the small space to her open door. She was a tiny shape huddled under the covers in the half-dark. Alarmed, I took off a glove and touched my hand to her forehead.

"I'm just having a little rest." Mother reached out a clammy hand. "How nice to see you." She squinted at me. "*Is* that you?"

I peeled off the moustache. "Where is Gaston?"

"Helping put up announcements," she said, her teeth chattering. "I thought I'd have a little sleep before I—" She began to cough.

There was blood in her spittle. Still? "I'm going for a doctor."

"I'm *fine*."

"I'll have those words engraved on your tombstone."

"That's not funny," Mother said with a laugh, which only made her cough again.

"No," I said, stroking her back. I could feel her bones. "It's not."

I was stirring the embers to get a fire going when I heard Gaston come in. It had been six Sundays since I'd seen him. His beard was longer, almost covering his chest. He had the diffident, gentle look of a monk, innocent yet wise. I embraced him. I hadn't realized how much I missed him. "Maman needs a doctor."

"She," he stuttered. He mimed her expression of horror.

I made a rueful face: of course. Mother had a mortal fear of being bled.

"She. Say." He pointed to Mother's room. "No. Sick."

And of course he believed her. He wouldn't think to doubt his mother.

He pulled a roll of papers from the waist of his breeches and handed them to me: Mother's annual contract with the theater, to be signed before a notary. It was that time of year. "Later," I said, putting the contract on the table, weighting it down with an earthen bowl. I could hear Mother moaning. "There's a doctor on the rue Tiquetonne," I said, looking for a quill and ink in the clutter and finally finding a vial illogically nested in the soup pot. Unable to find a quill, I used the end of my big iron key to scratch out the message on the margin of an old news sheet: "My mother is very sick. Please come see her." I handed it to him along with a silver écu, one of the two coins I was supposed to give the Widow Scarron later that afternoon.

Mercy me: the Widow. I'll figure this out in the morning, I thought, realizing that I would be spending the night.

THE DOCTOR STOOPED to get through the door in his tall cap. He was a young man, unbearded—he looked like a boy, his cheeks baby-pink.

"Go sit with Maman," I told Gaston. "Distract her."

Gaston took my head in his two hands, covering my ears and pressing gently. I'd never been sure what this meant; it seemed to be a consoling gesture. I rubbed his nose with mine: *Don't worry. Everything's going to be all right.*

He lumbered off. I listened for the door to Mother's room to close behind him. "May I ask you to remove your doctor's hat, Monsieur?" I said, turning to address the young man. "It may alarm my mother." I worried she was going to put up a fight. "I should warn you that she has a fear of being bled."

"First, the particulars," he said, fiddling with the clasp that held the contraption on. "I'm not used to this nuisance," he said, sighing when it finally gave way. "Her age, that type of thing." He stood look-ing for somewhere to put it.

"My mother is . . ." I paused to calculate. "Almost fifty," I said, tak-ing his hat and hanging it from a wall sconce. Half a century: imagine. "Her health is normally robust. She's never missed a day of work."

"What does she do?"

"Theater work," I said, intentionally vague. "This way, Docteur . . . ?"

"Baratil," he said, bowing. "And you are . . . ?"

"Mademoiselle Claude des Oeillets." I could hear Gaston hum-ming, Mother's chuckle. That was a good sign. Maybe she *was* fine. Maybe we hadn't needed to go to the trouble and expense.

"You're not . . . ?" the doctor said with a stricken look. "Your mother . . . she's not the actress, is she? La des Oeillets?"

I nodded warily. He would leave now. He wouldn't deign to treat a sinner. Maybe I could get the coin back.

He put his hands to his cheeks, like a girl. "Madame des Oeillets is a marvel! She's the finest actress in Paris. I've been to eight of her per-formances. No: nine. I saw her in *Sophonisbe* three times." He blushed in his fervor.

"My mother will be happy to know that, Docteur Baratil," I said, relieved, opening the door to Mother's small chamber.

"I refuse to be bled," she said glaring, her teeth chattering.

"Docteur Baratil is one of your fanatics." It was a word players used to describe the people who came to a show over and over just to applaud a particular player. "He saw you in *Sophonisbe* three times."

The doctor pressed his hands over his heart and bowed solemnly from the waist. "Perhaps I can help make you comfortable, Madame des Oeillets," he suggested, "without the loss of blood. Your admirers long to see you return to the stage."

Mother consented to an examination, but insisted that Gaston and I leave the room. We squatted against a wall, staring at the closed door, listening to the murmurs within. We'd grown up sitting on the ground—using chairs had been an uncomfortable adjustment. When anxious or worried, we often returned to our old ways.

We jumped up when the doctor emerged. My heart sank, seeing his eyes. "I'll accompany you down to the street," I offered.

It was raining, so we stood under an arch in the courtyard.

"A cold humor is dripping from your mother's head into her lungs." What did that mean?

"She has consumption," he said, swallowing.

I recalled the stories told by country people in my youth, how a dog demon would take over a person's body and eat his lungs. "What can we do?"

Docteur Baratil looked miserable. "Opium pills, if you can afford it. Laudanum, a new liquid form, is almost as effective and costs considerably less. Give her as much as she needs to be comfortable. Don't hesitate."

So. Only comfort—not cure. Was she dying?

GASTON TURNED FROM the wash-up area.

"The doctor says Maman is sick." I slipped off my cloak.

"No. Blood," he hummed.

I nodded. He hadn't bled Mother—but then he hadn't seen the point. "He said . . . He said it's going to take time." I kicked off my clogs, sending one flying.

I sat down, drumming my fingers on the table, staring at Mother's annual contract. "Gaston, I'm going to suggest"—strongly, emphatically!—"that Maman not sign this contract."

He stared, puzzled.

"Not this year." Maybe, with a long period of rest, Mother would recover. Maybe Docteur Baratil was mistaken.

thénaïs expected me back. She was approaching her final month and would be anxious, no doubt. After scrubbing Mother's room clean; after hiring a neighbor's daughter to come in every day to clear the garbage, gray water, and chamber pots; after deciding, yet again, not to tell Gaston—much less my mother— what the doctor had said, in truth; after persuading, with difficulty, Mother not to renew her contract for the year; after obtaining a vial of opium tincture and instructing the girl how to measure it out; after kissing my mother farewell and tucking her rosary under her pillow—I sadly took my leave.

"I'll be back soon," I promised. As soon as I could. Floridor and his wife, who lived close by, had kindly promised to look in every day, which was a comfort—but even so, I was heavy with concern.

I delivered the remaining silver écu to the Widow. ("There will be another coming," I assured her, mentally figuring the necessities I would have to forgo in order to save that much.) Then, heart- and bone-weary, I instructed the driver of my hired coach to head back to Saint-Germain-en-Laye. It was raining again, a spring shower. I closed the cracked blinds against the dreary landscape.

Easter was coming. I would make my first confession, do every penance required for my many sins. I would pray for Mother's recovery. (Surely the Virgin did not care if Mother was a player. Surely the Virgin knew her good heart.) I closed my eyes, tears spilling.

The rough tumbling of the coach wheels over cobbles jolted me awake. I wiped my cheeks dry. In the castle courtyard, a footman handed me down, protecting me from the rain with a leather ombrella.

I felt a guilty relief, stepping back into the ease of the Court. Perhaps here, in the realm of the blessed, prayers would be heard. Perhaps here, miracles were possible. I headed up the stone stairs to Athénaïs's suite.

"The Marquise is in her chamber," one of the maids informed me coolly.

I heard a man's voice from deep within the apartment, the faint sound of a woman crying. "What's happened?" I asked, alarmed, but the maid had insolently turned her back on me.

I hurried into the salon, burning at the slight. Athénaïs's staff were in league against me, resentful that I was in a position of confidentiality and favor: the daughter of an actress, no less. Fortunately, I ate with Athénaïs, and not below in the kitchens with the others, where I would be left to starve, no doubt.

I paused, puzzling over a bumper of wine that had been spilled onto the Turkey carpet. Five thick candles were burned down, the wax pooling. Cats were sniffing at a broken dish, helping themselves to cake crumbs and pâté. (Pâté? During Lent?) I had only been gone for one day, and the place was in shatters.

Apprehensive, I headed toward Athénaïs's bedchamber. I scratched three times on the door. No response. I tapped again, more insistently.

Monsieur Blucher opened the door. The *midwife*? Thunder. Had . . . ?

"It's your maid," he said, turning to Athénaïs, who was stretched out on the bed, her arm dripping blood into a bowl, her other hand pressed against her mountain of a belly.

So: the baby hadn't yet birthed, I realized with relief. But why was she being bled? Some women believed that being bled when pregnant would make the child quick and smart—but Athénaïs was not of their number, I knew.

"You've taken enough out of me, Blucher," Athénaïs said, rousing.

"Patience, Madame, the last bit is important." Blucher checked the contents of the blood-bowl.

"Don't 'patience' me, you idiot."

I put my hand on her shoulder. I'd had a lifetime of experience steadying a wavering temper. "He's going to do exactly as you say, Madame." I glared at the doctor.

Blucher's hands shook as he strapped Athénaïs's forearm to stop the flow, then wound a long strip of linen around her wrist. "His Majesty wishes me to return later this afternoon," he said sullenly, gathering his tools.

Athénaïs did not answer, her unbandaged arm now covering her eyes. I was startled to see that she was weeping.

I stepped into the parlor after the doctor. "Do you have anything to calm her?"

"We're in Aries?" He checked the astrological charts in his girdle book. "Bleeding from the forehead is ill advised. A sleeping remedy, perhaps?"

"Thank you, but we have that." Athénaïs was right. The man was a dunderhead. But why was she so distraught? "What happened, Monsieur?"

"There was a fulmination in the night, that's all I've been told. When the emotions are strong, the life of a womb-infant is endangered."

Truly! "You know the way out? Through La Vallière's suite?" It wouldn't do to have a midwife seen coming and going through the door to Athénaïs's rooms.

MERCIFULLY, ATHÉNAÏS HAD fallen asleep. I set the bloodied bowl and rags outside the door for the chambermaids to deal with. I found a stick of incense in a dish on the cluttered toilette table and lit it to cover the lingering smell of blood.

Athénaïs stirred, opened her eyes, but then closed them again. "It's cold," she murmured, turning onto her side, pulling a feather comforter over her.

I refreshed the fire and lowered myself onto the chair close to the bed. Something had happened, but I would have to wait to find out. I would have to wait, too, before I could ask leave to return to Paris. I had been foolish to imagine I could absent myself so close to the baby's birth. Patience, I told myself, leaning my head against the back of the chair, listening to rain pelting against the shuttered window, the wind howling.

·   ·   ·

ATHÉNAÏS WOKE IN early evening, as the call for Vespers was sounded. "Those damned bells," she said, stirring.

"How do you feel?" Blood had soaked through her bandage: I would have to change it.

"I dreamt I tried to kill the Limping One with a knife," she said with a loopy smile. "The holy whore." She laughed weakly.

"Why would you have done that, Madame?" Had it only been a dream? "Hold still, please. I need to change this bandage." I looked around for the supplies the doctor had left behind.

She laid her head back against the pillows. "Unfortunately, I didn't succeed," she said, using her free hand to wipe her eyes with a corner of a covering sheet.

I set her rebandaged arm down. "Keep it low, below your head." I gave her two opium pills and a glass of wine.

Athénaïs downed the pills with big, gulping swallows. "Tant pis," she said, handing the glass back to me.

I noticed a raised bruise on her cheekbone. She was regarded as the most beautiful woman at Court, but there were times, like this, when she looked not unattractive, but . . . I thought of the demons that could take over a soul. She was only twenty-nine, yet already she'd started to coarsen.

"The Limping One is with child," Athénaïs informed me, her voice thin. "By His Majesty."

I groaned in sympathy. The King had vowed to her that he no longer had relations with Louise de la Vallière, that she was his mistress in name only.

"He tried to stop me," she said, closing her eyes.

It hadn't been a dream. "What happened?"

"I tried to kill him too." Her voice tremulous.

Mon Dieu. I'd seen the scorn Athénaïs sometimes showed His Majesty—treating him like some slow-witted shopkeeper—but to strike out at him! "You must rest, Madame," I said breathlessly. *Calm.*

NINE DAYS LATER, Athénaïs's throes came on while she was with the King. Her cry was sharp, helpless—different from her moans of passion.

"It's begun," I told Xavier. "Her pains," I added, clasping my rosary. "She's early." Athénaïs wasn't due for at least another week.

I heard another cry. The King appeared at the door in his frilly linens. "Her waters—" He held up his soaked sleeve.

Just after three of the clock in the dead of night, Athénaïs gave birth to a son, who emerged with some difficulty, the wrong end presenting. He was small, with one leg dwarfed, shorter than the other, and strangely turned. (Yet another deformed infant from Athénaïs's womb: what did this signify?)

As soon as the baby was cut free, I swaddled and handed him to Xavier, who handed him in turn to Monsieur de Lauzun, Commander of the King's Household, who was waiting at La Vallière's door. Lauzun was to rush to an unmarked coach by the gate to the park and give the baby to the woman within—the masked Widow Scarron. The stealth procedure had all been worked out only days before. "Hurry!" I hissed. Before the baby began to howl.

Xavier disappeared, heading for La Vallière's suite.

"Well done, Monsieur," I told the midwife.

Blucher turned expectantly. I handed him a velvet bag of coins: the hundred gold louis were heavy. My own "reward" was only a tenth as much, but at least it would cover my family's expenses for the next little while. "From His Majesty and La Marquise," I said, looking over at Athénaïs, who had fallen, finally, into a deep slumber.

ON EASTER SUNDAY, I pushed my way through the throngs outside the Convent of Récollets. I'd made my first confession. I'd revealed my concern that I wasn't doing enough for my mother and brother, confessed to a slice of beef eaten during Lent, my sinful attachment to life at Court—the fine clothes, the food, the gaming, and partaking of spirits. I did not mention my visit to Madame Catherine. Athénaïs would not have wanted that revealed. I was keeper of her secret.

"I am sorry for these and all the sins of my past life," I said, fingering the coin I had brought to buy a prayer for Mother.

"Give thanks to the Lord for He is good."

"For His mercy endures forever," I intoned.

As I sat listening to the priest's words of absolution, I tried not to think of his garlic breath, vowing, instead, to improve, to curb my eating (I'd gained yet another stone) and save my earnings in order to provide for Mother and Gaston.

I was assigned penance for my sins—one Our Father, ten Hail Marys, and one Glory Be—yet even so, I felt burdened. Two nights before, La Vallière's cries had filled our rooms. She miscarried, but quite violently, very nearly dying. Athénaïs's response had seemed theatrical to me: staged. Something was amiss. She had woken several times in the night, tearing at her hair. "Catherine," she'd hissed several times over.

"No, it's me, Claudette," I'd assured her soothingly, yet wondering: had Madame Catherine something to do with what had happened to Louise de la Vallière? Was it possible that Athénaïs had given her rival *poison*? I was Athénaïs's confidential maid, but there were things even I did not know.

As I descended the church steps, lost in thought, a woman grabbed my arm. "Attendez!" A solemn procession was approaching. The King, dressed in a fox-collared robe, was accompanied by men of the Church.

Of *course*: he was touching for the King's Evil that day, dispelling the disfiguring disease with a pat of his royal hand. That explained the hundreds of grotesques on the streets. They bowed their heads, murmuring prayers as the silent procession passed by—a powerful display of spiritual kingship.

I stood watching the ritual healing, the King's solemn laying on of hands as he moved among the sufferers, sprinkling them with holy water, touching their tumors and making the sign of the cross over them. His Majesty went slowly through the motions of the ceremony with purpose. It was clear to see that he was moved by such suffering, clear to see that he longed to offer relief. With each cure—and there were many—people cried out with joy. It was proof—was it not?—of the miraculous nature of kingship, the Christ-like power of our good King.

Yet I knew all too well that players were often hired to perform the role of the "miraculously" healed—I'd done it more than once myself.

Even so, I wept at the sight of a girl leading her mother away, embracing her so tenderly.

Was the miracle of the King's touch nothing more than a performance? I longed to believe in wonders. How joyful I would be in the presence of a miracle. More than anything, I wanted my mother to be well. I wanted her to live.

turned the handle of Mother's door and pushed, but it held firm. I rapped several times, then pressed my ear against the planks. Not a sound. I put down my bags and rummaged for my big iron key to let myself in.

The door creaked open. Mother was standing before me like some ghostly apparition, dressed in a tattered nightdress and cap, a counterpane comforter hanging over her shoulders. "It's *you*," she said, reaching out for a wall to steady herself.

I embraced her. She was bone-thin in my arms.

"I'm better," she said, but visibly quaking. "You didn't lock the door."

"I will if you want, Maman," I said, bringing in all my things. We'd never locked it before. Was she in a fever?

"Why the bags?" she demanded.

"I'm staying for a while," I said, setting the string bags on the sideboard. They were filled to bursting with food from Athénaïs's abundant table—sweetmeats, figs, cheese from the Auvergne, fried sheep's testicles, a roast partridge in cabbage—all wrapped in cloths and tied up with pretty ribbons. "Like I promised." I'd even managed to get some of Athénaïs's opium pills by stealth.

Athénaïs had not wanted to allow me time away, but in the end it had been simple. She had to go north with the King and Court, and someone was needed in Paris in case the Widow had a problem with the bastard babies. (Heyday—I would even be paid.) "Where is Gaston?"

"He's at the theater. I think."

"Where's the girl I hired?" Ants were swarming over a trencher left out on the table.

Maman waved her hand through the air. "I let her go."

I groaned.

"She left her stool in *my* chamber pot!"

I made an incredulous scoff. She had a point. "I'll find someone new."

"I don't want strangers around. They sing off-key."

I felt too exhausted to do battle . . . *yet.* "I have some things for you," I said, opening my leather valise, stuffed full with Athénaïs's rejected garments—a silk chemise, two boned bodices and four sets of sleeves, several shawls and veils.

Mother brightened.

"Get back in bed and I'll show you."

I WALKED DOWN to the river, furious and frustrated. At a book-stand, a title caught my eye: *The Imitation of Christ.* It was a beautiful volume, bound in red leather and tooled in gold. It promised counsel on meeting adversity as well as reflections on death. On the frontis-piece, I saw that it was translated from the Latin by Monsieur Pierre Corneille.

Our Monsieur Pierre?

His Paris abode wasn't far: I would see if he was in. Maybe he wouldn't mind signing the book. I could give it to Mother as a present. It would strengthen us all.

I RESISTED EMBRACING Monsieur Pierre—outbursts of heart-fulness alarmed him, I knew. I hadn't seen him for more than four months, not since encountering him at Mother's performance in the disastrous premiere of Racine's *Britannicus.* "I've missed you," I con-fessed. His room was bright, but of modest size and cluttered, every surface covered with books and papers.

"Bah," he said with a smiling scowl. He had tufts of hair coming out of his ears. He looked like an owl.

I insisted he sit while I scrounged up the makings of tea. This took some doing, as the dishes and implements were in great disarray—worse even than Mother's. He had a girl to help, he said, but her mother was dying, so she hadn't been coming around as much. "My wife refuses to leave Rouen. She's convinced Paris is a city of cutthroats."

"Don't worry, I can manage." Was my own mother dying? She was ill—seriously ill, without a doubt—yet there seemed to be so much life in her (so much stubbornness). Her spirit was clearly strong.

I set the cups of tea on the table. "How have you been?"

"Pas mal." His hand trembled, causing his tea to spill, but he paid it no heed. He seemed pleased to see me, uncharacteristically prattling. He'd been to see Monsieur Molière's *The Miser* the day before at the Palais-Royal. The performance had been a disappointment, possibly because there was hardly anyone in the audience. Without all the courtiers, who was left in Paris?

Oui, I nodded. They'd all gone north with the King, following the royal progress through the Flemish lands newly acquired through the peace of Aix-la-Chapelle. It was to be a parade, a theatrical show of splendor and military might.

Getting Athénaïs packed had not been easy: she'd gained weight, and the gowns she wished to take were no longer comfortable, much less flattering. Then there had been all the commotion of departure: I'd never seen such chaos. The courtyard swarmed with pages, maids, valets, flunkies, carriages and wagons, pack mules and horses. There were thousands of men in the military escort alone. Even one of the King's former wet-nurses was part of the procession. (She kissed the King each morning, Athénaïs told me—something she thought was absurd but I found endearing.) The King's bed had been dismantled and sent on, an enormous four-poster construction draped in gold-embroidered green velvet, as well as all his tapestries and silver candlesticks. Moving a court was no small undertaking.

"And speaking of courtiers, why aren't *you* with the Court, headed to Flanders?" Monsieur Pierre asked.

"I'm needed in Paris," I explained vaguely. "Look what I just bought," I said, changing the subject. I showed Monsieur Pierre the lovely little book.

He was delighted. "I worked on this translation off and on for almost twenty years. It's as old as you are."

"You flatter me, Monsieur Pierre." Oh, to be twenty again.

"You're so pretty when you smile."

I smiled again. I loved this old man. "Would you sign it? It's a gift for Mother."

"You have such nice teeth," he said, standing unsteadily to rummage in the clutter of his writing table for a quill.

I surreptitiously found a rag to mop up the spilled tea.

"How's your charming mother?" He cut a few pages with a kitchen knife, then scratched out his name on the title page, sprinkled sand on it, and shook the book clean before handing it back to me. He looked at me over his sight glasses. "I was alarmed, I confess, to learn that Alix did not renew her contract this year. She's not well?"

I could not bear to look into his eyes.

"So, it's like that," he said softly.

I nodded. Like that.

other was awake when I got back, but in bed as I'd instructed. "I found someone to help me clean up," I told her. Yet another neighbor's daughter, free mornings and often some evenings as well. I'd already put her to work, clearing some of the mess.

"Do I have any say in this?" Mother demanded.

"We won't move a thing, I promise."

"You'll be throwing things out."

"We'll always ask you," I lied, knowing my mother would want to hold on to even the most moth-eaten rag.

"Is this supposed to prepare me for the beyond?" she asked, holding up Monsieur Pierre's book. "It looks like a prayer book with all these holy pictures in it."

"Monsieur Pierre wrote it." Or, rather, translated it from Latin. "He even signed it." I turned the pages. "See?"

"You know I can't read."

"I'm going to read it to you," I said, rearranging and plumping her pillows. "I thought you'd like the pictures." I could hear the new maid at work in the wash-up area, singing off-key. "He said to tell you that he'll be coming to visit." *Often,* he'd told me, his cheeks wet with tears.

IN A MATTER of weeks it became clear that my mother was truly dying. On the advice of young Docteur Baratil, she was put on a diet of tepid goat's milk for eight days, and after that, for three days, that of a cow. There had been hope of a cure, and she had, in fact, rallied, but only briefly. Now it sometimes seemed as if she was burning up from within. She kept to her bed and had to be helped to the chamber pot, her urine clouded and rank. The doctor called frequently—often in the morning and then again in the evening.

My own sorrow I could not face. Instead I focused on practical matters. I feared my mother would slip away without renouncing the stage, feared, too, that she would simply refuse—so I made the decision for her. "I've sent for a priest," I informed Gaston. It had been a grueling few days; we'd been sleeping in shifts. "To renounce," I clarified.

He pointed to our mother's room with a look of incredulity. He hummed one long drawn-out note. Then, "Accept?" he managed to say, haltingly.

I grimaced. "Not exactly."

Soon after, the priest arrived and, without ceremony or delicacy, proceeded to read out the statement:

With all my heart, I freely promise God not to act on the stage for the rest of my life, even if, in His infinite goodness, He pleases to return me to good health.

"Now you're to sign, Maman." I'd purchased a pot of lampblack ink and a swan quill in preparation. There must be no question, later, of the document's authenticity.

Gaston helped her sit up and put the leather portfolio on her lap.

Mother looked up at him. "You're so big now."

The priest cleared his throat, rocking on his heels.

I positioned the document in front of her.

"But what if there's a miracle?" she demanded, gesturing to her little Virgin propped in the corner.

I looked over at Gaston in despair. She wasn't going to sign.

Gaston knelt down beside her, humming, his gestures sweetly beseeching.

"It's not right!" She threw a scornful look at the priest.

I couldn't help but smile. She was feisty, even on her deathbed. "Maman, you don't want to go to Hell, do you?"

"I want to be with your father, I don't care where."

I groaned. I had no defense against this argument!

The priest reached for the paper, but I held the document firm. I couldn't bear the thought of my mother's body dumped unceremoniously into a pit with felons and sinners. She deserved a proper funeral, a proper burial—a proper eternity. *"Please."*

Mother looked at me with tears in her eyes. "And so, the final scene," she said with resignation, taking up the quill. She dipped the nib into the ink and slowly—ever so slowly—traced out the initials of her name.

IN THE DAYS and nights that followed, Gaston and I took turns sitting by our mother's bed, doing what we could to make her comfortable, giving her opium, and reading to her. I combed and dressed her thinning hair, made up her face as if for the stage, and adorned her in her beloved gewgaws.

"Your father liked this color on me," she said dreamily, fingering her sleeve, then fell into a deep sleep.

A STEADY STREAM of friends came and went as word got out: Monsieur Pierre, Floridor, and the players from the Bourgogne were daily visitors. Madame Babette showed up with beignets. Even our old landlord came with his wife.

Gaston moved a bench into the bedchamber for our guests, who lingered at Mother's bedside, praying, singing, telling stories—weeping and even laughing. Mother no longer woke, but I was certain she could hear and I knew how much she loved the sound of merriment.

By the fire, stirring a simmering cauldron of oxtail soup, I asked Floridor if he would deliver the eulogy. The dear man, so elegant and refined, began to sob with such violence that I poured him a mug of wormwood wine. He sipped at it delicately, holding it in his shaky hands. "You see? I'm all to pieces. Soon I'll be the only one left." The only player still living who had performed in the cursed *Andromaque* less than three years before. Of the four principals in that play, Montfleury had died, then Thérèse du Parc—and now, soon, my mother.

It was nearing midnight on the third day of our vigil that Mother breathed her last. Monsieur Pierre put down the text he'd been read-

ing from aloud: lines from *Sertorius,* lines from one of the great roles
Mother had played, a role he'd written for her, a role she'd helped
create.

Gaston cried out. I put my hand on his shoulder, suddenly unsteady.

"Peace now," Monsieur Pierre said, closing her staring eyes.

I WENT THROUGH the minutes, hours, and days that followed in
a daze. Gaston was twenty-four now, but the shock of our mother's
death rendered him a child once again. He squatted by the fire, humming, words lost to him once more.

I knelt beside him, trying to comfort. He looked at me helplessly,
locked in his grief. I pressed my forehead against his.

I, too, felt inarticulate and dazed, stumbling into furniture. Fortunately, I had taken care of quite a bit in advance: paying for a funeral
at Saint-Leu-Saint-Guiles; arranging for the burial; hiring callers to
walk throughout the city announcing the tragic news; making sure we
had a quantity of deniers on hand to throw down to the people who
gathered beneath our windows.

I was well prepared, but even so I found it surprisingly difficult to
deal with. Waves of tears came over me at unexpected moments. I even
began to feel faint in the lawyer's office, sending everyone scrambling
for nose cloths and salts. I had always been the strong and practical
one, the one who held my family together in times of need. Now I
could no longer count on myself. My mother—that charmingly will-
ful, exasperating child of a woman—was *gone.*

The day before the funeral, I tackled the chaos of Mother's papers
and discovered, in a basket under her bed, promissory notes, leases,
legal documents—all unopened, their wax seals intact. I hauled these
back to the lawyer, who studied them over, and then looked up at me
with sympathy.

The debts, as it turned out, were staggering.

As well as being responsible for my mother's obligations, according to the terms of the will I was now Gaston's legal guardian. "Don't
worry, Turnip. I will look after you." In truth I felt at a loss.

.   .   .

DIES IRAE! DIES ILLA! O day of wrath! O day of mourning!

On the day of the funeral, Gaston and I eased our mother's body into an oak coffin. She seemed small, birdlike, clothed in the simple blue linen gown she'd been wearing when she'd met Father. I'd wrapped her ugly shawl around her shoulders.

As the carpenter was about to bolt the coffin shut, I turned stricken to my brother. "What did we forget?"

He retrieved Father's rosary and the humble wood statue of the Virgin. I tucked them into the crook of Mother's arm, along with the key and chipped cup. (The corn-husk doll had long ago disintegrated; I regretted not having thought to buy carnations.) We each kissed her cold powdered cheek, and lowered the coffin lid.

I slowly descended the winding stairs to the street, following the coffin borne by Floridor, Gaston, and two strong actors from the troupe. A small crowd had assembled. The young doctor and Monsieur Pierre were there. Players of the Bourgogne hovered to one side, and a few vaguely familiar faces from the Marais to another, clustered around old La Roque, who'd become surprisingly stooped, his beard still divided into points, but gray. And many, many tearful strangers—Mother's ardent fanatics.

Monsieur Pierre stepped forward and offered his arm.

I nodded, fearful of speaking. I regretted not holding onto Father's rosary. I covered my face with my veil and slowly set off, following the coffin down the rue Saint-Denis to the church, someone behind playing sweetly on a flute.

I looked down at the cobbles. I thought of how Mother, Gaston, and I had walked down this very street after the flood so long ago. I remembered picking her up and twirling her laughing in the air. That's how I would imagine her—now and forever.

aint-Germain-en-Laye looked gray in the November drizzle, the river valley misting. No flags or banners were flying and the coaches were draped in black, due to the sudden death of Henriette, the King's brother's wife. The Court's mourning mirrored my own.

I nodded to the two guards stationed in front of Athénaïs's doors. I knew Miguel, but the other one was new.

"Madame de Montespan is not receiving," he told me officiously.

"Mademoiselle des Oeillets is Madame's personal attendant," Miguel informed him, ushering me into the antechamber. "We're taking precautions," he explained with a meaningful look.

I found Athénaïs sprawled on her bed, a heap of soiled linens on the floor. "I've just had a bouillon purgative—the usual humors kicking up, an excess of bile. Don't worry. I won't be bolting for the necessary for at least an hour, but until then I must not move. Shut the door, will you?"

I closed the heavy door, feeling strangely spectral. I was going through the motions, but my heart was elsewhere. Gaston had sobbed when I left. Floridor assured me that he would be fine. He and his wife would be looking after him, for the time being.

"I was sorry to hear about your mother. Monsieur Molière reported that the service was lovely."

"Thank you for allowing me the time to attend her," I said, straightening out the pillows that propped up her knees.

"Just think of all the mud you missed in Flanders. The roads were a nightmare."

Ugly Thing climbed down the brocade curtain and caught hold of the silk-braided rope, swinging. It seemed strange that life just went on, and on.

"Come here, silly monkey." Athénaïs made a clucking sound and patted the covers. "Pour me some wine, but test it for me first. I suppose you heard?"

I nodded. Madame Henriette had been young, gay, and vibrant when last I'd seen her . . . and now she was dead. "I know how fond you were of her," I said, sipping the wine and handing Athénaïs the glass. I paused before asking, "Do you think she was actually . . ."

"Poisoned? Of course she was," Athénaïs said, giving a nut to the monkey, but teasing him with it first. "I missed you, Claude—I admit it. I'm relieved to have you back. I couldn't sleep. My hair turned brittle, my nails chipped, and my face looked like a roasted truffle."

I smiled. "I'm sure you looked as gorgeous as always, Madame." Later I would give her a massage.

"And—mort Dieu!—I almost ran out of Voisin's remedies."

"I could have sent you a supply."

"Put something like that in the post? Monsieur la Reynie, His Majesty's beastly Lieutenant General of Police, has his spies open everything now, and that's just the type of thing he's looking for. Fortunately, my brother's wife had some. You're not in your courses, are you?"

I shook my head. What a strange question.

"His Majesty will be arriving soon—"

Of course, at three of the clock: the King ever punctual.

"—and I'm in no condition to receive him. All the milk I've been drinking—the so-called antidote against poison—has made me ill. I'd like you to stand in for me. *Lie* in," she added with a charmed laugh.

I inclined my head to one side. There had been times, of late, when my hearing had not been good.

"Oh, *you* know." She made a crude gesture. "He never takes long."

Ah, a jest. I slapped my thigh, feigning to make merry.

"Darling, you've been away from Court too long. You're acting like a rustic. I'm serious. The King must never leave my rooms wanting. You should have seen them in the provinces—the painted hopefuls practically lined up to be of service. There are too many beauties now at Court simply aching to oblige His Majesty, too many fathers pushing their daughters into his path. Which is why it's crucial that *all* relief"—she arched her painted brows—"come through me. I know I can trust you."

Trust me to have intimate congress with *her* lover? "Madame, seriously, I'm . . . I wouldn't know—"

"Are you chaste?" Athénaïs frowned. "At your age? You worked in the theater."

"My mother was strict." And actresses are not whores! I blinked back the tears that always seemed close.

"Well, all the better then. His Majesty will be delighted."

I turned away to hide the dismay—the confusion—I felt.

"What is it then? Are you unclean?"

Diseased, she meant. "Of course not," I said, offended.

"I do not offer this opportunity lightly," she said, impatiently now. "Consider how many people I employ . . . Almost one hundred? Including *you,* need I point out? All to be lost over your maidenhead? I thought you were more practical."

Ever-practical Claude. Claude who looked after others, cleaned up the messes. Claude who could not afford to be without employment—especially not now with Gaston to think of, Mother's debts.

I wiped my damp palms on my skirt. So: oui, of course, I would do it, have congress with His Majesty, offer relief. How hard could that be? He was well appointed and appareled. But more, he was an honnête homme—honest, decent, mannered, a true gentleman. I appraised the state of my chemise, trying to remember when I'd last bathed. Thinking of my great height, small breasts, my big feet.

"Just make him think you love him," I heard Athénaïs say. "That's all it takes to win His Majesty's heart," she added with a revealing hint of bitterness. "You're an actress: you can do that, surely?" She downed the last of her wine and held the glass up for more. "I'll tell you a secret: His Majesty is a passionate man, but the regal scepter sometimes fails. I've found that a bit of scolding helps. And, of course, there is our trusty *enhancer,* Madame Voisin's amatory assistant. With it, you'll have nothing to worry about."

,   .   .

AT THREE OF the clock, as church bells sounded mid-afternoon prayer, the King was announced, accompanied by a valet. *Xavier.*

I curtsied and took my usual position by the door.

"My condolences on your loss," Xavier said, once we were alone.

"That is kind of you to say." He'd always been someone I could talk to—but not this time. Not now. I'd never been in a man's embrace. I knew it would hurt, and I feared I would in some way fail.

"Perhaps I've not mentioned this to you before, but I was an ardent admirer of your mother."

"I didn't know," I said, moved. He had such nice eyes—smiling eyes, Mother would have said. *Would have.* I put my hand to my heart. How was it possible that I would never see her again?

I heard Athénaïs's voice, the King's low murmur. She was no doubt explaining the arrangement. Were kings accustomed to such things? "Excuse me, Monsieur Breton, but you should know that there has been a change of plans." It pained me to say, yet he had to know. "His Majesty will soon return—" My mouth was dry. I bit my tongue— a player's trick. "And he's to go in there." I indicated a door to a chamber. "Where I will be—" Waiting.

Xavier looked at me, perplexed. "His Majesty is to . . . with . . . ?"

I nodded, unable to meet his eyes.

A SMALL BED took up most of the room. Embers glowed in a corner fireplace. A glass of wine had been set on a tray, along with a salt spoon and the vial: Madame Catherine's "amatory assistant." Athénaïs must have arranged everything earlier, I realized, must have commanded a maid to prepare the room, set out the wine in anticipation of my return. I pulled back the heavy bed-curtains: the bed had been made up. Just to be sure, I pulled back the covers to check for evidence of mice.

I could hear the King talking with Xavier. I pulled my bodice ties, gradually easing them loose and wriggling free. I untied my skirts, letting them drop. Fortunately, I was wearing my best chemise. Fortunately, it wasn't stained. I shook the pins out of my hair and released my long braids, running my fingers through my hair, which fell to below my waist unbound, like that of a virgin bride. My feet might be big and my bosom small, but I was vain about my chestnut hair.

His Majesty entered as I was adding another log to the fire. "Mademoiselle." He closed the door behind him.

I stood awkwardly and curtsied. "At your service, Your Majesty," I said, testing the wine for poison and then offering it to him. He did not have his boots on. We were almost equal in height.

He regarded me ... with resignation, I feared. My heart sank. Now what? I smiled coquettishly—that look known to all players: a glancing up, then away, the head lowered, that edge-of-a-precipice trembling smile.

But he hardly noticed. He was having trouble untying the red bow at his neck. "It sometimes knots," he said as I helped him out of his shirt and breeches (which unfortunately reminded me of all the times I had helped Gaston disrobe).

His Majesty stood before me then: a man in clocked silk stockings. He was well proportioned, muscled, yet of modest parts—as the gossipers had long claimed. He was not in a manly state.

"Would His Majesty prefer I snuff the candles?"

"Don't, please. Thank you."

I didn't know what to do, so I took his hand and pressed it to my breast.

I HAD EXPECTED to be ravished, a virgin sacrifice. Rather, panicked at the thought of failure—as much for the sake of my pride as the loss of my employment—I was the one to persuade His Majesty.

After the business was done, he sat up. "Are you well?" he asked. I felt his hand heavy on my hip.

I opened my eyes, half expecting to see an entirely different world. I had been cut, as it was said. "Oui, Your Majesty." It had happened quickly.

The King stood and stretched, traces of blood at his root. "Merci, Mademoiselle," he said, gathering up his clothes. He still sounded so formal.

"Let me do that, Your Majesty," I said, and then realized that I shouldn't; I was bleeding.

"Merci," he repeated. "Xavier will help me." And then he was gone.

An animal of some sort was rustling behind the wall: a rat likely. I could hear Xavier's soft voice, the King's. I heard the King say, "I've a meeting with Louvois shortly."

And then there was silence.

I sat up. There, on the gold-plated tray next to the bed, he'd left a jewel—a domed ring of silver and gold with a large amethyst set into it.

I am a whore, I thought, slipping it onto my middle finger, wondering how much I could get for it. *Forgive me, Maman.*

CHAPTER 47

January 2, 1671
Theater of the Bourgogne, Paris

Dear Claudette,
    *You will be pleased to know that the King has increased the annual
pension to the Bourgogne. I suspect you may have had some influence
in this matter, and for this we thank you profusely.*
    *I wish I could be the bearer of only good news. It pains me to inform
you that dear Gaston disappeared yesterday afternoon. My wife and I
were taken up with New Year's Day visits, and then she noticed him
missing. Fortunately, we managed to find him—but with a warden
of the peace! Apparently he had "stolen" a glove—for one of his line
projects, no doubt. He's back with us, shaken and confused, but I don't
think it would be wise for him to live with us much longer. We love
him dearly, but what control do we have? We're in and out of the theater day and night, and if he does this again, it's doubtful that a warden
would let him go so easily.*
    My wife tells me that there is a house for fools in the Marais.
Yours always,
Monsieur Josias de Floridor

ATHÉNAÏS WAS IN her withdrawing chamber, reading her prayer
book by the light of the window. I hesitated. A maid is never to burden her employer with her problems. "Forgive me for disturbing you,
Madame, but—"

"Damnation!"

I turned to see the parrot on its perch.

"Silence, Jolie!" Athénaïs said, closing the breviary.

"Silence Jolie silence Jolie silence Jolie."

Athénaïs threw the beastly bird a cross look. "Cover him, darling, would you?"

I enticed the parrot onto my hand and into his cage, then threw the cover over him. If only life could be so easily managed.

"You're red, my dear," she said, stretching and yawning.

"I . . . I have a problem," I blurted out. "I need to bring my brother back here."

Athénaïs looked up from examining a fingernail. "Here at Court?" she asked with a frown.

"He could stay in my room. He's—" Gentle, no trouble at all! "He could help in the kitchens, fetch wood and water. He wouldn't cost you a sou."

"Claudette—" Athénaïs reached out to softly caress my arm. "Of course you know that's not possible."

I lowered my eyes. Of course. Simples were not welcomed in the realm of the blessed.

TWO DAYS LATER, a second message arrived from Floridor. *Come immediately.*

Roused by my shuddering sobs, Athénaïs looked in from her dressing room, her hair in a turban. She was giving an entertainment that evening in honor of a friend's engagement. It was to be one of her usual sumptuous affairs, with musical entertainment as well as performing dancers and even poets. She counted on me to manage it all, make sure everything went smoothly. "Madame, I'm sorry—I know this is . . ." I took a breath and pressed on. "It's about my brother again." I handed her the letter.

"The idiot?"

"He's . . . in jail!"

She squinted to make out Floridor's writing. "Which one?"

"It doesn't say." There were so many: Saint-Lazare, Vincennes, Conciergerie, Hôtel de Ville. I'd heard of their torture chambers.

"He wouldn't be in the Bastille."

No, certainly not—the Bastille was for political and religious prisoners, young noblemen whose families wanted them brought in line. Gaston would not be in such luxurious accommodations. Gaston would be in a cold cell, crowded with men and rats. I felt faint, my breath coming in gasps. Every time I imagined what he must be going through—his confusion and terror—I started to break down, my panicked thoughts racing. Even charity schools terrorized him! At the ring of a bell all the boys had to put their hands on their knees, then on the table, then clean their slate with saliva and hold it up for inspection. Gaston had failed at every step and had been punished brutally for it. I couldn't bear to imagine the torments he might now be enduring.

"Claude, where are the salts?"

"I'm well, Madame. I'm just . . . frightened," I said, leaning against the wall. I thought of the pillories, gallows, and scaffolds I'd seen in public squares. An execution always drew out a crowd. I'd seen a man drawn and quartered in Blois. Even with his arms and legs torn from him, he lived. "I have to go." My hand on the door.

"Wait." Athénaïs rang a bell and a footman appeared. "Ready my fastest coach," she commanded.

"Thank you, Madame," I breathed. *Thank you.*

"MERCI DIEU," FLORIDOR exclaimed. "I was just going to go out. I think he's in the Hôpital Général. But it's not really a hospital, it's a prison . . ." He paused, running his hand over his eyes. "For lunatics. It's run by the Company."

Ay me. "What did he do?"

Floridor threw out his arms. "Like before: he took something, but this time it was a nobleman's cane, left on a park bench apparently." He shook his head. "That poor boy."

The Hôpital Général was at a distance, so we took a riverboat. Coming into view, it looked like an enormous domed château. It took us some time to find out which building, which wing, which entry, which door. We were directed into a clerical office.

"We have, you must understand, over six thousand here," the clerk informed us wearily, leafing through stacks of notices, and then leafing through them yet again.

"He doesn't talk well," I told him. "Just a few words. He's a big young man with a long beard. He's gentle, childlike. He has his papers with him at all times." Ever since he could walk.

"Ah," the clerk said, studying a document. "Gaston."

I looked gratefully at Floridor. "He's *here*."

"But we can't let you see him," the clerk said primly.

"Why?" I cried out.

"He committed a crime. There are procedures."

I threw a silver écu on his desk. It bounced and rolled, but he caught it deftly. "My brother is a child in a man's body," I said angrily—*furiously*. "If you don't release him, I will be going directly to Monsieur de Mortemart, the Governor of Paris. And he will put *you* in chains."

Floridor regarded me with surprise.

"On whose authority?" the clerk demanded with an amused scoff, slipping the coin into a leather box.

I showed him my identification certificate, required at every city gate. "I am in the employ of Madame de Montespan—the Governor's daughter." I managed enough regality in my demeanor to convince him of the reality of my threat.

We were taken down into the dungeons. The stench was overpowering, the smell of rot and feces. And then there was a curious echoing hum, an incessant keening from what turned out to be hundreds—and *hundreds*—of rag-covered men lying on soiled straw. I saw their cringing fear of the brutish jailers, the welts on their backs, their limbs. I saw one lying dead.

And, at last, *Gaston,* squatting beside a man in an iron collar. He cried out when he saw us. I raised him up, weeping.

IT TOOK A long time to get my brother out of that hell, and then even longer to get him safely back to Floridor's house on the rue de la Comtesse d'Artois. I'd never seen Gaston so feeble, diminished. "I don't know what to do," I confessed to Floridor, huddling by the fire after I'd finally gotten Gaston to sleep. (Singing, singing . . .)

"In the morning I'll show you the place my wife found in the Marais," he said, and I sadly agreed.

Floridor, Gaston, and I set out at ten of the clock. I had tried to persuade Gaston to stay behind, but he'd wailed like a baby. "You must trust me," I told him sternly, "and do what I say."

It was a modest house, fairly small, at the back of a courtyard. I held Gaston's hand going up to the door. I could hear a boy crying within and I was tempted to turn away, but I owed it to Floridor and his wife to try.

The man in charge hardly looked at Gaston. "Papers?" he demanded. With trepidation, I handed him Gaston's certificate, which had been stamped at the Hôpital Général. "No criminals," he said firmly, closing the door in my face. I admit: I was relieved.

"You must find something. We can't keep on like this," Floridor's wife whispered to me as I took my leave the next day. "Josias would never refuse you, but his health is not good."

BACK IN SAINT-GERMAIN-EN-LAYE, I collapsed, weeping once again in front of Athénaïs. I couldn't help myself! I told her what a gentle soul my brother was, how profoundly I loved him, how puzzling he was—so ignorant and yet so wise—and how nothing I did seemed to help. "He would be perfectly at home in a monastery," I said, "but the Church would never permit it." Even a novice was required to read Latin. "A priest once called him the son of the Devil."

"Under the influence of the Company, no doubt."

No doubt. The Company's "influence" was insidious, a plague.

"*They're* the Devils," Athénaïs said heatedly. "Look how they threatened His Majesty over Molière's *Tartuffe*—"

And practically killed the playwright, so great was his distress.

"—forcing His Majesty to bow to *their* will. They aim to rule, but fortunately they are merely a faction, although a faction fueled by passionate hate and righteous conviction. There is nothing of Christianity in it," she said, sitting down at her escritoire. She wrote a short note, sprinkled it with sand and handed it to me. "Saint Francis is a small monastery I help support in Paris. They are decidedly not of the Company, I assure you. They will take your brother in."

I fell to my knees and kissed the hem of her gown.

"Claudette, really!" She laughed.

GASTON WAS UNSURE, I could tell. Too many people professing to help had hurt him.

"We'll stay the night, the two of us together," I promised as the gate opened. "In the morning, you can decide."

It was a humble establishment. Chickens pecked at our feet. Gaston giggled at their antics, which I took as a good sign. There were gardens of flowers and vegetables, two cows, a mule, and several horses. A black mutt with a comical face waddled out to greet us.

I rang a bell in the courtyard and a man in a patched robe came out. He greeted us with a dip of his head.

I explained that we wished to see the abbot. He smiled, oui, indicating that he was himself the person to talk to.

Rather taken aback by the "abbot's" humble bearing, I handed him Athénaïs's letter. Come with me, he gestured.

I did not need to stay the night. Gaston, on hearing the choir—on *joining* the choir—felt immediately at home with these gentle men. I lingered for some time and then slipped away uplifted, with a cautious feeling of hope in my heart.

CHAPTER 48

n the years that followed I often thought—with a glowing satisfaction—of Gaston's happiness in that humble little monastery. Crammed into the back of a pet-filled carriage on rocky, muddy roads, or racing over the new wide expanse between Saint-Germain-en-Laye and His Majesty's ever-expanding château at boggy Versaie (back and forth, back and forth), half listening as Athénaïs mused on about Court intrigues, complaining of the King's latest fancy, I would nod, staring out at the passing landscape, thinking of Gaston singing his beautiful heart out. He had found his calling.

But my own life . . . what did it amount to? Ropes of false gems, rabbit-fur wraps, secondhand leather gloves: the stage props of wealth and status.

An illusion?

I was envied, true, in a position of influence, the intimate confidante of the "shadow queen," considered to be the *real* queen of France, in fact. Athénaïs's estranged husband had finally granted her a legal separation and so, with the signing of a simple piece of paper, the world had shifted. No longer required to play the role of official mistress, Louise de la Vallière retired to a convent, leaving Athénaïs the undisputed victor.

The King built Athénaïs a château in Clagny. "It's not even suitable for an actress!" she'd exploded on seeing it. Cowed by her emotional fire rockets, His Majesty had had it torn down and was in the process of building a second, much grander château, one worthy of the queen that she was. The location wasn't far from Versaie—a leisurely half-hour walk, if that—but there was more of a breeze and a want of insects of the biting kind. It would have magnificent gardens, an orangery paved in marble, an extensive gallery—even a moat. With thousands of workers, it seemed to be springing up overnight (as if by magic, people whispered).

Athénaïs was fully in power, without a doubt, yet the higher her station, the more uneasy she became. She sent me more and more often to Paris to pick up beauty remedies, charms, and the essential "amatory assistant" from Madame Catherine. Sometimes she woke in the night screaming from frightening dreams (several times weeping over Alexandre, her beautiful lost love, her beautiful lost life). She ate compulsively . . . and drank. She had violent explosions of temper against the Widow, and even—twice—against the King himself. People began to refer to her as the Tempest, a dangerous and unpredictable force of nature.

I tried my best to soothe—that had always been my role. I massaged her shoulders and feet, made up her hair, and pinked her cheeks. "You're beautiful," I assured her, positioning the candles to throw a flattering light. "You enchant His Majesty with your eyes, your wit, your sensual allure." I worked with tailors and seamstresses to create unusual and arresting ensembles for her. I painted her face to illuminate her bewitchingly luminous eyes. In the theater, I had learned the arts of enchantment, skills Athénaïs made use of.

Skills she had *need* of, for La Vallière had been replaced with an even more threatening opponent: the Church. In the spring of 1675, Père Lécuyer, a priest at Versaie, dared to refuse Athénaïs absolution. I calmed her as best I could. "Talk to His Majesty," I whispered.

But the Church, more and more infused with the ideology of the Company, was not so easily dealt with—even by the King. His Majesty talked the matter over with his spiritual counselors and—repentant and clearly wary—reported back to Athénaïs that the consensus was that Père Lécuyer had only been doing his duty to God.

Athénaïs was overcome with fury, screaming that His Majesty was beneath her, a shopkeeper with bad breath! With a stoic expression, he tipped his hat (ever a gentleman) and left.

The next time, it was brave Xavier who brought the message. His Majesty's confessor, Père La Chaise, insisted that Athénaïs and the King live apart.

"And His Majesty has consented?" she asked coldly, imperiously.

"I'm afraid so."

"Did Louvois have anything to do with this?" she demanded with heat. Ever since she'd publicly shown her support for Colbert, the Minister of Finance, Louvois had been a thorn in her side. Any move she made to advance a cause—especially with respect to her family (and most especially her brother Vivonne)—the devious and chimerical Secretary of State somehow managed to prevent it.

"Perhaps indirectly," Xavier admitted. "Because of the coming war with the Dutch, Louvois has been urging His Majesty that he must prepare his soul to meet death."

"Because Monsieur de Louvois is such a caring individual," Athénaïs said, with clear but misdirected irony. It was true that Louvois cared only for himself and His Majesty, whom he revered with religious intensity.

Xavier wisely chose not to respond. "It's understandable that the King would not want to risk dying unshriven, Madame. He has decided to receive Communion at Whitsuntide."

"As he often does at Easter," she countered.

"Oui, but—" Xavier looked pained. This was not to be a temporary separation, as had been the custom during Lent in years past, he explained. Athénaïs was to move out of her vast, luxurious rooms at Versaie and into her château at Clagny. He paused before adding, somewhat apologetically, "And stay there."

I glanced at Athénaïs, alarmed. The château was not quite finished; there were laborers working there still.

"Furthermore—" Xavier took a deep breath before continuing. Athénaïs and the King were no longer to have contact (no carnal relations, was clearly meant). Nor was she to accompany His Majesty on campaign.

Athénaïs rose up out of her chair. I moved to her side (the better to contain her). "His Majesty received Communion in years past without such drastic measures," she observed with the appearance of calm.

True. Xavier cleared his throat. "His Majesty has been advised that the past practices were insufficient—that this is the only way for him to properly prepare to take the sacraments."

Only the pendulum clock could be heard in the silence that followed. Even the monkey had stilled, even the chattering parrot and snuffling pugs.

"Inform His Majesty that he need not fear," Athénaïs responded evenly—but not without a hint of contempt. "I would not wish to tarnish his eternal soul."

THE NEXT DAY, in a public display of subservience, we moved into Athénaïs's château at Clagny, in spite of the work still going on there. Athénaïs had been "allowed" to hold onto her apartment at Versaie, so the transition was not too rigorous, even with all the animals and birds. It was the stigma that was testing; everyone was watching, everyone whispering that the mighty Athénaïs had been banished.

Three days after Easter Sunday, we heard the boom of cannon. Athénaïs put down her cards. His Majesty was riding to war—without bidding her farewell.

In the months that followed, she put on a brave front. In any case, there was a great deal to do finishing the house and park. The King sent word through his Minister of Finance that he would pay for whatever she requested—and so she spent lavishly. She received visitors, even the Queen. Her sister and several friends came to stay with her. She took the soothing waters at Bourbon and devoted herself to good works.

Yet at night she woke in terror, plagued by a dream that she'd lost all her hair.

Bishop Bossuet—handsome, virile, full of God's grace, and one of the tribe we knew to be her enemy—came with messages from His Majesty. "The day of Pentecost approaches!" he announced with the flare of a tragedian. He led Athénaïs in prayer; she repeated the words after him with tears in her eyes. A great performer at the pulpit, Bishop Bossuet failed to recognize Athénaïs's own skill at illusion. Indeed, I believe she convinced him of her devotion—but as soon as he left, we began to plan her move back to Versaie in anticipation of the King's return.

· · ·

IN THE HEAT of a blooming July day, the King and Court returned from war, the noise and dust and general commotion unendurable. Athénaïs had changed her gown three times, and the ornaments in her hair twice. I'd given her an opium pill and lemon balm for nerves, but it hadn't helped. The Church had agreed that His Majesty could be allowed to call on her at Versaie, but only so long as she was chaperoned by an army of frowning virgins. (A plague of ancients, yet again.)

I prayed that the talisman Athénaïs wore tucked under her skirts would have the desired effect. "Madame Catherine vowed that it would," I assured her. It was a small silver medal—on one side was engraved the goddess Athena, on the other Venus flanked by demons. (A medal forged with human and goat blood, Madame Catherine had informed me. How do you get human blood? I'd asked, but she'd only laughed.)

Athénaïs wept on seeing His Majesty, bowing deeply before him. Even I thought her heart must be in it. His Majesty, his own cheeks glistening, led her immediately to her bedchamber and firmly closed the door against the crowd.

I glanced at Xavier. I was awed (if not a little uneasy, I admit) by her easy victory. Athénaïs clearly had the King entirely under her control.

HIS MAJESTY BECAME, once again, a daily caller. Athénaïs glowed with triumph. The virgin chaperones had been banished and the religious advisers thwarted. Xavier and I stood in attendance outside the closed door of Athénaïs's bedchamber. Louvois, Bishop Bossuet, and all their tribe—which Athénaïs and I now derisively referred to as the Company Faction—had lost the battle, true, but we knew that the war itself was far from over.

Ever vigilant, Athénaïs listened carefully to all that was said—and not said—at her popular salon. I did as well. As a mere attendant (and therefore invisible to the noble guests), I was able to observe. My years of training in the theater—the close study of gesture and voice—equipped me to interpret even the smallest motion: the flutter of an eye revealing a lie, the flick of a tongue across an upper lip indicating desire, the legs-spread stance of domination. I paid special attention to Louvois: his perspiring discomfort, his constant fussing with his wig and ribbons, the way he averted his eyes. "He's hiding something," I reported to Athénaïs.

The next afternoon, Xavier and I were startled by her raised voice, and the King bursting out of her bedchamber in his small linens. Athénaïs followed, waving a parchment in her hand. "You coward!" she exploded. "I *demand* an explanation."

His Majesty turned to face her, hands on his hips and his elbows out.

She shook the paper in his face. (Deus!) "Say something, you miserable creature!"

I rushed to close the windows.

"Calm yourself, woman," the King commanded, his voice low.

"How could my brother not be on this list!" she demanded.

Two maids and a butler appeared; Xavier and I quickly waved them away.

"Louvois made it; it's his list, not mine," the King said as Xavier helped him on with his breeches. "An error, no doubt."

She scoffed. "Then send for him!"

I lowered my eyes; it mortified me to see His Majesty humiliated.

"Now? But the Secretary of State is—"

"*Now!*" Athénaïs turned on her heels, slamming the bedroom door behind her.

I followed after her nonetheless; she had need of me.

It took a moment for my eyes to adjust to the gloom. I saw her slumped over her toilette table, her head on her hands, her shoulders heaving.

"Madame?" I put my hands on her neck, pressing my thumbs into her spine, caressing.

She raised her head and handed me the paper. It was a list of seven men—generals to be named Marshals of France, honored for exceptional achievement in battle. "I found it in His Majesty's leather jerkin."

"I see." Her brother Vivonne's name wasn't on the list, in spite of having distinguished himself in the recent war in Flanders.

"A rather conspicuous omission."

"Perhaps it was simply Louvois's error, as His Majesty said." I wondered if Athénaïs always went through His Majesty's garments.

"Hardly!" she said, wiping her nose. "I will *not* stand for it!"

XAVIER ANNOUNCED THE Secretary of State for War. Louvois was a big man, and if he weren't so pathetic, he'd be scary. He stood at attention in front of Athénaïs and the King, looking uneasy.

The King handed the list to Louvois and cleared his throat. "It's your list of the generals to be honored with a baton." A Marshal of France wore seven stars, and received a star-studded blue baton inscribed, in Latin: *Terror belli, decus pacis.* Terror in war, ornament in peace. "There must be some mistake: Madame de Montespan's brother Vivonne is not included."

Louvois stared at the list and then back up at Athénaïs and the King. He seemed flummoxed. "Forgive me, Your Majesty," he stuttered, "but—"

"But *what,* you ignorant fool!" Athénaïs exploded. Standing beside her, I felt the spray of her spittle.

"I will have your brother put on the list, Madame," Louvois said without looking at her.

"Admit that this was an intentional omission, Monsieur—*on your knees*!"

Louvois turned a violent shade of red. I feared he might have an apoplectic fit.

"Admit it! Admit that you did this to *spite* me! Admit that you are constantly looking for ways to thwart me and my family!"

His Majesty put his hand over hers. "Enough."

"Don't 'enough' me! Open your eyes. This man has evil intent."

But the King wasn't listening. Louvois was his "miracle worker" on the fields of battle—Athénaïs was powerless against him. "That will be all, Louvois," I heard His Majesty say wearily, excusing the Secretary of State before Athénaïs gave full vent to fury.

CHAPTER 49

That winter, I missed my courses for the first time. I attributed this to fatigue—constant nights accompanying Athénaïs to balls, feasts, and entertainments, followed by long hours at the gaming tables. At dawn, I'd often still be up with her, calming the anguish that followed a staggering loss.

It was easy enough to blame my irregularity on exhaustion, but when there was still no sign the second month, I began to wonder. Was it possible? Surely not. I'd just turned thirty-seven. Perhaps it was the change coming on early. Certainly I felt haggish, tired in my bones, weary as a twice-told tale. Maybe it was different for a woman who had never had a child, caused her to age early.

I sent a note to a midwife—a woman the maids talked of—and arranged to meet in her room near the market in Saint-German-en-Laye.

Madame Audouin was young—I took her for a girl. Even so, she spoke with authority: I wasn't going through the change. Au contraire: I was with child. "If you wish it to be otherwise," she offered in response to my look of incredulity, "I can help—but you'd have to act quickly. If you wait, you won't have a choice."

"No, no, thank you," I said, standing. How could it be, after all this time? I'd assumed I was conveniently barren.

"Perhaps you should sit for a moment," Madame Audouin offered soothingly.

"I'm fine," I said, giving her a coin and stepping into the chill wind.

. . .

A THOUSAND TIMES I resolved to "fix it" . . . and a thousand times I changed my mind. It was a miracle, surely, I thought, sitting through the church Jubilee celebrations, the once-every-half-century year in which all sins were forgiven. I marveled at my fullness, my aching breasts. Was *this* not forgiven? Even my profound fatigue now seemed a blessing.

As the world around me became loud and boisterous, preparing for yet another war, I grew quiet: I had a secret.

"You're mysterious these days," the King's valet Xavier said, "glowing. You must be in love." He said this with a brave tone.

I play-punched his shoulder. Yet he was right: I was. In love with the child growing within me.

PACKING FOR THE Court's voyage north (following, ever following the King's unrelenting battles with the Dutch)—I wrenched my back and had to spend a week in bed, fending off Athénaïs's doctor. I dared not let him near lest he perceive my condition.

Lying in my little bed, feeling the delicate flutter in my belly, listening to Athénaïs screaming at the maids, the page boys, her chefs, I tried to think of ways I might get out of my predicament. I dreaded telling her—yet I knew I must. Once Lent was over, she would begin drinking again.

But telling Athénaïs during Lent proved difficult. She was preoccupied with preparations for the voyage, subjected to the habitual enemas and bleedings recommended before travel. She was often in turmoil, and I knew it would be unwise to bring up anything troubling at such a time.

Yet I couldn't put it off. "Madame, I have something to tell you," I finally announced as we returned from Easter Mass.

"About Brinvilliers?"

"No," I said, taken aback. Daily, Athénaïs had been sending me to the market for the latest sordid detail regarding Madame de Brinvilliers's confessions to sodomy, incest, and murder. Athénaïs had become obsessed with the story of this Parisian noblewoman—"*new* nobility" it was always noted (as if that explained the woman's perversion)—the daughter of an administrator who had married into the Gobelins tapestry family, Madame de Brinvilliers had confessed in lurid detail to poisoning her father, her brother, her lover, and countless others, and to perfecting her deadly art as a volunteer at a charity hospital.

"No, it's nothing to do with the poisoner," I said, surveying the room, checking to make sure that the fire irons were well out of reach. "I'm afraid I'm not going to be able to go north with you."

"How is that!"

"I'm with child," I said bravely.

"You jest." She sounded more amused than angry.

I pulled my skirts around my hips, revealing my little belly.

"There are things one can do to fix it."

"I saw a midwife. She said it was too late." A half-truth.

"This is frightfully inconvenient," she said, rubbing the back of her neck. "Do you know who the father is?"

"I've only ever had congress with His Majesty!"

"Ah, my virtuous suivante." She rolled her head from side to side. "Damnation." She sighed as I stepped in to massage her shoulders.

"Damnation," Jolie echoed.

"Well ... His Majesty's valet will take care of everything. He'll find a home for it."

It. "What about His Majesty?" Shouldn't he know?

"Goodness, Claude, we must not burden him with such a matter."

"Of course not, Madame," I said, gently easing the tension I could feel in her muscles. *I'm sorry,* I started to say—but didn't.

THAT EVENING, XAVIER arrived to speak with me. "I've been informed of your condition. It will be placed with a family in the country."

It again.

He paused, swallowed, his Adam's apple bobbing. "I am required to inform you that His Majesty will never recognize it, nor in fact even be informed of it. Paternity cannot be proved."

I understood that Xavier was only doing his job, but even so, I was offended. "I don't expect anything from His Majesty. Only tell me, will the baby be placed ... not too far away?" My tone struck me as pathetically beseeching. Being with child had unnerved me, rendered me unexpectedly emotional.

"It is best you not have anything to do with it," Xavier said, yet with tenderness. "I'm sorry, Claudette," he said, reaching out to touch my shoulder.

I stepped back, away.

ATHÉNAÏS, THE KING, and all the Court set out, the long train of carriages and wagons and cavalry disappearing in a cloud of dust. I collapsed amid the wreckage of departure: the gowns and shawls not taken, the abandoned fans, skirts, bodices. But for the six girls who did the dusting, three kitchen staff, five gardeners, and the guard permanently stationed at the entry, I was alone. Even Gaston thought I'd gone north with the Court. I was invisible.

ON THE DAY of the Marquise de Brinvilliers's gruesome execution, I gave birth to a strapping big girl.

My little one, I cooed, which made the midwife laugh.

"That's no 'little one.' It took two swaddling cloths just to bind her," Madame Audouin said, handing me the red-faced wailing infant, tightly ensconced in linen.

"Sweet pea," I said, overwhelmed with an emotion that I knew beyond a doubt was love.

For a full month, I reveled in the luxury of being a mother, nursing my beautiful baby, waking with her in the bed beside me, sniffing and petting her. Singing to her.

I knew it was not to last. On a sultry July day, I heard the rumble of wagons, the carts loaded with regal furnishings, the beds, curtains, and kitchen implements sent on in advance of the Court's arrival. My life in seclusion was over.

Xavier arrived almost immediately. I had been scanning the horizon, listening for a horse. But of course he would not come on horseback, I realized, when a carriage came into view. He would come with a wet-nurse awaiting and a hamper of swaddle bands, petticoats, and double-cloths. I had been through this many times already, only now the inconvenient infant being rushed into seclusion was not one of Athénaïs's bastard babies—it was my own beloved Sweet Pea.

Xavier saluted and then bowed, sweeping his hat. "Mademoiselle des Oeillets."

"Monsieur Breton." He was thinner—months of riding on campaign had hardened him. He had a patch over one ear. "You're wounded?"

"Just a cut."

"Were you in battle?"

"Not so heroic. I fell setting up camp near Ninove."

I covered my smile with my hand.

"You look . . . beautiful," he said, as if surprised.

"How kind of you to say." I made the clown face that had always made him laugh.

But he didn't laugh, not this time. "You know why I'm here," he said gravely.

I led him into the withdrawing room where the traveling basket had been set. "She sleeps well," I whispered. "She won't be hungry for about two hours." I had nursed her shamelessly, like a peasant mother. "You have a good wet-nurse?" My feelings were betrayed by my voice, which grew tremulous.

"Certainly," Xavier said in hushed tones, but I didn't think it likely that he knew a good wet-nurse from a bad one. "Madame Colbert recommended her," he added, sensing my doubt.

"Ah," I said, relieved. The Minister of Finance's wife had a number of children. She would know. I cleared my throat. "Where is my baby to be taken?"

"I'm not to say," he admitted gently.

I felt my heart break.

"I'm sorry, Claude."

"Just go!"

"They're good people, caretakers of a château," he whispered, picking up the basket. He turned at the door. "In Suisnes," he added softly.

I stood frozen, listening to the door close, the muffled sound of voices, a carriage door, wheels rolling, horse hooves on the gravel. My knees gave way.

CHAPTER 50

thénaïs returned from the voyage north in the early stages of yet another pregnancy, up-throwing constantly.

"Darling, I'm ill today—too ill."

I heard her words with dread. The King was expected shortly. "Madame, forgive me, but I . . . I can't. My courses . . ." I put my hands over my belly. "They started this morning and they're heavy." The truth was that I didn't want to be of service anymore—not in that way. I didn't want to be used, even by a king.

"There are other ways to give relief," Athénaïs reminded me archly. She'd become vigilant with respect to His Majesty, displaying her charms artfully (if artificially), using all the magical talismans and potions she could buy. She had lost the bloom of youth and there were always women circling—young, voluptuous women whom the King regarded with the growing interest of an aging man. "You owe me as much."

That afternoon, I put drops into the King's wineglass, as usual. On impulse, I put a salt spoon of the "amatory assistant" into my own glass as well, and downed it in one go.

I placed the King's glass on the gold-plated tray and went into the closet, where His Majesty was waiting. Wigless and bootless, he sat perched on the edge of the bed. His legs, which had always been his best feature, had become even more muscled on campaign.

I set down the tray. I knew the routine well by now, but the drops had started a frenzied buzzing in my body. I felt my throat constricting and that alarmed me. I took the obligatory sample of the King's laced wine, then presented it to him, my head bowed—as if it were sacrificial holy water.

I am sacrificial, I thought as I sank to my knees before him.

WHENEVER I SAW Xavier accompanying His Majesty, my spirits lightened. As we stood side by side in attendance, as Athénaïs and His Majesty coupled, I plied him for news of my little girl. At first he was reluctant to say anything, but over time he weakened. It was his job to check, and in any case, he liked to talk of her. Sweet Pea had grown, she was sitting up, she had a charming smile. She'd cut her first tooth and was miserable, she was trying to stand, she could say a few words.

I lived for these scraps of news! "How often do you go to see her?"

"About once a month."

"How do you get there?" Suisnes, I'd found out, was not far on horseback, but in a carriage the journey would likely take days. One would have to first go into Paris and then take a coach south—but which road?

"I ride," he said evasively.

"The road to Brie-Comte-Robert is said to be fraught with bandits."

"Not really," he said, giving me the answer I sought.

THAT EVENING, I accompanied Athénaïs to a ball. "There she is," she hissed behind her fan as a young woman stepped into the room: Angélique, the girl the King was currently besotted with (in spite of the rumor we helped circulate that she had a contagious skin condition).

The room silenced, and everyone bowed low at her approach.

Zounds! They believed *her* to be the King's chosen?

Athénaïs wept that evening, back in the privacy of her chamber. "What in God's name can I do?"

"I have a number of things to get in Paris, and I'll be dropping by Madame Voisin's," I offered. "Why don't you write her a note, ask her for something . . . *stronger?*"

.   .   .

IT WAS A long trip to the Château de Suisnes, even in a hired coach. The driver got lost three times. Certainly, it would have been easier on horseback—or even on a mule—so it was with some relief when I finally arrived at a charming striped-stone château with peaked roofs and big arched windows overlooking a lush garden. Smoke—the only sign of life—curled up from one of its chimneys.

I heard a bark, and a man, a caretaker or gardener by his dress, rounded the corner with a bearlike dog on a rope, its tongue hanging down in the heat.

Monsieur de Maisonblanche, he introduced himself, a round little man with elf-like eyes and an enormous moustache.

"I'm sorry to have come so unexpectedly." I wasn't sure how to explain. "Is your wife in?" Perhaps it would be easier talking to a woman. "I'm Mademoiselle Claude des Oeillets," I confessed, unsure how that might be received.

Monsieur de Maisonblanche looked at me, startled, twirling one of the points of his mustache. "The girl's birth-mother," he said, his voice apprehensive.

"I've only come to visit. I'll be leaving well before dusk."

"That will never do."

"Pardon?" Was I not to even see my baby?

"You'll have to stay the night . . . Come, let me get your bag. I'll show you to Madame. You must be thirsty in this heat. Ah, the babe—wait till you see her. She's the light of our hearts."

"I'LL BE." Madame de Maisonblanche grinned, standing up in a row of turnips and wiping her hands on her apron. "Pardon my rags. We're not too fancy here when the owner is away. But then he's always away. You can call me Gaby."

I had worried I would be jealous of this woman, but I loved her immediately. "It's beautiful here," I said. A verdant meadow sloped down to a river.

"The baby is having her afternoon sleep," Gaby said.

I was ushered down into the lower level of the château—the

kitchen and service quarters—where Monsieur was building a fire. Doors onto the garden let in a flood of light. A bouquet of summer flowers graced a plank table.

"I thought we could have tea," Monsieur said.

"And maybe some cakes?" his wife added.

"Mais oui, cakes! Have a seat, have a seat," he said, jumping up to pull out a wooden chair.

I startled at a child's cry.

"Oh, there she is, right on the hour," Gaby exclaimed, disappearing down a passageway.

"She'll quiet with some nursing," Monsieur said, offering me a little cake of currants and raisins dusted with sugar. "We lost our own boy—maybe you don't know?—just before the Lord sent us your little one. Saved my wife from a bottomless sorrow. I'm afraid we're spoiling her some."

Gaby returned with the baby on one teat. "Look at her, so big," she said proudly, pulling the baby off and holding her up for me to see.

"That's good milk," Monsieur said proudly.

I smiled, aglow from tip to toe. The baby—*my* baby—had round cheeks and bright eyes. She had the King's nose and Mother's red hair.

Then she opened her mouth and wailed.

And Father's booming player's voice, I thought with a teary grin.

"Oh, that's enough of *that,*" Gaby said, clamping the baby back onto her breast.

LOUISE DE MAISONBLANCHE, she'd been christened. I watched, enchanted, as she slowly picked a crust out of her bowl and gummed it.

"Sometimes I can get her to use a spoon," Gaby said. "Here, sweet thing."

"I used to call her Sweet Pea," I said, watching in wonder as she latched onto the spoon and waved it around.

"I like that," Gaby said.

The baby banged the spoon on the tray with gusto.

"Now don't do *that,* Sweet Pea," Gaby said as the spoon fell clattering onto the floor.

Sweet Pea looked at her empty hand and then up at Gaby. She opened and closed her hand: bye-bye.

Ah, we two women sighed, making bye-bye motions like little fools. Sweet Pea chortled and did it again, enchanted with her audience.

I STAYED AWAKE late that night, staring at the stars through a narrow open window, staring at the crescent moon. I pulled the patched woolen blanket up over my shoulders. The coarse linens smelled of woodsmoke and the pillow smelled of duck. In the distance, I could hear wolves howling, one calling, another answering.

Like the evenings of my youth, I thought, falling into a deep, healing sleep.

IN THE MORNING, Monsieur de Maisonblanche offered to take me into the village to get the mail coach to Paris. My heart aching, I kissed my baby good-bye and climbed aboard the wagon with the basket of provisions Gaby had packed for me. I dared not look back for fear of weeping. I had chores to attend to in Paris, I reminded myself: purchases to make, Madame Catherine to see—Gaston to see.

"I have to go into town anyway," Monsieur de Maisonblanche said, clucking the horses. "Your beau will be coming in a week and we always like to have some beer on hand for him."

"My beau?"

"That stout fellow—rides a black mare with a white blaze."

"He's not my beau," I said, my cheeks burning. Monsieur de Maisonblanche thought Xavier was Sweet Pea's father!

Monsieur twiddled his moustache with a puzzled expression. "Are you sure?"

I laughed, nodding.

"Well, I'll be. The wife and I had him pegged: he carries on with the baby, just as if . . . just as if he were . . . you know." He blushed in consternation. "Well, it's none of my business, as the wife would say. You're a fine woman and that's good enough by us."

"Monsieur de Maisonblanche . . . If you don't mind my asking, is everything looked after? Are all your expenses covered? With respect to the baby, that is."

"Mais oui—Monsieur-*not*-your-beau makes sure that everything is paid for." He pulled the wagon into a lot by the main square. "And if he's not your beau, Mademoiselle, he sure as sunshine is a very good friend."

CHAPTER 51

t was nightfall by the time I arrived in Paris. The swans the King had recently installed on the Seine were sleeping, some standing on one foot at the water's edge, others floating like clouds on the water, their beaks tucked back under a wing.

I sat in my attic room staring into space, slowly eating one of the toothsome cakes Gaby had packed for me. Thinking of my baby, so healthy and lovingly tended.

I fell into a reverie, imagining living in that charming château with Monsieur de Maisonblanche and Gaby, working in the gardens together—raising Sweet Pea. A simple life, enriched by love.

THE RECEPTION ROOM at Gaston's humble monastery was scented with incense. A door opened and Gaston emerged, standing before me in hemp sandals, his long beard now almost reaching to his waist. He smiled to see me dressed as a man, in travesty.

"It's for travel," I lied. Later I would be going to pick up a parcel from Madame Catherine. "You've put on weight."

"You," he teased. "Too."

"I have a baby!" It was out before I could stop myself. "A little girl." I hadn't planned to tell him. I didn't know what he would think or how I would explain. "She's with foster parents in the country."

"Uncle?" he said at last, pointing at himself.

I nodded.

He did his happy dance, which made me laugh with joy.

"You are well? You look well." He had started as a novice and was now a choir monk. "The abbot wrote that you had something you wanted to show me."

He took my hand and led me through a series of schoolrooms, the public areas of the monastery. Boys of all ages sat at long tables, at work on hornbooks. They whispered amongst themselves, regarding us with curiosity. A few waved to Gaston as we passed. He was clearly well liked, which made me proud.

We came to a room lined with bunks. I noticed a signature line of a Gaston "project" near the door: a quill, a stone, a wilted flower.

He pointed to his chest. "Build," he stuttered, one hand on a bunk.

You? I dissembled my surprise: Gaston was hopeless at construction. I wondered if the bunks were for students. Some were small, others bigger.

"With." He glanced into the inner courtyard. "F-f-friend," he stuttered.

A tall young man in a tunic approached. "Mademoiselle des Oeillets," he said, bowing, nonplussed by my costume, my breeches and boots.

The birthmark on his cheek formed a perfect heart. Even so, it took me a moment to place him.

"Oui, I am Pilon," he said. "You remember? We met near a cave years ago—not far from Poitiers. Your family was camped there."

"You were leading a pack of boys," I said, breathless with the recollection. A lifetime ago! "Winter Swallows, and—"

"And you fed us." He had shy, bright eyes. "We meet yet again, but in more favorable circumstances."

Indeed! And then another thought, even more startling, came to me. "Are you the boy who saved Gaston during the flood, years back?"

"Friend." Gaston nodded, without stuttering this time.

"And now you are a novice here?" Life had so many surprises.

"Not yet. I am a postulant." Pilon spoke with an accent, but his French was excellent. Clearly, he'd been schooled. "They caught me thieving, but took me in anyway—thanks to Gaston." He cast a glance at my brother. "Does she know?"

Gaston made a rabbit nose ("non").

"Please, have a seat," Pilon said with the air of a gentleman, pulling out a stool. "We're excited to tell you about our plan."

The two young men sat opposite each other on bunks as Pilon explained: they would go out into the streets next winter, gather up Winter Swallows, the ones sorely used—offering them food, schooling, shelter . . . protection from the fleshmongers. Protection from the Bird Catcher.

"Live. Here," Gaston said slowly, proudly.

"With the help of the brothers, we'll educate them, set them up in a proper trade," Pilon went on. "Give them an opportunity to have another sort of life."

Their excitement was contagious. "This is wonderful," I said, greatly moved.

But, of course, it was going to cost. The fleshmongers would have to be paid off, the boys clothed and fed. "I will see what I can do."

he bells were ringing for midday prayer when I emerged from the monastery. There were heavy clouds to the south, but Madame Catherine's village of Villeneuve Beauregard wasn't impossibly far. I decided to walk. Dressed in travesty made me more secure, but even so I kept my eyes down and my stride purposeful as I crossed the rubble of the old fortifications near the Cour des Miracles, a hovel that housed the city's beggars and thieves.

By the time I got to the squat little church of Notre-Dame de Bonne Nouvelle, it had started to rain. I secured my moustache and turned onto the muddy road.

The door to Madame Catherine's house was ajar. It was no longer the humble plank door of years past. I lifted and dropped the heavy brass knocker three times, waiting for a response.

A roll of growling thunder was followed by a clap of lightning and a gush of blowing rain. I stepped inside to escape the storm. "Madame Catherine?" I called out. The small parlor smelled of gingerbread baking, which made me realize how hungry I was. I hadn't eaten since early morning.

I stood in the cluttered salon, dripping onto the floor. Was anybody even home? I felt in the cuff of my coat for the note, Athénaïs's request for something "stronger."

A sleepy yellow dog ambled into the room. Noël. I had befriended him on my many trips. He wagged his way over to me, pushing his wet nose into my hand. I took off my glove and stroked his head. The wind whistled and rattled the panes of the little window facing the street. It had blown up into quite a storm. "Madame?" I called out again.

"Marie Marguerite?" Madame Catherine appeared, holding a candle.

"Monsieur de Leu," I said, using the false name I always went by.

"Good Lord." Madame Catherine made her way through the boxes and crates, the books stacked everywhere. "Noël, what kind of watchdog are you?" she said, pulling the old dog's ears.

"Forgive me. The door was open." Madame Catherine had grown round as a biscuit, clearly well fed. As well, she'd taken to adorning herself with glittering gewgaws—of real gems, it appeared. I wondered how she could afford them.

"I'm expecting my daughter back from the market," she said, her left eye twitching.

"I knocked, but . . ."

"Acht. I didn't hear a thing. My old mother is in the kitchen, complaining of her joints. I give her remedies, but she doesn't use them properly and then she goes on and on." She went to the door and peered out. "Marie Marguerite should have been back long ago. She's going to catch her death in this storm. The girl has no sense."

I had only seen Madame Catherine's daughter twice before. Hardly sixteen, if that, lightsome but womanly for her age. She struck me as wily, in the manner of a fox. She would worry any mother.

"May God Almighty look over her," Madame Catherine said, signing herself. "Someone's going to have to. Would you care for a bit of gingerbread?" The dog yelped and Madame Catherine chuckled. "I know *you* would, you beast."

Hungry and chilled, I rashly accepted the offer, following the enchantress through the cluttered rooms into a warm kitchen. Everywhere I looked there were framed images of saints and crosses hung with rosaries as well as other, more mysterious and somewhat frightening images, one of snakes writhing, another a diagram showing parts of a female corpse. I followed her past an open plank door. Inside I glimpsed a room set up with copper vats and fat glass bottles with tubes running out of them. There was a smell of something burning, something noxious.

Was Madame Catherine practicing alchemy? The thought made me uneasy. Her lust for riches was more and more apparent.

In the kitchen, a crow jumped about in a wicker cage hanging from a meat hook. Madame Catherine introduced me to her mother, a nodding crone in the corner.

"I'm having an open house tomorrow, so we're busy," Madame Catherine said. A maid was stirring a cauldron on the open hearth. "It's rain or shine, so do come. I get the highest society—duchesses and marquises, even the occasional duke. Have some ale?"

There were three jugs on the table. "Thank you, mais non—I can't be long." I suspected she and her mother had both been imbibing. "I'm leaving Paris soon," I said, accepting a square of warm gingerbread slathered with creamed butter.

"Whereabouts do you live?" Madame Catherine asked.

She seemed cheery enough, as always—but there was something calculating and frantic about her now, her face contorting in a false grimace.

"Let me guess," her mother said, placing her palms on the table and closing her eyes.

Madame Catherine rolled her eyes. I noticed that she was using thick face paint: that was different, as well. "My mother knows everything there is to know about chiromancy and physiognomy, but a clairvoyant she's not," she said, disapproving.

"Wait. It's coming to me. Saint-Germain-en-Laye." The old woman looked over at me, pleased. "Or maybe around Versaie?"

"I'm afraid not." I began to perspire. I wasn't sure my disguise could hold up in a room of seers. "I'm from Meudon."

"Then you must know Madame de Verrue—or rather, the *Widow* Verrue," Madame Catherine added, taking the wood spoon from the maid and stirring the pot simmering on the fire. "She was married to the blacksmith, a bawdish man. He's worms' meat now, praise the mighty Lord." She glanced at her mother with what seemed a proudful glint. "His *depart* came as a great relief to the wife," she said, winking at me.

I was saved from answering by the sound of the front door slamming. "That had better be Marie Marguerite," Madame Catherine said, wiping her hands on her apron.

The girl appeared in the door, dripping wet and carrying a covered basket. "I hate these things," she said, dropping the basket onto the floor. The lid flew off to reveal a swarming mass of what looked like beetles.

I stepped back, repulsed.

"How many times do I have to tell you not to alarm them!" Madame Catherine clamped the basket lid back on. "It sets them off," she said, fastening the latch.

An acrid stench had filled the air. Blister beetles?

"They set *me* off," the girl said sullenly.

"What took you so long?" Madame Catherine's voice had a curiously pleading quality.

"Nothing," the girl said, popping her cheek with her thumb. There was something not right about her, something unsettled.

"I must be going, Madame," I said, touching the brim of my hat. It sounded as if the rain had let up. "Thank you for the gingerbread." I felt a little ill, in truth. I wondered what might have been in it.

"Are you sure you don't know Madame de Verrue?" Madame Catherine asked at the door, handing me a parcel of the usual powders and drops. Swiftly—deft as a pickpocket—she disappeared the coins I gave her.

"I keep to myself," I said, pulling the folded paper from the cuff of my coat. I hoped the ink hadn't run in the rain. "This is from my mistress."

Madame Catherine held the paper to the light, squinting. "She needs something stronger?"

"She said to tell you that the situation is desperate."

"Ah, her lover must be wandering."

He most certainly was.

"Tell her I can resolve the situation to her full satisfaction, but it will cost. It requires the services of a priest—"

That was reassuring.

"—but she herself will have to be present," Madame Catherine insisted. "No substitutes."

thénaïs tore open the packets from Madame Catherine and held the vial of drops to her heart. "I'll be needing some this afternoon. What did she say about—?"

"She said she could help, but you'd have to go in person."

Her old pug Popo snuffled at her feet. "But that's impossible," she said, scratching the dog behind his little ears.

"I told her that." It was difficult for Athénaïs to go anywhere undetected. "But she was firm. A priest is required, apparently, for some sort of ceremonial."

She frowned, considering. "Will it banish Angélique? Erase her from the King's thoughts?"

Oui: and all the other Angéliques swarming. "She pledged that it would, but at considerable cost: three hundred louis d'or—for the first ritual, that is. A second or even a third—which she recommended— would cost only a fraction as much."

Athénaïs's jaw dropped. "Did I hear you correctly? Three *hundred*?"

"And it would have to be paid in advance, I'm sorry to say."

"Where on God's earth am I to get such a sum?"

Yet what choice did she have? Her empire was in danger of crumbling. Without the King's favor . . . "Maybe you could tell His Majesty you need the money to cover a gambling loss," I suggested.

"He just covered one for seventy louis d'or." She fell back into the cushions. "Mort Dieu. Three hundred? That's a *lot* of money."

"His Majesty never refuses you, Madame. Imagine the cost were you to lose his favor," I added quietly.

.   .   .

SHORTLY AFTER, I donned my male attire again and returned to Madame Catherine, Athénaïs's gold in a hemp sack. The sorceress took me into a back room to count out the heavy coins. She bit into several and weighed them on a scale to ensure they weren't counterfeit. Her massive ropes of gems jiggled as she moved. "You'd be surprised how easy it is to make false ones," she said.

I thought of the flasks and vials I had glimpsed on my last visit, and wondered if this was a trade she herself indulged in. One didn't buy gems such as she wore from selling love potions and charms. "Have you ever tried?" I asked with an intentionally indifferent expression. On the table behind her was a thick book, covered in leather and embellished with intricately tooled metals. It looked to be a forbidden grimoire, a book of magic spells. I caught my breath. *Gospel of Satan.*

"That's the type of question a constable would ask," Madame Catherine said, pausing in her counting. Her piercing look was both wily and amused.

"Or a crook," I countered with feigned cheer, but a cold sweat came over me.

"Touché!" she exclaimed with surprising cheer. "Three hundred louis d'or," she pronounced, straightening the stacks. "I will send the priest confirmation that your mistress has paid," she said, scratching out directions to where the ritual was to take place.

I paused at the door. "And if it doesn't work, Madame?"

"Believe me," she said, clasping the heavy cross that hung from her neck, "this ritual involves the strongest powers. It never fails."

WE SET OUT well before dawn, Athénaïs disguised as a wealthy merchant's wife, I as her valet, both of us fully masked.

"You make the most charming gentleman, Monsieur," Athénaïs said as I helped her into the coach.

"You've said that before," I said with a smile, recalling that moonlit ride to the marshy field, the morning of the fateful duel. This journey, too, seemed dangerously illicit.

We made uneasy small talk all the way to Paris: the Widow—La *Marquise* de Maintenon now—had taken Athénaïs's eldest boy by the King to a spa in the mountains of Barèges in the hope of curing his feeble leg. He was seven, yet still unable to walk properly. "The Widow acts as if my children are hers," Athénaïs complained.

I agreed that the Widow took herself somewhat too seriously, especially now that His Majesty had rewarded her with a title and a château.

"*I* don't even have that," Athénaïs protested. As magnificent as her château at Clagny was, it didn't, in fact, belong to her, but to the Crown. "And as to a title . . ." She made a rueful grimace. Although officially separated, she and her husband remained married by law. Were His Majesty to give Athénaïs the title of duchess, her husband, by rights, would be a duke—and that, His Majesty simply would not abide.

And then Athénaïs got onto her favorite complaint of late, the inanity of the girl Angélique: beautiful, sixteen, and stupid as a brickbat. Even I was affronted at the way she put on airs, now even pretending to be pregnant by the King by stuffing her gowns with cushions.

"Soon His Majesty won't even glance at her," I told Athénaïs with satisfaction.

Once through the Paris gates, the coach headed out the rue Saint-Denis, past my old neighborhood and into the shanties. We slipped on our masks as the coach rolled to a stop. I handed Athénaïs down, wary of the shoddy surroundings. I was relieved to be greeted by an attendant in an elegantly embroidered justacorps. "Father awaits," he said, leading us into a sunny courtyard bursting with flowers. A gardener looked up from his work, then returned to clearing the ground of weeds.

The attendant ushered us into a small stone chapel lit by only two branches of dripping candles. He whispered instructions to me and left, the door closing behind him.

"Well?" Athénaïs's voice was muffled behind her mask.

I hesitated. What the attendant had told me was shocking. "He said you're to remove your clothes." And stretch out mother-naked on the table in front of the altar. Sacré coeur.

"All of them?"

"Except your mask." It had been a mistake to come. "Are you sure you want to go through with this, Madame?" The sweet scent of ambergris filled the air.

"I've already paid a small fortune," Athénaïs said, irritated, pulling off her gloves. She turned so that I could unlace her.

"Your chemise too, I'm afraid." At least a brazier had been lit and it was warm. I spread Athénaïs's blue velvet cloak over the table and helped her climb up onto it.

She stretched out, pulling the sides of her cloak up over her breasts and pubis. "Maybe I'll have a bit more of that brandy," she said.

"You finished the flask on the way down, Madame." Along with two opium pills, for nerves.

A door creaked open and the valet entered carrying a torch. He was followed by a priest, who smelled of tobacco. He had high coloring and a terrible squint. "Madame, your maid must wait outside," he said.

"She stays," Athénaïs said drowsily.

The priest scowled at me.

"I can be trusted," I said, clasping Athénaïs's hand, which was damp. The room was smoky; my eyes burned.

With resignation, he put a white napkin on Athénaïs's bare belly and set a heavy chalice on it. "You must remain absolutely still," he cautioned, his breath foul.

Had Athénaïs heard? "Madame?"

She nodded sleepily.

"She won't move," I assured him. His eyes rolled grotesquely in different directions.

"*In nomine magni dei nostri Satanas,*" he began. His voice—a curiously beautiful voice—echoed in the stone chamber. "*Introibo ad altare Domini Inferi,*" he intoned, and the valet, standing by the chimney, responded, "*Ad Eum Qui laetificat juventutem meam.*"

This wasn't what I had expected. It was like a Mass, but different.

Domini Inferi. Lord of the Grave.

Nomine Satanas. In the name of Satan.

I understood little Latin, but I knew enough to sense that Satan was being invoked. I clutched the cross at my neck with a trembling hand and glanced at Athénaïs. Was she sleeping? I wanted to wake her, put a stop to this!

The priest uncovered the chalice and raised it. The smoke of burning incense filled the tiny chamber. My throat burned; I coughed. I could hardly see through the thick haze. *"Veni Satanas, Imperator Mundi, ut animabus famulorum . . ."*

"Dominus Inferus vobiscum." Lord of the Grave, be with you.

"Et cum tuo," the valet responded. And with you.

A bell rang three times. A door creaked open and shut.

The priest was now hunched over a bundle on the sideboard. *"In spiritu humilitatis, et in animo contrito suscipiamur a Te, Domine Satanas; et sic fiat sacrificium . . ."*

Sacrificium. In *sacrifice?*

Something gleamed bright in the torchlight. A blade? And then I thought I saw the bundle move, but it was dark, too dark to be sure. A baby's sharp cry startled me, and then—chillingly—there was silence.

Athénaïs did not stir. Had she not heard?

"That's enough," the priest said, and the valet left with the bundle.

I held onto the table to steady myself. What had I witnessed?

"Speak your wish, Madame," the priest instructed Athénaïs, holding the chalice above her.

I touched Athénaïs's shoulder. "Madame?" *Was* she asleep? My mind recoiled from the thoughts that were forming—too horrible to believe.

"Speak your wish," the priest repeated, a little impatiently.

"I ask for the exclusive love of my paramour," Athénaïs said, her voice rasping.

Chanting, the priest spilled something dark from the chalice onto her bare belly. She giggled in protest as drops trickled down her sides.

The priest put the chalice back down on the sideboard and sounded a bell. He held his hands out over Athénaïs, his fingers hovering over her skin.

"Ecce sponsa Satanae." Behold the bride of Satan.

"Ego vos benedico in nomine Satanae." I bless you in the name of Satan.

I was shaking. I feared I might faint.

"Ave Satanas." Hail, Satan.

Athénaïs began softly snoring.

"In nomine Satanas. Amen."

"You may dress now, Madame," the priest said, and disappeared the way he had come.

"Madame?" My voice a croak.

Athénaïs stirred. "Is that it?"

"Don't move," I said. "I have to clean you." I used a nose cloth to wipe her belly. I sniffed the cloth: *blood.* Almost retching, I did my best to help Athénaïs back into her gown.

"What was that all about?" Athénaïs asked, lifting her mask. Her face looked ghostly in the candlelight.

"I'm . . . I'm not sure," I said, clenching my teeth to keep them from chattering. It was warm in the chamber, yet I felt chilled to the bone.

"So long as it works," Athénaïs said, securing the diamond-studded clasp of her cloak at the neck.

couldn't sleep for nightmares, the suffocating spirits that rose up in the dark. Even among the scented courtiers at Versaie, even in the blooming palace gardens, even deep in the heart of the palace Labyrinth, where I could usually find respite from my cares, even *there* I could smell ambergris, a haunting reminder.

Athénaïs seemed entirely unaware. Confident, she regained her wit, her humor, her charm. And now, with the King's ardor "magically" aflame once again, she was considering a second ritual to ensure her dominion over the royal scepter.

"Madame, please—*don't*."

"Claude, it works!" She leaned forward, peering into her looking-glass and stroking her chin. "I have nothing more to fear. This afternoon that trollop Angélique paraded before the King half-naked, but he didn't even lift his eyes."

I tried to swallow, my mouth dry. "But it's the Devil's power, Madame."

She burst into a gale of laughter. I'd begun to fear that she'd been taken over. Was she under a spell? Had her spirit been stolen?

"You're talking like a peasant," she said. "It has nothing to do with the Devil. A priest officiated, calling on the Divine."

"You were asleep. He invoked *Satan*."

"You keep telling me I was asleep. I wasn't asleep! Why are you not pleased? This is a miracle."

I wanted to cry. "Your eyes were closed. A swaddled baby was brought in and . . . and *murdered*." I pressed a hand over my mouth. I was sure of it now. A horror!

"You were seeing things. You took some of my opium pills, confess."

"The priest spilled the baby's *blood* on your belly, Madame. I smelled it."

Athénaïs snorted with amusement. "Next you'll be telling me there are werewolves in the garden."

There was no way to stop her. I heard my father's voice. *There are things we do not do, things we will not do.* My heart skittered, knowing the risks: Gaston could be forced to leave his beloved monastery, Sweet Pea could be taken from me—or worse. I arranged Athénaïs's silk shawl around her shoulders and stood back. I felt numb from lack of sleep. "I have to go," I said finally, bluntly.

Athénaïs pulled old Popo onto her lap and turned one of the pug's ears inside out, examining it for mites.

Had she heard me?

She folded back the dog's ear and set him down on the tiles. He ambled over to his pillow by the fire. "How long will you need, Claudette?"

Claudette. She'd first called me that at the ball at the Palais-Royal. We were so young. "Forever, Madame. I'm ... I must leave your service."

"Are you serious?" she asked, looking up at me, her enormous eyes searching.

I bit my lower lip. I'd known Athénaïs as a girl; we'd been through so much together. I understood her in a way nobody else did; understood her temper, her frustrations—her pain. I understood what she'd once had, and what she had lost. "My health has not been good."

She snorted. "Don't be ridiculous. You're as healthy as a beast of the field."

I felt a cat rub against my ankle. "I don't care to burden you, Madame, but I do have problems." My sleepless nights had weakened me; I feared the Devil's presence.

"I'll have my doctor attend you," she said kindly, applying the blade of a pair of scissors to her chin. It was a small pair used for cutting nails, but sharp as a razor, useful for eliminating unseemly hairs. "Just get some rest, my dear. You'll be fine. I'll have one of the cooks make you a healing gruel."

My ring of keys was heavy: I fumbled detaching it from my under-skirt. I clunked it down on the marble toilette table amongst her jumble of gems, the crystal perfume bottles with solid gold stoppers. "I'm serious. I can't be part of this." My voice quavered dangerously. "I'm leaving . . . today."

The frown lines between her brows were caked with powder. "Is it money you want?"

"It has nothing to do with money."

She stared at me, harder now. "You *are* serious."

"Oui, Madame. I am."

"And you actually think you *can* leave me?" She smiled, a cold mocking look. "Take back your keys, Claude. You're not going anywhere," she said, turning back to her image in the glass. "His Majesty will forbid it."

Was I indentured for life, a slave? I looked out the window. The brocade curtains had been pulled open, tied back with ropes of braided silk. The summer light was bright. "He would agree were you to press my case."

"And why, pray, would I do that?" she demanded, toying with one of her lovelocks. The stiff curl of bronzed hair was lacquered about her ear like a tragedy queen's.

I heard heels on the parquet outside the door, animals scurrying, the thrumming wings of a bird allowed to fly free. "Because there are things you would not want His Majesty to know," I said evenly.

She turned to me with tears in her eyes. "You're threatening me?" The spots on her cheeks stood out like those on a clown's sad face.

Her eyes, so transparent and blue, had always had a captivating power over me. I looked away. *Oui:* I am threatening you. It's all I have, all that is left to me, the knowledge of your secrets.

"You threaten *me?*" She stood with such violence that the table overturned, glass shattering on the tiles. The air filled with the stench of her musky perfumes. "Do you not understand that I am queen of this damned country!" she shouted, spittle flying in her fury.

A guard and a maid burst into the room. "Out!" she screamed, and they hastily backed away, stumbling over each other. She pointed the scissors at me. Although small, they could be deadly if aimed at an eye or the throat.

Shards of glass crunched under my feet. "An infant was murdered at that ritual," I said, my voice rising. I no longer cared who might overhear. "The priest spilled its blood on your belly."

"Don't lie to me, you whore." Her teeth, her lovely teeth, were stained pink from wine, like the teeth of the condemned at hangings. "There isn't a confession you've made to Père d'Ossat I don't know about. You think I didn't notice my missing trinkets, the opium pills that disappeared? Taken, you no doubt told yourself, to ease the pain of your floozy mother."

"You will go to Hell, Athénaïs."

"And you're so virtuous? You *used* me to fulfill your lusts. You're an unnatural woman, feigning to be above your station, among the quality. You think you *belong* here? You're no different from the beggar women in the market, your hand always out. You're loveless—and it's no wonder! You're a leech, one big hungry mouth, never sated, never satisfied."

I felt a choking sob rise up in my chest. "I *saw* it." I was bigger and stronger than Athénaïs—and quicker too, no doubt. My eyes on the scissors she held, I scooped up the splintered stem of a glass. "I've served you loyally, but I—"

I'm sorry, I wanted to say. Sorry for the monster she had become, sorry for the horrors I'd witnessed, been part of. The temptations I'd given way to. *Encouraged.* I'd given evil counsel.

"You thankless slut! I raised you up out of the gutter. I gave you everything! You'd have nothing were it not for me. I *bought* your idiot brother's salvation."

"For which I'll always be grateful," I cried, weeping now, buffeted by a confusing welter of emotions.

I glimpsed a hint of sadness in her eyes before she turned away. She stood still as stone. I waited, holding my breath, violently trembling.

"I will have your trunk sent on," she said finally.

I breathed with relief.

"To the world, this will be an amicable parting. You're never to say a word about what has passed. Understand? *Not one word.* Or—!" She faced me, her features hard. "Or I'll have your precious baby thrown into a bear pit."

Deus! I believed her, believed she could do such a thing. "I won't speak of it, Madame." I threw down the shard, as if it were a sword. "I vow to that—so long as my brother and daughter are not harmed." I was striking a deal with the Devil.

The pendulum clock chimed the hour.

"Damnation," the parrot squawked.

I turned to the door, glass crackling under my feet. Was it possible to walk away from this world, as if exiting a stage?

ACT V

LABYRINTH

(1680, Château de Suisnes)

CHAPTER 55

I was in the kitchen helping Gaby salt the Martlemas beef when I heard their dog, Bruno, barking, followed by the sound of horses and wagon wheels.

"Who could that be?" Gaby asked, tucking a stray curl under her crisp white bonnet. Monsieur de Maisonblanche had gone to the horse market early that morning and wouldn't be back until sundown.

We rarely had callers; it was one of the things I loved about my visits to Suisnes. After leaving Court—leaving Athénaïs—more than three years before, I'd sold my jewels and gowns. With that, and living sparely, I'd been able to get by, coming as often as I could to spend time in the country with my daughter, Gaby, and her husband . . . especially of late. Madame Catherine's arrest and horrifying execution had plunged Paris into an endless inquisition. The air of the city was foul with the scent of burning flesh.

La sorcellerie, daemonomania. In our enlightened times, witchcraft was no longer a punishable offense—but murder certainly was. The revelations, one upon another, had been shocking. It was as if a stone had been lifted, revealing a mass of maggots feeding on rot. Who could have believed that there were hundreds in Paris selling poison, and often to the *nobility,* members of the Court.

In spite of my hermetic life, I'd been suffering queasy fears. So many had been arrested, tried, and convicted. Who was exempt? Rumor had it that even Racine was to be tried, accused of poisoning Thérèse du Parc.

"Maybe it's Père Petit," my daughter said, sprawled on the stone floor with her wood dolls.

The cheerful village priest was a welcome visitor. "I don't think so," I said, lifting the child and setting her onto a chair. She'd turned four that summer and was growing tall as a maypole, her smocks already in need of lengthening. "He always comes on his mule," I explained, kissing my daughter's russet curls and setting the three dolls on the table in front of her.

Bruno barked again and a horse whinnied. "I'll go see who it is," I told Gaby, taking off my apron and hanging it over the back of a wooden spindle chair. I slipped outside and closed the door behind me to keep in the heat of the fire. A gust of bitter wind cut into my cheeks, making my eyes water. I wound my shawl around my neck.

A rooster crowed. Bruno had stopped barking. As I rounded the corner of the château, I saw that it *was* a carriage. The driver, a pudgy man in livery, was petting the dog, his matched team of four handsome blacks looking on warily.

"He gave my horses a fright," he said.

"He's big, but gentle," I said, taking Bruno by his rope collar. "Are you lost, Monsieur? May I help?"

"I'm looking for—" He withdrew a note from the cuff of his jacket and squinted at it. "Mademoiselle Claude des Oeillets."

Sun glinted off the official seal. "That's me."

"You're wanted."

It was a document from the office of Louvois, the Secretary of State for War. I struggled to control my voice, my sudden urge to run. Madame Catherine had been arrested at the doors of her parish church, having just attended Mass. "What's this about?"

"All I know is that you're to come with me," he said, almost apologetically.

"I'm afraid that's not possible. Kindly inform the Secretary of State that he may have the pleasure of my company in ten days, when I plan to be back in Paris."

"Mademoiselle . . ." The driver pressed his gloved hands together. "This isn't an invitation; it's a command."

From the Secretary of State. From *Louvois,* who was in charge of the poison trials. "May I have a moment?" I asked, overtaken by an inner trembling.

Tugging on Bruno, I headed back to the service entrance of the château, trying to compose myself. "I'm needed back in Paris," I announced, descending into the basement kitchen. The warmth of the blazing fire made my skin burn. I sighed dramatically—as if it were a mere annoyance. It wouldn't do to alarm Gaby or my daughter.

"Something to do with your brother?" Gaby asked, wiping her hands on her hemp smock.

"In a way," I answered vaguely. "I have to go to the city," I told Sweet Pea, unable to stop the catch in my voice. I pressed my cheek against her soft locks. "I'll be back soon," I said, wanting to believe it was true.

Calm! I admonished myself. "I'll bring you a toy," I promised. A spinning top.

THE HÔTEL DE LOUVOIS on the rue de Richelieu in Paris comprised an impressive block of stone houses. The iron-studded gates opened to let the carriage in. Guards were in evidence everywhere—it looked like a military encampment.

"Bonne chance," my driver said kindly, opening the carriage door and letting me down.

An officious valet and two guards—their hands on the pommels of their swords—showed me through a series of stately but unornamented rooms bustling with activity. Clerks stooped over documents and maps, ignoring us as we passed.

I came to an antechamber where three people—a man and two women—were standing. The valet scratched on the oak door, then slipped inside, the door closing behind him.

One of the women, a young sort with a rakish air, looked me over. I stared down at the floor.

"Mademoiselle des Oeillets," a clerk called out.

I was led through yet another series of rooms to a chamber at the back.

"Monsieur," I said on entering Louvois's cabinet, where he was seated at a tiny desk. "Monseigneur," I added, recalling something Athénaïs had said, about his vain insistence on the feudal title.

His considerable girth, lascivious lips, and small, appraising eyes always reminded me of a pig. I'd seen him many times at Saint-

Germain-en-Laye and Versaie, but even here, where he ruled, he seemed not in his element. There was something of the sloven in him.

Athénaïs had often mocked Louvois's boorish manners. Because of his insistence on being addressed as "Monseigneur," the nobility jokingly referred to him as *"Illustrissimus"* behind his back. Over the years I had heard other things about him as well, things that weren't laughable in the least: that he had no scruples, that his temper could turn violent, that he preyed on women, that he openly bedded the wife of one of his clerks. Players had always been wary of him, even when he was young.

Louvois pulled out a thick portfolio.

I stood before him, my hands clasped. I suspected he had his eyebrows plucked and colored. The chamber was lavishly furnished, yet nothing in it—not even the quill stand—had aesthetic merit. I recalled, with revulsion, the story of his killing a cat.

He cleared his throat, studying the papers. Reading, he reached over and rang a bell. A clerk popped into the room. "Was there not something in Voisin's confession?" Louvois demanded.

La Voisin. I was alarmed at the mention of Madame Catherine's name. It was rumored a register of all her customers had been discovered.

"Only that of the daughter," the clerk said.

Young, wily Marie Marguerite . . . ?

Louvois made a dismissive motion with his hand and the clerk backed out. "Mademoiselle des Oeillets, in my *discussions*"—he said the word with irony—"with several of the prisoners, your name has been mentioned." His voice was high and thin, nasal. Four of his teeth were capped with gold.

"*My* name, Monseigneur?"

"They say they have had dealings with you."

A chill came over me. "Monseigneur, respectfully, I believe there must be some mistake."

"The mistake is in jumping to conclusions." He made a tent of his fingers. His rings glittered with diamonds—gifts from the King, no doubt.

I smiled submissively. (Gritting my teeth.) I'd always gone to

Madame Catherine disguised as a man and under a false name. There could be no way—

"The Voisin girl—" Louvois riffled through the pages in the file, settling on one. "She has stated that you came to see her mother on a number of occasions."

Fear alerted me to play my part well. "I did consult Madame Voisin," I admitted in an intentionally confessional tone, "but only once, to get my fortune told."

Details made a fiction true. Who had told me that? Ay me. *Father.*

"This was . . . oh?" I looked upward. "Twenty years ago? She had a stand on the Pont Marie, before it was swept away by the flood. I was curious to know my future. She read my hand and told me I would marry, which I never did, so it was four sous wasted."

But Louvois wasn't listening; he was going through the papers in the file. Why were there so many? "And then there is the statement of Madame de Villedieu. She claims to have been your friend for more than fifteen years."

"That's interesting, Monsieur—Monseigneur—given that I don't know Madame de Villedieu," I said in all truthfulness.

"This was before you joined Madame de Montespan at Court."

I caught my breath at the mention of Athénaïs's name.

"You were mentioned by another prisoner as well. Monsieur Lesage, sometimes known as Monsieur du Buisson, or Monsieur Adam Coeuret." He stared at me.

"I do not know this man," I said with more emotion than was wise. Whatever I said must come from intentional devising. I must await my cue.

"He's a charming sort of charlatan, a man of many tales, many lives."

"A man of many lies!" I said heatedly, in spite of my resolve.

Louvois smirked. (Finally: a response.) "And then there is the statement by a priest—Abbé Guibourg."

I had never heard the name.

"A man whose eyes go—" Louvois pointed his two fingers in opposite directions.

A sick feeling came over me: I remembered. I shook my head.

"No recollection? Nothing at all?" Louvois leaned forward; he was enjoying himself. "Curious, don't you think, given these testimonials"—he thumbed through the papers—"made under oath, accusing you of procuring poisons for Montespan, partaking in an amatory Mass."

I felt tears pressing. It was all there, in that thick file. *How* was that possible?

Louvois crossed his arms and sat back. "You even stand accused, Mademoiselle, of plotting to poison His Majesty."

Deus! "On my *life*," I cried out, "put me before these people and you will see: they do not know me!"

here were two carriages in the courtyard, as well as six guards on horseback. Louvois and two clerks climbed into the coach at the front. A guard handed me up into the smaller, mud-spattered coach and then climbed in beside me. I sat looking out the window as we pulled onto the rue de Richelieu, en route to the fortress at Vincennes, where many of those suspected of dealing in poison were being held.

The guards riding alongside made a clatter. People stopped to gawk. I averted my eyes, knowing what they must think: that I was under arrest, that I was being taken to Vincennes . . . to prison.

I wiped away tears. Hundreds had been executed. That summer a woman had been sent directly from a hearing to the torture chamber, only to burn on the pyre the very next day.

The guard beside me shifted, leaning his head against the window. I was going to confront my accusers, I reminded myself—*not* be locked up.

Outside the city walls, we headed into open country. The horses were fast, the roadway covered with leaves. Soon, the towers of Vincennes appeared above the treetops. We stopped on the bridge over the moat as the massive doors opened. The coaches entered the vast courtyard and rolled to a stop in front of the fortress. There were cries from above. I looked up to see faces in the barred tower windows, both men and women, their hands reaching out. Madame Catherine had been held in this prison.

"Don't be stirring them up," the guard warned.

Following Louvois and his two clerks, the guard escorted me over another fetid moat and into the fortress. We descended narrow stone stairs. A thick stench permeated the air—the smell of people in chains. We entered one chamber and then another and another, finally coming to a large, dank room with benches in front of a plank table. A fire was smoldering; even so, it was cold. We were in the dungeons.

I was put in a dark chamber. A guard reappeared with a candle for the wall sconce. It illuminated a stained chamber pot set in a corner. "Merci," I said, gripping my trembling hands. Why was I being treated like a prisoner? The stench brought back memories of the flood—and Gaston's frightening imprisonment.

After a time, I heard men's voices, the clanking of chains, creaking benches. The door opened. Come out, the guard motioned.

I emerged into the room. Louvois was seated at the trestle table, his two clerks standing by, backed by five guards. Before him on a bench was a misshapen man in a matted, mud-red wig. Slowly, he turned to stare at me.

I vaguely recalled his pockmarked face. Then it came to me: he'd been a magician on the Pont Neuf. One of his tricks was to write a request to the "Spirit" on a note, which he enclosed in a ball of wax and threw into a fire. Then he would somehow bring forth the note with an answer from the "Spirit" scrawled on it. I had watched his act several times, trying to figure how it was done, but he was swift with his hands, and I could never devise the deception.

"Do you know this woman?" Louvois's nails made a scratching sound on the table.

The man stared at me, looking me up and down. I could not understand why there were no other women present. Why was I the only one? To be fair, a number should be present and the accuser should be asked to identify one.

"I do," he said.

I pulled in my chin, surprised.

"She's Mademoiselle Claude des Oeillets," he said, grinning at Louvois.

THE SECOND TIME I was brought out, there was a woman on the bench, and she was unable to name me. The third time, it was

Madame Catherine's daughter, Marie Marguerite. Her eyes were wild in her small face, her nose and chin inflamed with pustules. Not long before her mother had been burned alive at the stake, and now the girl was herself in chains. She'd had a wandering wit at the best of times, and now . . . now she was verily lunatic, I feared, watching as she stuttered and gasped, trying desperately to answer Louvois's questions: "No, Monseigneur, no, this is not the woman, Monseigneur, no, it was another, a short woman who came with the Englishman who spent his seed into a vial mixed with her monthly blood, the man who vowed to murder His Majesty."

"You do not know this woman? Are you sure?"

She was visibly shaking. "What was your question, Monseigneur? It's possible, Monseigneur, oui, I know her."

THERE FOLLOWED ANOTHER man—the Bird Catcher!—who was fortunately unable to identify me. I was beginning to feel hopeful, when I was shown in yet again.

A large man in a thread-worn cassock turned to look me over. He had the nose of a drinker and a mean squint. It was the wall-eyed priest.

"State her name," Louvois commanded.

"Abbé Guibourg," he said.

His voice—that curiously beautiful but terrifying voice—was the same.

"*Her* name," Louvois persisted wearily.

The priest turned one wandering eye toward me. I bit my lip to still the quivering. *Dominus Satanas.* Lord Satan.

"She's the one I was telling you about," he said slowly.

"Her *name.*"

There was a long moment of silence. I could hear workmen clanging on stone. I could not bear to look at him, but dared not avert my eyes, lest I be thought guilty. *Was* I guilty? I'd encouraged a ritual that involved a death, an innocent sacrificed. The memory clung to me like a curse.

"Mademoiselle Claude des . . . *Oeillets,*" the priest said.

.   .   .

I WAS RETURNED to my closet, shaken. I cringed as the door clanked shut behind me. I felt as if a pit-fall trap had opened under me, plunging me into Hell. How could he have known my name?

I thought of Madame Catherine and the day of her execution. Dressed in white and bound by rope, she'd been lifted onto a tumbrel. Children raced after her like excited monkeys. Approaching the Place du Grève, a dog had started to bark, the big yellow mongrel biting at the hooves of the horses—her dog, Noël. A horse caught its head with a kick. I heard its howls of pain and witnessed, to my horror, Madame Catherine struggling, falling, and screaming. The dog, trampled, gradually ceased to whimper. Madame Catherine pushed the confessor away, hurling his cross into the crowd.

She was strong in her rage; she surprised me. It took four executioners to drag her out of the cart. They clamped her to the stake with iron bands. She spat at them as they piled sticks and straw all around her.

A fury.

And now I stood accused. I squeezed my eyes tight, praying for strength. I longed for one of those improbable theatrical devices I often mocked, the *deus ex machina,* gods descending from the clouds to save the heroine.

O Mother! O Father!

Nil desperandum.

Father's wonderfully familiar voice came back to me. I was surely lost to him now, no longer his Good Knight Claudette. I thought of the innocence of my childish vow, my pure intent. I hadn't known, then, that there was no such thing as one true path, hadn't understood, then, that good and evil could be so intertwined, like a braid.

Father! What would you have me do?

Tell the truth.

I bowed my head. I can't.

Are you innocent?

I don't know.

You're not sure?

I went along. The powders, the drops, the charms . . . they did no harm, but as for that last—I don't even want to think of it.

Was it your doing?

I pressed a fist to my lips. I'd encouraged Athénaïs. I inquired on her behalf. I had even pushed for it, given evil counsel. It would never have happened had it not been for me.

The guard opened the door.

The room was empty this time, but for Louvois, a clerk, and several guards. "We have all we need," Louvois said, standing as the clerk helped him on with his cloak. "You will be informed when the trials resume, Mademoiselle."

I was to go to trial? *No!*

"A guard will return you to Paris, but do not consider fleeing," he informed me with a smirk, "for that will only reconfirm your guilt. We will always know where to find you—you *and* your idiot brother and daughter."

I reached out my hand in a pleading gesture—a gesture Mother had used onstage to great effect. "Monseigneur, I am innocent, I *swear*. You must hear me out!"

Louvois made an impatient motion to the guards: Take this woman away.

breathless trembling came over me. How had my accusers known my name? I thought of going to a lawyer, but who would dare oppose the Marquis de Louvois, the most feared man in France?

I counted my coins: I had just enough for a coach to Versaie.

THE PLACE D'ARMES in front of the château was teeming with workers, gangs of husky masons, glaziers, joiners, and carpenters. The sound of chisels tapping filled the air. A choking dust made everything look hazy, deceptively soft.

The driver let me down at the second set of gates. I stood, getting my bearings. So much had changed. Balconies and sculptures had been added to the original château and the windows looked bigger. An enormous new wing was under construction. Workmen swarmed up out of the ground like ants, building something underground—barracks for the royal troops, I surmised.

I approached the guards at the gate, relieved to recognize one of them.

"Good afternoon, Mademoiselle des Oeillets."

It reassured me to be recognized, greeted as a familiar. "Is Monsieur Breton on duty this quarter?" Praying that Xavier was.

THE NOISE OF construction reverberated throughout the cold marble halls. The King's rooms were crowded with guards, soldiers, servants, and citizens. Finally I spotted Xavier, studiously working at a table in a crowded antechamber, oblivious to the commotion.

He stood up, clearly shocked to see me. We nearly collided making obsequious gestures.

I tucked a stray hair behind my ear. I'd begun to go gray and no longer colored my hair with henna, no longer plucked and primped. I looked like a bumpkin, no doubt. "Forgive me for interrupting." I felt my cheeks burning. It had been years since I'd last seen him, years since we'd stood side by side in Athénaïs's rooms, pretending not to hear the sounds of passionate congress behind the doors. Even so, it seemed we'd never been apart. "How have you been?" His hair was brushed into a charming peak over his forehead. He'd gained weight, but still looked handsome.

He cleared his throat, making a sweeping motion over the papers that covered the desk. "Oh—"

"You're busy, I'm sorry." It was wrong to impose on him after all this time.

"It's only inventories of His Majesty's wardrobes—lists of what needs repair. Tedious work." The lines around his eyes crinkled when he smiled. "How's your—?" He glanced around. There were people milling about. *Daughter,* he mouthed. After I'd left Athénaïs's service, the King had stopped providing financial support for Sweet Pea and Xavier's visits to Suisnes had ceased.

"She's well." I could have said more—so much more—but it was not the time . . . or place. "I must have a word with His Majesty . . . *privately.*" I reddened, fearing how he might interpret my request.

"I'm afraid that's not possible."

Were all doors closed to me now? But of course, I realized with horror: I was suspected of trying to murder the King! "*Please,* Xavier, I—"

He put up his hands. "It's only because His Majesty is having a treatment, Claudette."

Of course: an enema, a bleeding, a purge—

I took a shaky breath before saying, under my breath: "I'm in trouble." *Serious* trouble.

He looked at me for a long moment. "It's cold, but might it be refreshing to walk in the gardens?"

"How about the Labyrinth?" I suggested.

· · ·

WE WERE ALONE, hidden by tall hedges. Even in the cool of late November, the air was scented from the blooms of the trees in the Orangery nearby. I traced Cupid's words, etched in stone, with the tip of my finger. *With this ball of string, I'll know how to find my way.* If only it were true, I thought, thinking of my complex entanglement.

"Shall we?" Xavier said, motioning to a bench.

"I'd prefer to go farther in." More hidden from view.

At the third fountain, we sat down. A blackbird, preening its dark feathers in the water, was indifferent to our presence.

Xavier leaned forward, resting his forearms on his legs. "I'm sorry, but I'm afraid I can't be long. His Majesty will be—"

"I won't keep you: it's about the Affaire." The Affair of the Poisons, people called it.

He dipped his head.

"Some of the prisoners at Vincennes—suspected poisoners— claim to know me, claim to have had dealings with me." I struggled not to burst into tears. The enormity of the charges was overwhelming. I thought of the pain of the fire. Such a horrible way to die! "I've even been accused—" I paused. *Dare* I tell him? "I've been accused of plotting to murder His Majesty."

Xavier reeled back. "I've not read that."

What *had* he read? "I would never do such a thing! You *know* that! I only ever wished to please His Majesty. He has been generous with me. Why would I want to harm him?" I was pathetically pleading. I knew I sounded ridiculous.

Xavier put his hand on mine, to calm. "Tell me."

Could I trust him? In the years since I'd left, I'd become accustomed to being with people who spoke from the heart—but this was not the case at Court. "I did go often to Madame Voisin, in disguise, to pick things up . . ."

"Love powders."

I flushed. Might he assume they were for my own use? "And liquids, which—which I put in His Majesty's wine." Such an admission could cost me my life! I pulled the hood of my cape snug around my neck.

He tugged on his bushy moustache. "Fortifiers, we call them."

"You knew?"

"His Majesty's valets are privy to the most intimate details of our sovereign's being. It's our job to know."

"Was the King aware?" The blackbird flew off, startling me.

"Oui et non: in a manner of speaking."

The never-ending charade of Court life. I thought of all our secrecy, making sure His Majesty was not present when the liquid—the "amatory assistant"—was put in his goblet. Yet he'd known all along!

"There is one other thing which I . . . I hesitate to mention." The words out, I had to proceed. "I accompanied someone to a ritual involving a priest."

"A Black Mass." He whispered the words so softly I hardly caught them.

Ay me. He knew about that as well? *Oui,* I mouthed, with a hint of a nod. "But I was only attending," I stuttered tearfully, my heart fluttering wildly.

"Madame de Montespan."

Swear never to betray a trust. I held my silence.

"You don't have to say, Claudette. I've read the reports."

Reports! Then did His Majesty know as well? Confusion came over me like a palsy. "That's why I left Madame's service," I said, letting out a deep breath. "And now . . ." My leather-gloved hands failed to cool my cheeks. Now *I* was to burn! "I am innocent of these charges."

"Then you need not fear."

He had such faith, it made me want to weep . . . weep, and rage. "You know, of course, what my going to trial would entail," I said. "If convicted, I would be required to make a full public confession at the doors of Notre-Dame." Madame Catherine had had to do so. I signed myself, weakened by the memory. "I doubt very much that either Madame de Montespan or His Majesty would want such intimate details made public."

Birdsong, wind. From far off the sound of string instruments.

"You would do that?" he asked with a tone of incredulity. As if I were impugning the Crown!

I was close to tears, close to keening like the prisoners in the Hôpital Général. The Court was a world unto itself. Versaie was far from

Paris, far from the smoke of the pyre. Had Xavier ever even been to a burning? Had he ever seen one up close? "Why—in the name of all that's holy—why would I *not*?"

"Because you are a loyal subject?" he offered, lowering his voice, "and a good woman."

I shuttered back tears. Oui: the Good Knight Claudette. *Do what is right, whatever the cost.* But it was so much more complex. Was I to protect the guilty, so that the innocent suffered? "I have a daughter, Xavier, a brother in my charge. I vow to you now: if I go to trial, I *will* make sure that all is revealed."

Church bells rang: both close and far away.

"Meet me back here before the lighting of the lamps," he said, standing.

CHAPTER 58

Shaken, I walked to the market. I had broken a trust. Worse, I had threatened harm to His Majesty: an act of treason.

I bought a wedge of rabbit pie—a leftover from the King's table the day before, "almost fresh." (Or so it was claimed.) It was rancid, but I ate it, washing it down with sour wine. Then, heart aching, I bought a tin spinning top for Sweet Pea at a toy stall. A thin maid from Athénaïs's staff recognized me, then looked away.

Where could I hide?

The little church in the village was dark as a dungeon and cold as stone. I bought a candle and lit it, but I couldn't even summon a simple prayer. I sat shivering for some time in the silence.

I HEADED BACK to the Labyrinth as the sun was starting to set. Xavier stood as I approached, his hat covering his heart. I felt dizzy, as if on a precipice.

"You will never be brought to trial, Claudette."

Would I be imprisoned then without a hearing? That happened often enough. A letter signed by the King—the dreaded *cachet*—could lock a person away, never to be heard from again. I was shaking. He helped me to lower myself onto a cold bench.

"I delivered His Majesty's order to Louvois just now," he said, baffled by my mute response.

"What does that mean?" I asked finally, taking a breath.

"It means you have nothing to fear." He held out his hands as if making an offering. "His Majesty understands that a public trial would not be in his best interest."

I bowed my head: merci Dieu. I searched for a nose cloth to wipe the tears from my cheeks.

"Louvois has been trying to prosecute a number of people associated with Madame de Montespan," Xavier said hesitantly, sitting down beside me. "Her sister-in-law, a cousin, others. I've been noticing this with suspicion, I confess. It's possible that the Secretary of State is . . . well, to be frank, *rewarding* certain prison testimonials."

Had it been staged? "You think Louvois gave the prisoners my name?"

"I think it's possible. *Why* I don't know."

"It's because he despises her." Her: Athénaïs. She'd mocked him, belittled him in front of the King, referred to him at salon gatherings as Monsieur Pig. She'd made him grovel! Was Louvois using the Affair of the Poisons as a private vendetta against her?

Xavier leaned forward, his hands on his knees. "Yet he dares not attack Madame de Montespan directly: she's the mother of several of His Majesty's legitimized children."

Louis Auguste, Louis César, Louise Françoise, Louise Marie Anne. A girl had been born two months before I had left, but I couldn't remember her name. Françoise Marie? She would be three now. I wondered if any other children had been born since, and if the eldest, the boy, could walk yet. "Have you spoken to His Majesty about this?" I asked.

"The King is not approachable on this issue. He's given Louvois and the judges full liberty."

I recalled the King's rage over that fateful duel, so long ago, his proclamation that "no one be spared." He was, indeed, firm: there was strength in that, but taken to brittleness it could be a weakness, too. I thought of the hundreds who had been executed. I thought of the guilty, yet alive. I thought of the wall-eyed priest.

"His Majesty asked me to give you this." Xavier reached under his cape.

The soft leather sack was heavy: coins, from the feel of it. I looked up at him, puzzled.

"It's rather a great deal, so be cautious."

For my silence, I knew: keeper of a secret. "I can be trusted," I said, feeling the weight of the coins. I handed the bag back to him. "But I don't need to be bribed."

"Claudette, please consider," he said, perplexed.

I'd always loved Xavier's eyes, his solid gentleness. I shook my head. *Swear to do what is right, whatever the cost.*

"Believe me, it's not about paying you off—it's for your daughter's care," he said with tenderness.

"You told His Majesty about my little girl?" The King's daughter too.

"I had to."

"What did he say?"

Xavier looked at me apologetically. "That you're never to come to Court."

Gladly!

"I'm sorry. But please—keep the coins."

"I can manage, Xavier." Court riches came with a price. "Inform His Majesty that I will honor his command, nonetheless."

"How is she?" he asked after an uncomfortable silence.

I clasped the brass locket hanging from a ribbon tied around my neck: inside was a strand of Sweet Pea's hair, together with a tiny image I'd drawn of her. It was a crude likeness—I did not have a talent for portraiture—but there was something of her spirit in it. "Growing," I said, tearfully relating her cleverness, her latest bon mot, how tall she was now, how pretty and pert.

"Like her mother," he said.

I turned to him, suddenly in the grip of an *impetuous tumult*. "Do you still have that rose?" I asked, flushing.

He smiled shyly. "Of course."

The birds began making a racket, a chorus of calls, a chorus of answers. I put up my hands in a gesture of surrender, tears brimming.

He pressed his hands against mine, palm to palm. "I've loved you for a long time, Claudette."

"Show me," I said.

One kiss revealed everything. I felt like Cupid flying.

EPILOGUE

(1684, Château de Suisnes)

CHAPTER 59

 walked through the rooms of the Château de Suisnes jingling a big ring of keys. The papers had been signed two days before, the money transferred to Monsieur François Pingré, the owner. The *former* owner, that is, for now the château was mine—made possible by an astonishing and totally unexpected windfall from one of Mother's "foolish" investments. (Thank you, Maman!)

I was filled with gratitude. At the full and blooming age of forty-five, I had everything I'd ever hoped for. I thought of the caves and campsites of my youth, the ramshackle rooms and grand palaces I'd slept in. Whether a roaming player or a member of the Court, I had been always on the move. Finally I had a place I could truly call home.

I went up the curving stairs and looked into each room. Sweet Pea—a long-legged eight-year-old with red curls and big feet—adored her new room under the eaves with its canopy bed. Even in the heat of July, it was cooled by the shade of the chestnut tree outside.

I looked into the four remaining upstairs rooms. The shutters had been opened and the rooms aired. Gaby had made them up nicely for my guests: a vase of freshly picked flowers adorned each toilette table. The fine muslin curtains in the room next to my own fluttered in the breeze.

I heard Gaby calling from downstairs. I followed her through the salon to the double doors of the library.

Shh, she gestured, her finger to her lips. She moved so that I could look through the doors. There, inside, was Sweet Pea, absorbed in constructing something—but what was it? She'd hoisted a rod between two shelves and was draping linens over it. Curtains?

"It's a stage," Gaby whispered, nudging me away so that we might not be discovered. "It's supposed to be a surprise," she explained in the basement kitchen, handing me an earthen mug of hot cider. "But I thought you should know." Newly baked loaves of bread were lined up on the plank table. The oxtail soup, chicken pot pies, crepinettes, beignets, tarts, and other sweets had already been prepared for this afternoon's feast. Venison was turning on the spit. A maid, a girl from the village, was just finishing cleaning up.

"Sweet Pea intends to put on a performance for us," Gaby said, taking off her apron. She was wearing her best gown, her church dress, a stiff taffeta in an ancient style, with enormous sleeves. "It's going to be a play—from something by Monsieur Corneille."

I frowned. My daughter had only just learned her letters.

Gaby grinned. "Of course it will only be a line or two, but all last week—while you were with the notary in Paris—she practiced, committing the lines to heart. Père Petit has been helping her. It was her reward for learning her catechism."

Our village priest had taught my daughter lines from a *play*? But then, Père Petit cast himself as a rebel priest who even talked to Huguenots. He once confessed to going to Paris to see a theatrical production, so perhaps it wasn't so surprising.

"I suggested she perform it after dessert."

"Good idea." I heard a coach and horses, and hurried up the stairs to look out the window that overlooked the courtyard. "Gaby, tell Sweet Pea that her uncle Gaston and Monsieur Pierre are here," I called down. And Gaston's friend Pilon. *And* two children?

"Christophe and Humbert. Twins," Pilon explained when I went outside to meet them. "Our newest recruits. We didn't think we should leave them alone just yet."

"Welcome," I said to the boys, who I guessed to be about six. "We have all sorts of treats for you."

I embraced Gaston, who had grown quite round with a long beard that he tied into a knot at his waist.

"So *here* you are," Monsieur Pierre said, approaching, leaning on a crooked wood cane. "All the way out in the middle of nowhere."

"I'm so glad you could come." I was shocked at how much he'd aged. He was almost eighty now, true, yet he seemed older than that, overly thin. It came to me that he could die at any time. Did he know how much I loved him? He had meant so much to my mother, my family.

I felt little hands around my waist. I grinned down at my daughter. "Sweet Pea, this is Monsieur Corneille—the *Great* Corneille."

"The playwright?"

Monsieur Pierre touched the brim of his floppy hat and my daughter made a charming curtsy.

"Why don't you show the boys your new swing," I suggested.

"The very image," Monsieur Pierre said, watching her skip off, the twins running after her.

I flushed. It was true: Sweet Pea looked very much like her father. I took Monsieur Pierre's arm, to steady him, following his slow, tentative steps into the house: *my* house.

EVERYBODY LOVED THE château, its vistas, its congenial ambience. They admired the gardens, Monsieur de Maisonblanche's friendly old bearlike dog, the cat's newest litter, the pigs, the mare, the cow. After Père Petit arrived, we all sat down to dine.

Père Petit said grace, giving thanks to the Good Lord *and* His helpmate, Madame Gaby, for the bounty before them, and to *her* helpmate, Monsieur de Maisonblanche, for his most excellent ale.

"Hurrah!" Everyone raised a mug.

The room hummed with talk of the war (briefly), the peace (thankfully), the Company (quietly, in whispers), and the King, whose conquests continued to bring him glory (unfortunately due to Louvois's evil genius). We raised our glasses to the memory of the Queen, who had tragically and suddenly died the year before. (It was rumored that the King had secretly married the Widow, something that must have enraged Athénaïs!)

There was also talk of Racine, who had long ago retired from theater to become His Majesty's official historiographer. (Clearly, the accusations against him had come to naught.) He was something of a bigot now, it was said, even condemning players and the world of the theater.

Over venison and chicken pie, Monsieur Pierre told us about the

Comédie-Française. The newly created government theater was an amalgamation of the warring troupes, intended to put an end to the War of the Theaters.

"Did you see their recent production of *The Cid*?" I asked.

Monsieur Pierre confessed that he had not had the heart to go, it had been so poorly cast. "I have no wish to spoil my memory of former glories," he said. "Let us raise our glasses to a truly great player, La des Oeillets. She made gods weep."

"Is he talking about Grandmama?" Sweet Pea asked Gaston, who was beside her.

"Oui," Gaston said, crinkling his eyes at his niece.

"To Alix!" we all sang out in chorus.

And to Father, I thought, saying a silent prayer. *Thank you.*

aby and I were setting out the snow custard and cakes when I heard a horse cantering down the laneway.

"Now who could that be?" Gaby said with a smile, tilting her head.

In the courtyard, I saw my stable hand taking the reins of a stout horse from a man in the King's livery. Xavier!

"I'm so glad you could come," I said, giving his cloak to the maid. "Put it in Monsieur's room, please." The room next to my own.

"Claudette—I'm sorry, but I'm afraid I must return to Versaie tonight," he said, embracing me tenderly. "As soon as my horse is watered and rested."

"Then at least join us for dessert," I said, crestfallen. It had been more than a week since I'd last seen him.

"This," Gaston said, rising as Xavier and I entered the dining room. "Is?"

"Oui, Gaston, this is Monsieur Xavier Breton, who I've been telling you about. But he can't stay long, unfortunately."

"I didn't want to miss this opportunity to congratulate Claudette on her new home . . . and to meet you," Xavier added with warmth. "She talks of you so often."

"Gaston, could you pour a mug for our guest?" I asked, noticing that Gaby was gesturing to me.

"We have a problem," Gaby said, letting me into the library, where my daughter was weeping.

"What's wrong?" I asked, stooping down beside the girl, the twins looking on perplexed.

Her shoulders shook. "I don't remember the words."

"If you like, I could help you," I offered, ignoring the fact that I was not supposed to know about the surprise. "I'll whisper them to you. I used to do this for your grandmama. It's what players do."

She looked at me in wonder. "You know the words?"

"That depends," I said truthfully, looking up at Gaby.

"It's a line from a scene—" Gaby wrung her hands. "But I don't recall which play."

"It's about a princess named Isabelle," Sweet Pea said, starting to weep again.

"Ah," I said. *The Illusion,* a light romantic comedy, was one of my favorites. "A beautiful princess."

"The most beautiful princess in *all* the world."

"I might know the words," I said.

"They begin with her saying not to do what we're told," Sweet Pea said with spirit.

I smiled. My daughter's interpretation was . . . well: inventive.

"But I can't remember what comes next."

" . . . not to do what we're told, when we detest what's been chosen for us," I prompted, imagining that my daughter thought this speech had to do with refusing to eat parsnips, rather than marrying a man she did not love.

"*That's* it."

"Perfect," I said, relieved that she had no intention of reciting the rest of Isabelle's passionate speech.

"And then Uncle Gaston is going to sing," she said.

"He is?"

"He said he would. And then, at the end, you come on and play a clown."

"I do what?"

"Monsieur Xavier says you do it wonderfully."

"Indeed," Gaby broke in. "He's been saying so for years."

"And I've never *ever* seen it," Sweet Pea said, striking an indignant pose befitting an actress.

.   .   .

I LIT THREE lanterns as everyone got settled in the library.

"Xavier . . . ?" He was deep in conversation with Monsieur Pierre. I stooped down beside his chair.

He turned toward me, lightly touching my hand. (*Oh,* how I love this man.) "Did you say something to Sweet Pea about me acting a clown?"

"Some time ago, *perhaps,*" he said—but looking a bit guilty, I thought.

"She's insisting I perform . . . tonight."

"This woman is the most exquisite clown imaginable," Monsieur Pierre said, pointing an accusing finger at me.

I'd never seen Monsieur Pierre so garrulous. I wondered what Monsieur de Maisonblanche had been putting in his mug.

"She's every bit as good as Molière," he went on, "may he rest in peace."

"*That* I'd like to see," Père Petit said, finishing off his third helping of snow custard.

I bowed my head at the reference to Molière. The wonderful play-wright had practically died onstage, playing the part of a man who was convinced he was dying. That the Church had refused him a proper burial enraged me still.

"Tra la la la! May the performances begin," Pilon called out, his voice deep and dramatic.

Gaby and I ushered everyone into the library. At the sound of Monsieur de Maisonblanche's horn (and the dog's subsequent bark of alarm), the twins somberly parted the drapes. Everyone applauded to see Sweet Pea draped in my shawl. She was trying hard not to giggle.

"Sometimes we are told . . . ," I coached gently.

"Sometimes we are told . . . by Heaven . . . *not* to do what we're told, when . . . when . . ."

"When we detest . . ."

"When we *detest* what's been chosen for us!" my daughter finished the phrase perfectly (in something of a rush). She curtsied to the cries of "Bravo!" and dove into my arms, ecstatic with her triumph.

"Well done!" Monsieur Pierre told her, patting her curls.

Gaston stepped forward and, with one hand clutching the tip of his long beard, sang "Le Beau Robert" in a voice so beautiful it brought tears to my eyes.

"My heart would die if I did not see you," I joined in on the familiar refrain, my heart aching with the memory of our mother and father singing the song together.

Sweet Pea squirmed out of my arms and pulled me forward. "Maman, the clown!" she announced, then leapt onto Xavier's lap, abandoning me on the makeshift stage.

I looked around the room at all the faces of my loved ones. I thought of the marketplaces of my youth, the crowds. *I love to hear people laugh,* Father had often said. So very long ago.

"With sincere apologies to my darling daughter," I began, "I have to confess that my clowning days are far behind me."

"Maman!"

There was a playful "Boo!" from Gaston, followed by laughter.

I put my hands on my hips and made a cross clown-face. My daughter giggled, but Xavier shook his head: *not enough.*

With a sigh, I obliged them with a simple, stomping shuffle.

Sweet Pea laughed and others guffawed. "Encore!" I heard someone call out.

Why not? I thought, and shuffled again, then flailed wildly, barely catching my balance.

A wave of laughter.

I scowled at everyone, which made them laugh all the harder. (Such fun!)

"Give your mother this," Monsieur Pierre said. Sweet Pea ran up to me with the bowl of apples from the side table.

I regarded the fruit with apprehension. Could I? I picked up an apple, felt its weight. I picked up another, and tossed one and then the other into the air. I frowned, concentrating, adding a third and then a fourth. I could still do it! Soon I was juggling five apples while pirouetting, everything on the verge of being out of control.

Bravo! Chapeau! Formidable!

"Oh, oh, oh!" Xavier cried out, laughing so hard he was gasping.

I let the apples fall into my skirts and curtsied.

"Maman!" Sweet Pea grasped my legs. "You're funny!"

And with that, the twins drew the curtains together. Gaby suggested that it was time for the children to go to bed and they were finally coerced, but only on condition that Monsieur Pierre go up with them and tell them a story.

I, aglow, stood outside under the star-studded sky with my sweet love, bidding him a tender adieu, and then watching him canter off on his good stout mare, waving and blowing me kisses.

THE VILLAGE CHURCH bells woke me the next morning. Zounds. I'd overslept.

I looked out the window at the bright summer sun, the leaves fluttering against a clear blue sky. I heard Gaby's laughing voice, someone plucking at the harpsichord. I heard the goat bleating. I heard carriage wheels, horse hooves. I heard a man's voice: Monsieur Pierre.

I sat up. Was he leaving? *Already?*

I threw on a morning gown and bonnet and slipped down the stairs. "Monsieur Pierre," I called out. "You're not leaving, are you?" His haversack was in the entry.

"There you are," he said, turning. "I've been up for hours."

Oh, dear.

"Gaston and Pilon and the boys are all ready to go. Something about school. They're out back having a last look at the pigs."

"Did you sleep at all?" I asked, adjusting the tilt of his hat, which was famously askew.

"Like a baby."

"Have you eaten?"

He made a droll face. "Your good Gaby is intent on having me fat as a Christmas turkey." He pointed his cane at a parcel. "She's sending me off with enough for thirty-six men."

"Come, sit with me for a moment outside. There's something I've been wanting to say."

He looked at me suspiciously. "Am I about to be scolded?" he asked, easing himself down next to me on a garden bench.

How dear he was. "It's just this: I'd like you to move out here, live with us." He was a widower now. We could care for him, look after him. I'd been giving this thought. "You could write here."

He made a rueful laugh. "I've no words left in me."

Each moment of life is a step toward death. Corneille's line came upon me unbidden. Sweet contentment had found me in my graying years. "Are you sure?" I said, almost pleading. I thought of my father's bones, abandoned in a rocky field. I longed to gather my loved ones near. "I could arrange for everything. You wouldn't have to worry about a thing. You'd have your own rooms." His very own messes. I touched his hand, his writing hand—the hand with which so many lofty thoughts had been inked. His skin felt papery, barnacled. "You've been like a father to me," I said, my heart both aching and full.

"I know, Claudette," he said, his eyes glistening, "but you don't have to worry about me."

Gaston appeared in the distance, Pilon, Sweet Pea, and the leaping twins trailing behind him.

I helped Monsieur Pierre to his feet. "Is it time?" he asked.

"Yes, time," I said.

Cradling a huge bouquet of flowers, Gaston raised one hand, fingers wide-spread.

"What is your brother saying when he does that?" Monsieur Pierre asked.

"He's saying he's happy."

Grinning, I thrust both my hands up high. *Double.*

"And what did you just say?"

"That I'm happier than I could ever have imagined."

Ten weeks and four days later, on the third of October, 1684, Monsieur Pierre Corneille—the Great Corneille—died in his rooms in Paris, on the rue d'Argenteuil, likely in the care of one of his daughters. On May 18, 1687, a little over two and a half years later, Claude des Oeillets died as well.

The King never legally recognized their daughter, Louise de Maisonblanche (who looked very much like him), but, through the persuasion of his second wife, Françoise de Maintenon—formerly the Widow Scarron, governess of the King's children by Athénaïs—the girl was informally recognized as "of the King's blood." As a young woman, she married well and had eleven children. On the basis of her "secret" lineage, two of her daughters were schooled at Saint-Cyr, Maintenon's school for daughters of the nobility. Throughout her life, Louise de Maisonblanche lived out of the public eye, and when at Versaie, remained veiled.

Very little is known about Claude's brother, Gaston, only that he seemed to require special care. He is, thus, my creation, an imaginative amalgam of several syndromes.

Many historians suspect Claude des Oeillets of crimes, including plotting to kill the King. I prefer the carefully documented work of French historian Jean Lemoine: *Les des Oeillets: Une grande comédienne, une maitresse de Louis XIV.* Claude did have to .confront her accusers, some of whom did claim to "identify" her, but Lemoine argues—with reason—that it was the work of Louvois, pursuing a vendetta against Athénaïs.

The most feared and hated man in France—but also brilliantly capable in matters of war (and thus indispensable to the King)—Louvois was described by his contemporaries as brutal and vindictive. He was guilty of many crimes, but not necessarily of some of the more intimate ones attributed to him here. After his death, the King was heard to say that he would never forgive himself for listening to Louvois, "a horrible man."

Jean Racine was accused of poisoning his mistress, the actress Thérèse du Parc, and a warrant was issued for his arrest. Nothing came of it, and how his case came to be so rapidly dropped is unknown.

As for Athénaïs, Madame de Montespan, nobody really knows for sure how guilty she was in the use of sorcery, potentially deadly poisons, aphrodisiacs, and Black Masses, but no historian argues for her complete innocence. In later years, she devoted herself to religion, and even sought out her former rival, Louise de la Vallière, as a spiritual adviser.

In the interest of a more dramatic narrative, I sometimes changed the timing of events. In Act II, for example, the events happened over a longer period of time. It is possible, if not likely, that Claude and her family arrived in Paris in 1658 (when, in fact, the Seine did flood), not two years later, in 1660. The King and his new bride were not in Paris until the fall of that year, and *The Golden Fleece* was not performed until the following spring. In spite of these and other shifts, squeezes, cuts, and additions to the historical record, I hope that something of the true spirit of the time is conveyed.

Also, in an attempt not to overwhelm the reader and, as well, to intensify the core relationships, I have pruned the family trees. A reader in pursuit of the historical record can safely assume that there were a great many more people about. For example, Claude had a second brother, François de Vin, and several cousins. As well, there were three additional Mortemart daughters.

The conflict between the theater, government, and the Catholic Church continued on for another hundred years, until the French Revolution. The Company of the Blessed Sacrament, like other religious groups of the day, acted in ways that could be seen as both positive and negative. As well as sponsoring hospitals and other works of genuine charity, they condemned players and were very active in censoring theater. They were, indeed, an extremist secret society, and in many ways more powerful than the King. Some even claim that they were plotting to overthrow the King.

I was first enchanted by the world of seventeenth-century French theater almost a half century ago—Corneille, Molière, Racine! I hope the French forgive me for giving their idols clay feet, but I will entirely understand if they do not. I also beg the indulgence of La Comédie-Française. Its creation, by royal decree, put an end to the theatrical wars of the period and ensured a certain stability in the lives of the players, but at the cost of creative vitality—initially. No longer, certainly. Some of the finest theatrical performances I have ever seen have been at La Comédie-Française.

For those readers who know and love Paris well, you're no doubt puzzled by the rue de la Comtesse d'Artois. Today that street is a section of the popular rue Montorgueil ("Mount Pride"), renamed during the French Revolution. Other streets: the rue Vieux Chemin de Charenton is now the rue de Bercy; the rue de Thorigny is now the rue de la Perle; the rue Neuve de Bourgogne is now the rue Française. The Rue Saint-Denis, one of the oldest in Paris, had different names in the thirteenth and fourteenth centuries, but I was unable to determine if it went under another name in the seventeenth.

For more detailed notes, please visit my website: www.Sandra Gulland.com.

CAST OF CHARACTERS

NOTE: *fictional characters are in italics. All others are historically based.*

THE DES OEILLETS FAMILY AND FRIENDS

Nicolas de Vin, known as des Oeillets—an actor.

Alix Faviot, known as Madame des Oeillets—an actress, Nicolas's wife.

Claude (Claudette) des Oeillets—their daughter and eldest child, aged twelve when the story begins.

Gaston de Vin—their son, seven years younger than his sister, Claudette, aged five when the story begins.

Pilon—a boy with a heart-shaped mark on his cheek, one of the Winter Swallows.

Courageux—a player with their former troupe.

Monsieur Martin—their first landlord in Paris.

Docteur Baratil—a young doctor.

THE WORLD OF THE COURT

Royalty and Inner Circle

Louis XIV—born in 1638, and therefore the same age as Claudette; known as the Sun King.

Anne of Austria—Queen of France, married to King Louis XIII; mother of Louis XIV and Philippe; on the ascendancy of her son Louis to the throne, became the Queen Mother; a woman of considerable piety.

Maria Theresa of Spain—wife of Louis XIV, Queen of France.

Philippe—younger brother of Louis XIV by two years: first in line for the throne and, as such, known formally as Monsieur. His bisexuality was tolerated by Louis XIV.

Henriette—Philippe's wife, the sister of King Charles II of England, known formally as Madame. She died young; poisoning was suspected but never proved.

La Grande Mademoiselle—the King's eccentric, feminist cousin, and the wealthiest individual in France.

Nobility and Courtiers

Gabriel de Rochechouart, Duc de Vivonne-Mortemart, referred to here as the Duc de Mortemart—father of Athénaïs and member of the great Mortemart family of Lussac in Poitou. One of the four First Gentlemen of the King's Bedchamber. Named Governor of Paris in 1669.

Louis-Victor de Rochechouart, Marquis de Vivonne—the Duc de Mortemart's only son, and Athénaïs's older brother, referred to here as Vivonne. A First Gentleman of the King's Bedchamber and later General of the Galleys.

Françoise de Rochechouart-Mortemart, here Mademoiselle de Tonnay-Charente—one of the Mortemart daughters. Adopting the name Athénaïs, she marries and becomes known to history as Madame de Montespan. Two years younger than Claudette, she is eleven when the story opens. *During her first confinement, Athénaïs goes under the name Madame de Sconin.*

Louis-Alexandre de La Trémoille, Marquis de Noirmoutier—Athénaïs's ill-fated fiancé, forced to flee France in order to escape punishment for his involvement in a duel in which his good friend the Marquis d'Antin was killed.

Louis Henri de Gondrin de Pardaillan, Marquis de Montespan—younger brother of the Marquis d'Antin, in the wake of whose death (see above) he marries Athénaïs.

Louise de la Vallière—the King's first mistress, referred to scornfully by Athénaïs as the "Limping One." An extraordinary horsewoman, and profoundly pious, she eventually was able to fulfill her desire to become a Carmelite nun.

Marquise de Brinvilliers—although her case preceded the Affair of the

Poisons by several years, her crimes (of poisoning her husband, her brothers and a sister, and even her father) sent a current of fear and suspicion through the world of the Court and set the stage for the rash of arrests, trials, and executions that followed.

Madame de Maintenon ("the Widow Scarron")—caretaker of Athénaïs's illegitimate children by the King ... and, much later, secretly the King's second wife.

Marquis de Louvois—Secretary of State for War and in charge of the Affair of the Poisons; a powerful man with a vendetta against Athénaïs.

THE WORLD OF THE THEATER

Playhouses

NOTE: *The theaters are listed in the order of their appearance in the story, not according to their creation.*

The Marais Theater (commonly called the Marais)—located in eastern Paris, in the area known as the Marais, meaning "marshland," which it had been in former times. Originally a jeu de paume (indoor tennis court), it was Paris's second public playhouse.

Theater of the Bourgogne—built in 1548 in what became Les Halles, the commercial center of Paris, the Bourgogne was Paris's (and France's) first public playhouse. During the mid-seventeenth century it was the home of neoclassical tragedy.

Theater of the Palais-Royal (Molière's troupe)—known from 1660 for the comic performances given there by a troupe of Italians and that of Molière, who shared the space.

The Comédie-Française—in 1680, by royal decree, the two major theater companies were merged to create the Comédie-Française company.

Players

NOTE: *The players' names given are, for the most part, their adopted stage names, not their legal names.*

Brécourt (Guillaume Marcoureau)—playwright and actor, excelling at comedy; initially with the Marais.

Étiennette, known as Mademoiselle—an actress and Brécourt's wife, initially with the Marais.

Floridor (Josias de Soulas, Sieur de Prinefosse)—director, chef, and principal actor at the Bourgogne.

Denis Buffequin—in charge of special effects at the Marais, called Keeper
of Secrets.

Monsieur la Roque (Monsieur Pierre Petitjean)—director with the Marais.

La Thorillière (François Le Noir)—a principal actor at the Marais, married to the director's daughter.

Marie—an actress, initially with the Marais, La Thorillière's wife and
Monsieur la Roque's daughter.

Marquise Thérèse du Parc—a popular actress who captured the heart of
Jean Racine, as well as, it is claimed, those of Molière and Corneille.
Initially with the Palais-Royal, she moved to the Bourgogne.

Molière (Jean-Baptiste Poquelin)—director, principal actor, and playwright of the Palais-Royal theater.

Madame Babette—a cleaning lady, noted for her wigs.

Zacharie Montfleury—a tragic actor with the Bourgogne, noted for his
girth, whose studied dramatic style is ridiculed by Molière.

Playwrights and Composers

NOTE: *It's not always easy to separate players from playwrights. Quite a
few, like Molière, both acted and wrote for the stage. Brécourt and Montfleury,
players mentioned above, both wrote plays as well as acted.*

Pierre Corneille—"the great and good Corneille," famous author of
The Cid. He is fifty-five years old when Claudette first meets him in
Paris.

Thomas Corneille—Pierre Corneille's brother; twenty years younger,
Pierre regards him as a son. A prolific and successful popular playwright, the brothers often worked together.

Jean-Baptiste de Lully (Giovanni Battista di Lulli in his native Italy)—
dancer, composer, proponent, and ultimate controller of opera in
Paris.

Molière (Jean-Baptiste Poquelin)—director and principal actor, as well as
playwright of the Theater of the Palais-Royal, excelling in comic sat-
ire. He is sixteen years younger than Pierre Corneille.

Jean Racine—a young, brilliant writer of tragedies, but an unethical person. He is thirty-three years younger than Pierre Corneille, his chief

rival, and seventeen years younger than Molière, who gave him his start by staging his first two tragedies. Racine betrays them both.

OTHER FIGURES OF IMPORTANCE

Père d'Ossat—a priest attached to Athénaïs's household.
Xavier Breton—one of the King's valets and Claudette's special friend.
Blucher—a male midwife, possibly the first, based on Julien Clément.
La Reynie—Lieutenant General of Police; considered to be the founder of the first modern police force.
Marie Angélique de Fontanges—the none-too-bright young woman who catches the eye of the King. At only twenty, she dies after the birth of a stillborn child, and was rumored to have been poisoned by Athénaïs.
Miguel—Athénaïs's doorman.
Madame Audouin—midwife in Saint-Germain-en-Laye.

The Church

Bishop Bossuet—a theologian and brilliant orator, renowned for his sermons. As Court preacher, he wielded a powerful religious influence.
Père La Chaise—the King's confessor.
Père Lécuyer—a priest at Versailles who refuses to grant Athénaïs absolution.

La Voisin Household and the Criminal World

Madame Catherine Deshayes Monvoisin ("La Voisin")—fortune-teller, palm-reader, abortionist, poisoner, witch.
Antoine Monvoisin—her husband, an unemployed drunk.
Marie Marguerite Monvoisin—their emotionally unstable teenage daughter.
Monsieur Lesage (also known as Monsieur du Buisson, Monsieur Adam Coeuret)—con man and poisoner.
Abbé Étienne Guibourg—priest who performs Black Masses; a poisoner.

Château de Suisnes

Louise de Maisonblanche ("Sweet Pea")—Claudette's daughter by the King.

Philippe de Maisonblanche—the girl's foster father and caretaker of the Château de Suisnes.

Gabrielle de la Tour ("Gaby")—Philippe's wife and the girl's foster mother.

François Pingré—owner of the château.

Christophe and Humbert—twin boys, Winter Swallows in the care of Gaston and Pilon.

Père Petit—the village priest.

ABOUT CURRENCY

Authorities differ regarding the value of the various coins of seventeenth-century France, complicated by the fact that coins minted in Paris were worth ten to twenty percent more than coins minted in Tours. But basically:

A denier was the smallest unit.

12 deniers = 1 sou (or sol).

20 sous (or sols) = 1 livre. (Note: there was no actual coin called a livre.)

3 livres = 1 silver écu, a large coin with the image of a shield on it.

6 livres = 1 gold écu; this coin was rare by the seventeenth century.

10 livres = 1 louis d'or (a gold louis). First minted in Paris in 1641, it had the image of the King on one side and a fleur-de-lis on the other.

In more general terms, one livre at this time would be worth approximately $40 U.S. A pichet of wine cost four sous, a meal of bread and meat with weak beer, five. The cost of one candle or a pair of wood sabots, one livre. Later in the century, it cost a gold louis for a seat in the first loge of a Molière play and thirty sous for the parterre.

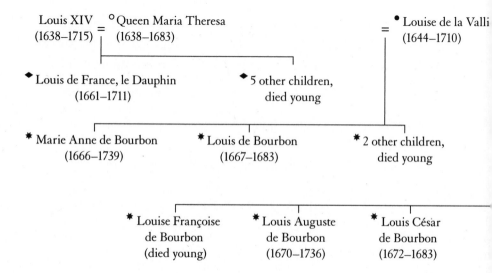

Louis XIV
(1638–1715) = ° Queen Maria Theresa
(1638–1683)   = • Louise de la Valli
(1644–1710)

◆ Louis de France, le Dauphin   ◆ 5 other children,
(1661–1711)   died young

✳ Marie Anne de Bourbon   ✳ Louis de Bourbon   ✳ 2 other children,
(1666–1739)   (1667–1683)   died young

✳ Louise Françoise   ✳ Louis Auguste   ✳ Louis César
de Bourbon   de Bourbon   de Bourbon
(died young)   (1670–1736)   (1672–1683)

o   Wife
•   Official mistress
◇   Occasional liaison
◆   Legitimate
✳   Legitimated, officially recognized
✗   Illegitimate, never officially recognized

(KNOWN) BIOLOGICAL DESCENDANTS
OF LOUIS XIV, THE SUN KING

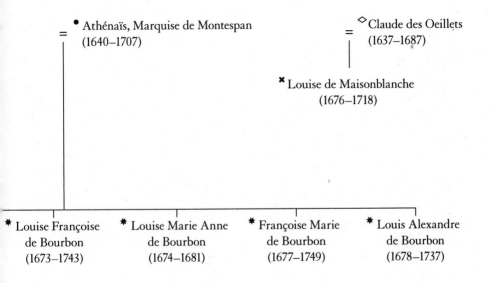

= • Athénaïs, Marquise de Montespan
(1640–1707)

= ◇Claude des Oeillets
(1637–1687)

✷ Louise de Maisonblanche
(1676–1718)

✷ Louise Françoise
de Bourbon
(1673–1743)

✷ Louise Marie Anne
de Bourbon
(1674–1681)

✷ Françoise Marie
de Bourbon
(1677–1749)

✷ Louis Alexandre
de Bourbon
(1678–1737)

GLOSSARY

Affair of the Poisons—the name given to the massive arrests, trials, and executions of people accused of poisoning and sacrilege (practicing black magic).

Alchemy—the study and craft of turning base metals into gold.

Amatory Mass—a Black Mass performed for the purpose of influencing a loved one.

Amphitheater—tiered benches opposite the stage, between the standing parterre and the front boxes. (Note, however, that the precise location of the amphitheater is debated.)

Angel Water (L'Eau d'Ange)—a fashionable seventeenth-century scent based on myrtle.

Assistants (or Helpers)—Viagra-like herbs believed to enhance sexual performance. (Also see *Blister beetle* and *Love powder*.)

Beignet—fried yeast dough, often sprinkled with sugar; similar to a doughnut, but shaped into a ball or square and without a hole.

Black Mass—a travesty of the Mass, celebrating Satan.

Blister beetle—a beetle that produced an irritating chemical that caused skin to blister (hence its name). The dried, crushed bodies of the beetle, when eaten, caused inflammation of the genital organs and was thus used as an aphrodisiac.

Burning Chamber (Chambre Ardente)—a basement room in which people suspected of poisoning and sacrilege during the Affair of the Poisons were tried. It was called the Burning Chamber because of all the candles needed to light it.

Burnt wine—spiced mulled wine, heated by plunging a hot poker into it.

Cachet—the royal seal, as in *lettre de cachet*.

Canonical hours—official prayers of the Catholic Church. Bells calling for prayer served as a way of telling time throughout the day and night.

> Lauds (Dawn Prayer)—3:00 a.m.
> Prime (Early Morning Prayer)—6:00 a.m.
> Terce (Morning Prayer)—9:00 a.m.
> Sext (Midday Prayer)—noon
> None (Mid-afternoon Prayer)—3:00 p.m.
> Vespers (Evening Prayer)—6:00 p.m.
> Compline (Night Prayer)—9:00 p.m.
> Matins—(Midnight Prayer)
> (Note that these times and patterns change from place to place and time to time.)

Claque—friends and family of a performer, who cheered and applauded; sometimes hired.

Clôture annuelle (recess)—a theater's annual three-week recess around Easter. Although no plays were performed during this period, it was during this break that the next season was planned, new works prepared and changes made to the plays in a troupe's extensive repertoire. It was also the period when players renegotiated their annual contracts, and new players were carefully considered.

Code of Chivalry—the Knights Code of Chivalry, developed during the Middle Ages, entailed valor, courtesy, sagacity, prudence, honor, honesty, faith, truth, charity, among a number of other virtues.

Deus ex machina—a Latin expression meaning "gods from the machine." In Greek plays, a crane was used to raise or lower gods onto the stage. More figurative, now, it's an improbable device used in a play to miraculously save the day.

The Dutch War—(1672–1678) a war which eventually pitted the Dutch Republic, Austrian Habsburgs, Brandenburg, and Spain against France, England, the Prince-Bishopric of Münster, the Archbishopric of Cologne, and Sweden. Louis XIV considered the Dutch to be trading rivals, seditious, heretics, and an obstacle to French legal claims on the Spanish Netherlands.

Fanatics—those who applauded a particular actor or actress; this is the origin of the word *fan*.

Farce—an endless variation on a theme, often involving sexual antics. The word is derived from the Latin *farsa,* which ironically means suffering.

Garçons de théâtre—theater servants, stagehands or errand boys who worked for a troupe, running errands for the actors.

Girdle book—a book tucked into a belt or hung at the waist.

Jerkin—a short, close-fitting garment, often sleeveless (rather like a vest).

Jeu de paume—a precursor of the game of tennis, played indoors. It was a very popular game in the early part of the seventeenth century, but lost favor under Louis XIV. A number of the abandoned courts were converted to theaters.

Jours ordinaires and extraordinaires—the theater week was divided into *jours ordinaires* (Tuesday, Friday, and Sunday) and *jours extraordinaires* (Monday, Wednesday, Thursday, and Saturday).

Justacorps—a knee-length coat which flared out from the waist.

Keeper of Secrets—the title given the machinist who creates the "magical" special effects; also called Great Sorcerer.

King's Evil—scrofula, a tuberculosis infection of the lymph nodes in the neck. It was preached that Saint Marcouf granted the kings of France the gift of healing this deforming disease. From Edward the Confessor on, a king was believed to be able to cure "the King's Evil" with his touch when his spiritual power was strong—just after he'd been newly anointed, for example, or shortly after he'd made confession and gone to Mass. It was also practiced by English kings.

Lettre de cachet—an order from the King, sending someone to prison, a convent, a hospital, or exile without the benefit of trial or appeal.

Litter—a chair or bed (often covered) carried by two or more men, sometimes called a sedan chair or palanquin.

Loge—box in a theater.

Loge attendant (ouvreuse)—the woman who has the key to a loge and attends to the needs of those patrons seated in it.

Love powder—a powder or tincture containing cantharides, more commonly known as "Spanish Fly," a potentially fatal ingredient that caused inflammation of the organs of the genital tract (and was thus used to treat impotence).

Machine play—a play in which special effects were achieved by the use of machinery.

Madame, Monsieur—when used as a name at Court, understood to be the King's brother and his wife.

Mushrooms—a game in which a woman would twirl and drop to the floor, trying to get her skirts to fall in a perfect circle around her.

Ombrella (or ombrello)—the original Italian word for an umbrella, from the Latin word *umbra*, for shade.

Ouverture—the day after Easter when all the theaters opened their doors to the public.

Overhire list—the list of part-time workers who helped to put on a theatrical production.

Paradis—the top tier (balcony) of a theater, where servants and relatives of the players were permitted to sit.

Parterre—an open area in front of the stage ("orchestra" seating today) where men, often rowdy, stood to watch a performance.

Pensions list—each year the King announced which playwrights and performers would be awarded a pension (what we would consider a "grant").

Petticoat breeches—wide, pleated pants that resembled a skirt, worn by men in Western Europe in the mid-seventeenth century.

Pit—see *Parterre.*

Pit-fall—a trapdoor on the stage floor, the means by which a character abruptly—alarmingly—disappears.

Poke—a bag hidden under a woman's skirts; the original purse.

Post chaise—a four-wheeled closed carriage.

Tant pis—"Too bad" in French.

Teethy—a very old word meaning testy and peevish.

Terce—see *Canonical hours.*

Travesty player—someone who played the part of the opposite sex in a play.

Turkey carpet (also known as Anatolian)—a hand-knotted or flat woven carpet made by Turks.

Unblood—someone not of the nobility.

Unities—from Aristotle's *Poetics,* three rules for drama: 1) unity of action (the play must be about one main action), 2) unity of place (the play must be set in one place), and 3) unity of time (the action of the play must take place in twenty-four hours or fewer).

Versaie—the Palace of Versailles in its early evolution.

Vespers—see *Canonical hours.*

Voyage—when a theatrical troupe makes a performance away from their regular theater in Paris, to travel to perform for the King, for example, wherever the Court resides.

Winter Swallows—country boys who migrate to Paris and other city centers during the winter months to beg.

Wormwood wine—a bitter tonic prepared by steeping a handful of wormwood in a gallon of wine. It evolved to become today's vermouth.

ACKNOWLEDGMENTS

Frankly, I was tempted to dedicate this book to John Golder, scholar of seventeenth-century French theater, so great is my debt. He generously answered my many (many!) questions over the years and provided a reading list that amounted to a master class in this fascinating subject. All errors of fact are mine, and mine alone—and when I do get something right, he is responsible.

Thanks also to the following academics who responded to my questions: Lynn Wood Mollenauer, author of *Strange Revelations: Magic, Poison, and Sacrilege in Louis XIV's France;* Holly Tucker, author of *Blood Work: A Tale of Medicine and Murder in the Scientific Revolution;* Jeffrey Jackson, author of *Paris Under Water: How the City of Light Survived the Great Flood of 1910;* and Virginia Scott, author of *Molière: A Theatrical Life.* Hilary Berstein and other scholars on the H-France list offered assistance, particularly Antoine Coutelle with information on Poitiers, and Jim Burrows on the approximate location of chez Duchesse d'Armagnac in Paris. Special thanks for the time and wisdom of two Corneille specialists of the Centre International Pierre Corneille: author and professor Myriam Dufour-Maître, and Evelyne Poirel, curator of Musée Pierre Corneille in Petit-Couronne.

Other guides on the long and winding research road include: Beckah Reed (visionary), Claire Naylor McKeever (actress), Frank Morlock (seventeenth-century enthusiast), Anne and Bruno Challamel (*toujours*), Katie De La Matter (seventeenth-century musicologist), Deb Reynold (clowning workshop leader), Phoebe Spanier (on seventeenth-century mirrors), and Monique Boulanger (for help with French translations). Social workers Lucy King and Fran Murphy shared their knowledge of

Asperger's syndrome (which Gaston has not, not truly). Pamela Grant, "Paris Story" tour guide, was fantastic. Special thanks go to Tanguy de Vienne, owner of the Château de Suisnes south of Paris, for a wonderful tour of Claude's lovely château.

To my editors, whose influence can be seen on *every* page of this novel: immeasurable appreciation. They are: my brilliant early-stage editors, Dan Smetanka and Fiona Foster; the inimitable Iris Tupholme and fiction editor Lorissa Sengara at HarperCollins Canada; bright spark and guiding light Melissa Danaczko at Doubleday U.S.; agent Jackie Kaiser of Westwood Creative Artists, my first reader and lead cheerleader.

A number of readers provided invaluable feedback on the manuscript at various stages: actress and creative spirit Ellen Stewart; seventeenth-century scholar Gary McCollim; writer and editor Jude Holland; fan-volunteer Deborah Schryer; authors Stephanie Cowell and Victoria Zackheim. Although Jordan Gentile was unable to review the manuscript, his fulsome and informed comments on my blog were always helpful.

Members of my two writers' groups saw this novel through various stages from mere scribbles to a finished book (a miracle): Jenifer McVaugh and Johanna Zomers of the WWW (Wilno Women Writers), and my ever-nameless San Miguel de Allende group: Beverly Donofrio and Susan McKinney. Thank you so much for your thoughtful feedback.

Additionally, and astonishingly, fourteen employees of Chapters/ Indigo bookstores across Canada volunteered to read and critique an early draft of this novel, forwarding me written reports. Their input was extremely helpful, and a number of important changes were made as a result. They are: Carlos Alonso, June Baxter, Martina Bracek, Ellen Clark, Gaye DeWolfe, Tami Grondines, Erin Legare, Beth MacDonald, Sheena Madole, Marjorie Morris, Lynda Parkinson, John Pickard, Jena Rayner, and Vivian Samoil. Thank you all!

The title of this novel was uncertain until the very end. Twice I solicited opinions on my Facebook author page. To all the readers who helped me arrive at a short list: thank you! Profound thanks, as well, to the members of the Fiction Writers Co-op, a powerhouse Facebook group, for giving a resounding thumbs-up to the final title *The Shadow Queen,* as well as emotional support and professional advice on all things to do with writing and publishing.

There are others, as well, working behind the scenes as this novel heads out into the world—people like James Melia and Nicole Pedersen at Doubleday, Doug Richmond at HarperCollins Canada, and Chris Casuccio at Westwood Creative Artists, but also many I've yet to even meet, people who are giving *The Shadow Queen* their professional best: I thank you!

And lastly, and always, wholehearted thanks to my ever-supportive husband, Richard, daughter, Carrie, and son, Chet, my home team.

About the Author

Sandra Gulland is the author of *Mistress of the Sun* and
the Josephine B. Trilogy, which has sold over a million
copies worldwide and is currently under development for
a television miniseries. Her work has been translated into
fifteen languages. She and her husband live half the year in
rural Ontario, Canada, and the other half in San Miguel de
Allende, Mexico.